Penthouse Uncensored V

Penthouse Uncensored V

By the Editors of *Penthouse* Magazine

WARNER BOOKS

NEW YORK　BOSTON

Part One contains the text of *Letters to Penthouse IX* copyright © 1999 by General Media Communications, Inc.
Part Two contains the text of *Letters to Penthouse X* copyright © 2000 by General Media Communications, Inc.

Warner Books
Hachette Book Group USA
237 Park Avenue
New York, NY 10169

Visit our Web site at www.HachetteBookGroupUSA.com.

Printed in the United States of America

First Compilation Edition: December 2004
10 9 8 7 6 5 4

Library of Congress Control Number: 2004105623
ISBN: 0-446-69355-3

Cover photo by Ghislain & Marie David de Lossy / The Image Bank
Book design by Charles A. Sutherland

CONTENTS

CONTENTS

Part One

～

Letters to
Penthouse IX

WAIT A MINUTE, ISN'T THAT YOUR WIFE WITH THAT GUY'S DICK IN HER CUNT?

*M*y wife Lori and I have been married for almost seventeen years, and at thirty-seven she's still a hot-looking lady. At five feet seven inches tall and a hundred and eighteen, she's still in good shape. Do the numbers 35-27-36 mean anything to you?

Recently, to make a little extra cash, she took a job in a titty bar. Last night was her first night.

We left the house and got to the club when they were opening the doors for business. Lori was nervous but wildly excited. I sat at the bar as the other girls showed my wife the dressing room and told her the rules. She could keep as much of her clothes on or get as naked as she wanted. She could do whatever she wanted for the guys, but she couldn't allow them to touch her.

I sat and talked to the barmaid and had a drink as Lori went to get ready. My cock was already hard, and there wasn't another soul in the place yet.

After several guys came in, the music started playing. The first dancer was a pretty girl who did an excellent job dancing. I was watching her when I noticed my wife come out of the dressing room. She was dressed in a skimpy little outfit that showed a lot of skin. It had a thong bikini that let her ass-cheeks show. She walked up to the bar and played like she didn't know me, ordering herself a drink. We'd decided to act this way all night, to add to the fun.

A couple of guys started talking to her, and I was excited with this arrangement, because I could watch as if I weren't her husband.

When it was her turn to dance, she went up on the stage. She danced to about six guys sitting in the front row. She was smiling, and one could tell she was having fun. On the second song, her top came off. I was hard! My wife was topless in front of half a dozen guys, onstage, stripping for the first time in her life. She was bending over in front of strangers who were giving her dollar bills. Her hands rubbed her tits and pinched her nipples. The second song wasn't even over before she was removing her bottoms, throwing them to the side and dancing completely naked (except for her heels) in front of guys with money in front of them. She was having so much fun, she'd have danced to them even if they hadn't been giving her money.

She came over to the end of the stage and smiled at me, giving me a very sultry look. Her pussy was completely shaved. I almost came.

She turned and went back to the guys in the front row, lay down on the stage and spread her legs. She struck many poses while rolling on the floor, most all of them showing her pussy. She looked especially good when she got on all fours, facing the guys on the other side of the stage. Her ass pointed toward those behind her, and her pussy was spread open for all to see.

The guys only a couple of feet from her cunt were leaning forward to get the best look they could. All too soon, her set of songs ended and she was off to the dressing room.

After she changed and came back out, she came to the bar. I started talking to her like we'd just met. It was fun role-playing. She was very excited about what she was doing. Her new outfit was just as sexy as the last.

When it was her turn to dance again, I went to the stage and put my dollars up. She was one hot number! I was so proud of her! She danced for me like she had for everyone else, squatting and spreading her legs. Her big clit poked out of her sexy lips. I stayed there as she went to the next guys, four of them celebrating a birthday. They mentioned this to her, and she did a special dance for the birthday boy.

Facing him and squatting with her knees on both sides of his head, she positioned her pussy just inches from his face. The guys sitting by his side were leaning to look at her cunt. She took the guy's hands and pointed both his index fingers up, then guided them down her tits to her nipples. One of the bouncers came over and motioned no to her, but she didn't care and continued for a few more seconds.

After she was done dancing this set and went to change, I went back to the bar and sat. She appeared later in another outfit and came to the bar to get a drink. Acting as if she was making small talk, she suggested I come downstairs and watch her. The birthday boy's buddies had bought him a lap dance.

I went downstairs and sat at the bar as she went to get him. I ordered a drink and waited. She showed up with him and I watched. She got topless as he sat on the couch. She danced and rubbed her tits over his body. According to the rules, his hands were on the couch back and he wasn't touching her. I would have enjoyed watching him feel her up.

I spent the rest of the evening watching her dance buck naked on the stage and give private dances on the downstairs couches.

One particular guy seemed to get her attention. He bought her a couple of drinks and she danced for him for three songs. I could tell she liked him. I went and sat at the stage to watch and listen.

They were making small talk and he was giving her a lot of dollar bills. He was telling her how much he liked her shaved pussy and her big clit. She just smiled and spread her legs, even going so far as to rub her clit with her fingers and spreading her pussy lips for him to see. I could tell she was getting off on what she was doing. It was highly erotic sitting two seats away, listening to a stranger telling my wife how hot she was and seeing her get sexually charged.

After changing again and coming out of the dressing room, she had on one of my favorite outfits: a one-piece, patent leather, crotchless teddy that's cut out around her tits, leaving them exposed. After more dancing, mainly to this one guy, her set was over.

She got dressed and went downstairs with this guy to give him a lap dance. I followed them about ten minutes later. Except for me at the bar and the bartender, they were the only ones downstairs. The couch they were in was at an angle, facing away from the bar. The guy was sitting with his arms on the couch back, Lori's knees straddling his legs.

She would take each tit in her hands and place a nipple on his nose before sliding it down into his mouth. He would eagerly suck it. I was surprised she was doing this. She whispered into his ear and he looked around the room and said something back. I could make out Lori saying, "He's okay," as she looked my way.

My wife's hands were in front of her as they continued to talk. As she motioned with her head for me to come over, her hands grabbed her tits again and she resumed sliding her nipples over the guy's face and in his mouth. As I walked up to them, Lori asked me to put some quarters into the jukebox. I walked around in front of the couch to the jukebox and, as I put coins in, I turned and looked at them. My heart leaped into my throat! I had a perfect view of a huge cock splitting my wife's crotchless outfit wide open, stretching her cunt lips as she had impaled herself on him. As she would raise herself to put her tit in the guy's mouth, his cock would slide partway out before she plunged back down onto it.

Her movements were so sporadic that you couldn't tell they were fucking. I sat down on a couch next to the jukebox so I could watch. When a song ended, they'd just sit still so some of the others who had come downstairs wouldn't know what they were doing. One of the other dancers entered the room just as Lori was coming, and hollered toward her that it was her turn to dance on stage. Lori bit her lip and nodded her head okay.

Then the guy tensed, and I watched as his dick slid out of my wife's stretched-wide cunt lips as she got up, his come shooting onto the floor. Lori gave him a quick kiss and ran upstairs.—
Name and address withheld

A DILDO WRAPPED IN A PUSSY INSIDE AN ENIGMA

The area was finally given a break from the scorching summer heat, perfect for lying outside and getting a tan. My house is surrounded by woods; the nearest neighbor is two hundred feet away, barely visible through the trees, allowing me to lose any inhibitions about sunbathing in the nude.

After covering my body with oil, I lay upon the blanket, enjoying the soft breeze, and started massaging my thighs and breasts, rolling my fingers over my nipples, which were quite taut by that time. Suddenly, I felt that hot surge coming up from my loins, and I knew right away that I was going to be a naughty girl.

I found myself rubbing my pussy and in quite a horny state of mind. In the distance I could hear the construction of a new high-rise apartment building, and I noticed that the voices of the workmen were a little clearer than usual as they echoed off the trees around me. Upon looking in the direction of the site, I saw that the building had now reached above the tops of the trees that surround my pleasure dome.

I could see the workers at the top of the structure, setting up the beams for the next story. Maybe that would be the penthouse floor, from where you could see for miles around all the homes below with their manicured lawns and glamorous swimming pools. One could even see my house, for instance. I grimaced at the thought of losing my privacy. On the other hand, this could lead to a new sexual intrigue. The idea of masturbating with my toys on my lawn, knowing that someone from afar could actually see me, was pretty exciting! So I went in to get my playthings to start practicing.

I returned to my playground, but before I resettled onto the blanket, I dove into my pool to completely refresh myself. The cool water felt so good as it reduced my horny fever and cleansed me of the body oil and sweat. I walked out feeling my long hair cling to my back as it dripped water down the crack of my ass. My nipples were so erect they ached at my touch. I left my skin glistening with the water as I nestled onto my blanket, placing my vibrators beside me. I glanced up to check that the workers were still in sight, and I thought to myself, Boys, I'm going to tease the fuck out of you!

I reached for my vibrator with the tingling fingers and held it against my pussy. I thought of the time I screwed my husband's boss right here beside this very pool. I acted like he was coming on all suave as hell, and I gave him the indication that I had no idea he was seducing me. But I knew it, and I didn't mind, because I'd wanted to screw him ever since we were transferred here.

I opened my eyes to see if my construction friends were keeping an eye on me, and I was pleased to see that half of them actually had binoculars. They must have been waiting for this day for a long time.

Back in my memory, I remember that while Dick's boss was talking to me about stock options and surreptitiously (he thought) staring at my tits, I just reached forward and cupped his nuts through his pants. He acted surprised, but he wasn't so surprised that he couldn't follow my lead and get undressed as fast as I did. While I remembered this, I stuck my vibrator halfway into my pussy, hearing muffled whoops and hollers from my distant audience.

Laying me back on a poolside chair, my husband's boss mashed my knees into my tits and slipped his huge cock into my tight hole. I must admit, it hurt a little at first (kinda like this dildo was doing now), but that only made the payoff that much more special. Once I got good and wet, his rod was slamming so deeply into me that I thought I was going to catch on fire from the friction.

I pushed my vibrator all the way into my hole, letting the little fingers explore every space there was inside me. Remembering my husband's face when he discovered me boning his boss brought me to a very loud climax. It turns out he'd been watching too.—*Name and address withheld*

YOU CAN HAVE THIS WONDERFUL PRIZE PACKAGE IF . . . THE PRICE IS RIGHT

My wife and I have been married for seventeen years. Although we are still very much in love, I must admit that our sex life is not what it used to be. Jackie is as attractive today as she was the day I married her. She is five two and weighs just over a hundred pounds. She has a gorgeous set of legs, her ass and bush are perfect and her tits are firm.

Needless to say, she still turns me on very much, but she has pretty much lost interest in fucking me. We tried doing different things in the bedroom, and these experiments served to rekindle her interest a bit, but soon her fire would fade again.

This has obviously left me very frustrated. The new things we tried turned me on so much that being denied them just added to my frustrations. I masturbated more often, relying on my fantasies for arousal. One of the things we did to add spice to our sex life was to take pictures and videos of ourselves. When I would be taking pictures of her posing in provocative ways, I would be thinking about her posing like this for other men and even screwing other people. The thought of Jackie fucking some good-looking guy while I watch became a very big turn-on for me. It was the main thing I fantasized about when I beat off. Before long, it was the only thing I thought of, and I started to think of ways to make it actually happen.

One night, while we were lying in bed, I decided to tell Jackie what was on my mind. I told her I'd had a dream about her fucking a friend of ours named Mark while I watched, and I let her know how much just thinking of it turned me on. At first she said

I was sick, but as I told her the details of the dream, how big his cock was and how wild she became while riding it and sucking it, she became hotter and hotter.

I started massaging her pussy as we talked about it. Her snatch was so wet and hot it soaked her panties. She started asking me questions about the dream, and when I filled her in on the details, she moaned and got even hornier. I reached for a ten-inch vibrator, and as I held it up, I said, "This is how big Mark's cock is."

She pulled her panties off and in a sexy voice loaded with desire she said, "Fuck me with that big cock of yours, Mark. Let Phil see how much I love your big, hard dick."

I slowly pushed the vibrator into her, and she went wild and started thrusting her hips, screaming, "Give me all of it, Mark, I want to feel your hard cock all the way up my cunt. I want Phil to see you fill me with your come."

I fucked her hard with the vibrator. She squirmed with pleasure as she neared orgasm. "Oh, yes, come for me Mark. Oh, Stubbly (Jackie's nickname for me), he's coming inside of me. I'm going to come too."

As she came, she reached down and pushed my hand to get the vibrator in as far as it would go. It all but disappeared into her hot box. Watching my wife come as she yelled another man's name drove me nuts, and my cock was ready to explode. I moved around so my dick would be near her mouth. She grabbed it and pulled it into her waiting lips, sucking me off like she had never done before. I was still working the dildo in and out of her, and I asked her what she was thinking about as she sucked my cock. She stopped long enough to say she was thinking about sucking off Mark while I watched.

Before wrapping her lips back around my cock, she asked me what I was thinking about. I told her the same thing, only with another well-hung guy who was fucking her as she sucked.

She moved her ass so it was above my face. We were now in a 69 position, with her on top. As I removed the vibrator, she lowered herself so I could lick her clit. In no time she was coming again, and as she did I exploded with the most intense orgasm I ever had. Jackie sucked my cock and swallowed every last drop of my come—something she had never done before.

After we regained our composure, I turned around and held her as we talked about what had just happened. She agreed that that was the best sex we had in a while. She said that the thought of her fucking someone else, not only with my approval but with me there watching drove her wild. She admitted that she often fantasized about men with extremely large cocks. (My own dick is barely five inches hard.) We discussed doing this for real, about how we would set it up, etc. As we talked about it, my dick began to rise again. Seeing this, Jackie mounted it and started to slowly fuck me while we talked. We both came again and fell asleep in each other's arms.

The next day at work all I could think about was what had happened the night before. I couldn't wait to get home and start making plans for our adventure. To my disappointment, when I got home Jackie did not want to talk about it. She said that what we'd done was okay as a fantasy, but she could never do it for real.

"But you were more turned on last night than I've ever seen you before," I said.

"I don't want to talk about it anymore," she said.

When we went to bed, I pulled out the vibrator again and started to rub it against her cunt. She told me to stop.

I rolled over and spent the rest of the night confused. Why was it that every time we found something we both enjoyed when it came to sex, she would refuse to do it anymore? I couldn't figure it out.

For the next three or four months, I kept trying to figure it out. Was the fact that she liked big cocks and that mine was not very large the reason our sex life was dying? I convinced myself that I just could not satisfy her. Maybe she had a lover. Although I wanted to see her fuck another man, the thought of her doing it behind my back made me mad. I became obsessed with the thought of watching her fuck some guy with a big cock. I wanted to see how she would really act. I wanted my wife to be sexually satisfied, and if I couldn't do it with my small dick, then I wanted her to have the big cock that she craved.

Still, I could only be happy if it was something we did together, not something she looked for on her own. I tried to be honest with her and tell her how I felt, but when I did she would say forget about it and quickly change the subject. This only helped to damage our sex life more. The few times we did attempt to make love, I started to have performance problems. This just compounded the frustrations.

Then there was a breakthrough. One night when we went to bed, she snuggled up close to me and asked, "If I were to tell you that I wanted to fuck someone while you watched, who would you want it to be?" My dick sprang alive and I didn't ask any questions. I just started to name a few of our friends that I thought she would like to screw. Although she agreed with some of the names I rattled off, she said she didn't think she could go through with it with someone she knew. I then suggested that we go out to a bar, pick someone up and bring him home and fuck him. She liked this idea but was worried that if she chickened out at the last minute it wouldn't be fair to the guy she brought home.

"I would feel bad getting some guy all turned on and then leaving him hanging," she said.

"Well," I said, "I guess you could always use your hand or your mouth to finish him off. Do you think you could do that?" I asked.

She thought a minute and said, "I guess."

We were getting horny now and I said, "We can always hire someone."

"Hire someone, eh." The thought of paying someone to fuck her seemed to make her even hotter. "That's right," I quickly added, "we wouldn't have to worry about how he felt with having me be there or anything."

"Where does one hire such a person?" she asked. I had no idea, but I told her, "There are several male escort services around. I heard that that is what they are for. We'll have to call a few."

"Not we. You," she replied. "Wouldn't you want to pick out the guy?" I inquired. She was now stroking my cock with her hand as she moved her mouth down to it.

"If this is going to happen," she said, "you will have to make all the arrangements. You know what I want. I'm not going to mention it again. You just tell me when," and then she slurped my rock-hard dick into her mouth. We made fantastic love all night.

For the next couple of days I racked my brain on how to set this up. I had no idea where to find a male prostitute, and I was too embarrassed to ask anyone.

One Wednesday evening, as I was getting out of the shower at the health club I go to, another guy that I'd seen but never met was just going in. He was about thirty-two years old, five eleven with a muscular build and a cock that hung about six inches— soft! I estimated that it had to be at least eight or nine inches erect. I remembered having thought on many occasions how much Jackie would love that cock. I'd been thinking so hard about finding a male prostitute, and the solution was right here in front of me. Jackie would love this guy. Now all I had to do was get him to like the idea.

I hung around the club awhile until Alex came out. I said hello to him as I approached, and he said hello back. He asked me what I was doing and I explained I was waiting for some people, but that I didn't think they were going to show. He said he was going to a bar he usually goes to after his workouts and asked if I wanted to join him. I said yes.

Once we were in the bar we started to talking, and eventually the conversation turned to sex. I asked him if he had a girlfriend, and he said, "I've been out of circulation for so long that I don't know how to meet women anymore. Besides, I don't need a relationship, just some wild sex."

Bingo!

I took advantage of the opportunity and started telling him of my wife and our plan. He sat there in shock as this practically total stranger told him of how he was supposed to hire a man to bring home and fuck his wife.

"Since you're looking for wild sex and I'm looking for someone to satisfy my wife, maybe we could help each other out," I told him. "Interested?"

Not knowing what to say, he said, "It depends. What does she look like?"

I pulled out a picture of her taken at the beach and showed it to him. When he saw the picture of my wife, he exclaimed, "Wow, what a fox. You're serious, aren't you?"

I assured him I was and that if it wasn't him, it would be someone else. He eagerly agreed and we set it up for the following Saturday. He would come to our house and pretend he was a hired gun, so to speak.

I didn't say anything to Jackie until Saturday afternoon. When she got back from her weekly errands, I helped her with the bags and then kissed her. "Tonight's the night," I said, out of the blue.

At first she was unsure of my drift, but then a look of panic came over her face. "Tonight? Oh, my gosh. When? Where? I don't know if I'm ready," she blurted out.

I kissed her again and smiled reassuringly. "You have until eight o'clock to get ready. He's coming here."

I went out to buy some booze, and when I returned she was in the bathtub getting ready. I went into the bathroom and she was trimming her pussy. "Why are you doing that?" I asked.

"I want everything to be perfect. But I have to keep stopping because when I put my fingers near my snatch I start to come," she explained.

"Well, I'll let you get ready," I said, and I left the room. When she came out, she started asking me all sorts of questions about the guy. I just assured her she wouldn't be disappointed. We picked out what she was going to wear. Sheer black G-string panties that barely covered her pussy lips, thigh-high stockings and black high heels. Over this she wore a white polka-dot sundress that was very short and low-cut in front and clung to her perfect hourglass figure. She was gorgeous.

"I'm nervous. What am I supposed to do?" she asked. I lit a joint and said, "That's easy. Relax, fuck him any way you want and have the time of your life."

It was seven o'clock. An hour to go and I couldn't wait.

The bell rang at eight on the head. I answered it and Jackie went to the living room and waited. She had smoked a couple of joints and downed a few drinks to loosen up, and she was glowing. I walked Alex into the living room and introduced them. It was obvious from the look on her face that she liked what she saw. They sat down on the couch making small talk.

I excused myself to go and make drinks. I went into the kitchen and made them, then lit a joint and smoked it. I wanted to give them some time alone to relax. When I brought the drinks back they were sitting right next to each other. Jackie was asking him about his line of work. I was worried that Alex might blow it and give away that he wasn't a pro, but he handled it well and played right along.

"When I have the opportunity to be with a woman as beautiful as you, I don't consider it work," he told her. "Believe me, the pleasure is all mine."

"Let's hope not," she teased as she moved toward him and they locked lips in a deep French kiss.

It was started and there was no turning back. As their tongues worked, their hands were exploring each other's body. Alex pulled my wife's dress aside and cupped her breasts. He kissed his way down her neck and took her hard nipples into his mouth. His hand found her thigh, and he slid under her dress and found her wet bush. Jackie was totally into it now, and she let out soft moans as Alex fingered her through her panties and sucked her tits.

Her hand was on his swollen dick, massaging it through his pants. She started fighting with the zipper, trying to get at it.

Alex got up and started to undress. Jackie did the same as she let her dress fall down her body. When Alex saw her standing there in her G-string, stockings and heels, he grabbed her and pulled her to him, kissing her as his hands went to her ass and fondled it.

She pushed away and sat down, helping him finish undressing. When he pulled his shorts down, his erect cock sprang out. It was easily ten inches. Jackie was awed at its size. She wrapped her hand around it and started stroking it as she exclaimed how beautiful it was. She started licking it up and down the entire length, then she slowly took it into her mouth. She began sucking it in more and more. My cock was ready to burst through my pants as I quickly got undressed.

I stroked my pecker slowly as I watched my wife suck Alex faster and faster. Alex warned her he was about to come, but she was loving his dick fucking her mouth so much that she couldn't stop and he exploded into her mouth. She swallowed as fast as she could, but there was so much that some ran out of her mouth and down her chin. She was fingering her soaking wet snatch with her left hand as she milked every last drop of come from his dick with her right. She eagerly licked his cock clean, then wiped the come from her chin and swallowed that up, too.

Alex's cock remained hard as he sat down and started to pull Jackie's panties off. His hand went to her cunt and he buried his middle finger in it as their mouths met. Jackie spread her legs wide as her hand expertly stroked Alex's cock back to a full erection. Alex got on his knees and buried his face into my wife's burning pussy. She screamed with delight as he fucked her with his tongue. Never in my life have I seen Jackie so wild with lust. She came with a screaming fury, and she grabbed Alex's head and pressed it hard into her crotch.

As she came, so did I, stroking my cock furiously. I swear, my come shot three feet into the air.

Alex stood back up as my wife's legs wrapped around him. Her pussy was rubbing against his stomach as they kissed and tried to catch their breath. "Let's go into the bedroom. I want you to fuck me with that gorgeous cock of yours. I want you to fill me with your come," she said. As they walked into the bedroom, my wife took hold of this man's cock and led the way. She looked back at me and asked, "You coming, Stubbly?"

"I'll be right there," I replied.

They went ahead and I got our camcorder. I guess they couldn't wait, because by the time I got in there they were already in a 69 position, with Jackie on top devouring his cock and Alex on the bottom with Jackie's pussy hovering above his mouth. I started the camera and zoomed in on Jackie as she slowly deep-throated Alex's tool. She would let the head pop out of her mouth and lick his shaft up and down, then she would suck the entire length back in. I had no idea how she got that thing all the way down her throat without gagging, but she did. Alex was alternately tonguing and fingering my wife's love box. They were totally oblivious to anything else going on.

Alex's cock swelled even more and he was about to come again. Jackie pulled his rod out of her mouth and said, "Not like this. I want you inside of me."

She moved around and positioned her waiting cunt lips above Alex's dick. She lowered herself onto it, guiding the swollen head into her. She let out a gasp as she took about half of his length in. She worked herself up and down on his cock, each time taking more of it in until she had all ten inches of him inside her. She rotated her hips for a few seconds, then leaned forward and started to kiss him.

She would slide up and he would suck her tits, then she would slide back down on his cock and their tongues would meet.

Each time she slid up, about six inches of his dick would be exposed. When she slid down, he would bury himself in her. They fucked real slow like this for quite a while before Jackie sat up and started to quicken the pace. She rode up his pole until just the head was in her and then she rode it back down.

As they moved faster, she suddenly jumped off and turned

around on her hands and knees. Alex did not have to be told what to do. He quickly got up and entered Jackie from behind, thrusting his entire ten inches into her all at once. She let out a gasp as she put her shoulders onto the bed, arching her back to push hard against Alex, making sure she had every inch of his cock inside her. Alex started to fuck her hard, pulling out and thrusting in. He was hitting home so hard his balls were slapping against her stomach. With each thrust Jackie would push her ass to meet it. I had a good angle with the camera and got a good view of that monster cock going in and out of my wife's snatch. Stroking my cock with my free hand, I was ready to come again.

Jackie was now completely out of control. As she met Alex's every thrust, she came so hard that she made Alex's dick start pumping come deep into her tunnel. As Alex continued to hammer her, his come started to run out of her cunt and drip down her legs. His big cock was wet with her juices and his own jism. Jackie was biting the bed to keep from screaming. As they both reached the end of their orgasms, they collapsed onto the bed, exhausted. Alex wound up spending the night, fucking my wife several more times.

My wife and I have since had several experiences where I was able to watch her get totally satisfied. Hiring a "pro" to get started helped Jackie over any inhibitions she had. She goes out now and picks guys up and brings them home to fuck while I watch. She has seduced several of my friends and has fucked three guys at once while I videotaped them.—*P.M.*, *Truth or Consequences, New Mexico*

PARTY ANIMAL UNLEASHES INNER BEASTS

Since my husband and I moved to our new neighborhood, I've really been wondering about myself and my sexuality. I was once rather active and have had quite a few guys, but since we got married seven years ago, it's just been Bill and I. After the bizarre events that took place last week, though, I've been reevaluating my priorities.

We were invited to a party. I only knew a few people there, and those only slightly. They all seemed to be an average group of professionals, similar to ourselves.

One of the first people I met was Cynthia. She was young, friendly and likable. She had a pleasant smile and very pretty eyes, dark and deep. You could see her trim, athletic body very clearly through the thin summer dress she wore. She was good-looking but didn't really make an issue of it or anything. I had a little chat with her just as we got there, about how Bill and I were getting on in our new home and his new job and all. I didn't think much of it at the time, just the pleasant chitchat that people exchange.

A little later I caught sight of her among the other guests, chatting with some guy. I didn't know him. I later found out that his name was Mike. The way she smiled at him and stood close to him, and the way she fiddled with the belt on her dress, made me think there was something going on between them. As it turned out, they'd never met before that night.

A little while later, on the way to the kitchen to get another glass of wine, I caught sight of her sitting on the couch, grinning across the room at Mike. He was smiling back at her, obviously enjoying her attention. It kind of amused me.

On my way back I caught sight of Cynthia and Mike in the hallway by themselves. They were pressed against one another, talking very intimately, while his hands ran up and down her body. She seemed to quiver at his touch. I watched this teasing and bantering, feeling a little ashamed of myself. No one else was paying any attention—or maybe everyone else just had the good taste to ignore them.

But I was fascinated and kept out of sight, watching their flirting advance to outright lust. His hands began to clutch her ass more firmly. Her ass-cheeks were so round beneath the filmy dress. Cynthia, who was obviously getting off on his attention, squirmed and grinned up at him. Her eyes darted to his lips, as if enticing him to kiss her. He basked in this for a moment (as did I, observing unseen) and then leaned slowly down to kiss her, her expression encouraging him.

Just then the music suddenly changed from a slow song to loud, pulsing, dance music. Cynthia yanked herself away from Mike, then pulled him behind her into the living room. I discreetly followed, lingering at the edge of the crowd. Some people were dancing in the middle of the room, and that's where Cynthia and Mike started to move to the throbbing rhythm.

She moved like a dancer, her whole torso gyrating in a slow, slinky grind against him. Her dark eyes flashed up at him, a sultry smile on her face. I was obviously not the only one watching them because, before long, they were the only ones dancing. Everyone else had stepped aside to make a circle around them.

Her dancing was a blatant seduction. She might as well have been wearing a neon sign that flashed "SEX" as she slithered about, undulating her hips seductively and rubbing her ass up against him. Mike seemed momentarily taken aback, as if too embarrassed to keep this up.

She squatted low before him, keeping in perfect rhythm with the music, and gave him a look that said, "Are you man enough to go for it?" as she shimmied up against him. She made sure the whole length of her body made contact with the very evident bulge in his pants. From that point on, Mike accepted her challenge. There was no turning back for either of them.

She lifted her leg and wrapped it around his waist. His hands clutched at her ass, holding her up as she ground her pelvis into his. Their eyes locked. It was clear to everyone by now that she had nothing on beneath her dress.

The people around me were all amazed—some fascinated, others amused, still others embarrassed. I, too, wondered how anyone could make such a spectacle of themselves, but I could not look away. Then I noticed that Bill was on the opposite side of the room from me, and his eyes were also fixed on Mike and Cynthia. Then Bill looked across the room and our eyes met. An electric shock seemed to pass through me as I looked at Bill. I shuddered with excitement while Cynthia and Mike pushed their erotic romp even further.

As she twisted herself around and back and over, gyrating to the pulsing music, her dress loosened and her right breast tumbled out, her nipple erect and dark. Some of the audience snickered, some clapped and cheered and some, perhaps unsure if she was aware she was exposing herself, felt a little uncomfortable.

But she leaned back against Mike, arching her back and thrusting herself forward as he reached around and clasped her naked breast. As she grinned at the crowd, making sure that we were all watching, her eyes connected with mine and she winked at me. That's when I knew the naked tit wasn't an accident.

As she stared at me, Mike's other hand worked its way down her body, easing her dress up her thighs, revealing the little clump of hair beneath. I couldn't keep from looking down to see her pussy. The thin line of her labia was clearly damp. I must have gasped or looked stunned, for when I looked back into her eyes, she seemed to laugh with delight at my shock.

She then twisted around, her dress above her waist, and jutted her naked ass out. She started to gyrate her round, white ass-cheeks. I was fascinated by the sight of her cheeks squeezing tight, then releasing and spreading before clenching again. She didn't protest in any way when Mike pulled her flimsy dress up over her head, leaving her entirely naked.

I looked across the room at Bill. From the look on his face, I could tell that Cynthia was giving him the eye. But not for long, because it was soon obvious from her lewd and passionate kisses that Mike again had her full attention.

The people around were either getting into it or were growing even more disturbed. One woman was so outraged she dragged her reluctant husband out in a big huff. It was kind of funny—I knew how the woman must have felt, but there was no way I was going to miss any of Cynthia's extraordinary performance.

I watched her coil and curve her sinewy body around Mike. I watched her tongue lap hungrily at his. I watched her thrust her pussy against him, welcoming his fingers as they prodded and parted her lips. She spread her legs to make sure everyone could see all the action. I was stirred—repulsed yet fascinated. I had never seen anything like this. Cynthia was exuding pure, raw lust. She didn't care what anyone thought—I think she was beyond caring. She was into some amazing zone of sensation where her body and mind fed not just on Mike, but on all the eyes trained on her—on her saucy little tits rubbing against his body, on her ass swinging about in proud display, and her pink cunt, all spread open and moist. The harder Mike thrust his finger in, the more she splayed herself for all to see.

Next she began tearing at his shirt, and then she yanked open his trousers and jerked them down and off. I held my breath and sensed everyone around me do the same. We all wondered how far she would take this.

Mike's prick was fully extended and already leaking pre-come. He, too, appeared to be in a trance as Cynthia kneaded his balls and stroked his long shaft. She then dropped to her knees before his cock, as if praying to it. She kept massaging it and caressing her face with it. Her cheeks were getting sticky with its fluids. All the while she grinned up at Mike, her eyes dancing with delight.

Then she looked around the room at all of us, making eye contact with as many of us as possible, including me. I shuddered as she looked right at me and crammed his prick into her mouth. She let out a moan, savoring the taste and texture with unabashed enjoyment.

I began to feel almost faint as my own body quivered beyond my control. Across the room I saw Bill in a similar state, his crotch not just bulging, but with a damp patch starting to show.

Beside me, some guy was standing very close, his breath coming fast and excited, warm on my neck. A clearly sexual energy

emanated from him, and most definitely from me too. Around
the room people were smiling, their bodies moving, their own appetites stirred. Sucking and slurping sounds could be heard over
the music as Cynthia filled her mouth, then moved around and
up and down that sleek, wet staff. She was in a frenzy, attacking
Mike's dick with total abandon, as if she had lost all control of
herself.

But she was actually very much in control. She pulled Mike to
the floor and laid him down. His organ, pointing up ramrod
straight, gleamed with saliva. I had a clear view as she squatted
over his face. Her pussy hovered over his mouth. He reached up
and delicately spread her open with his fingers. She smiled lasciviously at his touch, her eyes darting about the room, making
direct contact with her rapt audience. Then she lowered herself
as his tongue darted out, lapping at her wet lips and hair. She
gasped, like a laugh and sigh combined. Her eyeballs rolled back
and forth and she continued to pant and whimper.

She seemed so completely outside of herself, or so far into herself, that she was no longer present. She seemed lost in a welter
of extraordinary sensations beyond description. But then her eyes
would come back to us, checking up on us: were we still here?
Still watching and enjoying her total exposure? As if that fed her,
she'd disappear back into herself, to feed that tongue lapping at
her clit.

Cynthia shifted away from Mike's face and, like an agile cat,
turned her back to me and poised herself over his magnificent
cock. Again she looked around the room, then glanced over her
shoulder at me, before smiling down at Mike and sliding down
onto his prick, letting it slip deep into her.

I gazed, enthralled, at her pussy, all red and wet as it swallowed
up his cock. She rode up and down on his shaft, slowly at first,
then quicker. Her round white ass was spread wide and her little
asshole winked at us as she plunged up and down with unrelent-
ing force. Mike thrust up into her in perfect rhythm.

It was an awesome spectacle that left me limp and damp. Cynthia was taking us all with her, to the very threshold of total sexual release.

She rode Mike's prick with total abandon. Her head rolled and jerked, her legs pulsed, her buttocks quivered. Little shrieks and moans burst out of her. Her eyes, now glazed, roamed the room to seek us out, her conspirators in wanton carnality. The whole room throbbed to the rhythm of their fucking, and I thought it was actually possible I myself would come just standing there watching this exhibition.

And then, at the last possible moment, she lifted herself off him as that cock popped, and a fountain of white jism gushed up and out. Mike filled the room with his roars at each spurt. It splashed onto his belly, gushed onto her arm, her tits. She leaned down to catch some in her mouth.

The whole room seemed to convulse as Mike roared and erupted. I nearly passed out. Thank God for the guy beside me or I would have hit the floor.

Giggling, Cynthia licked the come off his prick and slurped it up off her lips. She made it look so delicious, I could almost taste it myself. Then everyone started to applaud and cheer. The man beside me let go of my hand to clap, and I had to steady myself before I could join in the ovation. The tension in the room had been released. We all breathed easier.

The party broke up soon after. What can you do after that? Some hurried upstairs to the bedrooms to indulge their urges in more private quarters, others, including us, hurried home to their own bedrooms.

That night I sucked and fucked Bill like I never had before. Together we connected with something we'd never touched. We followed Cynthia's ground-breaking trail and unleashed the rawest, most primal parts of ourselves. I could never do what she did, but I have to admit I envy her. I'm also grateful to her for showing us the way. —*J.G., Cincinnati, Ohio*

ANNIVERSARY COUPLE CELEBRATES
BY GIVING A FAIR SHARE FOR CAB FARE

My first experience with two partners happened on the very date of my third anniversary of marriage to Ian. Ian is tall, very muscular and extremely well-endowed, both physically and sexually. I am always very satisfied with him, but the turn of events on this particular night led me to want even more.

We went out to dinner at a romantic Italian restaurant, where we shared two bottles of wine. After dinner we strolled along the river and smoked a joint. It was a beautiful night. I was more than a little buzzed as well as somewhat turned on. As we turned away from the water and walked back toward a busy street, we embraced in a long, heated kiss. We then hailed a taxi to take us to our next stop, a local club for some dancing.

In the back of the taxi, Ian began to stroke my bare legs, tracing little circles, getting closer and closer to my moist heat. I was wet already. He leaned into me and kissed me deeply, sliding a finger into my unclad pussy. I glanced up and caught the driver watching us in the rearview mirror.

Ian leaned down a little farther and pulled the strap of my dress off my right shoulder. As he hungrily brought his mouth to my right breast, the driver's eyes bored into us. I realized I didn't care in the least—in fact, it turned me on.

Ian kept up his attention to my pussy with his finger until I begged for more. He clumsily unzipped his trousers and let his rock-hard dick come out. He pulled me over on top of him and my wetness took him in with the greatest of ease. After just a few strokes, I was jerked to attention when the cab rolled to a stop.

The driver was staring intently into the rearview mirror. We sat still and acted, unconvincingly, as if nothing was happening. The driver said, "You guys are killing me."

Red-faced, I answered, "We're sorry. We didn't mean to get carried away." Cabbie, as I'll call him, was apologetic for interrupting and explained that this was a first for him. He admitted it was making him so horny he could just burst.

To my total surprise, Ian, after making sure I didn't mind, asked the cab driver if he wanted to join us. Strangely enough I realized I wanted them both, and said so.

Ian asked the driver to guess what I love the best. When he said he didn't know, Ian responded, "You know what she likes? She really loves a tongue in her. You want to taste her?"

Cabbie jumped at the chance. He got out of the cab and came around to open my door. He gently turned me sideways in the seat, then spread my legs and shoved his face between them. He licked and sucked and tickled my clit. I thoroughly enjoyed it. He continued this as I lay back and began to suck my husband hungrily. Then, all of a sudden, I felt a huge rod thrust inside me. I knew it must be larger than Ian's, because it seemed to tickle all the way to my stomach. For a minute I completely forgot about my mouth. Ian quickly reminded me by guiding my head back up and down. All this was most thrilling, and exhausting too!

We skipped the dancing and went straight home, with a free cab ride, of course. Ian and I showered together and made beautiful love under the cascading water. Soon thereafter we snuggled into bed together.

I felt a little guilty for a few minutes, but Ian held me tighter, placed a gentle kiss on my forehead and whispered, "Happy anniversary, my love." I felt completely at peace and we slept a deep sleep together.—*T.L.*, *New York, New York*

HOLIDAYS AREN'T BORING WITH A WIFE LIKE HIS

Well, anybody who says that holidays are boring is wrong. It all started on the Fourth of July. My wife Lanie and I decided to attend the picnic at the local park. We both like to go every year because we get to talk to a lot of old friends whom we don't see very often, while downing a few cold ones.

This year Lanie really dolled herself up for the occasion, and was looking extremely edible. She's twenty-nine years old, five foot ten and has a great figure. She was wearing tight, faded jeans and a tasteful blouse left unbuttoned enough to reveal some sexy, tanned cleavage. To top it all off she was having a great hair day. To sum it up, Lanie and her sexy ass could stun the average male in seconds.

When we arrived at the picnic, it was a typical mob scene, but the crowd in the beer tent was kind of thin.

Lanie and I got a couple of beers from the bar and somehow got into a conversation about fantasies we used to have. Things started to heat up a bit from all the sex talk and Lanie's slinky body. She was getting me hot without even trying. I suggested to Lanie that we play a little game. I would pick out a guy who I thought would be a good sex partner for her and she would select a woman for me. With a little giggle and a smile, Lanie said okay.

I scoped out the tent and saw a guy who looked just right for Lanie standing by the entrance. I pointed him out to her. "Check out the dark-haired guy with the green shirt and light-colored jeans." Lanie smiled and said that he looked interesting. I have to admit that I cheated a bit. I'd seen Lanie checking out this guy when we'd walked in. "Now it's your turn," I told her.

Lanie's task was going to be much harder than mine. She was having trouble finding a woman she thought would appeal to me. She finally picked someone she thought was right for me: a short blonde with a bad attitude whose clothes didn't really fit well. "Nice try," I said, "but she's not for me." There just weren't any sexy women there that night.

As Lanie and I got up and started to walk around, we bumped into an old friend of hers. I figured I'd let them catch up a little and excused myself to fetch a round of beers. As I walked up to the bar to order, the guy I'd selected for Lanie was there, watching the football game on TV. I asked him who was winning, and we soon got into a conversation about sports. We introduced ourselves. His name was Andy.

My beers finally came and I figured I'd better return. The last thing a man wants to do is leave a horny female by herself. When I got back I found her standing there alone. As I handed Lanie her beer, I told her whom I'd run into at the bar, and her face lit up with excitement. I asked her if she wanted to meet Andy. I told her he seemed like a really nice guy.

We walked over and I introduced them. Right off the bat I could tell they hit it off. We all started talking, and I could tell that Andy was attracted to Lanie. It was pretty obvious to me that she was wet for him. After several beers and many laughs, I asked Andy if he wanted to come to our house and watch the rest of the football game. He seemed kind of unsure, but I convinced him with the promise of better booze and good food at the house. Andy said he'd follow us in his car.

I could tell Lanie was happy with the invitation. By this time hormones were pouring out of us, and if anything sexual was going to happen, it was going to happen soon. On our way home I asked Lanie what she thought of Andy. She smiled and said, "Todd, you know what happens to me when I drink. I get very horny. If his cock is like the rest of him, he'll be perfect." I'm proud that Lanie can tell me anything because our marriage is so secure.

When we arrived at our house, I turned on the game and broke out the Jack Daniel's. We were all soon laughing it up. By now Andy and Lanie were checking each other out, but trying not to be too obvious. Lanie and I looked at each other and I could tell she was thinking of making a move, but to be honest I didn't think she had the nerve.

Lanie excused herself and went into the bedroom. Andy and I talked and watched the game. At this point, we were flying high from the drinks and I asked Andy what he thought of Lanie. "Todd, you're a lucky man to have such a sexy woman," he replied, but I think he knew what I really meant.

A few minutes later Lanie came out wearing nothing but a skintight, white see-through teddy, with white stockings and white pumps. Our jaws dropped. With her bronze skin contrasting with that white teddy, her golden nipples erect and her shaved mound dripping wet, Lanie looked incredible. Andy and I were speechless as Lanie twirled around, modeling for us.

"So what do you think boys? Do I look good enough to eat?" she asked coyly. I couldn't believe my eyes. She walked over to where Andy was and sat down next to him, spreading her legs and languidly stroking her wet mound. Andy and I were still in shock. Neither of us could say a word. "Todd," Lanie said, "you are going to sit there and watch me and this stranger fuck and suck."

That's when it finally hit me. Earlier, Lanie and I had been talking about our old fantasies, things that we'd never had the nerve to make happen. Lanie had always wanted to get it on with a stranger and never see him again. Just pure lust with a stranger, nothing more. My fantasy was to watch some guy, either a friend or a stranger, balling my wife. Well, it looked like both of our fantasies were finally going to come true.

Andy looked at me, confusion on his face. I just said, "Go for it. Just don't hurt her and don't make a baby!" Andy smiled. I could tell he couldn't wait to explore her mound.

As Lanie rubbed her wet throbbing pussy with one hand, she started stroking Andy's bulge with the other. They both started to groan, and Lanie's box actually started dripping. Andy reached over and replaced her hand with his as he leaned over and started kissing and sucking her neck. Deep groans came from Lanie. I could tell she was loving it. I was going crazy. My pole was like cement. This was incredible. I couldn't believe it.

Lanie pushed Andy down onto his back and said, "I'm going to fuck your brains out. I'm going to fuck you like you've never been fucked before." She bent over and pulled out his rather large cock. She groaned as she slid her tongue around him. Andy started moaning and held the back of her head to steady her while Lanie worked her magic. The stranger was finding out how good Lanie was at giving head. After lapping him for a minute, she lay back and told him, "Eat me."

Andy leaned over and started rolling his tongue over her wet clit. Andy was a pro and it didn't take long for Lanie to explode. "Now ride me hard and don't stop," Lanie instructed. Andy slipped it in and started riding her. I don't think they noticed, but I had my cock out and was going to town as I sat there watching all this. After some wild riding, Lanie made me get the K-Y jelly from the bedroom. They kept going while I got it. When I returned, Lanie was on all fours waiting for me.

"Give him the K-Y," she told me. I did, and Lanie told Andy to put some on his cock and her asshole. I was shocked. Lanie never wanted to have anal sex before, but she was going for it all. Andy slowly slid his cock into her well-greased rectum. Lanie started to scream with passion. "Faster, faster," she yelled. "Pump my rump." Andy went faster and was almost there. "Before you get there, pull it out and squirt it all over my cheeks," Lanie told him. Andy pumped harder and harder. "Keep going," Lanie encouraged. Finally Andy pulled his cock out and spurted all over Lanie's butt. Wow! What a trip this was!

After Lanie and Andy cleaned up in the shower, Andy left knowing we would never see him again. Lanie gave me a great blowjob, and told me, "I hope you enjoyed it as much as I did."

It was the best sex I'd ever seen. Who says holidays are boring?—R.G., *Harrisburg, Pennsylvania*

BLAME IT ON THE BELLBOY
WHEN A SHY WIFE GOES WILD

What follows is a true experience my wife and I would like to share with your readers. We are an average couple in our early forties, and what happened brought us closer together than we had ever been before.

I had been married to Beth for fifteen years. Like many marriages of that length, ours was in sort of a down period as far as sexual excitement went. It was not that Beth is unattractive. She is a pretty five-foot-six-inch woman with shoulder-length brown hair, a trim figure, lovely long legs and beautiful 36C breasts. I guess you could say she's easy to look at. It was just that, after fifteen years I was bored with the same old thing. To add to that, Beth was never very inventive. Though she was really hot when the right buttons were pushed, she never tried to vary the routine. She always dressed conservatively, even though she had a great body. She was a virgin when we married and I was the only man she'd ever had.

A couple of years ago, I read an article in a magazine about men who liked to watch their wives with other men. At first the idea seemed strange to me. I figured if I ever saw my wife with someone else I would flip out. But, to my surprise, the more I thought about it the more turned on I became.

I began to imagine Beth trying to attract other men. I thought about her showing herself off to other men or being made love to by someone else. At first these thoughts proved to be very confusing for me. However, the more I thought about it or read about it the more real and exciting it became. When I had these thoughts while we made love it seemed to heighten my pleasure. I began to be consumed by the idea of my wife teasing or making love with another man.

When we went out on our boat I would talk her into removing her suit or taking off her top to sunbathe. All the while I assured her nobody could see her, but all the time I was hoping somebody would.

This went on for over a year. Every letter I read in men's magazines about women making love to men while their husbands watched turned me on more. I would read the letter and imagine the woman was Beth. Needless to say, I got myself off time and time again with this fantasy.

I began to buy Beth sexy underwear and nightgowns, low-cut blouses and short skirts. Every purchase was made with one thing in mind: to show her off to other men. My goal was to make my average wife so desirable that she would be hounded by other men. Sometimes she wore the clothes I bought her and sometimes she didn't. I didn't have the courage to tell her what my motive was.

To celebrate our fourteenth wedding anniversary, we went to Toronto for the weekend. It would turn out to be a truly momentous weekend. After years of trying I finally talked Beth into going without underwear on Friday night, our first night in town. We were going out to dinner and the theater. She reluctantly agreed because it was our anniversary and she wanted to please me. It was a real turn-on to know that under her very modest button-front dress she was nude except for her thigh-high nylons.

As we walked down the hall to the elevator I noticed how her breasts swayed and undulated under the thin material of her dress. Her nipples became erect from rubbing against her dress and their outline was very evident as they pushed against the material.

In the cab on our way to the restaurant, I ran my hand up her leg until it made contact with her uncovered cunt. This was a first for us both. Her pubic hair felt like silk, and she was so very warm. As we sat in the dark backseat of the taxi I gently stroked her. She leaned over to kiss me, moaning ever so softly into my mouth. All the while I was hoping the driver would see what we were doing.

After a great meal with a couple of bottles of wine followed by a wonderful play during which we teased each other, we headed back to our hotel. We decided to walk since the weather was nice. We walked arm in arm, kissing and laughing, feeling very much in love. Twice along the way I pulled Beth into the shadows of a building to kiss her and feel her up. I managed to open several buttons on her dress during our passionate embraces. I was thrilled when I realized that she was not aware they were open.

As we walked along, a little tipsy and both of us quite horny, I glanced over and saw that her dress, shifting with her movements, occasionally exposed a side view of her lovely breast right down to the nipple. I had a raging hard-on as we walked through the hotel lobby and she unknowingly exposed herself to some lucky onlookers.

Once in our room we had several more drinks. I was sitting in a chair by the window, looking at downtown Toronto. Beth stood at the foot of the bed. She walked toward me with a seductive smile as she reached down to unbutton her dress. When she discovered the open buttons on her dress, she gasped in shock.

"Oh, no. I must have exposed myself to half of Toronto tonight. I'm so sorry. I shouldn't have had so much to drink. Please don't be mad. I just wanted to celebrate with you."

I got up and held her. I knew the time had come. It was now or never. I said, "I'm actually very turned on by the thought of some other guy seeing you like that. I know it sounds crazy but you're a beautiful woman and I enjoy the way men look at you." Beth looked a little stunned.

"But you're so jealous. Are you just saying that or do you really mean it?"

"I'm very serious," I said. "Sometimes I imagine other men watching you, or being with you. Tonight, walking around the city knowing that you weren't wearing anything under your dress, with other men so close, had me excited from the moment we left the room. Beth, I love you more than anything in the whole world. I hope you don't think I'm disgusting."

She said she loved me and that anything we did together to please each other wasn't disgusting or wrong. She said she loved me so much that she would do anything for me.

"Even flash other guys?" She kissed me and said, "I'll do whatever I can to please you."

We fell onto the bed and made passionate love. We didn't

close the curtains or turn out the lights. Afterward, Beth got up and walked over to the window and looked out at the city. She looked beautiful standing there, her breasts firm, her nipples large and hard, her legs long and inviting, her ass so very pert and smooth.

Seeing her at the window gave me another hard-on. She walked over to the bed and took my cock in her mouth.

The next morning we ordered breakfast from room service, and I was in the shower when it arrived. When I came out of the bathroom, it was obvious that Beth had answered the door in her robe. Through the thin white cotton, I could see the slight dark shadows of her pussy and her nipples. The sway of her breasts made it clear she was naked underneath. In the past, she would have gotten dressed before letting anyone in, but today she was evidently feeling a little looser.

I told her she looked great and that room service must have enjoyed their stop at our room. Blushing, she admitted that the bellhop who had delivered breakfast had checked her out, even though she was probably old enough to be his mother. She said it was kind of fun knowing that he was looking at her with obvious lust. She also admitted that teasing him had been kind of exciting.

I leaned back in my chair and opened my robe to show Beth the huge hard-on she had just given me. I said, "Just imagine what that guy would have done had you been wearing some sheer negligee."

"I didn't bring one with me, so I guess we'll never know," she sighed wistfully.

I told her it was still fun to think about and, with that, I drew her down on the bed and made love to her. Just before I came I whispered how turned on she had made me by turning on the bellhop. We both had powerful orgasms. The only thing Beth could utter was that it was the very best she had ever had.

Later that day we passed a lingerie display in a large department store. I pointed out some of the sexy negligees to Beth. I told her I wanted to buy her one, adding that she might have a chance to use it before we left. She reluctantly agreed. I felt like she might be humoring me.

I was looking for just the right one when I heard Beth say, "Boy, this one's beautiful." She was holding a long black nightgown, sheer except for black satin stripes. It came with a matching robe that tied at the neck and hung partially open. Then she added, "But this is more revealing than anything I have. I don't know if I could wear this. It's just too much. I wouldn't be very comfortable. Let's look for something else."

"If I was the only one to see it and I like the way it looks on you, why not get it to make me happy. Nobody else will ever see you in this." That seemed to reassure her, and I bought the gown. The rest of the day, I told her how much she turned me on.

In bed that night, I began to kiss and suck her nipples, while my fingers stroked her cunt. She became very hot and excited.

I whispered in her ear how much she turned me on and how wonderful she was for letting the bellboy see her. She grew more highly aroused, moaning with each stroke of my finger.

I told her the bellboy must have gotten a huge hard-on just looking at her. "Right now, he's probably making love to his girlfriend, thinking of you," I said. "It turns me on to know that other men want you, but you're all mine."

As I continued to arouse her with my fingers, I asked if she liked teasing the bellboy. She moaned a little. I asked if it made her feel good to know she could turn a man on like that. She moaned again.

When Beth was about to orgasm, I asked if she would do it again. She moaned, "Yes, oh yes! Anything for you!" and, with that, I took her over the edge to a shuddering orgasm. Without hesitation, I crawled on top of her and sunk my throbbing cock into her hot, moist pussy. We fucked well into the night.

The next morning, while Beth was showering, I laid out her new finery. When she saw the negligee on the bed she said, "I don't know about this. If the bellboy sees me in this he might get the wrong message. He might think I really want to, you know, do it with him."

I told her that would be my ultimate fantasy. She asked softly. "Do you really want to see me make love with another man?"

When I told her it was my deepest desire, she kissed me and said, "I would do anything for you."

Beth took her time dressing. She applied her makeup carefully, and even darkened her nipples with lipstick. Her hair was brushed and hung down around her shoulders like silk. When she had finished her nails, she stood there looking at me and I told her she was the sexiest woman in all of Toronto.

In her new gown, her nipples and breasts were clearly visible, as was the dark triangle between her legs. She said, "I'm really nervous. I hope I can go through with this." I poured her a drink to help her relax and ordered breakfast from room service.

Then I laid her down on the bed and told her I was going to help her relax while we were waiting. I knelt between her legs, and raised her gown. Before me was her beautiful pussy. I inhaled her aroma and began to run my tongue up and down her slit. I tongued her clit and made it stand proud. I inserted my tongue and then my finger into her hole. She began to moan. When I moved up to suck her nipples through the gown, they were larger than I had ever seen them before. Her thighs and buttocks grew moist with her juices. For twenty minutes, I kept her on the brink of pleasure.

When we heard the knock on the door, I gave her cunt one last lick, and then we stood up. She adjusted her robe, and stood there, her cheeks flushed, her eyes glazed. She wore an expression of pure lust, and her nipples were obviously erect through the sheer material of her gown. Best of all she smelled of sex. Her thighs and cunt glistened, and gave off an aroma of womanhood. She was ready.

She kissed me and went to the door, while I stepped into the bathroom and turned on the shower as we had planned.

Beth opened the door and let in the bellboy. He was about

twenty-two years old and very good-looking. His eyes lit up when he saw my wife. She slowly turned and walked into the room, directing him to bring the tray in. She took her time getting her money, giving him a good look at her luscious body.

From my vantage point behind the partly opened door, I could see them in a mirror on the wall. He had a noticeable bulge in his slacks. He couldn't take his eyes off her and the longer he looked the harder his cock got.

Beth handed him some money and told him to wait. She looked at me from across the room, then smiled and said, "I don't seem to have any more money for a tip. Maybe there's something else? From that bulge in your pants I bet you could think of something."

I saw the bellboy move to Beth's side. He kissed her neck as his hand came up to caress her breast. As he lowered his hand to her dripping cunt and felt it through her gown, he asked, "What about the guy in the shower?"

"Don't worry. He likes it when I fuck other guys," Beth said. With that, she turned and kissed him full on the lips, then guided him to the bed. I stepped out of the bathroom, still staying out of sight, my cock throbbing. I was about to live out my ultimate fantasy.

I watched as Beth disrobed him. When she pulled his slacks and underwear down, his nine-inch cock sprang to attention. It was much longer than my six inches and a little larger in girth.

Beth dropped to her knees and began to blow the stranger. It was a delight to see my wife of fifteen years sucking this young man's cock. She moaned with every thrust as he slid it in and out of her mouth. She acted as if she couldn't get enough.

After five minutes or so he stood her up and peeled her gown and robe off. He gasped when he saw her body, and laid her back on the bed.

I moved in to get a better view. As he kneeled and buried his head in her crotch, she looked at me and said, "Come here, honey. Be with me."

Aware of me now, he started to pull away from Beth's juicy snatch but she put her hand behind his head and guided him back between her thighs.

I walked to the bed and she took my hand and guided me down so I was next to her on the bed. She leaned over and kissed me, and then started to talk to me in a soft whisper while he ate her cunt.

"Honey, he's licking my pussy. He just put his tongue in my hole. Nobody else except you has ever done that to me. It feels so good. Just think, someone I never met before is eating me. I'm letting him do it to me for you. I'm so hot I can't wait until I can feel his cock in me. It tasted so good and it felt so big and smooth. I loved it in my mouth. Do you want him to fuck me now? My cunt is on fire. I already had two orgasms but I really need to feel him pounding into me. Tell me if you want me to let him fuck me, honey. Tell me if you want this man's cock buried deep in your wife's pussy. I want it bad, honey. Tell me it's okay."

"Fuck him, Beth. Fuck him good. Let him pump you full of his hot come. Do it for me, baby." I kissed Beth again and she moaned into my mouth as she had yet another orgasm.

Beth guided the bellboy up and began to lick her juices from his face. "Fuck me for all you're worth," she said. "I want your big cock in my pussy."

When the stranger lifted her hips, about to penetrate her, Beth stopped him and told me to watch his cock enter her pussy. I slid down until my head was about a foot from her moist cunt. She reached down and guided the head of his cock to her opening. Ever so slowly he began to sink his big prick into my wife. I watched until it was buried to the balls. When he slowly withdrew, his cock was covered with Beth's juices. Her pussy grasped his dick as if trying to prevent it from ever leaving her. He soon established a steady fucking rhythm, and Beth moaned with each stroke. They fucked furiously.

After a few minutes, he rolled onto his back and Beth rode his cock. As she bounced up and down I stood by watching. She took my hand and pulled me to her, and kissed me as she fucked him. He rolled Beth onto her back again and began to pound her. I could tell he was about to come. Beth had me lie down next to her, and she was kissing me when the stranger stiffened and moaned. As I lay there kissing my wife, another man was pumping her cunt full of jism. Then Beth moaned and stiffened as she climaxed. Her legs were wrapped around the bellboy, holding him deep in her cunt.

I watched him pull out, and his large, softening cock was covered with their fluids. As he stood up and began to dress, I sat between Beth's spread thighs, gazing at her freshly fucked cunt. Her pussy hair was soaked with their sweat and juices. Her lips were swollen and her slit was oozing another man's come. It flowed from her cunt down between her ass-cheeks and pooled on the bed beneath her. She looked more beautiful and desirable than I had ever seen her.

As I heard the bellboy close the door behind him, Beth gently stroked the back of my head, and slowly pulled me forward, directing my face to her dripping pussy.

To my surprise I ate her out. I then moved up and kissed her. Just as I was sinking my cock into my wife's well-used pussy, she licked my face clean and tried to suck my mouth dry. We fucked until one that afternoon. It was the best sex we ever had. Beth is now a changed woman and every day is as exciting as the first.—
Name and address withheld

COUPLE'S NEW MOTTO: IF THE SHOE FITS, BARE IT!

I'm a forty-seven-year-old man blessed with a wife twenty-one years my junior. I met her four years ago at a local college where I was taking a refresher course in real estate. We dated for about one year before getting married. We had both been raised to believe in a strict moral code; so—although we did plenty of petting and necking—we didn't have intercourse until our wedding night.

It wasn't until a year and a half later, however, that we opened up to each other enough to discuss our sexual fantasies.

We were reading the "Someone's Watching" section of *Penthouse Letters* when my wife suddenly confessed that she was a closet exhibitionist. Nothing, it seemed, turned her on as much as the idea of cockteasing men by exposing herself to them in public places. Fortunately, this was one fantasy my wife could easily accomplish. She is an extremely attractive woman who has little trouble arousing men even when fully clothed.

That very night my wife and I agreed that we would try to fulfill her fantasies. After working out certain guidelines to minimize risk, we embarked upon our new sexual adventure. I'm writing this letter in order to share some of the great experiences we've had.

At first we started off simply. One day we got on a bus together and pretended not to know each other. My wife sat across from a nerdy, pimple-faced eighteen-year-old who had "virgin" written all over him. I sat nearby. She was wearing a short skirt over a pair of sheer, white panties. Slowly but surely she hiked up her skirt and parted her shapely thighs. I don't know which popped out further, the kid's eyes or the bulge in his pants.

Several times we've gone to adult bookstores together, knowing they're excellent places to hunt for horny men. Upon entering a store, my wife would browse the shelves of steamy X-rated materials. She assumed a variety of provocative poses beneath walls covered with photos of flesh.

But soon, reaching for the top shelf and letting a guy glimpse her firm, panty-clad ass wasn't enough of a thrill for her. She began making eye contact with her victims, especially the young, well-built ones. She'd wink and leer at them and slowly circle her lips with her hot pink tongue. Sometimes, when she thought it was safe, she'd lock eyes with a guy, reach her hand underneath her skirt and finger herself to a powerful orgasm. I began to think she wouldn't be happy until she had guys dropping their pants in public and beating off. Several times, we had to leave the stores in a hurry, fearing for her safety.

As her nerve increased, we tried wilder and wilder things. Once, she arranged to have a masseur come to our home. I hid in the closet while he gave her the massage. To tell you the truth, I almost pitied the poor guy as I watched my young, sexy wife tease the hell out of him. She let him touch and rub oil over every part of her nude body. But (because of an agreement we had made earlier) she wouldn't touch him back; nor would she allow him to relieve himself in any way. After he limped out the door, I came out of the closet and we had great sex.

The last incident I'll share took place in a shoe store of all places. We entered the store about ten minutes before closing time, when the store and the mall surrounding it were nearly deserted. I told the clerk that my daughter needed a pair of blue shoes to match her blue panties. My wife then lifted her skirt, took her panties off and handed them to the startled young clerk. She then sat down demurely and waited for service. The clerk was back out with a pair of shoes before I could even blink. A second clerk also materialized, ready and willing to provide my wife with any service she might require.

My wife allowed each clerk to fit one shoe. Even though there were two men on the job, it took a lot longer than usual. It's quite possible they were distracted by the view.

Suddenly, with both clerks still kneeling before her, my wife spoke up. "Do you like feet?" she asked them coyly.

The clerks nodded dumbly.

"I just figured that since you work in a shoe store, you must really like feet," she continued. "Would either of you like to kiss my feet?" she asked, wiggling her manicured toes in front of their eyes.

The clerks said nothing but the next thing I knew, I was witnessing the wildest thing I had ever seen: two young guys we had never met before were kissing my wife's feet and rapturously sucking on her toes as if they were small, hard cocks.

I could tell that my wife was really hot for these guys, so I let things go a little further than I normally would have. I handed her a dildo and said, "Show the guys what you do at parties." She immediately grabbed the dildo and crammed it into her tight, wet twat. She was on fire now, and the two clerks were devouring her with their eyes. I handed her a second dildo and, after lubricating it with her juices, she forced it up her ass.

At this point, I suggested to the guys that they give her a hand. (I think they would have done so whether I wanted them to or not.) They brought my wife to an unbelievable orgasm. She then brought out the guys' cocks and masturbated each of them to orgasm. Later she told me that it had been only the second time she had done that to a man besides me.

I love showing my wife off and she enjoys it too. Our sex life is now very satisfying because we dared to let our fantasies come true.—K.L., Muncie, Indiana

MORE SHOE STORE HIGH-JINX! WILLING WIFE SHAKES HER BOOT-Y

Heather is the most wonderfully sexual woman I have ever met, and it has been my great pleasure to be married to her for the past sixteen years. She is more than willing to accommodate my perversions and more than able to think up many of her own.

Heather is also a real beauty. She stands five feet, nine inches tall and has light brown hair that cascades over her shoulders and around her angelic face. Her body is perfectly proportioned. Her breasts are gorgeous and are adorned with large dark-brown areolae and nipples that stick out a full half inch when aroused.

To top it all off, Heather has remained in tremendous physical shape. She walks five miles every day, which keeps her body as hard and shapely as a granite sculpture. Her long, firm legs are strong enough to squeeze the come right out of you when she wraps them around you to fuck.

Needless to say, when Heather walks by men, they (and their cocks) sit up and take notice. This brings me to one of my favorite pastimes: I love to watch men looking at my lovely wife. The more she shows, the better. I love it, and you better believe she likes showing off as well.

One day, about two weeks ago, Heather and I took a day off from work and decided to go shopping at a new mall located about ninety miles from our home. We rose at six in the morning to make the one-and-a-half-hour drive. When Heather came into the kitchen that morning my dick immediately sprang to attention. She had on a tight semitransparent top through which I could clearly make out the outlines of her large nipples. She also wore a black, pleated miniskirt. Her long, slender well-tanned legs were bare. Her outfit was topped off by a pair of three-inch high heels.

The moment I saw her, I wanted to lay her on the table and bury my face in her sweet pussy; but the day was young, and her outfit (as well as the mischievous twinkle in her eyes) told me to wait and see what the day would bring.

We arrived at the mall just as it was opening for business. After about half an hour of window shopping, we bought some coffee and seated ourselves on a bench near the top of a spiral staircase. I soon noticed that Heather had not chosen our bench at random: anyone coming up the stairs had only to glance slightly upward to see her lovely legs. Soon a well-built man with a mustache started to ascend the stairs. When Heather spotted him she slowly uncrossed and re-crossed her legs. This caught the man's eyes instantly.

Pretending she was looking over her shoulder at a store window, Heather seductively spread her legs once more, giving the young stranger an unobstructed view up her skirt at (I assumed) her customary lace panties. At this point our young voyeur tripped and nearly fell down the stairs. Watching his reaction made me hard as stone.

After teasing a few more passers-by, we got up and continued our stroll through the mall. As we walked hand in hand, Heather turned to me and asked if I had enjoyed the show so far. I gave her a kiss on the cheek and briefly placed her hand on the raging hard-on hidden in my jeans. "Judge for yourself," I said.

Our next stop was a shoe store. Stopping in front of the store, Heather pointed out a good-looking young man helping an older gentleman try on shoes. With a twinkle in her eye, she announced that I too needed a new pair of shoes. I entered the store alone while Heather went to the bathroom to freshen up.

The young salesman, whose name was Ross, was quite helpful. I had been trying on shoes for about ten minutes when Heather waltzed in looking incredibly sexy. She sat in a chair directly across from me. Spotting her, Ross dropped me like a hot potato and instantly turned to help her. Looking at Heather, I couldn't really blame him.

She told him she would like to try on a pair of red heels. Ross looked at me and I told him to go ahead and wait on the young lady since I was really in no hurry. Ross turned back to Heather, gently raised her foot up onto his stool and removed her shoe. As he did so, Heather let her thighs fall slightly apart. It was only then that I discovered that Heather had not worn her usual panties. She was wearing a pair of hot-pink crotchless panties with black, lace trim. Ross froze as he caught sight of my wife's beautiful pussy. Then, without a word, he rose to retrieve a new pair of heels. When he returned, he again placed her foot on his stool.

Leaning back in her chair, her nipples taut against her tight top, Heather once more spread her legs for all to see. Her pussy—which she keeps shaved clean from the top of her pussy-lips all the way to her asshole—was cherry red from excitement. The lips were full and succulent, and her love juice glistened as it flowed down to her asshole. It was the most unbelievably sexy thing I have ever witnessed, period.

I was more turned on than I ever imagined possible, and I imagine the same was true for Ross. He looked over at me and I just shrugged my shoulders. Since we were the only three people in the store and I had made no sign of objecting, Ross decided to go for it. He turned back to Heather and ran his hand lightly up the inside of her thigh. Heather closed her eyes and spread her legs even further.

Encouraged, Ross tossed caution to the wind.

Slowly sliding forward on his stool, he inched his hand higher and made contact with Heather's hot, wet box. Heather emitted a low guttural moan. He then started to gently caress my wife's lovely pussy. He inserted two fingers into her cunt and began to massage her clit with his thumb. Heather was hot as fire. She began to rock back and forth on his fingers, riding them as if they were a hard, throbbing cock. The juices flowed over his fingers and dripped onto the faux-leather chair. Within minutes Heather was in the throes of an intense orgasm. She threw her head back and grunted loudly. Her cries of passion were so loud, I was afraid a crowd might gather in front of the store.

After Heather had settled down she stood, straightened her clothes, thanked Ross and walked away. I soon followed.

I met Heather down the hall from the store. Without saying a word, we hurried to the parking garage and climbed into our minivan. I lay her down on the back seat, dropped my pants and draped her long legs over my shoulders. With one swift thrust I buried my diamond-hard cock in her wonderfully hot canal. Neither of us lasted more than three minutes before we simultaneously came.—J.F., *Minneapolis, Minnesota*

IT TOOK BEAUTIFUL STRIPPERS
TO EXPOSE HER PASSION FOR HIM

I have been an occasional reader of your magazine for many years. Like many of your letter writers, I didn't think I'd ever have the opportunity to write a letter of my own. As a married thirty-five-year-old with children, I thought my glory days were over; but on one September day, I was proven wonderfully wrong.

I work at a franchised national chain in a middle management position. One September day I had to go to a meeting in a large city with another manager from our firm. The other manager is a beautiful lady in her early thirties. In spite of her beauty, I had never considered trying anything with her because I knew she was happily married with a nice house, a sweet dog, a two-car garage and all the other accouterments of a dull but happy life.

Sioban and I had a good relationship at work but other than an occasional collision in the hallway, we had never had any physical contact. I must admit, however, that I treasured those encounters and had often dreamt about how things might develop from these encounters.

Anyway, on the day of our trip, I went to pick Sioban up at her house at six in the morning. The city was about three hours away so we had to get an early start. As I pulled into Sioban's driveway, she walked out of her front door, looking as beautiful as ever. She was wearing a light blue dress that fit rather snugly around her ample bust and waist line, but was loose and flowing below her waist.

She got into my car with a big bright smile and a grand good morning. We headed for our destination chatting about our work, our mates, vacations and various other safe subjects. All of a sudden, though, Sioban asked me if I intended to visit the strip joint that all of the other men in our office frequented whenever they got the chance to visit the city. I was actually kind of shocked by this comment and I just laughed it off by saying, "Yeah, right!"

Shortly thereafter, we arrived at the hotel where our meeting was to take place. As we walked in through the huge front entrance, I kept picturing how nice it would be to have a private meeting with Sioban in one of the hotel rooms.

The meeting was pretty much a standard affair. It ended with a buffet lunch, but Sioban and I blew it off and decided to eat somewhere a little more interesting. We proceeded downtown to an old building that had recently been converted into a series of shops and eateries.

The restaurant we chose had an old-world ambiance and great food, but it was the conversation I enjoyed the most. It was very intimate, kind of like a first date when you get as much from looking deeply into your date's eyes as you do from the conversation. We spent a lot of time discussing past relationships. The conversation was at times intense, but always very pleasant.

Once in the car, Sioban asked me if I regretted missing out on the strip joint. I thought to myself: This is the second time this woman has brought this subject up. Could she actually be interested in going there? So I turned to her and said: "Do you?"

Sioban blushed and averted her eyes. I asked her if she wanted to go there with me. After what seemed to be an eternity she responded, "If I said I did, would you tell anyone back at the office?"

I assured her that I would not, because I didn't think it would be a good idea for my wife to find out. As we discussed what we were about to do, I noticed that she was no longer her usual calm cool self. She was nervous, but it was much more of an excited nervousness than an apprehensive one. It was obvious that she could hardly wait to get there. I didn't tell Sioban, but she wasn't the only one.

I paid her cover charge and we entered the smoke-filled front door. It was midafternoon and the place was far from packed. Only one of the three stages was being used, so I guided Sioban towards an empty table about ten yards away from it.

The dancer teased for a while before finally removing her

g-string. She teased and rubbed her twat in several guys' faces and collected as many tips as she could before the song was over. I had to explain to Sioban how the whole thing worked. It was arousing just telling her about the process.

After a couple of different dancers had performed, Sioban asked if I was going to sit up near the stage. I didn't want to act like a chicken, so I assured her that I would and asked if she would join me. She declined and said that she would keep an eye on me from the table.

I got to the stage just as a very well-endowed, dark-haired dancer stepped into the spotlight. At this point, there were only two of us up near the stage: myself and an older man who must have weighed a good three hundred pounds. The dancer (her stage name was "Ginger") gave me more than my share of attention. Toward the end of her third song, she reached down my pants, gave me a quick squeeze and nodded at the audience as a sign of approval. After getting an appreciative chuckle from the crowd, she asked if I would like a private dance later. I tucked a buck into her garter and said, "You betcha!"

When I sat back down at our table, I noticed a big smile on Sioban's face. I smiled back and asked her what was so funny? She said she thought that the way I tucked the dollars into the dancer's garter was really cute. I asked again if she wanted to move closer to the stage but once more she declined.

A few minutes later, Ginger came to our table, grabbed my hand and said, "It's your turn, honey!" She pulled me out of my seat and led me to the back corner of the club. This part of the club was designed for only one thing: private dances.

Ginger was good and she knew it! She worked me over in every possible way short of giving me a blowjob. About halfway through the song, I noticed that Sioban had moved to a different table, one which allowed her to keep a closer eye on my activities.

When the dance was over and I had caught my breath, I asked Ginger if she could arrange to have one of the dancers put on a special show for Sioban. She agreed that this could be arranged and took my money.

I returned to my seat. Sioban and I talked and watched a few more dancers until a dancer named Tammy showed up to show us her stuff. She began to strip in front of us, shaking her tits in both of our faces. Then, gradually, she began to pay more attention to Sioban. I could tell Sioban was excited and so could Tammy. Soon, Tammy was dancing solely for Sioban's benefit. Her bra came off and her large firm breasts bounced free. Then she leaned over and swayed her breasts just inches from Sioban's upturned face.

As Tammy worked on Sioban, she occasionally paused to give my swollen cock a rub and me a big wink. When the show was over, Sioban smiled but didn't say much. After watching a few more dancers perform we decided it was time to head home.

As we headed for the car, neither one of us said anything. Once in the car we didn't say much either. Instead, Sioban turned to me without a word, put her arms around me and began to kiss me—a French kiss at that!

The only sounds in the car were moans of passion. Sioban rolled toward me so that her chest was rubbing against my arm. I slowly put my right arm around her and began to rub her back. She responded by going straight to my swollen groin. The heavy kissing went on for a few more minutes before I pulled away from her to gaze into her eyes for a moment. Then I told her how beautiful I thought she was and softly kissed her.

Without speaking, she grabbed my hard cock and began her intense kissing again. I slowly moved my hand to her tits. I massaged her breasts through her dress. Her nipples were erect and her breasts were very firm. In fact, the only thing in the car firmer than Sioban's chest was my aching cock wrapped in her right hand.

Next, I popped the top two buttons on her dress open, revealing a bright red lacy bra. After enjoying the feel of her breasts through the silky material of her bra for a while, I found the front release clasp on her sexy bra and used it. Since her large globes were now exposed for all to see, I suggested we move the car to a more secluded spot. She agreed and temporarily released her stranglehold on my swollen member.

As we drove to the rear of the parking lot (neither of us wanted to take the time to drive any further), she told me how she had long admired me and how watching the dancers grabbing my crotch had looked like so much fun that she just couldn't keep her hands off of me when we got in the car. I didn't argue. I just parked the car and grabbed her again, picking up where we'd left off.

Sioban picked up where she'd left off too—at my belt buckle. It didn't take long for her to release my manhood and suck it deep into her mouth. Back at the strip club, I had pictured Ginger doing this to me, but I had never dared hope that Sioban's lips would be wrapped around my penis that very evening!

While Sioban was working away, my hands roamed over as much of her body as I could reach. It didn't take long for me to unload in her mouth. She moaned with pleasure as I filled her up. She kissed her way up to my mouth and I could taste my own juices as I probed her mouth with my passionate tongue.

Our kissing continued as I resumed massaging her tits. Finally, she undid the last few buttons of her dress. The final button revealed red panties matching her red bra. (I almost came a second time just at the sight of them.) Traces of her bush were poking through the lace on either side of her tiny panties. I worked my mouth and tongue down from her face, stopping briefly when I reached her tits and belly button. When I reached her aromatic crotch, I paused and kissed her mound. Then I worked at her inner thigh with my tongue, kissing and licking along the edge of her panties. The aroma of her wet twat was driving me wild.

My first foray beneath her silky panties was limited to just one finger. The warm slickness of her pussy lips tempted me to slip my finger inside her, but I waited. Her panties were now stained by the abundant moisture running from her slit. I continued to kiss my way around her groin before finally pulling her panties to one side and revealing an absolutely beautiful pussy. Her curly black hair was neatly trimmed, leaving just a narrow swath of carpet at the top. The sides of her dripping slit were perfectly clean-shaven.

I dove in head first, working her clit over and occasionally letting my tongue stray to her opening. As I happily tongued away at her, she moaned as if she hadn't received this kind of service in years. Before long she was trembling with pleasure as a powerful climax overcame her. Her screams of pleasure quickly quieted to heavy breathing as she returned to reality.

I kissed my way back up her body to her mouth. I kissed her, letting her taste her own juices. This was wonderful, but the job wasn't done yet—my rigidity had returned. I slowly slid my prick up and down the length of her slit, stopping briefly when Sioban moaned, letting me know I had made contact with her clit. After a few moments of this, she grabbed my ass and pulled me in as deep as I could go. We both started going as if there was no to-morrow. I looked and watched my dick pumping in and out of her beautiful, black-haired pussy and glistening with its shiny coat of vagina saliva. The sight of this brought me to the brink once again. I got kind of worried about coming inside her, so I asked her permission.

"Please do," she answered. Her words released the floodgates. With a loud cry I exploded within her. With my cock still erect and inside of her, we kissed and caressed for a few minutes before getting dressed. As I looked out of the car, I noticed that the parking lot was much more crowded than when we'd first entered the car. Some cars were only ten or twelve yards away. How could they have not noticed us?

Anyway, we both got dressed and commented about how much fun it had been, and how we had never expected something like this to happen, even though we had both wanted it to happen for years.

We had an enjoyable conversation on the way home. Sioban

had to use a Kleenex to mop up her panties because my semen was running out of her. After the sun had gone down and we were nearly home, Sioban leaned over, gave me a big smooch and said that she had really enjoyed our trip and that she couldn't wait to go again. She also wanted to make sure that I kept our little secret.

With a big smile on my face, I assured her that I would. I drove the rest of the way home with the windows down, hoping to air out the car. It had the unmistakable odor of passion, and my wife would no doubt recognize it.

The next day at the office, it was business as usual. We both acted as if nothing had happened. Now every time that I see her walk down the hall my mind wanders back to that special day in September. I just hope that I don't have to wait till next September to go again.—F.G., *Boston, Massachusetts*

SHRINKING VIOLET BLOSSOMS BENEATH THE STROBE LIGHTS

My wife Nancy had a part in a play that ended in two weeks. To celebrate, I took her out for an expensive dinner, and then dancing at a new club. My plan was to see how she would behave in a club if I wasn't around. While we were dancing at the nightclub, I got a prearranged message on my pager. I pretended to use the phone and then went back to Nancy to tell her I'd have to be gone for at least an hour. If I had to be gone longer, I added, I would leave a message on our home answering machine. Nancy offered to leave with me, but I told her to stay and have a couple of drinks because I would probably be back. I then pretended to leave the club. My friend Steve, who works at the club, led me to a small room where I could watch Nancy through a two-way mirror. She was sitting at a table near the main dance floor. It took less than a minute for a guy to sit across from her and buy her a drink.

At that point, I noticed a group of three well-dressed black men in their mid-thirties checking her out. They were seated in a semi-circular booth—one of those old-style ones with a curtain that could be drawn for privacy. By their table, a magnum of champagne was being chilled. The nicest looking of the three men got up and approached Nancy. He was probably six-five, and he was wearing an expensive Italian suit. Steve had rejoined me earlier, and he now informed me that the black guy's name was Jim, and that his two friends were Tim and Doug. "Jim's a real operator," he added as he left the room.

After a while Jim asked Nancy to dance. She seemed a little tipsy walking toward the dance floor. Jim folded Nancy in his big arms. Soon he started rubbing her back. Eventually his hand was squeezing her ass. Nancy reached around and pushed his hand away, but it soon drifted down there again. After pushing him away a couple of more times, she gave up and nestled closer to him.

I guess this was the encouragement Jim needed. With his hand between her legs, Jim said something to her and she nodded. The guys pushed the table out a little bit and drew the curtain. From my vantage I could see everything, while from down in the club, you'd have to go out of your way to get a peek.

Nancy climbed onto the table and turned to face Jim. She reclined on her back, resting on her elbows, her pussy right in Jim's face. She lifted her ass up off the table and he removed her thong, balling it up and putting it into his coat pocket. He then pushed her dress up and spread her legs. Slowly he ran his tongue up and down the seam of her little red bush. Tim and Doug just smiled and sipped their champagne, watching the proceedings with relish. It wasn't long before Nancy was moaning and pulling Jim's head into her crotch. Finally, she began trembling as a huge orgasm coursed through her.

When she had caught her breath, Nancy sat up on the table

and pulled the dress over her head. The guys' eyes nearly popped out of their sockets when they saw how big and firm her tits were. All Nancy had on now was a pair of black stockings and high heels. She reached over, undid Jim's buckle, unzipped his pants and pulled down his slacks and underwear. Out sprang a huge black cock nearly twice as big as mine. Nancy grinned devilishly, wrapped a hand around it and gave it a few pumps. Then she leaned back on the table and let her legs dangle over the edge.

Jim stood before her, and with his hand he guided his cock up and down along her wet slit, coating it with her copious juices. Then he slowly started to penetrate her, inching his way deeper with each stroke.

Nancy's box is really tight, so I wasn't sure he'd be able to fit it all in; but after about twenty strokes he was buried to the hilt and his big balls were draped over her asshole. There was a look of sublime satisfaction on Nancy's face when she realized she'd taken his whole cock inside her.

Jim proceeded to give her a nice slow fuck. With each stroke, he pulled his cock nearly all the way out and then slowly slid it back in till it disappeared inside her. Doug and Tim, not wanting to be left out, leaned in from either side to suck on a tit. Nancy's nipples are really sensitive, so I knew this would get her super hot. Jim then started fucking her harder. Nancy met his every thrust, trying to get every inch of his dick inside her. Soon she was squirming about so much, Doug and Tim had a hard time keeping their mouths on her nipples.

This scene was better than I'd even imagined. Nancy's milky white skin contrasted amazingly with Jim's deep umber. The sight of that huge, black, glistening hose stretching out her little pink slit was making my heart pound and my dick ache. I knew he was reaching places inside of her I'd never been.

Nancy was so transported by the fucking Jim was giving her she didn't even notice when Doug took his mouth off her tit and opened up the booth's curtain. The dance floor was treated to the sight of a lovely young redhead, totally naked, her legs spread wide to accommodate the immense black cock ramming into her. Jim lifted her legs onto his powerful shoulders and really started giving it to her. Nancy panted and writhed, yelling at him to fuck her even harder. Finally she began convulsing and tossing her head from side to side as a massive orgasm swept through her.

I guess the sight of her come sent Jim over the edge. He growled and his thrusts became short jabs as he blasted his cream into my wife's spasming pussy. He shot the first few spurts deep, then he pulled out and sprayed thick jets of gooey cream all over her pubic hair.

Just then, a song ended and people started clapping. I thought Nancy would turn fifty shades of red when she realized she'd had an audience. But, to my utter dismay, she smiled, stood up and took a bow. She was shiny with sweat, her nipples were stiff and aroused and her pubic hair was visibly matted with come. While everyone watched, my wife got on her knees in front of Jim, sucked the come off his dick and zipped him up.

By now it was getting late, and (perhaps due to Nancy's fine example) the club really started to hop. I saw women dancing topless and a guy getting a blowjob from a cute blonde.

After they finished their champagne, Jim took Nancy by the hand and led her, like his personal slut, up the stairs and into the VIP rooms. Doug and Tim went along. I had to go down a corridor and look through several different two-way mirrors before I found where they went. My efforts weren't wasted.

They were in an empty room that had an upholstered table in the middle of it. Jim told Nancy to lay back and spread her legs. She willingly obeyed. Tim and Doug then undid their pants. Their cocks were as big as Jim's. Doug's was even a little thicker. When he slipped that thing into Nancy's slick cunt, she just about went crazy, but her moaning was soon silenced when Tim pushed his tool into her mouth. When passers-by saw that a hot young redhead was being doublefucked by two big black men, they came in to watch.

Soon a good-sized crowd had gathered. A nice-looking

brunette in a minidress leaned over, braced herself against the table with her arms and started wiggling her ass provocatively at the guy behind her. The guy lifted her dress, freed his cock and penetrated her. She formed an "O" with her lips and began grinding her hips, all the while staring in rapt arousal at Nancy.

Nancy was well worth staring at. She was on her back, her legs spread wide and Doug's dark meat sliding back and forth in her wet pussy. Her sweet lips were wrapped around a second, big black cock, and she was massaging her own breasts and tweaking her nipples with her hands. She seemed to be coming every two minutes.

It was so incredible. I had to remind myself time and again that this was my wife down there, enjoying the thrill of carnal pleasures in a room of strangers.

The two guys picked up the pace as they approached their climaxes. Nancy thrust her pelvis to meet each of Doug's strokes even as she gently stroked Tim's big balls, trying to coax the cream out of them.

"Here it comes baby," Tim bellowed. His cock started pulsing and a torrent of come erupted into Nancy's mouth. She tried to swallow it, but she was panting so hard that much of it spilled over her lips and chin. Suddenly she started shaking wildly. Tim's cock slipped out of her mouth and she gasped, "I'm coming! I'm coming! Fuck me, yeah, fuck me!"

Doug bore deep into her, groaned and filled her box with come as her hips shook wildly.

A minute later, the brunette and her guy went into their own orgasms. Then, without taking her eyes off Nancy, the brunette removed the cock inside her and took off her dress. As Doug and Tim backed away from the table zipping up their deflated dicks, the brunette climbed up and started sucking Nancy's nipples. Seconds later they were kissing passionately, mixing saliva and jism with their tongues.

A few moments later, the girl shimmied up Nancy's torso and

put her knees on either side of Nancy's head. Her come-soaked pussy was just inches above Nancy's face.

My cock got even harder when my wife reached up and pulled the girl's hips down so that her chestnut snatch landed on her open mouth. I could see Nancy's tongue probing vigorously, causing the girl to let out a long, low moan.

She rode Nancy's face for a while, then turned around and went down on her. Now they were locked in a furious 69. It seemed like they were competing to see who could make the other one more excited.

I thought Nancy had won when she slicked her index finger with saliva and worked it into the girl's asshole, but then the girl did the same to Nancy. Finally, they exploded together, hips shaking and tongues writhing against spasming pussies. It was quite a scene.

The girl climbed off Nancy and they both stood up. Their faces were shiny and slick with juices and perspiration. Jim handed Nancy her dress and she put it back on. Then Jim, Tim and Doug escorted her out of the club. It was three-thirty in the morning.

I left the club by a back door and raced home to wait for Nancy. I was so worked up by what I'd seen, that I couldn't wait to fuck her silly. Once I got back home, however, it quickly became clear she wouldn't be back anytime soon. I paced, looked out the window and drank beer as the hours passed. There was no way I could sleep—not with all the images of Nancy's night out playing in my mind.

At dawn a shiny black Jaguar pulled into the driveway and deposited my disheveled wife at the doorstep. She was tired, a bit hungover and her pussy was stretched and sore—I could tell by the way she was walking.

She said she'd been to an all-night party. All in all, she said, she'd had a great time and she'd tell me about it after she'd had some sleep. As soon as she woke up that afternoon, I got the whole story, never letting on that I knew most, if not all of the details already. The only thing I didn't know was where she'd spent the time between leaving the club and getting home. She said, "When I get good and horny sometime, I'll tell you all about it."—R.R., *Marietta, Georgia*

SHE'S SPENT A LIFETIME MOONING, AND SHE'S HAPPY TO SHOW YOU HOW

My wife Janie and I are both thirty-three and have been happily married for nine years. Janie is a very sexy and passionate woman. Her shapely long legs make heads turn wherever we go. Janie's auburn hair matches her lovely bush but what's most impressive about Janie is her luscious ass, which she just loves to have licked and fingered.

Janie has always been very sexually active. After we were married, Janie would tell me about some of the more memorable fucks she'd had while I played with her wet pink slit.

She'd ask her dates to stick their tongues and fingers into her pussy and asshole, which was especially sensitive, and she told me how when she was fucking, she enjoyed feeling the hot come squirt in and fill her cunt. But what really surprised me was when Janie revealed to me the thrill she got from mooning.

My wife, though sexy, also has a very sweet and proper appearance and I was astounded. At parties Janie would hike up her skirt and pull her panties all the way down her legs when she was dared to moon. She said the guys would nearly fall over themselves and I couldn't blame them.

One particularly memorable night, I invited two of my most muscular friends over to help me move our new furniture into the living room. After they finished moving, Janie brought out some beer for us all. I could see Janie was excited by Mark and Jerry by the way she kept looking at their broad-muscled chests and arms.

When Mark kidded Jerry that he had done most of the heavy

lifting, Janie stated that she could have lifted the couch herself. Then Janie said that she used to moon and any girl that can moon can do anything. The guys kidded her and said that girls didn't have the guts to moon. At that Janie stood and turned her back to the guys.

She hiked her skirt up to her waist to reveal her pink satin panties, then she hooked her thumbs in the waistband and slowly lowered them to her ankles, completely exposing her creamy-white ass. Mark and Jerry were speechless as she spread her legs wide and bent over.

Janie looked back at us between her long legs and said, "No guts to moon, huh?" All eyes were glued to her spread cheeks revealing her puckered asshole surrounded by curly hair with her full cunt lips protruding.

Janie remained in this pose for a few seconds before she straightened up and pulled up her panties. I was rock-hard after having witnessed this scene, which I had only fantasized about before. I knew Janie was hot, too, by the way her pussy glistened.

I wanted Janie to show the guys more and I wanted to be there to see it. I retreated into the adjoining room and waited for Janie to break away. She soon excused herself and sauntered up to me. I told her it had excited the hell out of me when she showed the guys her ass. I asked Janie if she would like to have sex with them and she said yes.

I reached into her panties and slipped a finger into her dripping hole. She was hotter and more excited than ever before. I told her my plan and then said, "Go for it."

I told Jerry and Mark that I would be going to the store for some more beer. I went out and made my way behind the bushes which covered the living room window. I had an unobstructed view of the entire room and the open screen allowed me to hear everything.

Jerry brought Janie the last beer and they continued to chat. Mark really started to tease Janie. "When guys moon, they do it

for a full minute," he said. Then Jerry said that she still looked
too prim and proper to moon.

To these comments Janie replied, "Mark, kiss my ass!" Mark
jokingly got down on his knees at Janie's feet, but she was serious.
She turned her back on him and knelt on the couch. Once more
she pulled down her cute lacy panties just enough to expose her
full butt.

Mark knew an opportunity when he saw one. With my wife's
ass only inches from his face, he started to plant kisses on her soft
cheeks. Then Mark tugged her panties all the way down her long
legs and left them at her ankles. Jerry started to squeeze an ass-
cheek as a huge boner filled his pants. Watching my buddies feel
and examine my wife's beautiful ass got me yanking at my own
hard-on.

"Make sure you hit the bulls-eye," Janie whispered as she
reached back with both hands and spread her cheeks apart to reveal her asshole. Mark sank his stiff tongue all the way into her
butt. Janie moaned in ecstasy, which caused Jerry to remove his
trousers and start jerking at his meat. He too watched as Mark alternately licked Janie's butthole and pussy.

Janie groaned hoarsely and Jerry knelt by my wife's face. She
hungrily gobbled up his hot cock and began slowly sucking it as
Mark flicked his tongue deep into her cleft. Then Mark stood up
and unzipped his pants to reveal his ten-inch member.

He placed it at the entrance to my wife's vagina and slowly
started to push its entire length in. Janie growled deeply and continued to deep-throat Jerry's cock. Mark wet his finger and
pushed it all the way into her asshole as he continued to ball her
vigorously.

I watched with mounting excitement while Janie was getting
it from both ends. Mark then pulled his boner out of my wife and
lay down on his back. Janie straddled his lap and reached back,
sinking his swollen cocktip into her wet hole. I watched in fascination as her large hairy cunt lips enveloped the head.

I could hear the liquid sound of her wet snatch as it slowly swallowed the entire shaft right up to his balls. Janie started to ride him while moaning in ecstasy. It was so freaking hot watching Mark's huge dick appear and then disappear into my wife's pussy. Then Jerry, his cock still wet from my wife's saliva, stepped behind them and placed his cockhead against Janie's butt-hole.

He inched his meat into her hungry rectum as he moaned in pleasure. They got into a slow, deep rhythm and the sounds of lovemaking filled the room. They fucked like this for fifteen or so minutes before Janie bucked into a deep orgasmic moan, whereupon both Mark and Jerry let go, filing her butt and cunt with a double load of come.

As my buddies removed their shrinking cocks from Janie, I saw their sperm dripping from her snatch and asshole. Janie then kissed Jerry and Mark and told them good night.

When I entered the house I knew Janie was still hot and horny, and one look at my hard-on told her I had witnessed the whole scene and enjoyed it. Janie quickly undressed me and straddled my face as she lowered her buttered pussy onto my mouth. We slipped into a 69. She took my throbbing member into her throat. I could taste my buddies' salty come mingled in with hers as I dug my tongue deep into her well-lubed pussy and then her asshole.

It became too overwhelming and I shot my load far into Janie's sucking mouth. I tongued her clit into another shattering orgasm. We slept like logs and woke up the next afternoon, fully rested.

Over a late breakfast Janie started to tell me more mooning stories, but this time I believed her one hundred percent. I'd seen the evidence with my own eyes, and I couldn't wait to see more. My wife's hot ass looks so much hotter knowing that other guys have seen it.—*Name and address withheld*

RENO ROMP RAISES STAKES FOR MARRIED COUPLE

My wife wanted me to write this letter and describe what happened on our trip to Reno last week.

Beth is a very beautiful forty-two-year-old woman. This is the second marriage for both of us. We have been married for twelve years, and have talked many times about past relationships, so I know Beth had quite a sex life even before me. When we were dating, she openly confessed that she'd once been fucked by three guys at one time. Each of the men, she said, had exceptionally large penises, which they had used to fill each of her available orifices. As she told me about this story, which she went into in great detail, Beth got incredibly turned on, and we ended up having one of our best sexual experiences ever.

In Reno, we found ourselves at the blackjack table with this guy named Larry. He sat next to Beth. We started talking and soon we were all getting behind in the cards so we decided to play the slot machines. I asked Larry what he did, and he answered he occasionally acted in adult movies. A look crossed Beth's face I will never forget.

After Beth and I went back to our room to get ready for dinner, she was curious and couldn't stop talking about Larry and how sexually charged everything was in Nevada. "Sex is in the air out here," she said. "It makes it hard to think of anything else. I wonder if Larry has a big dick, he's a good-looking guy," she said.

I told her guys in that business did not necessarily have to be well-endowed but it helped if they were short on looks, sexual stamina or acting skills. I could tell she was thinking about it and getting turned on, so I told her if we saw Larry later that evening we would ask him up to our room for a drink. With that, she went wild. We went to bed and had one hell of a fuck as we talked about what he would do to her with that big dick.

When we did get around to dinner, she asked me if it would be alright if we went through with our fantasy. "Oh, baby, this is for you, whatever you desire," I said, agreeing to go along with her fantasy. After dinner we went back to play blackjack, but we didn't see Larry. After an hour I told Beth I was going to the restroom. Instead I went looking for Larry, who I found playing the slot machines. I walked over and asked him how he was doing. "Pretty badly," he replied. I told him we were not doing so hot at blackjack either.

"Why don't you come to our room for a drink?" I asked. There was an implication in the tone of my voice, and an understanding passed between us with nothing said.

You should have seen Beth's face when we walked up. When we got to the room, Larry said he would go and get the ice. When he left the room, Beth gave me a big kiss. "What should I do?" she asked nervously. I ran my hand over her pussy.

"Don't worry," I told her. "I will take care of everything." At twenty-six Larry was considerably younger than us so I knew we were in for some hot and heavy action. After three drinks, which I made doubly strong for Beth, I asked Larry about some of the pornographic movies he'd made. He told us about one that was very good because the female costar really got into it. She was a good fuck so it was more than a job for him. I told him we had seen a few movies, and most of the men had large cocks. I asked him if his was big, and he said, "a little bigger than average."

Beth had not said a word. "I bet Beth would like to see it, wouldn't you, honey?" She just nodded her head. Larry looked at me. I told him to take his pants off and walk over and show his cock to Beth. He stood up and pulled his pants down. Out fell his dick, which although it wasn't erect, was so long and fat that my wife said, "Oh my God! It's as big around as my wrist."

He walked over to Beth. She reached out, took hold of his dick and played with it lovingly. Once, when she pulled her hand up to the head, there was a drop of clear come on the tip. She took it off with her finger, then licked it off, giggling like a school girl. Larry helped her to stand and we both undressed her. He gave her a deep kiss while he moved his dick into position between her legs. I could tell he was on her love-button because she started to moan and shake. Larry picked her up then put her on the bed. Beth looked up and said, "Fuck me, Larry. Please fuck me."

Larry got between her legs while Beth raised her knees to make room for him. She closed her eyes as he put the big head of his cock to her pussy. As the head went in, she looked at me and said, "Oh my God, it's so big it's beautiful." Larry started to slowly fuck her, putting more and more into her with each stroke. He moved faster so she raised her ass off the bed to meet him. Then she started to scream, "Fuck me, fuck me with that big cock!"

Beth put her arms around his neck and her legs around his ass. She screamed out, "I'm coming, oh baby, I'm coming, fuck me, yeah!" All the time he was giving her long hard strokes. Beth was trying to get it all as she raised her ass off the bed, to milk him dry, something she does to me all the time. He fell on top of her as he moved it in and out. Larry rolled off on his side as Beth screamed "No, no don't take it away from me."

Larry told her what a great fuck she was. He was not done, however. She put her hand on his dick, which was still hard. She put as much of his cock into her mouth as she could, holding onto the base with her hand. Then she said, "I have to have more, I can't stop."

She got on top, put a leg on either side as she guided his cock back into her pussy. Then she rode him like a wild woman, screaming, "It's so deep. He is fucking the hell out of me." Beth moaned from deep inside her body.

"Baby I'm going to come with you," Larry yelled.

Beth screamed, "I can feel you coming. I'm coming too! My whole body is coming." She fell on top of him as she went limp. He pushed her over on the bed as he got up but she didn't move. Her pussy was open and the bed was wet.

"You're a great fuck," Larry said.

Here was a professional, calling my wife a great piece. It made me proud to think someone in the sex business would find my forty-two-year-old wife so desirable. I was beaming like I'd won first prize at the high school science fair.

Beth was mopping up the spunk between her legs, smiling at both of us. "You are not bad either. Either one of you."—*T.H., Denver, Colorado*

WIFE BECOMES A PARTY FAVOR

I wrote you a letter a few weeks back about my wife's very first multiple-partners experience, which occurred this past winter. We have subsequently joined a swingers' network and enjoyed some good and bad multiple-partner relationships. One in particular helped us discover that my wife prefers having sex with multiple black partners.

A few weeks after we had joined the swingers' club we received a member number and password that allowed us access into the online network, which you can browse by area code or by zip code. Upon returning home from work one day, I came across a message on the answering machine. It was from another member, who said he had received my wife's message and was returning the call. He also left a number and address where he could be reached. When Brenda arrived home I asked her about the message. She said that she had contacted a few different members the past several days, and that this must have been one who was calling back.

Later that evening Brenda returned the man's call. As she was sitting down at the table she asked me for a pen and paper. After introducing herself she started talking and writing down some vital information on the piece of paper. She wrote, "six-foot-three, two-hundred-twenty-five pounds, black, well-hung, good shape." She spoke for a half hour or so. Finally, she told him that everything sounded pretty good and that she would get back with him to possibly set up a time to meet.

After she hung up, Brenda asked me my feelings. I wanted to know if he had a partner, and if it was just going to be him and her, or if others were going to be involved. Brenda said that he discussed just the two of them. If I was interested in doing more than just watching, she said, this was fine by him. He said that if we were interested he could definitely arrange for additional people. I told her to give me a few days to think about it.

A few days had passed when she brought the subject up. I told her to give him a call and make the arrangements. Later that night they agreed on a date and place. We were to meet him at his apartment that coming Saturday around seven. He was having a small party and we were invited. We were going to play it by ear. We live in Cincinnati and his apartment was located in Dayton, Ohio, which is about a forty-five minute drive. We left a little early to make sure we had no problem finding it. We also wanted to get there a little before the party started so we could talk with him and see what he was like.

We arrived at his place around seven, found his apartment number and knocked on the door. A tall, well-dressed black man answered the door and introduced himself as Tim. He asked if we had any problem finding our way. We introduced ourselves and he invited us in.

Tim told us that he had been a member of the swingers' network for a few years and that he was pretty happy with most of the people he had met. We were there for about forty-five minutes when there was a knock on the door. As Tim got up to answer it, Brenda looked at me and said that she was feeling pretty comfortable. I turned to see who was at the door. I noticed three other black men walking in. They introduced themselves as Brad, Anthony and Mike. Each one was checking out Brenda as she stood to shake their hands. Tim then told us that maybe a few more people were going to show up, but that was going to be it.

Tim put some music on the stereo, and Brad asked if anyone

would like something to drink. We sat around talking for a little while and drinking a few beers. Mike took out a small bag from his jacket and asked if anyone wanted to really get the party going. He rolled one up, and as we passed the joint around things started to loosen up for everyone. After a few more beers and a couple more joints, Tim went over and turned the music down low. Then he hit the VCR and put a videotape on. The porno flick starred two black studs and one white chick. He then turned to Brenda and said, "I thought things were starting to get a little boring. This might loosen things up."

Brad, who was sitting next to Brenda on the couch, put his arm around her and said, "I got something that will loosen you up." He then began to take his hand and run it across her chest, stopping on each tit to give it a little squeeze. I got off of the couch and moved over to a chair in the corner of the room, where I could see Brenda and the couch clearly. When I got up Tim took my place. He reached down and spread Brenda's legs apart. Brenda suggested that they find a more comfortable place, one with a little more room. Anthony then came over and took her by the hand and said, "Sounds like the bedroom to me."

Once we arrived in the bedroom, Anthony told Brenda to remove her clothes and lay down on the waterbed. Tim looked over at me and asked if I was okay and comfortable with what was going on. I told him to go ahead. As I stood there watching Brenda undress, Tim went over to a closet and removed a shoe box, placing it on a table next to the bed. By this time Brenda was down to her panties and bra. She removed her bra, revealing a soft, firm set of breasts. As she took off her panties, exposing a shaved pussy, everybody let out a collective sigh of admiration.

Tim told her to take the shoe box and lay down on the bed. He told her to open it and take out whatever appealed to her most. Brenda opened the box and dumped the contents onto the bed— three sex toys in different shapes and sizes. She chose a battery-operated dildo that stroked up and down with multiple speeds. Mike told her to put it into her mouth and suck it.

She began to lick and kiss the head of the toy, then turned it on to let it stroke and hum inside her mouth. After just a few minutes of this she took it out and inserted it between her pussy lips, turning it up to full speed. Her nipples were like bullets and her toes were curling as the buzzing toy moved against the pleasure center at her clitoris. She looked over at us, fucking herself, and said that the real thing would feel a whole lot better.

"We got plenty of the real thing, baby," Tim said.

The group proceeded to remove their clothes. Brad was the first to approach her. His cock was huge. I then looked around at the other three, who were also positioning themselves around the waterbed. Their cocks were nothing to be ashamed of either. All four were hung, especially Mike. His was not only long but very round. As Brenda laid there still stroking herself with the dildo, Brad knelt next to her face and started to stroke his cock. When he rubbed it on her erect nipples, Brenda reached over and guided it toward her lips. She licked the cockhead and, little by little, inserted the bulbous knob into her mouth.

Tim was removing the dildo from her pussy and positioning himself between her legs. He placed her knees forward, exposing her wet, hot pussy. He thrust his swollen black cock into Brenda's pussy with one fast stroke. Brenda let out a few groans and moans, while Mike and Anthony were getting into position. Mike moved to one side of her face, while Anthony got behind her at the top of her head. They each placed their cocks next to her face.

Tim was pounding her pretty good, while she was taking turns on the three cocks in her face. Tim finished fucking her and buried his face in her pussy. Someone eating Brenda's pussy was all it took for her to come.

She was moaning and writhing around, having one long, multiple orgasm. Anthony told Brenda to get on her hands and knees. As she knelt on the bed Anthony positioned himself next to her rear, and began banging away with fast, hard thrusts. Brad had gotten underneath her and was licking her pussy while she gave head to both Tim and Mike.

Tim then got out of bed and went into the bathroom. He was only gone for a few minutes when he returned with a jar of Vaseline. Anthony opened the jar while still fucking away. He inserted a few globs on his fingers and began to rub them inside Brenda's asshole. As soon as he touched it, she jerked her head back and said that was one thing she did not do. Tim said that with four guys and only two holes they needed a little more out of her.

I know that I had tried several times over the years to have anal sex with Brenda, but I never could accomplish it. Anthony took his fingers and slowly began to probe her rectum. Once it was inside and he began to slide his finger in and out, Brenda willingly put her face down on the bed and stuck her ass invitingly into the air. It still took her several minutes to let him penetrate her. Every time he would try she would lift up off the bed and say, "I do not think I want to do this."

Finally, after some convincing, he took his cock and started to enter her juiced-up asshole. The tip of his head went in gradually. Once in, the rest of his head fell into the tiny crack, which gaped widely to accept the stem of his manhood. Anthony stroked with steady thrusts.

Mike was getting a blowjob while Brad positioned himself underneath Brenda, who was forcing her pussy down onto his cock. Finally, he got her into a position so he could enter her cunt. I sat there in front of the bed and could not believe that my wife was taking on all three men at the same time. Each of her holes was plugged and she was loving it. I couldn't let a good thing pass. I had to try it one time, easing my rod deep inside the tight clasp of her anus.

When I was finished getting her in the rear we dressed and left the room so Brenda could get cleaned up. When she entered the living room I asked her if she was all right. She said that she was fine and that what had happened was the best sex she had ever had. Tim asked that we stay, and we took him up on his offer. I do have to admit that since that night anal sex with my wife has just been great.—*T.L., Cincinnati, Ohio*

MARRIAGE MADE IN GANG-BANG HEAVEN

I recently began buying your fine publication. My wife and I enjoy it immensely. Reading the letters from husbands who enjoy watching their wives with other men has led us to believe that our relationship is not as unusual as we had once thought.

Cheryl and I had been living together for over four years, and we enjoyed what most people consider an open relationship. We had agreed that we could date others; however, I never felt the urge to do so. I was a virgin when we met and had always been quite shy around women. Cheryl had been quite promiscuous throughout her high school and college days and she saw no reason to alter her behavior just because we were living together. Cheryl is five feet tall and has long red hair, perky tits and a vivacious personality.

About a year ago I started to get the feeling that Cheryl was less than excited whenever we made love. In contrast to our lovemaking when we had first met, Cheryl rarely climaxed. In fact, while Cheryl continued to see other men on a regular basis, whenever she and I made love she acted rather indifferent to my efforts to bring her to orgasm. It was on one such night, after vainly trying to bring Cheryl to orgasm, that I confronted her with the problem. "Honey, I'm so sorry. I love you so much, but I'm afraid I'm going to lose you if I can't make you come," I said. Cheryl seemed touched by my concern but she didn't spare my feelings.

"I'm sorry Mike," she said. "Don't take this the wrong way, but

I just can't get turned-on with you like I used to. I still love you, but I guess I just like to make love to bigger guys."

I was heartbroken but gradually got over my hurt with the assurance of her love and support. Since that night Cheryl and I became even closer. She began to freely discuss her sexual needs with me, treating me as she would a close girlfriend and confiding all her secret desires and longings. During this time, I began to work on my skills at licking and sucking Cheryl's juicy pussy. It was something I had always enjoyed but never felt like I had completely mastered. I concentrated on it like it was a real task, and I became a cunnilingus expert as a result. I got to the point where I was able to bring her to orgasm most every time we made love. My tongue was one little talented teaser.

For my own sexual release, I began to masturbate more and more, not only when Cheryl was out with one of her lovers, but also while hearing the juicy details upon her return. Although Cheryl never actually refused me sex, it was clear that upon returning home after a passionate lovemaking session, she preferred me to lick her pussy clean while bringing myself off.

Over time I began to have the urge to actually watch Cheryl make love to one of her lovers. Just imagining one of her big studs move up between her legs and insert his thick shaft deep inside her eager pussy gave me an immediate erection. When I brought this up she said she would ask Bob, one of the men she was currently seeing, if he minded if I tagged along on one of their dates.

Bob was a guy she had met at her health club and they had been carrying on an affair for over three months. Cheryl had told me about several of their previous dates and it seemed that Bob really encourages Cheryl's exhibitionism, going as far as having her do a sexy striptease in front of two of his envious friends.

As a condition for letting me accompany them, Bob had requested that Cheryl abstain from sex for two weeks before their date. Cheryl told me that Bob wanted her to be extra horny, and as for me, well let's just say that it took quite an effort not to masturbate while anticipating the upcoming event. At her suggestion, Cheryl and I spent the entire day before her date shopping for a sexy new outfit.

I took a special interest in helping her choose extremely provocative clothes, including a tight black miniskirt and a sheer white blouse. Cheryl also selected white fishnet stockings along with a lacy white garter belt and G-string panties. To top off the look we got a sexy pair of black platform shoes with five-inch heels.

Throughout the day Cheryl continually teased me, saying things such as, "I'm in the mood to be really fucked hard tonight. Wait till you see Bob's cock, it's huge."

It was all I could do to keep from coming as I sat on the edge of the bed, massaging my rigid member and watching Cheryl dress. It's become something of a ritual for me to help Cheryl prepare for her dates. Earlier that evening I had carefully shaved her pussy until it was smooth as silk. As she dressed for a date, Cheryl performed what I like to think of as a reverse striptease, and I often ended up jacking off. Tonight was no different.

I watched her bend over to fasten a delicate gold chain around her ankle. I was quite close to orgasm when Cheryl noticed me in the mirror.

"Oh Mike you are a naughty little boy, aren't you? Don't come yet, though. Wait until later, okay?" giggled Cheryl as she straightened the seams in her stockings. I reluctantly took her advice and tucked my erect cock back into my pants while she continued to primp.

Cheryl had just put the finishing touches on her makeup when the doorbell rang. I quickly excused myself to answer the door. Cheryl said she would be about twenty minutes more and so I offered Bob a drink while waiting. I felt a sharp pang of jealousy as I saw that he was extremely handsome, well over six feet tall with a strong, muscular physique. At the same time my cock stiffened as I imagined Cheryl making love to this Adonis.

Bob wasn't paying much attention to me as he surveyed the living room from his seat on the couch. It was clear from the way he looked at me that he considered me a nuisance, so I resolved to be as inconspicuous as possible throughout the evening. Nevertheless, I tried to start up a conversation by remarking, "You know, Cheryl says that you and her have had a lot of fun over the past three months."

"Yeah, man, you could say that. Your woman sure does like to fuck. That's for sure," he said with an arrogant flourish. I was about to respond when I was interrupted by Cheryl bouncing down the stairs to meet Bob. She greeted him with a lingering French kiss.

On the way to the restaurant, I drove Bob's Lincoln Continental while Cheryl and Bob made out in the backseat of the car. After a quiet dinner, Bob and Cheryl spent an hour dancing at a local nightclub. As she and Bob danced, I could see her grinding her pussy against his crotch. Watching Cheryl's blatant seduction, I developed a raging erection. After a particularly sexy dance, Bob and Cheryl returned to our table and said, "C'mon boy, let's go. It's late and your girlfriend says she needs my big pole."

Cheryl ran off to the ladies room as we exited the bar. While walking to the car, Bob told me how he planned on fucking Cheryl on the way to his house, but that he didn't want me hanging around after that. Although I was quite disappointed that I wouldn't be able to watch their entire session, just the thought that my beautiful girlfriend would soon be spreading her legs for this stud had my cock straining in my pants. When we reached the car, Bob climbed in the backseat while I got behind the wheel.

It was only a couple of minutes before Cheryl joined Bob in the backseat and we were soon on our way. As soon as I had driven out of the parking lot, Bob unzipped his pants to unleash his hard cock. "Suck it baby," he growled. Cheryl immediately leaned over and began to mouth his swollen rod. I glanced into the back and saw a sight I'll never forget. Cheryl was kissing the head of an absolutely enormous cock. It must have been at least ten or eleven inches long and three times as thick as my slender rod. My cock had formed a tent in my pants as I frantically tried to find a secluded spot to observe Cheryl and Bob. It took about five minutes, but I soon found a deserted street and quickly pulled the car over to the side. By this time Bob was lying somewhat uncomfortably across the backseat and Cheryl was on top of him, straddling his huge cock. Her blouse was unbuttoned to expose her firm tits and her skirt was bunched up around her waist. I immediately pulled out my cock and began to stroke it.

It so happens that earlier that day I had purchased a diamond engagement ring and I had hoped to ask Cheryl to marry me the following week while on our annual vacation. However, the beautiful sight of Cheryl impaled on Bob's massive pole inspired me to ask Cheryl to marry me then and there. When Cheryl heard my proposal, she just giggled, "Of course I'll marry you, Mike. I love you." Hearing these words, I was ecstatic and immediately pulled out the diamond engagement ring I had recently purchased. Cheryl didn't even miss a beat as she continued to rock back and forth on Bob's dick while allowing me to place the diamond ring on her finger. "It's beautiful, sweetheart. I love you," declared Cheryl, leaning over to give me a kiss.

When Cheryl leaned forward to kiss me, Bob's cock slipped out of her pussy. Bob pulled Cheryl back toward him while furiously roaring, "What the fuck is going on? I thought I told you I don't want this wimpy guy anywhere near you tonight!" Cheryl immediately turned her attention back to Bob as she cooed, "Oh, Bob, I'm so sorry. He won't get in the way anymore, I promise. Come on, you get on top. I want you to fuck me hard." She then lay back on the seat while Bob positioned himself between her luscious thighs.

All the while I continued to stroke my dick. I noticed Cheryl's diamond engagement ring sparkling in the moonlight as she reached between her legs to insert Bob's swollen rod. The lust and pride I felt when I saw her ring made me truly appreciate the fact that we were to be married. It was a truly incredible sight as

I watched my fiancée with a muscular stud between her legs, her platform shoes draped over his broad shoulders with his glistening manhood pounding in and out of her soaked pussy. The car was rocking back and forth with Bob's thrusts, and Cheryl's moans and whimpers of orgasm created a real soundtrack of lust.

As I watched I felt an incredible craving to feel, taste and even smell my wife-to-be's delicious body. Remembering the angry tone of Bob's earlier remarks, I realized that for tonight at least Cheryl was to be Bob's alone. Grasping about for some method of enjoying all the beautiful sensations of my fiancée, I finally reached over the seat and grabbed Cheryl's discarded G-string. Clutching it in my hand, I immediately brought it up to my nose and savored the delicate smell of her perfume mingled with the musky scent of her pussy. As I watched Bob thrust in and out of Cheryl's cunt, I slipped the silky panties over my hard cock and began to masturbate in time to their lovemaking. It was only a matter of minutes before Cheryl's cries of pleasure triggered my orgasm. I squirted my pent-up sperm all over the tiny white triangle of her panties.

"Oooh, yes, yes. Fuck me harder!" moaned Cheryl as Bob brought her to yet another climax with his driving penis. Meanwhile, even a stud like Bob had his limit as Cheryl's skillful caresses coupled with her luscious pussy pushed Bob to the limit.

He threw his head back and growled, "I'm coming, baby!" while unloading his seed into the depths of her pussy. After Cheryl and Bob had straightened up, I drove them over to Bob's house.

"Would it be alright if I came in for awhile?" I asked, as I carefully parked Bob's car out front.

"No way! I promised Cheryl I'd let you watch us once, but I'm not going to have you hanging around my house. You can get the bus down at the corner," responded Bob. Cheryl noticed that I was very disappointed.

"Just a minute, Bob," she said. "I've got an idea. Mike, why don't you take out your dick and play with yourself for me." I wasn't sure what to do, but one look at Cheryl leaning forward with a mischievous grin and I immediately unzipped my pants to free my soft prick. "C'mon Mike, stroke it. Make it hard," urged my fiancée. I began to slowly stroke my cock with my right hand while fondling my balls with my left. "You liked watching me fuck Bob, didn't you Mike?" teased Cheryl as her eyes never left mine. "Did you see how many times I came? His cock is so big I just can't get enough of it. It feels so good when he's inside me I just want to fuck forever," cooed Cheryl.

Giving Bob a sexy smile she reached over to run her hand over his crotch. I was quite close to coming for the second time that evening when Cheryl reached down between her legs and scooped up some of the copious semen leaking out from her pussy. She then brought her fingers to my lips so that I could smell and taste the remnants of their coupling. "That's it Mike, lick it up," whispered Cheryl while I licked and sucked her fingers clean, savoring the delicious taste of Cheryl's juices coupled with Bob's tangy semen. Bob, meanwhile, was chuckling softly, as he found the whole situation quite amusing. I ignored him completely, however, as I continued to stroke my manhood. Cheryl's sexy teasing soon brought me to another tremendous orgasm as I spurted semen all over my hand.

As soon as I had finished spilling my load, Bob ordered me out of the car. I stood there, come dripping off my hand as Cheryl and Bob walked up the steps to the door. I longed for another opportunity to observe their passionate lovemaking, but it was not to be. As I learned later, Bob and Cheryl spent the remainder of the evening together engaged in a fabulous sex session. I took almost an hour to get home where I ended up masturbating to one more tremendous orgasm while just imagining Bob and Cheryl engaging in all manner of erotic escapades.

Cheryl and I were married last September in a beautiful small chapel in the mountains. We had planned on spending our honeymoon at a nearby resort, so after saying our goodbyes to the guests at the reception, we drove off to the resort. What I didn't know was that Cheryl had planned a surprise for me when we finally reached our hotel. It was almost ten when we arrived. Following the custom, I lifted Cheryl up and carried her through the threshold into our suite.

As soon as I had closed the door, out came three enormous men from the bedroom. All three of the guys were well over six feet tall and played for a local semipro basketball team. "Congratulations Mike, my name is Larry and that's Bill and Jim. Let me be the first to kiss the bride," laughed one of the guys as he took Cheryl from my arms and gave her a wet kiss.

I guess I must have looked pretty shocked as Cheryl giggled, "Surprise, honey. I thought you might want our wedding night to be extra special, so I invited some friends. Why don't you pour us some champagne to celebrate while we get comfortable in the bedroom."

In Larry's arms Cheryl looked like a tiny doll. As he walked into the bedroom my cock stiffened at the thought of these massive men making love to my bride. I poured five glasses of champagne while shedding my clothes. As I entered the bedroom, I noticed that even in her five-inch heels, Cheryl was over a foot shorter than any of the guys. Two of the guys had sandwiched Cheryl between them. While Larry was kissing my wife, Bill was intent on unzipping her dress. It wasn't long before Bill had unzipped my wife's wedding dress, tugging it down over her hips and tossing it unceremoniously into a corner of the room. Cheryl's bra and panties didn't last long either, leaving my lovely bride wearing a white lace garter belt, sheer white stockings and white satin heels.

My cock was near bursting as I watched Cheryl slowly unbutton Larry's shirt to expose his muscular torso. She covered his chest in kisses, slowly working her way down toward his crotch. Cheryl then undid Larry's belt and unzipped his slacks, pulling them down around his ankles. Cheryl repeated her actions with Bill and Jim until all three men were standing in their underwear.

With a naughty little smile over at me, Cheryl knelt down in front of them and slowly tugged down first Bill's then Larry's and then Jim's underwear to reveal their semihard cocks.

"Oh, wow, I love your big cocks," moaned Cheryl as she began licking and sucking Larry's large rod. It grew to at least ten inches! Next, Cheryl turned her attention to Bill. Within a couple of minutes his prick was also fully erect. Bill and Larry had by far the largest cocks I had ever seen, but when Cheryl had finished with Jim, I was shocked to see that his manhood was almost as big as my forearm!

As I learned later, Cheryl had contacted them through a local swingers' magazine and she had carefully culled the ads looking for a group of well-endowed men. My pretty bride was absolutely fascinated with their cocks as she alternated between each of them, kissing and licking up and down the entire length of their shafts.

After enjoying my wife's oral worship of his cock, Bill lifted Cheryl up and placed her on the bed. He immediately moved up between her outstretched legs and began to rub his giant cockhead between Cheryl's juicy pussy lips. Just the touch of his prick on her clit excited my wife.

"You're going to like this, baby," Bill said.

"Hey, ditto, my man," Cheryl retorted. "You are going to like this, too."

I saw Cheryl shudder as the monster cock penetrated her inner walls. It wasn't the first shudder nor would it be the last. I wasn't sure if it would fit in my wife's tight pussy, but with her copious juices easing the way, Bill's meaty cock was soon buried balls deep.

I couldn't have imagined a more incredible wedding night as I softly rubbed my throbbing penis. Larry was standing near me sipping his champagne as he chuckled, "Man, I couldn't believe it when your wife said she wanted us to fuck her on her wedding night. But hell, it sure looks like you are enjoying yourself."

"Yeah, she's the greatest," I responded. "This is kind of a twist on the old bachelor party routine, isn't it?"

I couldn't help but bless the luck that had brought us together. From my vantage point all I could see of my wife was her clean shaven pussy, the soft creamy globes of her ass-cheeks resting on the bed, and her high heels kicking wildly in the air. Jim was seated on the bed next to my wife and he was running his hands all over Cheryl's firm tits, pulling and teasing her erect nipples. I was stroking my cock when Jim reached back with one hand and began to toy with Cheryl's pink asshole. This in itself was enough to give me a tremendous climax as I spurted semen all over my wife's moist panties.

Bill continued to fuck my bride for almost thirty minutes as Cheryl experienced numerous orgasms. Larry and Jim were becoming somewhat impatient as they awaited their turns, so they stood at the edge of the bed while Cheryl eagerly alternated on sucking their glistening rods.

Since I had previously brought myself off, I was able to hold back, timing myself so that at the same instant Bill threw back his head and grunted, "I'm coming," I came too, shooting my cream for the second time all over Cheryl's panties.

When Bill pulled out of my wife, he got up off the bed and invited Larry to take his place. Larry immediately mounted my wife, using his large cock to fill and engulf her completely. As soon as he started thrusting she began to climax once again.

"Baby, you've got one hot little pussy. I'm going to make sure you don't ever forget this night, that's for sure," Larry said as he banged her box.

Hearing this, Cheryl glanced over at me and sighed, "I love you, Mike. So far this has been the best day of my life."

Cheryl's attention was soon diverted by the pleasurable sensations emanating from her busy love-canal. Larry fucked my wife for at least thirty minutes, pounding her with a steady, pulsating beat until he came in a rush of orgasmic bliss.

Larry was quickly replaced by Jim, who eased his enormous rod into Cheryl so that she sighed in pleasure. I didn't know she could take so much loving in one setting. They fucked for almost twenty minutes, both of them heaving and writhing as Jim's cock slammed against Cheryl's heated twat. I masturbated to another incredible orgasm watching them climax together.

When Jim finally pulled his cock from my wife, I immediately leapt onto the bed and began to kiss and caress my sexy wife. She was numb with pleasure, I thought, but still able to accept my attention.

I had a decision to make. I knew there was no way my cock could compare with the three massive members that had recently entered my pretty bride. Rather than fucking my sweet bride, I decided to lap up the juices oozing from her opening. It turned me on to think I could ingest the fruits of all this lust. Cheryl's pussy was so loose from Bill, Jim and Larry's huge cocks that my tongue immediately slipped deep inside her.

The taste and the smell was pungent. Gobs of tasty semen, mixed with the copious outpouring of Cheryl's vagina, flooded into my mouth. I noticed her snatch was warm to the touch, a result of all the incredible friction and the huge demands placed on her sex by the three hunks.

"Oh, Mike, that's it. Suck the come from my pussy," moaned Cheryl as she rolled over on top of me, grinding her creamy snatch into my face.

The next day Cheryl would be sore, but for now she egged on my cunnilingus technique with total enthusiasm. For the next ten minutes I licked and sucked every drop of juice from Cheryl's pussy, taking extra care to dart inside the walls of her cunt and titillate the knob of her clit as I did. The three guys were taking a smoke break as we performed our little marital ritual for them. Cheryl was squeezing her nipples as I rimmed her asshole and cunt with my moistly elongated tongue. We finally maneuvered into a 69 and she sucked my throbbing erection until I pumped what little sperm remained in my balls into her silky mouth.

Even after I had come, I remained so engrossed with licking

and sucking Cheryl's pussy that I didn't even notice her sucking Bill's cock. Before long I felt Cheryl's hands on my head as she pushed me away so that Bill could move up between her legs. The two of them began to fuck hard and fast. Bill's hips looked like a rivet machine, blasting my wife's tender hole with feverish intensity. Soon they were joined on the bed by Larry and Jim. By this time I decided to give the four of them a little privacy so I quietly left the bedroom. I promptly fell asleep on the small couch in the other room.

It was almost three in the morning when I awoke to find Cheryl's lips on mine. "Oh, sweetheart, I love you," she whispered while taking my hand and leading me into the bedroom. The guys had just recently left and the room still had the musky aroma of semen mixed with Cheryl's pussy juices. Cheryl was exhausted from her sexual marathon so we both instantly fell asleep in each other's arms.

Since our wedding, Cheryl and I couldn't be happier. She has a small group of lovers to choose from. About once a month she will invite one or more of them over to our house for a wild session of fucking and sucking. On these occasions, I'll sit quietly nearby, masturbating to one orgasm after another. I can't imagine a more perfect marriage.—*M.R.*, *Phoenix, Arizona*

HAPPY COUPLE GETS AWAY TO PLAY, WITH ONE BEST FRIEND AND TWO STRANGERS

I have read in *Penthouse Letters* about husbands watching their wives make love to other men, but never figured I would be involved in it myself. I was never sure how I'd feel about it, either.

My wife is thirty-seven and I'm thirty-three. Gina is five feet five inches tall, has beautiful, platinum blonde hair and 34B boobs tipped with sensitive, lickable nipples. Her best feature is her butt. She weighs under a hundred pounds, so you can imagine she's got a tight little "microbutt." It is incredibly shapely even at this age.

We both keep in tip-top physical shape by exercising, playing baseball and tennis, biking and so forth.

During a troubled time in our relationship, she used to sneak off with a coworker to "talk" at a park near where they both worked. They only kissed; it never went any further than that. I had a sixth sense something was going on and asked her during the heat of lovemaking if she had ever kissed her coworker, Bobby. She whispered no, but then immediately changed it to yes as she quickly decided to get it off her chest, since it had been bothering her. While I was certainly turned on, I was also upset, and asked her to cease the physical part of the relationship with Bobby. She did that in one more trip to the park the next day.

Fast forward to Christmas of last year. We drove across the state to her hometown to celebrate Christmas with her parents. While we were there we saw her old best friend, Tracy, who had just gotten divorced. Tracy is thin and striking, though very small-breasted. Such a pretty face, with brilliant green eyes looking out through long, kinked blonde hair. She has an all over tan that she gets at the exercise club she practically lives at.

I asked Tracy if she had the cash to go with us to Jamaica to celebrate our tenth wedding anniversary and Gina's birthday. She said yes, and the trip was on.

The whole thing was a surprise, so Tracy stayed at another friend's house the night before we were to leave. When Gina woke up I presented her with two of the three tickets. She packed her suitcase excitedly as I shuffled the kids like playing cards to a variety of friends and relatives.

When I returned, Tracy had arrived. We walked in to let Gina know that Tracy was coming with us.

Gina was thrilled, and traveling was a breeze. We arrived in the afternoon, got our act together at the hotel and went in search of some serious eating and drinking. As we danced through the night, Tracy, Gina and I all became a lot closer. We giggled, drank and became physically festive. Both girls were wearing minidresses that clung to their bodies.

I took some liberties with Tracy on the dance floor, with double entendres and tight dancing during the slow songs. Of course I made sure Gina got equal treatment. While I never got a full hard-on while dancing with Tracy, I knew she felt me at half mast, because I was holding her so tightly and she whispered that what I was doing felt so good.

We all stumbled back to the hotel in a drunken stagger. No one bothered to turn a light on as the moon shone in, giving us just the right amount of ambient romantic illumination. I quickly got cleaned up in the bathroom, and came out in just my underwear and cutoffs with the top button undone. Gina and Tracy lay on the two beds giggling and toasting themselves with tequila shots.

Their dresses had ridden high on their thighs, exposing their panties. Gina wore thigh-high black stockings under her black dress, with oh-so-French-cut black thong panties. Tracy had red panties on under her red dress and no stockings, since her tan legs were something you never wanted to cover.

I attacked Gina. Tracy ripped off her dress, revealing her red bra-and-panty set, but just as quickly got in under the covers. She rustled around under the sheets removing her undergarments, which she threw on our bed as I disrobed Gina. We're not exhibitionists, so we threw the covers over us as I got my two stitches of clothing off as well.

Tracy was obviously beginning to masturbate under her blankets, holding one hand behind her head, lying on her side, and the other buried in her pussy. I played happily with Gina's nipples and pussy, and we both started to moan quietly.

I teased Gina's pussy lips with my penis, then finally plunged in with one long stroke. From then on I didn't stop until we both came about five minutes later, sweat on our brows. I lay next to Gina, listening to Tracy frigging herself, and rubbed Gina's clit. I stared over at Tracy. We locked eyes as she brought herself off in a very obvious way. She came violently, then licked her fingers clean. Gina came shortly after that from my finger ministrations.

I had another boner from watching Tracy and Gina, but Gina'd had enough, and Tracy wasn't ready at that point to schtup her best friend's husband, even with her best friend there.

I asked Tracy to turn on the lamp in the corner of the room for some ambient light. Then I arranged Gina and Tracy on either side of me, both very naked, and both talking very dirty, while I showed them how I masturbate. It took about ten minutes of teasing, with both of them blowing lightly into my ears, before I erupted my second geyser of the night past my left ear as I lay on my back.

The next day we rode bikes and hung out on the beach. Little was said of the night before. What were they plotting, I wondered, but then I decided my imagination was a little overactive.

Night number two was more subtle, as we didn't dance but went to a very laid-back bar, where everyone was chatting quietly and drinking conservatively while being friendly. We went back to the hotel room, none of us certain what was to transpire. The amount of alcohol we'd consumed certainly helped us figure things out. Gina and Tracy lay in their respective beds. I washed up, and when I came out of the bathroom I switched off the TV, turned the stereo on and proceeded to do a mock strip. I can't dance worth a lick, but was down to my silk Speedos in ten minutes. The girls played along, pointing out that I sported a "semi."

Tracy had on frayed faded cutoffs and a white vest, with a white teddy underneath. She sat upright on the bed and opened her legs. I sat back into her. Gina joined us as well, lying atop my chest. We took in each other's smells and lightly caressed each other. Tracy had started wetly kissing my neck, unbeknownst to Gina, which made it more erotic. I turned my head to kiss Tracy directly, and Gina got up to move back to our bed again, simultaneously whipping off her jeans and T-shirt.

Gina watched as I made mad, passionate love to Tracy, all the while masturbating up a storm herself. Seeing Tracy in her white teddy was too much for my tender mind. I quickly unsnapped the garment's crotch and plunged my tongue deep inside her warm, waiting vagina, at the same time reaching up to fondle her nipples underneath her teddy. As she neared orgasm I got up and mounted her quickly. Excited beyond belief, both of us came within thirty seconds. Fortunately, to save face, I was able to stay hard after coming, and I continued to plug away. About ten minutes later we both fell in a heap, after a second intense mutual orgasm, and fell asleep together.

On day three we went to a nude beach to enjoy the sun. Unfortunately, there was more cock than cunt, but I didn't feel the need to have a perpetual boner all day, so that was fine by me. Tracy and Gina seemed to be enjoying all the attention they received, as they went topless part of the day and nude for about an hour at the end. When they did I had to plunge into the ocean to hide my erection.

We went dancing again that night, because it was our last night. We ran into several of the guys they had seen at the beach earlier that day. Tracy and Gina both admitted to me that they were very horny, because they already knew which men had the biggest penises.

Gina started hinting that she wanted it to be a night for her to get some fresh man-meat. I told her to go for it. After all, I had just schtupped her best friend, so who was I to argue. Gina was making her desires quite obvious with her dirty dancing, and periodically told me some of the men were pressing their legs and penises into her crotch, which was making her crazy.

Gina and Tracy picked two guys, and we went back to our hotel suite. Both girls were wearing one-piece Lycra outfits that consisted of shirts and shorts rolled into one. They were so tight they could have been painted on, and they wore only thongs underneath. Tracy and Gina are not models, but they have their curves in all the right places.

More drinks flowed, and one of the guys had some pot, so

everybody enjoyed that, and got nice and relaxed. We all lay around together in an assortment of poses, and our clothes came off, slowly but surely.

When we got hot and heavy, I was with Tracy. My wife Gina was flat on her back with an eight-inch penis in her pussy and a six-inch penis in her mouth. She was moaning uncontrollably, something I had never seen her do before. I was lying on my back as well, and Tracy kept asking me if I liked watching that other guy's dick slide into Gina. I told her I did.

Tracy used her mouth on me, sucking me slowly and gently while I watched Gina. When my excitement got to be too much Tracy jerked me off lovingly into her waiting mouth. All the time I was spraying my sperm my eyes feasted on Gina being jammed in two orifices.

Gina told me to come over to the chair next to the bed so I wouldn't miss any details of what was about to happen. Gina announced that she had never had anal sex, and that she wanted to try it with the guy who had the six-inch penis, since she thought it would be the easiest to accommodate. I was desperately jealous, since I had always wanted to do her butt, but had only gotten my head in before she decided my penis was just too wide for comfort.

Gina lay on her belly, spread-eagle, all four limbs flung wide, no clothes and no blankets hiding her beauty. Ronnie, the guy with the six-inch penis, was working his dick along her thighs while the other guy rubbed some oil into her butthole, slowly inserting his finger to get her loose and slick.

I was rock-hard as Gina moaned with each thrust and Tracy licked my penis and caressed my balls again and again. Gina looked me right in the eyes and groaned as loudly as I'd ever heard her before as Ronnie slowly inserted his cockhead. Five minutes and about a quart of oil later he was all the way in.

They put pillows under her to raise her butt, which made her look all the more sexy. The other guy quickly got underneath Gina and entered her vagina with his penis. Gina said later that she had the longest, most intense orgasm of her life at that point, as they developed a very slow rhythm. She moaned, "Oh, honey, I feel him all the way up my ass, and it feels so good."

She felt so free that she came again when Ronnie started to fuck her ass more quickly. He stayed all the way inside her as he came violently. Gina yelled, "Ah, sweet Jesus, he's coming all the way up my ass. Oh, it feels so good." Tracy sat on my dick, her back toward me, and rode me for all I was worth. I came quickly, and had to send her over to the other guy to be fucked so she could come as well.

So, not only did I get to see my wife make love to another man, I got to see her do it with two men and watch while one took her anal cherry. That was quite a vacation.—*P.S., Trenton, New Jersey*

THEY MET THE COUPLE OF THEIR DREAMS AT A SMALL SWING CLUB IN THE BIG CITY

I've read so much in *Penthouse Letters* about swinging. Even though the subject never fails to give me a diamond-tipped erection, I was not sure about trying it. I finally did, though, and oh boy, did it ever change my life for the better.

This took place several years ago now, but I remember it better than I do what happened to me yesterday.

My husband and I had been married for about ten years, and our sex life needed a good airing-out. We had once gone to a club in Houston that had turned out to be a swingers club. We went with it. That was the first time I had sex with a man other than my husband. Jack and I did a lot of talking after that first swing, and we both decided we wanted to try it again.

One Saturday afternoon Jack suggested we drive into Houston and go to the club for a little fun. I was thrilled. I thought and thought about what to wear. I wanted to dress sexy, like most of the other women at the club. I wanted Jack to be proud to be seen with me. I chose a wrap blouse, with no bra, and a skirt to match. I wore white lace panties and no hose, just sandals. I'm five-three, with long brown hair and nice-sized tits with large nipples. I love my husband, and was looking forward to learning some new sexual techniques to try on him.

On our trip into Houston, Jack and I did a lot of laughing and talking. My pussy was getting wet just thinking about what might happen. The club wasn't very big. It was like a neighborhood bar. Most of the people there seemed to know each other. It had a comfortable, homey kind of feeling.

There were several people dancing when we entered. I had butterflies in my stomach from anticipation. We ordered drinks and sat listening to the music. It was a little early and we had a table to ourselves for a while.

Soon two other couples sat at our table. They seemed nice, but the guys didn't really spark my interest, and I don't think the women interested Jack either, although he did dance with one of them.

A couple of guys from other tables asked me to dance. I enjoyed the attention, and didn't mind that they copped a feel or two. I liked it, as a matter of fact, but we just didn't click. One guy asked if we'd like to come meet his wife, but she had already picked some other guy to swing with.

I wanted to find a couple that my husband and I could both enjoy swinging with. Then Rand came to our table, introduced himself and asked Jack if he minded if I danced with him. Jack said it was fine. I'd been enjoying watching the other dancers fool around. A couple of women were dancing in their sexy undies. Then they took their bras off, and the other dancers closed in around them so the host couldn't see what was going on and put a stop to it.

Rand was not tall, but I really enjoyed dancing and talking with him. Something clicked inside me, and I knew that I would enjoy exploring him and seeing how his dick felt inside me. The more we danced the bolder Rand got. He started feeling me up. He had one hand on my ass, and the other was playing with my tit. His dick was rubbing against my cunt. My pussy was getting wetter and wetter.

We started kissing, and I got even hotter. I wondered if my husband was watching, or if he was doing the same thing to some other woman. The thought of him watching really turned me on.

Rand said that he would sure like to fuck me. He said that he would bring his wife over to meet my husband. He was hoping they would hit it off and we could all go to their house for a party. When Rand took me back to our table I told Jack that we'd been invited to Rand's house if he was agreeable. Rand went and got his wife and introduced her to us.

Her name was Sue, and she seemed really nice. Jack asked her to dance, and Rand and I had one more dance too. This time we both did a little more exploring. I was happy, when I looked over, to see that Sue was pressing her big breasts into Jack's chest. He had a big smile on his face. When we all got back to the table we were all in favor of going to Rand and Sue's place.

Rand asked me to ride with him, and Sue rode with Jack, in case we got separated. The minute I got into Rand's Honda Civic he gave me a long kiss, tongue and all. My pussy was drenched, and needed attention. It did not take Rand long to have my tits bared to the world. He felt them, then kissed me again. My nipples were both standing at attention. We hadn't gone far when his hand was on my knee, squeezing it. He moved his hand ever so slowly up to my panties. He was exploring my cunt through my thin, white, lacy panties.

I put my hand on Rand's crotch, and began playing with his peter through his pants. It wasn't long till it was hard as a rock. We continued playing around all the way to his house, with me damn near nude most of the way. My breasts were bared and my skirt was up around my waist as we sped through Houston.

*   *   *

Somewhere along the way we lost sight of Jack and Sue. We waited in the driveway till they pulled up next to us. Of course we were a little busy necking while we waited. I'd never been so bold before. While necking, I hauled out his beautiful dick and began to stroke it. He was fingering me, with my skirt pushed out of the way and his finger snaking up the leg of my panties. I had my first major orgasm the minute he touched my boiling cunt.

I think he would have fucked me in the car if they hadn't finally driven up. We headed into the house, and straight to the master bedroom. It was a big room, with a king-size bed. There was a bathroom off this room, and in a corner was a wooden box about the size of a desk. I asked Rand what that was for, and he told me it was a darkroom, where he developed pictures. He said he'd take my picture later if I didn't mind.

Then he walked over to me and began kissing my neck and lips. Slowly he took off my top, and gave my nipples a quick, sucking kiss. Very nice. As we kissed, he put his hands on my hips and slowly pushed my skirt to the floor, along with my slip. All I had on was my panties. Rand stepped back and took a look. He said I was beautiful, but he wanted me naked, so he took off my white lacy panties. I watched as he stripped his clothes off, then he led me to the bed.

He spread my legs wide open, getting a good look at my hairy pussy, before he jumped in and began licking my cunt. My juices were so thick, he said, he just had to fuck me, right then and there. He slowly moved up and put his hard dick into my hot cunt. He started slowly, but before long he was flying along, and all the time his dick was rubbing my hard clit.

I can't tell you how many orgasms I had, but it damn sure felt good. Pretty soon Rand filled my cunt with his hot love-juice. We were out of breath, so we just lay in each other's arms for a while.

When we had recovered, Rand sat up and asked if I would mind if he took my picture. I didn't mind, so he went to get his camera.

He told me I could pose any way I wanted. I sat up in the middle of the bed, with my back to the headboard. I raised one leg up and crossed the other one over, and Rand took my picture. Having my picture taken in the nude turned out to be a real turn-on for me.

Rand joined me back on the bed. He said it would be a while before he could get it up again, but he sure wanted to fuck me again. While we were waiting I rubbed his back. He rolled over on his stomach, and I straddled him and began rubbing softly.

I don't know how long I rubbed for, but I could tell he was ready for me to rub something else. He turned over, and I rubbed his chest, his arms, his legs, but I ignored his dick. I could tell it was getting to him, but he didn't say a word. Finally I took his semi-erect dick in my mouth and began to rub my tongue around the head. Rand moaned, enjoying my tongue-lashing.

He asked me to stop and let him fuck me again, so I did. He thrust into me and started hammering my pussy fast and furious. I was wondering if Jack could hear the sucking noises. The more I thought about it, the more noise I made. It didn't take long before Rand shot his load in me again.

When our breathing slowed down, I could hear moans coming from out front. I was so happy. Rand suggested that I clean up a bit, and then we would go see what Sue and my husband were up to in the other room.

When I came back from showering Rand had on a robe. I didn't feel like wearing anything so I followed him into the living room nude. There sat Sue and Jack. She had on a housecoat too, but my husband was nude. I smiled at Jack, and he gave me a loving smile back.

Rand and I sat across the room from them. We had a nice talk.

It was getting late, and Rand said he wanted to take me back to the bedroom for another quick fuck. I followed him. He sat down on the edge of the bed and pulled me to him. He sucked one nipple, then the other, while his hands explored my body.

I was getting turned on all over again. Rand noticed this, and guided me back to the bed. He didn't lie on top of me. Instead he slid his butt and dick up between my legs while his legs moved past my butt. We were in kind of a sitting position. Rand slid his dick back into me and began rocking back and forth. It felt wild; a new part of my cunt was being massaged. Rand kissed me and played with my breasts as he moved. My cunt contracted around his dick and that was all there was to it. He came again.

We slid down in the bed and held each other for a while. Rand said he'd sure enjoyed our lovemaking.

I dressed, while Rand sat on the bed and watched me. We walked back to the living room. Jack and Sue were just coming out of the other bedroom. Jack was still getting dressed. We said our goodbyes to Rand and Sue and headed for our truck.

I was a little tired, but exhilarated too. I slid over close to Jack as we drove off, and put my hand on his leg. We started talking about the evening's fun. I could tell that he was getting horny. So was I. He opened my wrap blouse and let my breasts out. He was tweaking my nipples with his free hand. I was having little spasms each time he did it.

We had not gone more than a mile before he pulled off the road. He had his hands in my panties, pulling them off. He asked me to move over and lean up against the door so he could eat me. I moved over and spread my legs wide apart. Jack dove for my pussy. Each time he batted my clit with his tongue, I came. I suddenly realized that I still had Rand's come inside me. Jack was bound to be tasting it. I don't know how many times I came before Jack slid up and stuck his dick into me. I exploded again in another orgasm. He pumped away for a while, then he filled me with his come.

Jack pulled up his pants, but didn't fasten them. I slid back over close to him. I had no idea where my panties were, but I didn't need them. We played with each other all the way home.

When we got there we drifted off to sleep. I'm not sure what time we woke up, but we were still horny, and made love again.

Our little swing kept our love-life heated up for several months. I learned to be more adventurous sexually and more vocal about what I wanted and needed. We met Rand and Sue again at Lake Travis, and it was as much fun as the first time. Camping out and skinny-dipping can really turn a person on—not to mention the pictures we took of each other.

We lost track of them finally, but we think of them often. They will always be special people to us. Just writing this made me as horny as on that memorable night. I sure would love to meet up with them again.—*N.K., Galveston, Texas*

A HAPPY CUCKOLD MANAGES TO PUT HIMSELF IN THE PICTURE AT LAST

When I married Adele I introduced her to *Penthouse Letters*, and since then she has also been reading it regularly. Adele often gets inspiration for various adventures from what we read.

I often read letters from horny guys getting their jollies watching other men fuck their wives, and I always get so turned on that I wind up beating off. To be truthful, I would also get very envious. Ever since we got married I've fantasized about seeing some well-hung stud fuck my lovely wife. Adele knows how much I've wanted to see her with another man, but she always steadfastly refused to grant my wish.

Her reluctance wasn't based on any great disdain for taking another man to bed. Adele was twenty-two when I married her, and she willingly admitted she had been with numerous men before me. We slept together on our very first date, which she said was common practice for her. When I proposed to her, she was hesitant, saying I fit her ideal in every way except one: I wasn't as well-endowed as other guys she'd been with. She said I just didn't satisfy her in bed.

Adele finally agreed to marry me, but it was understood she would share her bed with other men. In our four years of marriage

Adele has had numerous lovers, maintaining at least one full-blown extramarital affair at all times. She doesn't neglect me, either emotionally or sexually, regularly giving me fantastic blowjobs. She also lets me fuck her now and then, usually serving me sloppy seconds. She loves for me to go down on her when she's been with another man, and I've learned to at least tolerate the taste as I lick my wife's swampy, sperm-saturated snatch.

In spite of all this, though, Adele refused to let me watch her have sex with another man. To her, making love was intimate and personal, not something to be done in front of an audience. She loved to read about other women doing just that, but refused to do it herself.

Yesterday that all changed. It all began with Adele going to work out. She loves the gym because it's such a good place to meet prospective lovers. With her good looks and fantastic body she always has several guys hitting on her when she goes there.

I stayed home, as usual. When she got home she had a real surprise for me. She told me she'd been talking to a guy at the club and he was coming over in half an hour. Now, Adele has brought guys to our house on a couple of occasions during our marriage, but it's very rare. But Richard was married, so she couldn't meet him at his house.

Adele asked if I would straighten things up a bit while she went upstairs to get ready. Adele keeps the house very neat, so it took me just a few minutes to pick up the newspapers I'd strewn around and pick up the toys our oldest son had left on the floor when he went to bed. Twenty minutes later, the doorbell rang.

When she returned she was wearing only a very short, transparent nightgown. It was black, barely covered her crotch and hid nothing. Adele's fluffy blonde pubic fuzz was clearly visible, and her smallish breasts were in plain view. Her nipples were standing out, firm and erect.

Richard's eyes opened wide at the way she greeted him, and a broad grin appeared on his face. My eyes opened wide also.

Standing there in our doorway was a handsome, very well-built, extremely dark-skinned black man. I had not expected that. This was to be her first experience with an African-American.

No sooner was the door closed than Adele was in Richard's arms making out with him. She didn't even bother to introduce me.

Their mouths met in a tongue-probing kiss, and Adele's abdomen ground against the bulge in Richard's slacks. His hands went under her short nightie, gripping her bare ass-cheeks as he pulled her hard against him. His mouth moved to her neck and ears, and Adele got hotter and more passionate than I'd ever seen her in my life.

Her hands clumsily fumbled with the zipper of his trousers, trying to free his manhood. He kept mouthing her neck, and I heard her gasp. "Uh, uh, oh, oh yes. Keep doing that. Yes! Don't stop, keep doing that."

Richard's powerful hand was up under her nightie between her legs. Adele's lower torso was frantically twitching as he fingerfucked her. His entire hand was already wet with her juices, and I could see she was about to come. Adele closed her eyes, shuddered, moaned loudly and a flood of juice came out of her, further coating his hand and running down her inner thighs.

"Where's the bedroom?" I heard Richard gasp.

"No," I heard her respond. "Just fuck me. Here, now. I want you in me now, Richard. Fuck me now."

Richard pulled his hand from between my wife's legs. As he helped her work his trousers and his boxer shorts down his legs I heard Adele say to him, "Just remember what I said earlier. I can't take a chance on getting pregnant, so don't come in me. Okay?" Richard nodded as he gave a few tugs on his huge cock to bring it to full hardness.

I saw Adele look down between them and smile when she saw his rigid cock sticking out. She looked back up at him, smiled and then feverishly began kissing him. Adele was hotter than I'd ever seen her. She literally climbed up his body.

Richard's hands grabbed my wife's butt and helped support her as she grabbed his shoulders, hoisted herself up and put her legs around his waist. Adele's hot gash lined up with the head of Richard's prick and she sank her crotch down on it. I was undoing my own trousers by then. I took out my dick, stroking it as I watched my wife impale herself on Richard's cock.

They were only a couple of feet from the closed front door. Richard took two choppy steps and leaned her against it. The door banged and rattled as Richard began thrusting at her. I could tell they weren't going to last long, and I knew I wouldn't either. As Richard lunged at her, Adele worked her wet, slick tunnel up and down his thick shaft.

I heart Richard grunt, then saw him stiffen and I heard him moan. "Gotta come, Adele. Oh God, I gotta come. I'm gonna come in you. Yes! Yes! Coming, oh shit, coming." When he did that, I heard my wife give out a deep, guttural sound. I also saw her thrust at him, hold and shudder as her orgasm hit her. Richard pushed in to the hilt and really pinned Adele to the door as he shot his wad. She was crying out, shaking, appended to Richard's body, as they climaxed. Seeing them in the throes of an intense mutual orgasm, I shot my wad on our living room carpet.

Adele went limp and Richard's knees buckled as they finished spending. For a second I thought he was actually going to fall.

Richard regained his balance, though, and helped lift Adele off his body. She just hung onto his shoulders and leaned against him.

Richard spoke first. "I'm sorry, I couldn't pull out. I got too worked up. I'm sorry."

Adele looked up at him, grinned and replied, "I'm not." She then kissed him, passionately, for a long time.

When she ended the kiss she looked at him and said lovingly, "Now we can go to the bedroom. If you can get that hard again, you can do me some more. Interested?"

When they were gone, I looked at our front door and saw a

wet, sticky spot, the mixture of Richard's come and my wife's juices.

Richard wound up staying in our bedroom with Adele a full two hours. I beat off again as I listened through our bedroom door. I could hear Adele's moans of pleasure and the headboard of our bed thumping against the wall as Richard repeatedly fucked her. It was past eleven when he finally came out. A smug smile my way and a nod was his only acknowledgment of me. He left without our having even been introduced.

I guess I'll be seeing a lot of Richard around here from now on.—V.S., *Akron, Ohio*

THE GREAT OUTDOORS HAS NEVER BEEN GREATER FOR THESE LOVERS

My lover Rosie and I decided to watch an X-rated movie one night recently. We sat close beside each other on the sofa, started the tape and were soon getting hot from kissing and watching the writhing bodies on the screen. Rosie's hard nipples stood up under her shirt, and I couldn't resist gently pinching them.

It wasn't long before she slid off the sofa onto the floor in front of me, unzipped my pants and freed my cock. She ran her tongue slowly up and down its full length before taking the tip into her mouth. I was transfixed by the sight of her full lips sliding down the shaft, and it was the visual as much as the physical sensation that made my cock so hard.

Once she had me good and wet, Rosie stroked me with her hand and fondled my balls until a drop of clear, sticky come oozed from the tip. Rosie licked it up and told me she loved the taste.

I asked her to turn the TV off so we could concentrate on our own pleasure. Rosie stripped off her jeans and panties. Running a hand over her partially shaved mound, then slipping a finger inside to spread the gathering moisture over her labia, she straddled my lap. She slowly lowered her hot, wet pussy down over my cock. We both watched as her beautiful sex swallowed me deep inside her. I groaned with pleasure as she slid all the way down to my balls. Rosie began fucking me while I kneaded her large breasts. The feeling was incredible, perfect.

I suddenly got the urge to make love standing up, so I reached under her legs and grabbed hold of her bottom. She was surprised when I stood up, still holding her, and continued pumping into her. Recovering quickly, and delighted with our new position, she held onto my shoulders, and wrapped her legs around my waist, bouncing up and down on my cock. Rosie got very excited and asked me to fuck her from behind, definitely our favorite position.

We went into the dining room and Rosie leaned over the table. She reached back to spread her lips, and I rubbed the head of my cock along her pussy. The pink folds glistened with her juices. I held her by the hips and slowly drove my full length deep into her. She moaned with pleasure and so did I. I started to fuck her faster, and she responded with cries of "Oh God, it feels so good!" and "Fuck me harder!" Rosie came twice. Each time she stopped pushing back against my hips and just stood with her mouth open, unable to make a noise, her legs rigid and her body trembling from top to bottom.

By the time she came the second time I was getting close to coming myself. I told her she felt so good that I had to slow down to make it last. I asked if she would suck my cock some more. Rosie loves to suck me until I come in her mouth, and she eagerly agreed. I suggested we try something a little different: going out onto the back porch. Rosie just grinned her sex-hungry grin at me and out we went. It was a warm summer night on the New Hampshire coast, clear and still. She sat in a lounge chair and began to drive me wild again with her mouth while I stood in front of her. Her sucking soon made my knees weak, so I asked if she wanted to try something really daring—would she like to fuck out in the backyard, down in the grass. She was hesitant at first, but some passionate kisses and stroking of her pussy persuaded her to try it.

I took her by the hand and led her out the screen door and down the steps into the moist night air, enjoying the heavy, expectant feeling in my balls that I get when I've been putting off a good orgasm. Rosie got down on her hands and knees in the dew-covered grass. I then gripped her firmly by the hips and kneeled behind her.

Neither of us could believe we were really about to fuck outdoors, where we might be seen by neighbors out for a walk or drivers passing by. But we were so hot to fuck each other by this time that we couldn't have stopped even if we had wanted to try. I slid my cock teasingly between Rosie's thighs, and she reached back to guide me into her. We wasted no time and started pounding into each other. Rosie and I both came quickly in a hot, sweaty, mutual orgasm, shuddering with pleasure, certain someone would hear our moans in the dark.

It seemed like a long time before we were able to regain our senses and move again. Finally we helped each other up off the grass and ran back into the house, laughing at the craziness of it all. Rosie is a wonderful lover and that was one midsummer night that I'm glad wasn't a dream!—*S.T., Portsmouth, New Hampshire*

COLLEGE STUDENT GETS AN EDUCATION FROM GIRLFRIEND'S MOM

My girlfriend Gwen and I are seniors at a small college. Gwen is a cute girl, with small breasts and a nice little ass. Her idea of sex, though, is to give me an occasional hand-job, or maybe a suck on her little A-cup titties. Gwen refuses to let me fuck her, as she intends to remain a virgin till she's married. I've never even laid eyes on her pussy. I've often thought of breaking up with her, just to satisfy my need for a good fuck, but I decided to stick it out.

A couple of weekends ago, Gwen went away on a ski trip to Colorado. I was just getting out of the shower when there was a knock at the door. I pulled a towel around me and answered it. I was greeted by a hot-looking blonde babe who introduced herself as Rachel. "I'm Gwen's mom," were the first words out of her mouth, followed by, "The way you look in a towel, it's no wonder she likes you." A little embarrassed, I invited Rachel in, though I told her that Gwen was gone for the weekend.

"It doesn't surprise me," Rachel said. "Gwen invited me up to spend the weekend and now she isn't here. She was never terribly considerate." Rachel was the total opposite of her daughter physically, with a pair of nice big boobs and a fine-looking ass. I could already tell they had different views about sex. Rachel asked me if Gwen had given me blue balls. I confessed she had. Smiling, Rachel said that, in that case, maybe she hadn't wasted a trip after all.

Next thing I knew, my towel was on the floor and Rachel was rubbing my cock and French-kissing me. Sinking to her knees, Rachel touched her tongue to my cockhead, slowly circling that sensitive organ with the warm, pink tip of her tongue. My cock disappeared into her mouth and she proceeded to give me a wild blowjob.

Rachel didn't have to work long before I let loose into her hard-working mouth. She swallowed my entire load, then kept my dick in her mouth, sucking very gently, until it went limp.

"That's just a sample of what we can do," Rachel said, smiling as she undressed and lay back on the floor. "Now it's your turn to do me." I sucked hungrily on her hard, hot nipples while feverishly fingering her clitty. "Come on, baby, give it to me hard. I love feeling like a slut," she cried. She was creaming in no time. "Please. Get your fucking cock inside me," she begged. "Fuck me hard." I buried my bone deep in her sloppy pussy and fucked her fast and wild for another several minutes, thoroughly enjoying her eager cooperation before coming at last inside her.

Rachel and I showered together and went out for some beer. On the way back home Rachel sucked me off in the car and asked me if I had ever fucked a woman in the ass. When I confessed I hadn't, Rachel purred that it was time I had a lesson. "I've been itching for a good butt-fucking," she told me, "and your young, hard dick is perfect for the purpose."

We went into the bedroom. Rachel took a jar of Vaseline and coated my cock. She got on all fours on the edge of the bed. I stood behind her and aimed my erection, which was harder than hell at the prospect of what we were about to do, at her tight brown hole. I plunged my dick into her butt.

"Come on, butt-fuck me," she howled. "Plunder my ass. Do me like you'd like to do Gwen." I banged her hot butt for a good ten minutes, then filled her asshole with come.

We fucked each other silly for the rest of the weekend. As Rachel was leaving she told me her pussy and ass were sore, and I started to apologize. "Are you nuts?" she asked. "It's the best feeling on earth. It's going to keep me reminded for the next couple of days of everything we did. Every time I think about it I'll have to beat off."

Gwen came back on Monday, and everything has gone back to the way it was, but I keep thinking about the weekend and shaking my head. I can't wait to see what the future brings.—M.O., *Des Moines, Iowa*

YOU DON'T HAVE TO TEACH THIS OLD BABE
ANY TRICKS

My mother suffered a stroke that impaired her speech and weakened her right side to the point where she cannot care for herself. Business commitments kept me from traveling to North Carolina to be with her immediately. By the time I could arrange the trip, Mom had been returned to a nursing unit at her retirement community.

I arrived at the nursing unit in the middle of a violent thunderstorm. I was only able to visit with Mom for a few minutes before the unit closed to visitors for the evening. My mother's friend Erica escorted me from my mother's room. On the way out I asked Erica to suggest a nearby motel.

Erica suggested that I stay in her apartment. I gratefully accepted.

Erica and I hurried through the pouring rain, but we were both drenched by the time we reached the front door of her apartment. She instructed me to get out of my wet clothing, and then disappeared. She returned shortly, wearing a short terry cloth robe tied at the waist. I stood before her, naked except for my wet cotton briefs. Erica smiled, commenting that if she was fifteen years younger I would not be safe parading in front of her dressed as I was.

Later, as we sat drinking coffee, I took a good look at the lady who had come to my rescue. Erica was much younger than my mother, probably in her early sixties. Her black hair was highlighted with gray. Large glasses were perched on a small pointed nose, and lines were carved deep into her stately, handsome face. Plenty of skin was exposed from her neck to the point where her robe overlapped, but there was no hint that any portion of her breast was about to be exposed. Erica's hips were wide, her butt more than ample, but her legs were still shapely and toned.

Erica finished her coffee. She placed a pillow and a single blanket on the couch and quietly retired to her room. I realized my underwear was still damp, so I removed it and drifted off to sleep.

Before my sleep-filled eyes could focus I was greeted by her cheerful voice. "Good morning. You must have had one hell of a dream." Erica sat on a chair next to the couch on which I reclined. It was several seconds before I realized that I had kicked off the blanket during the night. My entire body was exposed, and I was painfully aware that my erect cock hovered above my stomach.

I sat up, aghast. Very matter-of-factly, Erica asked me to keep myself hard. Before I could respond, there was a knock at the door. Erica tossed me the blanket, which she had folded and placed by her chair.

As I spread the blanket over me, Erica let a totally gray, stocky lady into the apartment. Brendenna took a chair, while Erica forced her way onto the end of the couch. Erica apologized for my lack of formality, explaining that I wore nothing other than the blanket, placing her hand firmly on my thigh.

"Yeah, right," Brendenna said, her voice filled with disbelief.

"See for yourself," Erica replied, tossing the blanket over the back of the couch.

"Oh, my God. Look at that boner," Brendenna squealed. "You sly old slut."

Erica gently grabbed hold of my erect cock. Brendenna watched momentarily, but quickly excused herself. Erica told her not to let the door hit her in the ass on the way out. Erica continued to gently jerk me off.

Brendenna and Erica, it turned out, regularly swapped stories about their sexual encounters. Erica confessed that her stories were pure bullshit, and she suspected that Brendenna's were too, but she was never quite sure. This was Erica's chance to give her stories some credibility. I didn't care what her motivation was, I just wanted to get my rocks off. Suddenly the senior tease stopped stroking my cock, saying she shouldn't be doing this.

I grabbed her around the waist, pulling her on top of me. I

kissed her passionately. My tongue explored her mouth as I slid my hands inside her robe and lifted it off her shoulders. I sucked on her little tits for all I was worth.

Turning my attention to my dick, I tried to guide it to her cunt. She stopped me, explaining that she would need some Vaseline. I decided I could get her juices flowing. I buried my face in her crotch, licking and sucking every crevice of her cunt. I massaged her buttocks as the horny old lady rode my face. She bucked and thrust her hips into my face harder and faster with every stroke. Her cunt now moist, I tried to lick my way up her body so I could bury my prick deep inside her. Erica was no longer interested in cock. She pushed my head back down between her legs.

Somewhat disappointed, I licked and sucked on her clit. Erica pulled my head against her crotch. I licked faster and faster until she exploded.

We lay caressing each other while Erica calmed down. The doorbell rang.

Without bothering to cover herself, Erica answered the door. Again Brendenna entered. Brendenna apologized profusely for the intrusion, explaining that she had left her purse by the chair. "Oh, stop, Brendenna. I knew it was you. I knew you'd need another glimpse of my young man," Erica insisted.

Erica took a wide stance in front of me, pulling my face to her cunt. As Brendenna watched, I buried my tongue in Erica's pussy. She fucked my tongue in a nice, slow rhythm. With Brendenna still looking on, Erica pushed me onto my back, grabbing hold of my cock on the way down. Then she straddled me, aiming my erection at her pussy.

"Eat your heart out," Erica cried, smiling at Brendenna as she impaled herself on my dick. Erica bounced on my cock, telling Brendenna how good it felt. Brendenna left before I came. My cock wilted too soon for Erica to get off again. Erica was not going to be denied, though. She planted her pussy over my mouth, insisting that I suck her to another orgasm.

My sister cannot believe I am already planning to visit Mom

again. But since Brendenna has invited me to stay with her this time, I think I will hurry back.—N.T., *Toronto, Ontario*

AN OLD LOVER COMES OVER
TO SHOW OFF HER NEW TALENT

A few years ago I was in a situation where I'd been dating the same girl on and off for years, but just wasn't getting what I needed from her. One night, when I was working at my computer, an old ex-girlfriend called me, and we started to chat. Eventually the conversation got around to sex. We started to get into a deep conversation about how we would like to get together and do it. Well, my girlfriend was going home early the next day, so we set it up that Regina would come over after she left, and we would fuck.

Regina came over, and was sitting on the edge of my loft bed, undressing. She was down to her bra and panties, and all I had on were my boxers when I got a phone call and had to climb down. I was the sports editor of the school yearbook, and the call was from the managing editor. Regina followed me down and was rubbing my cock while I talked. It was soon hard as a rock. It was, like, impossible to get this guy off the phone, but I finally managed it, then crawled back up to the loft and begged Regina to suck my cock, which she proceeded to do in great fashion.

She was licking and sucking my shaft and playing with my balls, then using her hand to jack me off while using her mouth on my balls. She even stuck her finger in my ass, because she knows I love that. I was grabbing her hair and moaning when she deep-throated my rod. I can't take much of that, and I blew a huge load, which she noisily gobbled.

After I blew my load, Regina just kept right on sucking my dick, which never went soft. She was running her tongue up and down, sucking my balls into her mouth from time to time, and even licking my asshole. After a while I blew another load into her mouth. It was so cute when she looked up and asked me to fuck her silly, a drop of my come dripping out of her talented mouth.

We rolled over. Regina mounted me and began to ride my hard cock for all she was worth. She was sliding up and down my shaft at blinding speed. Her tits were softly calling my name, so I began to squeeze and suck her nipples. That sent her over the edge, and she began heaving her hips around in sharp, spastic little move-ments. She held my shoulders hard and suddenly went still. All I could feel was her pussy pulsing around my cock, trying to milk me of what little semen I had left. She'd had a little orgasm, but Regina wanted more, and began rubbing her clit against my pubes in short, hard thrusts. Soon she was screaming and grab-bing at my chest.

Without a pause, we rolled over and I mounted her. I began to slam my cock into her as hard as I could, and she was loving it. She kept looking into my eyes and saying, "Come on, come on. Come in me." I fucked her for what seemed like an eternity.

She wanted me to fuck her from behind, knowing that it is my favorite position. I slid my cock into her cunt from the rear and began to fuck her in good, long, steady strokes. She was playing with my balls and fingering her clit as her juices poured out of her and down both of our legs.

All at once Regina turned and looked me in the eye, then asked me to fuck her ass. I had never done that to her, but she had told me that she had let her last boyfriend, who has about a nine-inch cock, do it to her. I was ecstatic! I have always wanted to fuck her luscious ass.

I reached into a nearby drawer, got a tube of lube out and coated my cock with it. I stuck a finger in her ass to loosen her up, then placed the head of my cock at the entrance to her anus and began to push.

She was so tight that it was really hard the first few tries. Her ass finally gave way, and I was in with one huge stroke. Her passage was so tight and hot. I slammed my cock all the way in on every stroke.

Finally she said she was getting a little sore, so I pulled out, not expecting to get any more that morning. Regina surprised me by taking my cock right back into her mouth. She was giving me the blowjob of a lifetime. I was getting close to blowing another load in her mouth when she slipped two fingers into my ass. That proved to be my final undoing, and I shot my third load of the morning down her throat.

At that point we were totally spent, and just lay back and talked about past lovers. We haven't fucked since then, but I am hoping one day we'll get together again. Maybe next time she'll even fuck my ass.—H.G., *Billings, Montana*

THE OLD TOOL SHED,
WHERE FANTASIES ARE BORN AND SATISFIED

About ten years ago I was home from college, preparing for my senior year. Both of my parents were working so I used my time at home doing yard work and minor house repairs. But I had another motive as well: the girl next door. She had also just finished her junior year, but at another college. Boy, did I have the hots for her.

I used every possible excuse I could to go into the yard wearing almost nothing, with the hope of catching her eye. My favorite shorts were an old pair of cutoffs with a large rip across the back. Of course I wore no underwear, and several times I caught Gillian looking my way when I was bent over to start the lawn mower.

One particular day she was sunning herself in an unbelievable bikini. I had just mowed the front yard of my parents' place and was sweating up a storm. We lived in a small town and the property was large, although our houses were not far apart. Gillian watched me closely as I mowed the backyard. As I neared her I could see her erect nipples pressing against her bikini top. I immediately had a hard-on. At first I thought I should turn around and conceal it, but I changed my mind and mowed near enough to her that she could plainly see my dick's outline in my tight jeans. Then she winked, and that was all it took.

I turned off the mower and went her way, noting that she was as hot and sweaty as I was. After all, the sun was bright. "I see a young man who needs a bigger pair of shorts," she said. I asked her if she thought they should come off, and she gladly offered to help. "Not here, though," she said. "My parents could catch us." We ran to an area near the back of the yard, next to a tool shed. No one could see us there unless they were looking from one of the large upstairs windows. But we would hear her parents when they returned, and we could split from behind the house before they got inside and up the stairs.

It seemed as if the gates of heaven had opened when she began stroking my crotch. The top of my cock stuck out of my jeans as she rubbed. Our tongues met. I removed the top of her bikini. She unzipped my cutoffs and squeezed my rod, causing a small stream of pre-come to run out and onto her hand. She licked it up as I bent down to kiss her again. We tumbled together to the ground where I pulled off her bikini bottom and dove into her wet pussy. Our bodies slithered easily against each other as the sweat lubricated us, and I tasted salty perspiration mixed with her love juices. I entered her from on top and pushed so hard that I could hear her ass tearing the grass. I was about to come like never before, but she told me not to.

Instead, she instructed me to sit up and lean back against the shed. "Scoot closer to me," she demanded. As I did so, she swallowed my throbbing member into her mouth so far I thought she would choke. She reached under my balls and began rubbing the sweat around and toward my asshole. Then, with a sudden push, her sweaty finger slid into my ass. She developed an unbelievable rhythm, sucking my cock and pushing her finger slowly in and out of my butt. I was delirious.

As I pushed my dick into her face, I wanted more of her finger in my ass. But when I pushed my ass down further onto her finger, my cock slid away from her mouth! The exquisite joy and tension were driving me crazy! My own pumping got faster, until Gillian knew the moment was near. Watching her suck me, with one hand on my pole and the other on her clit, sent me into ecstasy. I told her I was going to come, and she pulled my cock out of her mouth to watch. I erupted with a thousand pounds of pressure per square millimeter.

Come went everywhere! There is nothing remarkable about my prick, but when I shoot it seems like it will never end. That had been true since I first masturbated, and still is today. After a few jets, Gillian tried to swallow the rest of my cream, but it just kept going, and when she pulled my penis out again, still spasming and dribbling, she grinned and giggled like a little kid.

After resting her cheek on my spent rod, she reached up to offer me a gentle kiss. I had tasted my own come once before, but this time it was much more salty because of the sweat. Gillian and I lay together awhile before noticing that we were covered with grass stains and come. Then we heard a car in the driveway in front of her house. Gillian kissed me and ran into the house naked. As I quickly put my shorts back on, I looked up to see her wave from her upstairs bathroom window before jumping into the shower.

Then I noticed something else. On the opposite end of the upstairs level was a full-length window in a separate bedroom. Gillian's nineteen-year-old brother was standing there with his pants down to his knees pulling on his pecker. Evidently he had been watching us the whole time, and was now so involved in his own fantasy that he hadn't noticed that we were finished. I watched as he exploded come on the window, then I snuck away.

Gillian and I had other adventures, which I'll relate in later letters.—*H.P.*, *Sarasota, Florida*

ONE-WOMAN LEAGUE OF NATIONS OFFERS MORE THAN HANDS ACROSS THE WATER

My wife Allison and I are avid readers of *Penthouse Letters*. We've recently developed a hobby which may be of interest to your readers. In brief, this hobby consists of her seeing, from amongst her lovers, how many countries she can collect.

Allison is a gorgeous blonde who sticks out in back and front in an enticing way. We have been very happily married for eight years. Our sex life at first was outstanding, but over time it gradually deteriorated. For some time, we had discussions as to what to do about this. Finally, Allison suggested that what she needed was more variety in her sex life. I agreed that it would be good to try this out, even though she wouldn't agree to my following the same course of action.

My wife works in an office where there are many visitors from other countries. It seemed the ideal setup for our new hobby. The male visitors are all capable, sophisticated gentlemen, generally without any accompanying spouse, who have an appreciation for good-looking girls and a desire for blonde Americans and their sexual favors. In addition, they stay at elegant hotels, which are quite suitable for extramarital sex events. The fact that these eligible studs are here for only short periods of time eliminates the problem of possible long-term emotional attachment.

So, we began the "foreign assistance project," and it has turned out to be a huge success. A little flirtation from Allison almost always brought forth an invitation for dinner and a few drinks afterward. This would be followed inevitably by an invitation to the stud's bedroom, with invariably interesting results.

In the first year of the game, Allison chalked up the following countries for her collection: Canada, Costa Rica, Ecuador, France, Honduras, India, Ireland, Japan, Liberia, Nigeria, Russia and Saudi Arabia. She had many exciting experiences, and even learned some new tricks, which happily she shared with me in both words and action. For example, there were some interesting variations of cunt-eating from the French entry, some new twists in the cocksucking field from a Saudi prince, and a new position for fucking from the Honduran.

Allison's goal is to be sucked and fucked by macho guys from at least half the countries in the United Nations. In any event, our sex life has been greatly enhanced—my wife's by the additional and greatly varied activity, and mine by the terrific improvement in our joint lovemaking, as well as the thrill of hearing about her sexual exploits with so many different men. The only problem is that I can't get her to permit me to undertake a similar project. However, I'm trying hard to convince her, and very much hope that I'll soon be successful.—*L.L.*, *New York, New York*

THE BIGGER THE BETTER,
SAYS ONE WOMAN WHO HAS BEEN THERE

I've seen in many sex surveys the question of whether women prefer large penises to smaller ones. For my part, there's no question. I prefer the big ones.

Several years ago I met Georgie at a going-away party for one of my coworkers. He was slightly younger than I am, tall and slender, with a dazzling smile.

Georgie and I hit it off immediately, and by the end of our second date I knew that I would be sleeping with him. To skip the preliminaries, we ended up at his place. After some kissing, he removed my top and began to gently suck on my nipples. He then moved further and started to caress my moist pussy. I was getting hotter by the minute. When he finally moved between my legs and started licking me out, I came within seconds. Georgie was patient, though, and ate me to two more fantastic orgasms before coming up for air.

I felt that I should do something to return the favor so I began to remove his pants, which of course he had no objection to. When I finally grasped his cock in the dim light, I thought to myself, this can't be real. I couldn't see exactly how big it was, but I could definitely tell it was bigger than any cock I had held before. I couldn't even get my hand around it. I did my best to give him a good sucking, but it consisted mainly of licking the shaft and the underside of his balls. After several minutes of my eager if unsuccessful attempts, Georgie suggested that I lie down.

I was a little apprehensive at first, but when I felt the bulbous cockhead touch my pussy lips I knew that I wanted it all inside me. Georgie rubbed his monster at the entrance of my cooze for a minute, then started to make his entry. As his cock slowly nudged forward I could feel my pussy stretch to let him inside. He wasn't even fully inside when I felt a climax building. I came once very powerfully, and then began a succession of what I can only describe as miniorgasms. After about every fifth miniorgasm I would have another huge one. And he wasn't even all the way in yet! Finally Georgie got all the way inside me, and truly gave me one of the best fucks I've ever had. He pumped in and out with a steady rhythm that rolled me from one orgasm to another.

When he finally came he was so deep inside that I could feel his boner twitching and spurting his load. We lay still for several minutes, and even after he had stopped coming I had another climax.

The next morning in full light I was able to really take a look at that monster, and was truly amazed to discover that it was even bigger than I had thought. I once measured it at just under eleven inches long and five inches around. One time I climaxed a total of twenty-three times with the help of Georgie and his fabulous tool.

We continued to see each other for several months, until Georgie was transferred across the country. I've heard that he is married now, and I can't help but be a little jealous of his wife and the great sex she's having with him. I have been with a few other men since Georgie, but none has ever been able to drive me the way he could.

To sum up my feelings about big cocks: Ladies, if you've never had a monster dick churning inside of your pussy, you are truly missing out on one of the most pleasurable experiences a woman can ever have. Of course, if Georgie hadn't been so patient about getting me good and wet and ready for his monster, I might have been less enthusiastic, but the combination of a big dick and good technique is unbeatable.—R.G., *Boston, Massachusetts*

NOW THAT YOU'RE GROWN UP, YOU CAN SCREW RIGHT HERE IN THE FRONT SEAT

My wife and I were returning from a vacation up north when I asked her to play a game to kill time on the road. We started asking each other questions that we had to be completely truthful about and both answer.

One question she asked me was, "What would you do if you could be a member of the opposite sex for a day?" Part of my answer was that I wanted to have sex with two men and a woman at the same time. Roxanne asked me how I would feel if she did that. I said that I didn't know, but that I would be as supportive as possible.

One question I asked was, "What was the most erotic thing you've ever done in a car?" Roxanne said that hers was giving me a blowjob while a friend of ours was in the backseat. That was mine as well, actually, but she asked me to tell her about something else I'd done. I told her about a girlfriend who had stripped while we drove down the interstate so that I could masturbate her. After she came, she knelt on the seat with her ass against the window, so that truckers could see her pussy, and she gave me a blowjob.

Roxanne asked me if I wanted her to do that. I felt selfish, but said, "Sure!"

Roxanne pulled off her sweater, dress and panties and placed her back against the passenger door. She spread her legs, one foot on the dash and one on my seat back, so that I could easily get at her pussy with my free hand. I could smell the sweet, pungent aroma of her sex and it made me dizzy with lust. When I stroked her pouting labia with my fingers she was soaking wet. I plunged into her with my forefinger, and she softly and sexily moaned and moved her pussy against my hand for more penetration. As her moaning became louder and her bucking became more urgent, I put two fingers into her and began to rub her straining clit with my thumb. She looked so beautiful, caught up in herself, with her hair in her face and her exquisite skin pale in the cloudy moonlight.

Soon her breathing quickened and she began to shudder as she frantically impaled herself on my fingers. The orgasm that rocked her seemed to start deep in her stomach, and rolled out to her sexy toes and fingertips.

Once Roxanne caught her breath, she decided it was my turn to come. She unzipped my jeans and delicately began licking and sucking my cock. As she went down on me, she made little moaning sounds and began to sway her beautiful ass. I began to rub her bottom with my right hand and slid a finger into her soaking pussy from behind. The more I masturbated her, the more enthusiastically she worked her mouth and tongue on my dick.

I started to gently finger Roxanne's asshole between rubbing her ass and fingering her cunt. She stopped sucking me long enough to push her long red curls aside and say, "That's it. Shove it in there, Christopher! I want to feel you in my ass!" I was already loving the feeling of Roxanne working on my cock as I attempted to drive down the coast, but I was elated by her request.

I began to finger her harder and with a more deliberate rhythm. She responded by sucking me more vigorously and moaning around my cock with each stroke. Roxanne's mouth and moans were slowly but surely driving me to the edge, and I was more than ready to come.

I said, "Suck my cock like you mean it, girl!" With that encouragement, she began bobbing her head and sucking me like never before. I kept saying "That's it! Suck it like you mean it!" I continued to shove a finger into her butt, and soon felt myself going over the edge. I exploded into her warm, waiting mouth with an orgasm that left me quivering and breathless.

Roxanne kept sucking me until I was hard again. Then she sat back against the passenger door. With her legs spread wide, she plunged two fingers into her cunt. After a few seconds, she pulled them out so that I could taste her wonderful juices. She was so wet and tasty that I was quickly ready for more driving fun.

Roxanne was ready for some driving fun too, but the driving she wanted was my cock in her glistening pussy. She leaned forward slightly and said with authority, "I want you to stop the car and fuck me. Now!" Then she began sucking me again while I looked for a place to pull off the road.

We parked in a turnout in front of a farm. Roxanne reclined her seat as far as possible while I stripped. She turned around and lay down on the seat with her bottom slightly raised so that I could fuck her from behind. As enticing as fucking her was at that moment, I couldn't help stopping and sampling her sweet pussy. After a few licks she looked over her shoulder and said, "Fuck me, damn it!" I raised myself level with her ass and slowly pushed my throbbing cock into her. She was so hot! It felt like the muscles of her vagina were pulling me into her.

After a few minutes like this, we switched our positions so that she was facing me with her knees up high. I started with long, slow strokes again as Roxanne quietly exhorted me to fuck her. I started talking to her about the earlier fantasy of being with two men and a woman at the same time. I asked her if she would like someone to fuck her from behind while someone else worked his cock into her little mouth and down her throat. Would that turn her on? Would she cry out with pleasure?

Needless to say, all this fantasizing and her hot body had made me pick up my pace. I was tearing in and out of her pussy like I was one of the men I had been describing. It was incredible! We were making so much noise I'm surprised that the farmer didn't come outside to see what was going on. Roxanne began to come again, with another tremendous rolling orgasm. I love looking into her eyes while I can feel her coming.

We quietly put our clothes back on and started down the coast again toward home with a twinkle in our eyes and the smell of sex filling the car.—C.L., *Palo Alto, California*

TALK ABOUT GETTING IT ON BEHIND
YOUR PARENTS' BACKS!

There's a thrill to screwing in secret, right under the nose of someone who has no idea of what's going on. My wife and I were near the end of a long trip, vacationing with both sets of our parents. My wife Lisette's parents were driving the minivan, my parents were in the middle seat and we were in the back. The interstate stretched for miles ahead of us, and we sat silently in the dark, for after a week together there was little small talk left. Lisette had fallen asleep with her head on my lap, and I was in that mesmerized state you get in when waiting for the highway to end.

I felt her stirring as she woke up, and reached down to stroke her head. In response she lifted my T-shirt and kissed my belly. I absentmindedly reached out and stroked her tits and felt a shudder go through her body. To my amazement, I felt her hands on my zipper. She was soon digging into my open fly to expose my cock, which lay flaccid beneath my jockey shorts. I wondered just how far she was planning to go, right there in the car with both sets of parents. I didn't have to ask. She let me know that she had decided to suck my cock.

In complete silence, she surrounded my drooping dong with her lips and began to suck gently. Her mouth covered my prick completely, the warmth of it like a blast furnace in the air-conditioned minivan. Her attentions soon caused my cock to grow and fill her mouth. Her lips slid up my pole as it expanded. Soon only the glans was covered, and her wonderful tongue ran swirls of delight around the tip of my cock. She sucked gently, and very lightly, never hard enough to make a telltale slurping sound and draw attention to us. With exquisite slowness I felt her lips slide down my cock, a band of liquid heat surrounding my manhood, until I was fully sunk between her lovely lips, then another achingly slow withdrawal as she pulled back.

I worked hard to keep my breathing steady, even as my body was sent racing by Lisette's attentions. Once again she clamped my glans between her lips and began to suck, drawing my juices from the depth of my balls. I felt the excitement begin to rise, felt my balls tighten and my prick get even stiffer. It was all I could do to maintain my silence when I began to pump my come into her mouth. Lisette maintained her steady sucking, draining me silently in the backseat of the van. At last the rush was over, and to my amazement neither set of parents had noticed a thing.

Lisette let my prick drop out of her mouth and rolled over. I quickly slid the strap of her halter top down one arm and pulled back the cup to expose one tit. With trembling hands I began to play with her nipple, gently pinching it and rolling it between thumb and forefinger. I could feel it hardening as I played, and soon the rhythmic motion of her head in my lap told me she was enjoying the attention. I reached my hand farther down, sliding it under the band of her shorts. The angle was wrong to be able to penetrate her warm bush, so I contented myself with sliding my fingers over her slippery cunt hair and cupped my hand over her clit. Using short strokes, I massaged her and felt her hips begin to move.

Keeping time with her motion I rubbed her clit, feeling her tension build. I felt her hand grip my arm as she grew more excited, her lips firmly sealed to keep from making a sound. I kept rubbing and nearly lost my arm as she tightened her grip on it. At last I felt her hips rise in the seat, and she drew in one sharp breath as she went over the edge. I struggled to keep rubbing her clit as she came, slowing as she rolled over the peak. At last she lay still on my lap, and we continued down the highway. With no one but ourselves having any idea what had just happened.—K.T., *Saint Paul, Minnesota*

SHOWERING AT A TRUCK STOP
LEADS TO A HIGHWAY FUCK STOP

Sally and I were going away for the weekend, and we had to hurry and get on the road. We hit the freeway wearing shorts and shirts, nothing fancy. We had a four-hour drive, and only five hours to arrive, get cleaned up and be ready to attend a play with my parents.

While we were driving we came upon a truck stop that advertised showers, so we decided to get cleaned up there. We separated to our respective locker rooms and agreed to meet at the grill. Forty-five minutes later she came out, looking absolutely stunning. Sally is five feet seven inches tall, and has a very nice figure. She was wearing a loose white blouse that buttoned up the front, a black skintight miniskirt and white heels. I got a hard-on just looking at her. Sally walked up and said, "Do you like? I bought this outfit to wear for you tonight." I was so stunned I couldn't answer.

We jumped in the car and hit the road again so we wouldn't be late. I couldn't keep my eyes off her. The bulge I was sporting grabbed her attention as well. That was all the signal she needed.

Sally turned in her seat so that her back was against the passenger door, put one foot on the back of the seat and the other on the dash. She pulled up her skirt. To my surprise, she wasn't wearing any panties. She slowly started rubbing her pussy and asked, "So you didn't answer my question. What do you think?"

I growled, "I want to eat you."

"Not yet, my hasty friend," she responded. "I have a lot more planned for you."

She started rubbing harder and faster. I could smell her excitement, and my cock felt like it was going to burst through my pants. I started fidgeting in my seat, trying to get more comfortable, but it didn't help. Sally leaned over and took my cock out of its cloth prison. She leaned back and rubbed my throbbing muscle with her foot. Reaching up, she undid her blouse. I started stroking myself. When Sally saw this she removed her hand from her cunt and stuck her fingers in my mouth. "Find somewhere to pull over," she moaned. "I want to fuck you."

She returned her hand to her cunt, at the same time leaning over to suck my aching dick. I found an isolated road and pulled off. Once we were parked, Sally pulled my pants down around my ankles, then lay back on the seat.

I slid down and started eating her pussy. Her flowing juices were sweet as honey. Her moans became louder and louder until she screamed out, "Fuck me!" I didn't need to be told twice. I propped her up on all fours and fucked her doggie-style. The way she controls her muscles is fabulous. She gripped my tool tightly. I pushed and pushed, working my prick in and out of her clenched cunt, and we both came with a roar. I pulled out, leaned down and cleaned her of both our juices with my tongue, then shared the cream with her in a passionate tongue kiss.

We pulled ourselves together and hit the road again. We arrived with ten minutes to spare. When we approached my folks they commented, "You two sure look happy this evening!" We looked at each other and just smiled. It was the most wonderful experience I've ever had.—*P.D.*, *Taos*, *New Mexico*

LOOKING FOR SOMETHING DIFFERENT, SHE DECIDES TO TURN OVER LEIF

I was at my boyfriend's apartment one evening while he was still at work. Ray's roommate Leif was there too, and looking good, as always.

I was wearing tight sweatpants. When I bent over to pick something up, I felt a hand on my butt. I let Leif have his way for a moment before I spun around and asked him what he was doing. "Sorry, I just couldn't resist," he said.

I told him he'd better watch it. "I have been watching it," he stated with a sly smile that drove me crazy. "I watched it twitch around here in those short shorts you wore all summer, and now I've watched it twitch around here in those tight sweats all fall, and I couldn't resist touching it." I was already worked up, knowing he had been eyeing me as much as I had been eyeing him.

"I don't think so," he responded sarcastically, when I told him he might get slapped. Leif and I have gotten along well since we first met, about nine months ago. His muscular build and his "country coolness" to my flirting have had me hot for him ever since.

I asked him what it was he liked about my short shorts. He said, "Come here," and led me to his room, where he handed me a beat-up old tank top. "This would go good with those shorts," he said. Making him turn his head, I slipped out of my sweatshirt and into the flimsy top. My 36D boobs weren't too well covered up by the little bit of material, and the fact is my nipples were about as hard as they could get. "It doesn't go so well with those sweats, though," he mused. "Go put on something that looks good with that top and you'll look the way you do when I fantasize about you."

I couldn't resist playing with my boobs as I stood in front of a mirror getting ready to change into a pair of pink G-string panties.

I was soon standing in front of him. His eyes ran slowly up and down my body. "You mustn't like the change, since you're not fondling me like you did in the kitchen a while ago," I complained.

"I might get slapped," he responded.

"I don't think so," I laughed, and moved toward him. Leif's hands played over my boobs, then crept behind me to outline my tiny panties. He picked me up and carried me into the living room. Once there, we kissed for the first time, our hands exploring each other's body. I love to talk a little dirty while having sex. Ray hates it, but I was hoping Leif would feel differently. I knelt before him, undid his pants and said, "I can't wait to suck your dick." That sly smile came over his face again, and I nearly ripped his pants in my hurry.

Soon I was sucking the most beautiful cock I'd ever seen. I positioned myself so that Leif could play with my butt while my head went up and down his shaft. "I want you to come in my mouth, but not until after you fuck me," I told him in between slurps, gazing into his eyes, with his cock resting on my lips.

We switched positions, with me on my knees on the edge of the couch and him directly behind me. He gave me the best tonguing I had ever received. I squealed as his tongue ran up my crack and stopped long enough to tease my asshole. (I love to play with my asshole, but Ray doesn't like that either.)

Soon Leif was sliding his big cock in and out of me. "I want you to fuck me in the ass," I said. I got on all fours, with my butt up in the air, and he slowly worked his big cock into my ass. It felt so good I could hardly stand it, and I knew right then that Leif and I were going to be making love a lot more in the future.

We switched positions several more times, and he was on top of me, driving away, when I realized that Leif was ready to come. "Come in my mouth," I begged.

He sat on the couch and I lowered my head, waiting for my prize. It wasn't ten seconds before he gushed his come into my hungry mouth. I slurped and played with his load, then climbed onto his lap to share it with him in a lingering kiss.

I love Ray, but I really love fucking Leif. I later told Ray that I had given Leif a blowjob that evening. He looked at me funny, but said he knew I wouldn't be able to resist Leif for very long. He even said he didn't mind, because Leif is a good buddy and had recently gone through a rough breakup with a girl he had dated for several years. Now Leif and I fuck each other a lot, sometimes even when Ray is home. I don't know how long he'll stay cool about it, but for the moment I have a perfect world.
—S.B., *Pontiac, Michigan*

ONE LARGE HOUSEGUEST

When my husband called from his office Monday afternoon to inform me that his old college roommate was in town on business and would be spending the rest of the week with us, I was not very happy. I had been complaining for several months about Joe's lack of attentiveness to my sexual needs and viewed this as just another excuse for him and a boon companion to hit every singles bar in town and run up a world-class drinks bill while I sat at home with a bad case of the hornies. But much to my delight our houseguest turned out to be exactly the right medicine for my problem.

The next morning I had to run some errands after Joe left for work, and didn't get back home until about ten o'clock. As I walked down the hall past the guest bathroom I saw that the door was slightly ajar and heard the sound of the shower. Glancing through the cracked door from where I was standing in the hallway, I could see Danny's reflection in the mirror. He was in the clear-glass shower enclosure, and the water streamed down over his naked body as he lathered himself with soap. I shivered with excitement and anticipation. But I couldn't get a full-frontal view of him in his present position. "C'mon, baby," I whispered, "turn just a little bit more." When he did, I gaped in astonishment at the marvelous sight that presented itself.

Danny's cock hung down nearly halfway to his knees. Even in its flaccid state it had to be eight or nine inches in length, and it was twice as thick as my husband's larger-than-average tool. Without even thinking about it, I slipped my hand under my dress to touch myself and found my panties were already damp from excitement. I somehow knew that if I didn't go for that prize prong now I probably would never get up the courage again. Within seconds my clothes were on the hallway floor and I was stepping into the shower with Danny.

His eyes nearly bugged out of his head when my twin 38Ds pressed against his hairy chest and my hand grasped and started stroking his hambone.

"Lucille," he mumbled, "are you sure you want to . . . ?"

"Yes," I told him, "I've been sure what I wanted since I first saw you last night." Danny's lollapalooza was now half erect and so big that I could barely get my hands around it. He needed no further encouragement. Now his hands were all over my wet body. He fondled and massaged my tits, caressed my ass, explored my hot and welcoming pussy.

When I felt his dick as he rubbed the head up and down in my crack, I nearly lost it there and then. "If you keep that up for very long I'm going to come," I told him.

"That's what it's all about, isn't it?" He had a big grin on his face as he concentrated on my throbbing clit. I couldn't hold back any longer and exploded in a quick but intense climax that caused my body to shake uncontrollably.

"Wow," Danny said when I had calmed down a bit. "You are one very hot lady, aren't you?" And he continued, "Now that you've had the appetizer are you ready for the main course?" I nodded. My body was still on fire with lust. Danny grasped the cheeks of my ass and easily picked me up. He lowered me slowly onto his cock. I moaned as he slowly eased me down that massive rod until it slipped into my cunt, buried to the hilt. The sensation of being that full of cock was unbelievable. Without either of us even moving I started coming again in one long, shattering orgasm that seemed to last for five minutes.

When I realized Danny had not come yet and that his massive prong, still hard as a rock, was still buried in my pussy, I knew what I wanted next.

"Let me down, lover," I told him, "I want to suck you off." I immediately dropped to my knees in front of him and sucked that large muscle into my mouth. Pumping his thick shaft with one hand and fondling his huge balls with the other I blew him in a near frenzy. Now I felt another climax building inside me. I was so hot I knew that when he started to climax I would go over the edge for the third time.

I heard Danny start to moan and felt his stretcher twitch in my mouth and throat. Seconds later, he erupted, filling my mouth with so much come I couldn't swallow fast enough. I had to release that cock and he shot several streams of jism onto the glass shower door and onto my avid face. As expected, this set me off again. I shuddered as another orgasm rolled through my body until I thought I would pass out.

We had been at it for so long the water had gone completely cold. We were so hot for each other we didn't notice the change in temperature. Danny laughed and shut the water off before helping me stand up. Then he kissed me hungrily. "Goddam, Lucille, that was fantastic!" he said, "but what the hell do we do for an encore?"

I gave his cock a gentle squeeze before answering. "Well, baby, it's only Tuesday, so we've got the rest of the week to think of something."

And believe me, we did. But that will take another letter.
—O.P., Kansas City, Kansas

CLEANING UP AT THE DRIVE-IN

I am a regular reader of your journal and enjoy very much the spectacular pictorials and stimulating articles. I would like to share one of my recent experiences with your readers.

Not long ago, I acquired a used van. I quickly seized the opportunity and invited my girlfriend Barbara out to a flick at the local drive-in. I was uncommonly lucky this night and we were into each other's pants in minutes. I loved it when she ran those luscious lips over my throbbing johnson as I thrust my face into her cavernous gorge. Then I licked her labia and let those pussy juices slowly trickle across my countenance while at the opposite pole her throat anxiously awaited delivery of a hot load of semen.

Suddenly we were interrupted. A gentleman rapped on the window and politely asked for a light. It was obvious from the bulge in his pants that he had had a good look at what was going on in the van. We did the only gracious thing and invited him to join us. He seemed hesitant at first. My girlfriend went into a frenzy when he unveiled a twenty-centimeter cock. She begged him to shove his rotor-rooter into her plumbing. He was not prone to argue, and he immediately complied. Actually, at this point I must admit that I was getting pretty excited at the sight of his enormous shaft as it penetrated the depths of Barbara's dripping cunt.

He was extremely polite, and after depositing his load of jism he invited me to clean up. I eagerly jumped in and ate his hot come out of her inflamed pussy. As he got dressed and left for his own car, we thanked each other and agreed to meet again.— M.P., *Louisville, Kentucky*

SAMPLING A VINTAGE WINE

This all happened when I visited my older brother Jim in Carson City. He said he had promised two girls that he would help them move the next morning and that I could just stay in bed until he got back. But I was up before he was, so I drove him over to the girls' place in my pickup truck and dropped him off. I went on to an X-rated movie house, which can't be found where I live. But after four films in one hour I decided to go and help with the move.

That's when I met Jane, a twenty-five-year-old redhead who obviously had her eye on Jim, and Vanessa, a beautiful twenty-eight-year-old woman who I will surely remember for a long time. We finished the move in about three hours and after one case of beer. Then Jim and I went home to clean up and allow the girls time to straighten up their new place. Jim told me the girls had invited us to come over that evening and play some cards, and he also said we might not be going home that night. I thought he might not come home, but I was pretty sure I would. I didn't think Vanessa would be interested in someone six years younger. But I'm glad to say I was wrong.

After a tour of the house we all sat down at the dining room table to play spades. The conversation soon turned to sex, and the more we drank and smoked the more open we all became. When the talk got around to birth control, and both girls assured us that everyone was safe, I began to feel maybe Jim was right about not going home. Vanessa and I were partners, and after we lost in the card game we suggested that we all go in the living room and listen to music. But no sooner were we all comfortable than Vanessa said she had to run out to the liquor store, since it would be closed the next day, Sunday. Vanessa and I went together, and since we had had no dinner, we also bought the groceries for a meal for all of us. By the time we got back, Jim and Jane were in the bedroom, which was fine. It gave me a chance to be alone with Vanessa. When Jane and Jim came out of the bedroom the steaks and French fries were cold. Neither of them complained.

We talked until it was late, and we all agreed it was best for Jim and me to spend the night. It seemed a dream come true to me. Vanessa and I went in her bedroom and simply held each other close for a long time. Then we fell onto her king-size waterbed. I had never even slept on a waterbed, and I certainly had no experience in what was to follow. I tried to be subtle in getting off Vanessa's clothes and my own on the waterbed, but I was woefully clumsy. It was then I began truly to appreciate who I was with and to treasure the experience. Things were awkward and getting worse when Vanessa gently suggested, "Why don't we get off the bed to take off our clothes?" That doesn't sound like much, but it opened a line of communication that stayed open for the rest of the night. We undressed, and I marveled at Vanessa's pendulous breasts, her full ass, and her mature figure.

We wasted no time in getting back in bed and it was continuous ecstasy from then on. We started by kissing and fondling each other but the pace quickened when Vanessa kissed and licked her way down to my blood-engorged prick. Cocksucking is too crude a phrase for what she did for me that night. I've had other girls give me head, but she was practicing an art. I had never experienced the feeling that went through me then. She slowly ran her tongue up and down my shaft, then sucked it as contentedly as a newborn baby at its mother's breast. As much as I was loving it I didn't want to come in her mouth, so I turned her around so that her pussy was over my mouth and returned the favor. I have always loved the joys of cunnilingus. Although I don't feel I am an expert, I certainly practice whenever I can. As I kissed, nibbled and gently sucked the lips of her vagina she reached down and guided me to exactly where and how she was excited the most. I'm a fast learner. I redirected my attention to her now stiff clitoris and flicked my tongue over it as I massaged her breasts with light circular strokes. Before long she moaned, "I'm coming." As I quickened my strokes both on her breast and on her clit she reached a quiet screaming orgasm.

I couldn't believe how naturally everything had happened. We took a break, joking around and caressing each other, but not for long. As soon as we caught our breaths we took up where we had left off. This time, after a little more foreplay, I had the privilege of sinking my roscoe deep into her warm moist pussy. Now I know what paradise is like—and for once I knew I had all night and day if I needed them. I was in no hurry. Both of us savored every sensation with easy, full, rhythmic strokes. When I reached the point of no return I slowed my pace to make it last. Vanessa started nibbling my neck. She said she was about to come again and wanted us to come together. We did, matching one another's strokes and intensity precisely, thrusting in perfect unison at high speed. I was amazed to find that after I came powerfully and thoroughly I had no need to stop and rest. It was like defying gravity.

Our night together was over after about three hours and three climaxes. Vanessa had to leave town, but she came back the next day and brought with her a film projector. Jim was working that night, so I went over to the girls' house alone. Jim would join us later. I had told the girls of Jim's aversion to X-rated films, so the three of us watched several together. These were the first girls I had ever known to show any interest in them. As we watched the fuck-flicks, Vanessa said that she was getting excited and had already creamed her jeans. We decided it would do Jim some good if he saw a few X-rated films. As soon as he arrived, I rolled one. Vanessa was sitting at my feet, which gave me the opportunity to reach down and remind myself just how perfectly round and firm her breasts were. Jim raised no objections. From the sound of things, he and Jane seemed to be exploring their possibilities. Before long we all went to bed. I don't know about Jim but my night was, like the whole weekend, unforgettable. I know that a time like that may never come again but I live in hope.—G.D., *Fargo, South Dakota*

WORKS HARD, KEEPS CLEAN

I've read your magazine for years and never believed even half of the encounters I've read until recently. I was earning some extra money to pay for a blind date my friends had set up by cleaning out the basement parking lot and trash room where I live. I was hot and horny and the job was dirty and smelly.

I was almost through cleaning the trash room Dumpster, reaching over it to pick up a stray newspaper, when a paper bag of garbage slid down the chute. It burst and showered garbage on my head and back.

"Great!" I complained as I picked eggshells and coffee grounds out my hair. "I can't wait to get my hands on the dope who did this." I went up to my apartment hoping to avoid running into anybody when to my dismay the elevator stopped at the floor just below mine.

Standing there was the most gorgeous brunette in three counties. She snickered at first at my garbage-bedecked appearance. But then a look of comprehension came over her face.

"Oh my God," she gasped. "I'm sorry. That was my trash that hit you." To make amends she offered me the use of her shower and laundry room to clean up. I had nothing to lose, so I accepted. The brunette, who introduced herself as Colleen, led me to her apartment. She said to leave my dirty clothes on the floor when I climbed into her shower. Colleen took the clothes to her laundry room while I scrubbed myself clean. I wondered as I soaped myself if my hostess looked as hot without clothes as she did in them.

As if in answer to a prayer, things took a turn for the better. I'd barely finished washing my hair when I suddenly heard a husky feminine voice.

"I need this too," said Colleen. "Mind if I join you?"

"No indeed," I said, over my delight and confusion. "No problem." Then my eyes popped at the sight of her grapefruit-sized breasts. As I backed away in the shower stall to give her room as she stepped under the water, my gaze immediately zeroed in on her firm and generous ass. She looked over her shoulder and saw me soaping up my chest.

"Would you wash my back?" she asked.

"Sure," I said, with sincere enthusiasm. I lathered up my hand and worked my way slowly from her freckled shoulders down her splendid tapered torso. She leaned slightly forward and tensed when my hands briefly cupped her full breasts.

I knelt behind her then, and gently soaped her ass. I spread the cheeks as she spread her legs and leaned forward. The sight of Colleen's hairless snatch was as arousing as her moan of approval when I gently touched her labia. I gently washed both her legs, then stood back and suggested it was my turn.

Colleen faced me and her eyes focused on my semi-rigid prick. "You missed a spot," she said. "I think I can fix that." She took the soap from me and knelt down. Then she slowly lathered first my pubic hair, then kneaded my balls. Now there was nothing semi- about my erection. She gripped my cock to pull me under the stream and rinse me off. Still kneeling, she took my newly washed John Thomas between those luscious lips. She started at the base and licked and kissed her way up to the tip. Then she sucked in my stiff shaft as if she hungered for it.

I was already horny, so I soon shot a load of come into her mouth. She swallowed every drop. We washed again and dried one another off. I sat on the couch in the living room wearing a towel.

"It'll be about an hour before your clothes are dry," Colleen said when she returned. "Would like something to eat?" She took off her T-shirt and lay down on the couch with her legs apart and her pussy open to me. I dived into her honey-pot like an Olympics competitor. I think I proved I could give as well as take. I licked circles around her mound of Venus, then worked my way to her sweet-tasting twat. I watched her pinch her nipples as she clutched my head and pulled my tongue deeper into her honey-pot. I puckered my lips and sucked her pussy hard. Now I had another roaring erection, and I pulled my face away from her grotto so that I could slide my cock into this eager pussy. I prolonged our pleasure with long hard strokes. Then we switched positions. She straddled my prick and her beautiful tits bounced wildly as she bounced happily on it. I lost track of time, but I know we came together, with me shooting what seemed like buckets of jism and Colleen's pussy lips happily squeezing out every bit. She fell down on me exhausted and I held her close.

Needless to say, I now make this place the cleanest building in town.—P.C., *Calgary, Canada*

THE TRUTH, SO HELP HER

I know you don't receive many letters from women and I suspect few of the stories are true, anyway. But here is a true story from a woman that your readers may like.

My name is Georgia. I am a twenty-five-year-old homemaker. I am petite and sport strawberry blonde hair almost down to my waist. I have green eyes and measure 35C-23-35. I'm probably attractive—I get a lot of longing looks—and I am definitely a nymphomaniac.

I love my husband dearly but he does not satisfy me. This, coupled with his absences on sales trips, often leads me to seek extramarital pleasures. Yesterday's adventure was fairly typical.

The telephone rang and woke me at nine a.m. It was my friend Callie inviting me for coffee. Usually, with Callie, that means a session with her in bed as well. She is thirty years old, five-foot-six, 36C-24-36, black and beautiful. Callie is addicted to the way I lick her pussy. Yesterday, we had our morning coffee, jumped in bed, and did a lot of petting. Then I ate her pussy.

Once Callie came, it was my turn. I tend to flow like a river when I reach a climax, and Callie drinks it all up greedily.

By eleven, our fingers and tongues having done all they could, I was out cruising the local roads looking for likely sites to stage a breakdown and break out the air mattress I keep handy in the back of the van.

As usual, I was rewarded. There were a couple of good-looking guys among the good Samaritans who stopped and, also as usual, both gentlemen elected to drop their pants upon invitation. I always wear a garter belt and stockings under a loose short skirt when I'm cruising. Leaving my underpants at home helps, too. The men are understandably in a hurry.

Home, showered and changed by four is a must since I'm screwing the paperboy. I enjoy Herbert mostly because he was a virgin until I broke him in, and I can still safely dispense with condoms. Like any eighteen-year-old, that lad can get it up again in a hurry. A few sucks help sometimes, in an emergency. I try to meet and seduce a college student at least twice a month. Needless to say, the males are easy, once you overcome their fright. You have to spend a great deal of effort becoming a young woman's friend and confidante before you can bed her.

Whenever my husband is away I spend part of an evening at a second girlfriend's home. Bernice is a call girl. She is quite pretty and consequently very busy. Because I am not interested in the fee part, she never minds letting me take on a couple of interesting, well-hung Johns.

I typed this letter with a vibrator in my pussy, so please overlook any errors. And guys, if you see a blue van and a lady in distress one afternoon on a side road on the west coast, stop and say hello!—B.M., *Pacifica, California*

SHOWTIME FOR SUZETTE

I have been an avid reader of your magazine for years, I can't believe I finally have a story to write about. I have a passion for exotic dancers. I love to watch them dance and strip. Lap dancers are my favorite. My girlfriend knows about this and dances for me at home. She is quite attractive, with a fine body: small and firm breasts, flat stomach, nice hips. Her tight, bouncy butt is probably her best feature.

Until recently I was her only audience, although her home dance routines are excellent. She seems to take naturally to the art of stripping. When we took a trip to Baltimore where there are a lot of bars that feature exotic dancers, I talked her into going into one of the bars with me. She was reluctant at first, but I told her she could just watch the other dancers and maybe pick up a few pointers.

When we got ready to go to the bar, she wore one of her stripping outfits from home. It included black lace thong panties, thigh-high stockings, a white lace bra under a lace top that is quite transparent and a black spandex miniskirt. She looked great. You could see her dark nipples through the lace top and when she sat down her skirt rode up to show a lot of thigh. If she spread her legs a little you caught a glimpse of her panty-covered pussy. I told her sincerely I was sure she would probably look better than most of the dancers, but she didn't believe me. In fact, she got a little apprehensive, not really sure if she could go out in public dressed in such a revealing outfit. Little did she know that

before the night was over I was hoping that she would be showing off all of her body.

I suggested we have a couple of drinks and a joint for courage,
and we did. She always gets real horny after smoking so I knew
everything would work out fine.

Walking through the hotel was an experience for her. She really turned a few heads, which helped build her self confidence.
When she got into the cab her legs opened up and the cab driver
got quite a view. We were on our way to a very enjoyable evening.

The bar we chose was a little more upscale than most, and it
was crowded. It had a large stage in the center and there were
smaller ones in dark corners for the lap dancers. When we entered the bar the featured dancer was just finishing her routine.
As she removed her G-string she rubbed her middle finger along
her pussy lips and into her slit, then licked her fingers. The crowd
really loved that and so did I. Turning to my girlfriend I said,
"Now there's a new trick for you, Suzette." Suzette nodded, enthusiastically, and watched the dancer closely. She was really getting excited by the dance. And even with all the professional
dancers around, a lot of guys were checking her out. That got her
even more excited.

We found a seat at the bar and when she sat she gave everyone
a good view of her crotch. I asked her how she felt about showing her pussy off. She said she wasn't sure. "What do you think
about everyone seeing my pussy?" she asked me. I told her I not
only didn't mind but was hoping she'd go a little further, let
everybody see all she had.

Suzette loves to fuck and suck cock but she was not sure she
could strip in front of all those horny men. She protested that she
was not attractive enough, I told her I would prove her wrong. I
found the manager and told him I had a girl who wanted an au-
dition, that she was a little nervous but wanted to try out. We
walked over to her and I introduced him.

"Call me Jim," he said. "If you're nervous, come to my office and dance for me there." Suzette said she would only do that if I accompanied her. The manager said, "No problem." Then he asked if she knew what the men might want her to do.

Suzette said she had a pretty good idea, and that she understood there were rules about touching and stuff.

Jim said men would pay more if she let them touch her. "Some might want you to suck their cocks while you dance," he added.

Suzette said she wouldn't suck anyone's cock but mine. The manager said that was up to her. All this was quite an advance for Suzette—from not being sure about dancing in the nude to talking about sucking some strange guy's cock.

In his office, Jim put on some dance music. He and I sat in chairs in the middle of the room. It was show-time. Suzette danced around the room, slowly at first, and let her skirt ride up. As she danced over to Jim she pulled off her top. When she reached him, he stroked each of her breasts.

She pulled away from Jim and slipped off her skirt, leaning over to give us a full view of her ass. Now dancing only in her bra, panties and stockings she really got into it. I didn't know how far she would go but I soon found out. She danced over to the manager and asked, "Do you want the works, sweetie?" It was obvious to me Suzette had overcome a lot of her shyness.

"Give it your best shot," he panted. She unhooked the bra and it fell away. Then she placed his hands on her tits. He fondled each nipple. She bent closer so he could kiss her nipples. Then she pulled away and danced over to me. I ran my hand up her inner thighs and fondled her pussy. It was soaked. I asked her if she wanted to stop now.

"I'm doing fine," she said. "I'm not going to stop now!"

"Do whatever you want," I encouraged her. Suzette danced back to Jim and stood between his legs. She put her hand on his crotch and grabbed his prick through his jeans. Jim opened his belt and gave her better access to his cock. She sat in his lap and rubbed his prick all over her legs and pussy. Then she removed her panties. When she slipped them over her legs you could see just how wet her pussy was.

"Let us see how wet your pussy is," I asked her. She put Jim's hand right on her honey-pot. When she removed it she licked her cream off his fingers.

What a turn-on! She was really putting on a good show. Now Jim told her she could dance later in the evening, but first invited her to suck his cock. He wanted her to suck his cock!

Jim had said the right thing. He then got the blowjob of his life. Suzette knelt in front of him and slurped his cock into her mouth. She licked and sucked it, then took it all down her throat. It did not take long for him to come, and she swallowed it all. As she dressed, he told her she could dance for him anytime.

We returned to our seats to await her turn, but that will be another letter.—G.C., *Kenosha, Wisconsin*

GETTING TO KNOW A NEW NEIGHBOR

In our six-year relationship my former girlfriend Louise and I have spoken of many fantasies. Some we fulfilled. Others will always remain just fantasies. Either way, we love sharing them.

One very hot fantasy was our all-time favorite, and it included another man—a threesome. The idea of watching Louise wrap her soft wet lips around a thick, long hard cock made us both extremely horny as well as creative. One night we had smoked a good joint and got pretty drunk. I lay down in our bedroom. Louise stayed in the living room to watch one of our favorite porn movies. (You guessed it, a threesome.) Later Louise came into the bedroom. I was stroking my hard cock. She liked to watch me jack off. She climbed in next to me and asked what I was thinking of. Well, I first told her of how horny I got just watching her get excited as we talked about our threesome fantasy, in which she fucked a man with a thick hard cock as I watched. Then I would lick all the juices from her well-fucked, ruby-lipped pussy. "His come too?" she asked. "Yes, everything from the lips to the deepest point of your sweet cunt," I answered. She kissed me gently, gave my hard tool a peck, ran her tongue over the crack of my ass and told me not to come until she got back. She wanted to finish the movie. She was wearing a sexy black G-string and a teddy I had bought for her. She loved to show it off. Moments later I heard her open the patio door, as we often do to cool off the apartment when there's a breeze. Then I heard a rustling of clothes. I assumed Louise was getting comfortable on the couch. But then I heard slurping noises and very soft moans of passion. Louise loves to play with a monster-size dildo as we watch our movies, so I thought nothing of it. The sound of the TV got louder, as did the moans. It all sounded like good hot sex. A half-hour later Louise turned off the TV and came to bed. She was naked and I felt a light film of sweat on her body. I was nearly asleep and my cock was soft now.

"I'm going to get your cock fat and hard," she said, "and then you're going to fuck me to an earth-shattering orgasm." She kissed me deeply, groaning passionately, and ground her honey-pot against my John Thomas. I realized then that she reeked of sex. Her lips were all swollen, as if she had just finished giving a well-hung stud a dedicated blowjob.

My cock stiffened. "Please eat my pussy," she begged. I spread her legs and dove into a very wet and puffy-lipped pussy surrounded by matted pubic hair. Her cunt was filled with come. I smelled and tasted another man's jism and his musky sweat.

So Louise had just finished fucking another man. But who? How? I loved it.

"Eat me," she cried again. I can't remember being that excited. Like a mad pussy hound I explored every crack and fold of her sweet cunny. "Oh yes," she shouted, "eat my pussy good." I swallowed every drop of fuck-juice in her quim. "Do you like my pussy? Do you love the taste?" she cried.

I growled deeply, grabbed her ass, rubbed the honey-pot all over my face. "I've never tasted your pussy like this. The taste and smell makes me hornier than I can ever remember. I love the taste of your pussy!" She came immediately. Her body shook as never before. Her screams of orgasm pierced the night. "Yes, oh yes. I'm coming," she cried. I played with her clit as my tongue made deep passes through her beautiful pussy.

Finally, she pushed me away. She could take no more. I rolled her over on her stomach and with one stroke easily thrust into her asshole the entire length of my very hard nine-inch cock. She arched her back and made the penetration even deeper. I fucked her with long leisurely strokes. "Your cock feels bigger than ever," she said. "Fuck me." She looked up at me over her shoulder as I lunged within her. "Why are you so horny?" she asked.

"The smell and taste of your sweet pussy does that to me," I told her, my voice husky with passion.

I didn't want to let her know I knew her secret. She reached back, grabbed her ass-cheeks and spread them even wider. I exploded with an orgasm surpassing all others I had ever had. I kissed her face and neck, telling her how much I loved her. We soon fell asleep.

The next morning while drinking my coffee on the balcony, I saw our newly moved-in next-door neighbor, also outside and reading his newspaper. His robe opened slightly to reveal a robust chest and a flat stomach. I introducing myself and he uncrossed his legs to shake my hand. That revealed his monster cock. I kept glancing at it as we spoke. It was at least ten inches long and thick as a Coke can. This, I realized, was the man and the prick that had deposited the load of jism that I had eaten out of Louise's pussy. The new neighbor made no attempt to hide his prick as we continued to make small talk. He leaned his head back to soak up the morning sunshine and his legs widened to show off a large pair of balls. He knew my eyes were fixed on his cock. He also knew I would be less embarrassed if he looked away. He was enjoying my curiosity.

My cock began to thicken as I pictured Louise's hot mouth trying to swallow his prong whole. I could almost see her lips and tongue massaging this mammoth cock. I fantasized her straddling his cock, and this made my prick peek out of my robe. I couldn't help but picture him fucking Louise doggie-style, thrusting deep inside her. My hand had now begun to stroke my own hardened tool. He looked up and asked, "What's on your mind, neighbor?"

I realized what I was doing and was embarrassed. I answered, "Women must love your cock, eh?"

"Yes, they do," he said. "They like it any way, from sucking it to my fucking them doggie-style."

I immediately came on myself.

"Damn," he said. "What can you be thinking of?"

"Well," I said, "I love the fact that you are fucking my girlfriend. We always fantasize about her and another man—hoping his cock looks like yours."

"Then you know?" he asked.

"Yes, I do," I said, "and when she came back to bed, I cleaned out her come-soaked pussy and swallowed every drop."

He looked surprised.

"Relax," I said. "I would like to keep this our secret."

"Fine, anything special you want me to do?"

"Yes," I said. "Fuck her good and deep and have her suck every inch of your cock. Fuck her in every position, and come in her doggie-style."

"You got it," he said.

"When the time comes," I said, "I would like to have a threesome with you and Louise."

"Sure," he said. "We would have a great time."

"So, tonight, same time?" I asked.

Just then I heard the shower going, and went to join Louise. I knew the evening would be fantastic because, knowing I'd be watching, he had promised to fuck her well.

That evening I tried to replay the night before. This time I crept to the living room and watched my new partner in fantasy.

I loved the whole thing. I came all over the curtains, watching them fuck in every position. His handsome cock was like a giant piston as he thrust deep in Louise's cunt. I have never enjoyed sex or fantasy so much. I rushed back to bed just as they both orgasmed. Again she ran to me, spread her ass-cheeks and sat on my face.

"Eat me. Lick my hot pussy," she cried. Again I swallowed her come and his. It was fantastic. My orgasms were so powerful I almost fainted. He certainly filled her up with his seed.

Louise and her not-so-secret lover have repeated this hot and nasty sex session about fifteen times now. I know she wants to tell me, but deep down she realizes I know. For now, things are too good to blow her cover.

Sometimes I watch through the cracks. Other times I lie in bed and listen to their cries of passion, always waiting for my turn in the fantasy. Soon I will share with you our threesomes.—A.B., *Fort Lauderdale, Florida*

CHICAGO COPPERS DISPLAY IRON-HARD RODS
IN STEEL TOWN, USA

I'm writing this letter to let you know about an amazing event that I experienced, and which I am finding impossible to forget.

Alex and I have been partners for about seven years. Not sexual partners, squad partners—we're cops. We both work the juvenile section of our police department.

Last month Alex and I went to a convention in Pittsburgh for five days. We spent the first night there checking out the town and doing some drinking. The next day we had to sit in seminars all day long, and by the time evening came we were ready to let loose again. We went to our room and cleaned up, and then we went out to dinner. After that, not wanting to spend a lot of money, we picked up a couple of fuck magazines and went back to the room. First thing I did was take a shit, and while I was in the bathroom I decided to wash my face, using one of the hotel washcloths. When I came out of the bathroom, Alex was lying naked on his bed reading one of the magazines we had picked up.

We've been to these conventions before, and we've learned a lot about each other. After being partners for as long as we have, you know so much about the other guy you don't even think about it. I probably know as much about Alex's personal habits as his wife—that's how long we've been together.

I grabbed one of the other magazines and lay on my bed, going through and looking at the great-looking cunts which were plastered on every page. After a while, I looked over at Alex. His prick was starting to grow out of the dark pubic hair which covered his balls and cock. Alex saw I was looking and said, "Man, I'm horny."

"Me, too," I said. "But don't forget, we promised our wives we would not fool around with any women on this trip."

Alex said that still did not stop him from being horny. As we lay on the two beds, I noticed that every once in a while Alex would pull on his cock, making it grow even larger than it was before.

Now, reading the magazines and watching Alex pull on his prick was about all it took for my own prick to start getting hard. Alex kept reading and pulling his cock when all of a sudden he said to me, "Hey, read this letter," and he passed the magazine to me. The letter was about two gay men and how they liked to suck each other off. After I read the letter, Alex asked if I had ever done anything with a guy. I told him that once, when I was in the army, this guy and I fooled around and jacked each other off. Alex then said that once, when he was in college, he and another guy on the football team sucked each other off.

"Get the fuck out of here," I said. "You, king dick of the Ninth Precinct, have sucked cock?"

"What did I tell you, man. Yes, I sucked a dick."

"What was it like? I mean, what did it taste like?"

"I don't even remember, brotherman. It was a long time ago. I barely even remember doing it. It's more like I remember remembering doing it. You know what I mean?"

"No."

"Well . . . ah hell, forget it. What do you remember about jacking another man off?"

I told him that it was a lot of fun at the time. Alex and I kept talking, and soon the conversation turned to the things we did with our wives. The longer we talked, the harder our cocks grew. Alex's prick had a drop of pre-come hanging off the tip which looked like a pearl in the light. I told Alex how one night, when my wife and I were having sex, she was in a silly mood and after she sucked my cock she came up and kissed me, squirting the last few drops of my own come into my mouth. Alex, at hearing this, reached over and took hold of my prick and started rubbing it back and forth.

"Alex," I said, "we have been through so many things together, if you're interested, we can try something together."

When Alex heard this, he moved over to my bed and placed his head on my thigh. When he saw that I was receptive, he moved around on the bed so that his prick was just an inch away from my mouth. I watched in amazement as Alex moved his own head and in one quick movement caught the head of my cock in his lips and sucked with just a slight amount of wetness covering my prick. After a minute, Alex's saliva covered that entire length of my cock. As Alex worked on my cock, I pushed my tongue out and took a drop of pre-come from the head of his prick. It was not salty or bitter, just sticky. Then I moved my own head and let the head of his prick slide into my mouth. The warmth of his prick was a surprise to me, and the soft skin felt very good in my mouth.

I sucked on Alex's hard prick for a while, then let it slip from my lips and took one of his balls into my mouth. After sucking on his balls, I slipped my tongue to the base of his prick.

"Please take my cock back into your mouth," Alex implored me.

As I let his prick reenter my mouth, Alex let mine slip from his mouth and yelled that he was going to shoot a load, begging me not to stop. I felt Alex's prick grow in size, and then I felt it start to pulsate between my lips. All at once, Alex grabbed the back of my head and rammed his prick all the way to the back of my throat. Alex moaned a loud moan as shot after shot of his warm come splashed down my throat. I felt like I was in Paris or Budapest or some other place I've never been, but I was happy to be there. Feeling that gusher go off in your own mouth and knowing that it is due to your own ministrations, is the most amazing experience in the world.

After Alex was finished coming and I had licked his prick clean, Alex asked me to stand up next to the bed. When I was standing, Alex got on the floor and knelt between my legs, reaching a hand around my ass and pulling my cock deep into his mouth. Alex then started to push and pull on my ass, which caused me to fuck his mouth. I knew that at this pace I was going to come in no time at all. As Alex kept sucking and licking the head of my prick, my legs started to shake and Alex had to hold me up.

First gradually and then quickly, I felt my load of come start at my toes and move through my body. When I warned Alex that my come was on the way, he pulled me closer to him. Faster and faster his head moved. Then my come came rushing up from my balls, through my cock and onto Alex's tongue. Load after load shot out of me and into Alex's mouth. After he finished swallowing every last drop, we fell together on the bed and rested.

After that, the rest of the trip was spent in our room finding out all we could about each other.—*F.W.*, *Chicago, Illinois*

LITTLE GUY FEELS STRONG WHEN HE FEELS BIG GUY'S COCK BEHIND HIM

My story starts about two days after my wife left me for, in her words, a "real man." To put it plainly, this guy is six-foot-two, weighs one hundred ninety pounds and, to hear my wife tell it, is hung like a horse.

I am a rather small man—five-foot-eight, a hundred and thirty—and I have a very small cock. But when we married we were both virgins, and for a couple of years my wife was satisfied—probably because she didn't know what she was missing. Then she met Arnold at work, and they had an affair. Soon she told me to hit the road because she had found a real man that could fuck like a wild man.

Two nights later I was sitting at a bar trying to drink my problems away. This club is next door to a large motel and truck stop. I picked this spot because it has lots of truckers who come in to drink, and I thought that I might feel more manly being around these guys.

After a while, a trucker sat down beside me at the bar. He was a large man with a beard and a rather large beer belly. His voice was very deep and his eyes had a rather vacuous look in them. He was dressed in tight pants and a T-shirt. His arms were very muscular and hairy. He also had a bulge in his pants that no one could help noticing. But at that time, I had no interest in other men's cocks, only the lack of mine.

We started talking and doing some serious drinking. After some drinks I was getting pretty drunk and started telling him my troubles. He was a good listener and told me that he felt bad for me.

Well, around two in the morning, the bar gave last call, and I was drunk as hell. My new friend, Gene, asked me where I lived. I told him across town. He said he had a room at the motel and that, since I was too drunk to drive, I should stay there the night.

We left my car in the bar parking lot and walked the short distance to the motel.

His room was small but clean. Also, it only had one bed, but he told me not to worry, we would be fine.

Well, I hardly remember getting undressed and into bed.

I don't know how long I slept, but something woke me up. I was still a little drunk and had a hard time remembering where I was, but knew someone was in bed with me, because there was a large hand rubbing my ass and a great mass of hair against the back of my neck. The face behind the hair was licking and biting my neck.

I could feel the hand going inside of my underwear and then a large finger sliding up and down the crack of my ass.

Suddenly I remembered where I was and whose hand it was. What a crazy night, I thought.

Finally, I asked Gene just exactly what he thought he was doing.

"You feel just like a girl," was all he said.

At first I thought I was with a crazy man, but then I thought about it and it made perfect sense. Except for the fact I don't have tits and a pussy, I am like a girl. I barely have any hair on my body, and my skin is soft and smooth like a girl's. Gene said that my ass was so round and firm that he couldn't help himself. It felt faintly intriguing to be attractive to someone, even though the someone in question was kind of like that big hulk of a man in *Moby Dick*. I thought I might as well relax and enjoy the attention.

Then Gene started removing my underwear, rubbing his hands and then his legs all over my fine little behind. All the while he was still nibbling my neck. It tickled, especially with that beard.

Needless to say, I was apprehensive, but my life had taken such a strange turn that anything new is welcome.

Gene then lifted my top leg and started sliding a very large dick between the cheeks of my ass. Then, still nibbling my neck, he reached a hand around and started tweaking my nipples.

I don't know what happened, but suddenly I was very turned

on. Like I said, it was nice to feel attractive to another person after feeling inadequate for so long. I had heard how much pain is felt the first time someone gets fucked up the ass, but I needed the human contact. I then relaxed and started moving my ass against that great cock. Gene asked me if this meant that I wanted to fuck. In a very small, feminine voice that surprised me, I said yes.

With that, Gene got up and went into the bathroom. When he came back he left the bathroom light on and the door about half open. As he walked back to the bed, I could see him clearly, completely nude, for the first time. That is when I realized I was in for a wild night. Gene was every inch of six feet four inches tall with very wide shoulders and a massive chest. His legs looked like two oak trees, very thick and muscular. His whole body, including his shoulders and back, was covered with thick, black hair. And between his legs was the biggest, thickest dick I have ever seen, and that's not counting the two huge balls that hung beneath his ass.

He was standing next to the bed, and suddenly I had a very strong urge to touch him. I slid across the bed and very softly caressed his balls. Then I ran my hand up and down that beautiful cock. It wasn't all the way hard yet, but it was already eight inches long and as big around as my fist.

Gene then put his hand behind my head and pulled my face to his nuts. At first I only let them rub against my face. Gene asked me to lick and suck them. I slowly ran my tongue over and around each nut. I found that they tasted great, all sweaty and salty, so I took one in my mouth. It filled my entire mouth, and I tried hard not to bite him. The smell of him intoxicated me (even more than I already was) and I felt like I was on LSD.

After I licked and sucked both nuts, Gene moved me over on the bed and lay down beside me. In a gruff voice that I found made me weak and very ready to love him, he implored me to suck his dick. I had never done this before, but being a man I knew what would feel good. I slowly ran my tongue around the head of his dick, letting my saliva run down the shaft and onto his legs and balls. I then took the shaft into my mouth and started slowly swallowing that monster an inch at a time until I had about half of it in my mouth.

When I couldn't take any more, I started sliding my mouth up and down very slowly, being careful not to let my teeth hurt him. Then I started going faster and, to my surprise, taking more and more dick down my throat. I wasn't even gagging. Gene started moaning and bucking his hips. I knew he was going to come, so I increased the speed and just kept swallowing dick. At last Gene grabbed me behind the head and pulled my head down real hard. I could feel the head of his dick at the back of my throat, his balls slapping me in the face and gobs and gobs of come squirting down my throat. I lay very still and swallowed all of his love jism that I could.

He shot off for a minute or so, and I felt like his cock was filling up my entire skull. After he was all done, I savored his dick as it went soft in my mouth.

We both fell asleep that way, with my face between his legs.

Later I was woken up by Gene pulling me up in the bed. He started kissing me on the mouth and I responded by kissing him back. He gave me a real hard French kiss, and then he spread my legs. He then started nibbling and sucking my neck, working his way down my front, covering my tits, belly, thighs and ass-cheeks with warm, wet kisses. This got me really turned on. He then put two pillows under my ass and spread my legs wide apart. He then produced a jar of K-Y jelly and started rubbing it on his big cock and putting some on my asshole. I knew then that it was going to happen, that in a few moments that big dick would be up my ass and I would be in for the biggest new experience of my life since I was born. I was excited. I had made up my mind that this would be my life from now on.

Gene started rubbing the head of his dick around the edges of my anus. Then I felt the head enter me. The head of his dick was so big and my ass was so tight that it was a difficult thing to pull off. But there was no turning back. As Gene stared passionately into my eyes and I stared back, I thought of all the women who would have killed to be in my position.

Gene then started slowly putting more and more dick up me until I didn't think I could take any more. In the woman's voice I had developed, I suggested that maybe that was enough. But Gene said that I was going to be his woman completely. With one huge thrust of his large body, he drove that whole ten and a half inches all the way up my ass. I was screaming with ecstasy, and Gene answered my cries of passion by saying, over and over again, "Oh, yeah. Oh, yeah. Oh, yeah."

Gene lay still until his cock settled in my ass, and then he started slowly fucking me.

Then the magic started. This ass-fucking I was taking started to feel better than anything I had ever done before. So good, in fact, that I started moving under Gene as he would pull his cock out until the head was barely in and then slam it back in, up to the nuts. This went on for a very long time. Then Gene started moving faster and faster, moaning loudly, those huge nuts slapping me in the ass. Then with a mighty thrust, he filled my ass with sweet come.

The next morning, he woke me up by putting that big thing back up my ass again. This time was even better because I had experienced it before.

When I went into the bathroom to shower, I looked in a full-length mirror on the bathroom wall. I looked like hell. I had hickeys all over me and large, dark circles under my eyes. But I felt great. Gene and I parted company promising to see each other often, which we have.

That night I realized I loved this kind of sex, so I decided to do all I could to become a woman—short of surgery. Since then I have started taking female hormones, had all the hair removed from my face and body and let my hair grow down to my butt. I wear clothes that show off my long legs and round, feminine hips. I now have more boyfriends than I can count. I still pick up men at bars and, when possible, I ride up and down the interstate with the top down on my car, trying to attract truckers. I also stop at rest stops and truck stops and fuck these great guys. Most of them already know I have a very small dick between my great legs, but some of them have had their dicks sucked by me and not known that I am a man.

None of them would have been pissed off, mind you, because I give the best head on the East Coast.—*Name and address withheld*

JACK-OFF BUDDY HELPS OUT A FRIEND IN NEED

The following events happened over twenty years ago. This is the first time I've told anyone. While you're reading, please remember that truth is sometimes stranger than fiction.

During our senior year in high school, when we were both eighteen, Allen and I were neighbors and best friends. I spent a lot of time at his house after school because both of his parents worked. He had his own room and he had an older sister with fabulously large breasts who was in the habit of going braless. In time, we became jerk-off buddies, using Allen's large collection of magazines.

We'd sit side by side on the edge of Allen's bed with the door locked as we stroked our erect cocks while reading his latest magazines. Allen often reminded me that he admired my cock because it was so large. I had a very thick, six-inch circumcised cock with a large head. Allen had a thin cock barely five inches long with a small head partially covered by his foreskin. What he lacked in cock size, Allen made up for with a pair of enormous, low-hanging balls. He also shot off huge loads of come—about two tablespoons compared with my one teaspoon. I enjoyed watching Allen fill up his cupped left hand with huge loads of hot jism. One time, when I had trouble shooting off, Allen rubbed a handful of his hot come on my cockhead until I shot one of my best loads ever. I really enjoyed the feel of his hot sperm and slippery hand on my cock. Allen realized how much his hot jism turned me on because I practically passed out afterwards.

The next week, Allen came up with yet another way to jerk off. We both sat on his bed facing each other with our legs spread wide. Allen put his thighs over mine and we moved closer until we were cockhead to cockhead, sitting on top of an old towel. We'd shoot our hot sperm all over each other's organ. Allen always came first, shooting gobs of gooey sperm all over my cock, pubic hair and balls. As his hot spunk covered my organ and dripped down to the towel, I'd shoot my load—aiming at the huge balls hanging low between Allen's legs. Because I had a longer cock, I was practically touching Allen's balls when I shot off. I always hit my target.

Allen was a jerk-off expert. He taught me to wait for at least three days so I'd shoot a bigger load, to take a hot bath so my nuts would hang down like his, to fondle my balls before I shot off and to use a greasy finger to play with my asshole. In early summer I managed to get poison ivy on both of my hands and one of my arms. I had to wear cotton gloves on my hands to keep it from spreading. After about a week, I was extremely horny, but I wouldn't touch my cock with my hands and I couldn't jerk off with my gloves on. When I told Allen about my problem, he told me to come over on Saturday night and he'd help.

On Saturday night, Allen locked the door to his room and told me I had to smoke hash with him and get high. He dimmed the lights, told me to strip and complimented me on my large penis, as he usually did. I was so horny that my cock had juices dripping out of it. Allen told me to kneel on the floor and put my head and shoulders down on a pillow. I got into position with my ass up in the air as Allen lubricated his hands and began fondling my cock and dangling balls. My cock snapped to attention as he began greasing my asshole. This was the highlight of my life: I was extremely high and my best friend was handling my swollen, throbbing genitals. Allen stretched my asshole with one finger and then with two until I was fully relaxed. Then he put his thin cockhead against my asshole and very slowly penetrated my ass. When his rod was fully inserted, I could feel his warm thighs against my hips, and then he began stroking my greased cock. In this position, gravity caused my balls to hang toward the head of my cock so that he could stroke my cock and fondle my nuts at the same time.

Allen moved slowly in my ass—in deep, then back out. I never would have believed a real cock would feel so good in my asshole. His hips rocked back and forth and his heavy nuts bounced against me. He began to moan, and then he shot a huge load of come inside me. As he blew thick wads of jism in my asshole, I felt a pressure build up in my balls. They drew closer to my body and I knew I was going to shoot an extra big load of come. When I exploded, the first spurt rocketed out and splashed against the bottom of my chin. Allen slowly milked my cock and balls, giving me sufficient time to shoot six hot wads of jiz on the floor. It was the best come of my life, and the largest load I'd ever shot.

For the next three weeks Allen serviced me every two or three days. When the poison-ivy rash completely healed, I paid Allen back by helping him jerk off at least once a week for the entire summer. I enjoyed cupping his long, heavy balls in my left hand as I reamed his asshole with my left thumb. With Allen facing away from me, I'd reach around his hips with my right hand to slide his foreskin back and forth over his glans until he shot his usual huge load of come. Allen would tell me when he was going to come so I could quickly get my left hand in position to catch his hot load. I'd rub his hot jism on my cock until I shot off, too. By the end of the summer I'd become a jerk-off expert. I could get Allen so hot that he'd shoot his first wad of come almost three feet—we had a contest and I measured it.

Today, just thinking about that summer makes my "trouser

snake," now very thick and seven inches long, crawl down my leg and protrude out of my shorts. Honey is oozing out of the slit and my cockhead is throbbing near the bursting point as the poison-ivy summer adventure replays itself in my mental VCR. What a summer that was.—*Name and address withheld*

IT ALL HAS TO START SOMEWHERE, AND IT MIGHT AS WELL BE UP THE BUTT

Let me come right out and say it: Being bisexual is the best of both worlds. I have been married for almost twenty years. The two finest sexual things that I can think of are putting my cock in my wife's sweet, juicy pussy and wrapping my lips around a hard, thick, well-shaped penis.

My wife loves for me to tell her about the experiences of my late teens that helped me discover my bisexuality and my love for cocksucking.

One of my close friends was a stocky, hard-muscled boy who loved to have his cock sucked but would never suck anyone else. The strange part about Chip was, he felt that if you put a dick in his mouth it would make him queer, but he had no problem receiving a blowjob. Gradually he loosened up and began taking it up the ass. This is the story of how I took his virgin ass.

A week after we graduated from high school, we were fooling around in Chip's bedroom when I asked him if I could suck him off.

"Gladly," he said. "A hole's a hole, and I'm horny as hell."

"Great," I said, "thanks a bunch."

I lightly licked the head of Chip's cock and it twitched. I had sucked cock before, and I moaned in anticipation of that thing growing ever bigger. First it was a little small in my mouth, but soon it grew to where it perfectly filled my lips.

*   *   *

Wrapping my thumb and forefinger around the base, I sucked on the top third of his cock while stroking the rest with my fingers. Chip put his hands on the back of my neck and started fucking my face. Soon I could feel his dick going down my throat as if my mouth was one big pussy.

"I'm coming," Chip screamed, and I was in heaven. When that warm juice started pulsing down my throat, I nearly came in my pants.

When Chip was done, I looked up at him and said, "My turn, right?"

"If you think I'm gonna suck your cock, my man, you've got another thing coming."

"Okay, let me cornhole you, then."

"You want to stick your dick up my ass?" he asked.

"Indeed I do," I assured him.

"Okeydoke."

First thing I did was stick my tongue up Chip's ass, getting it all nice and lubed. Then I spit in my hand and rubbed it all over my cock. He was very receptive and I shot right inside. My cock was rock-hard, and his ass was so nice and tight that I dropped my load after only a few strokes.—*Name and address withheld*

IF YOU CAN'T BE WITH THE ONE YOU LOVE, LOVE THE ONE YOU'RE WITH

Sex with a man had never crossed my mind. When I was single and chasing women, I had been given a few blowjobs by a couple of my male married friends. I could never really understand why they would want to give head to a man when they were happily married, but I didn't argue. And now that I'm married, I have no need for sex with a man.

One night last week, however, while my wife was away, I went out drinking with an old friend of mine. When we returned to my home, I took him to my guest house. Since we were both drunk, we fell asleep in the guest-house bed.

In the middle of the night, still half asleep, I was stroking my dick to hardness. Something didn't feel right, however, and when I opened my eyes and looked down, I realized that it was not my own dick I was stroking but my friend's. He opened his eyes and we stared at each other in bewilderment. Then we laughed out loud. The warmth and texture of my friend's growing cock in my hand had my cock as hard as a rock.

Figuring he ought to return the favor, he grabbed my cock and started stroking it like I was stroking his. It had been a long time since another man had touched my cock, and I must say that it was refreshing, because he knew what he was doing.

Without hesitation, I leaned over to start an adventure I will never forget. I viewed the object in hand as my own. I lowered my lips around his shaft as far as my mouth would allow, closing my lips around him just tight enough to have the proper pressure.

Then I slowly slid my lips up and down the shaft, feeling the texture of the skin as it slid over the inner hardness. The swelling veins really turned me on. I moved ever so gently over the outer skin with my lips, up and down, up and down.

I stopped occasionally to run my tongue along the shaft to the head of his cock and around the bottom side of his helmet. Then I returned to my up-and-down movements on his stiffening rod. As I went up and down his cock, I could feel his thighs and butt tighten, and then his nectar erupted and shot down my throat. It was great—warm and sweet. His globs were so big that I felt like I was eating raw oysters.

As I cleaned off the subsiding shaft, I realized that my friend was still stroking me off. My rod had never been so hard. With a few more strokes of his hand I exploded like I never had before.

I have come to the conclusion that this form of masturbation can only be accomplished by another man. I still prefer women

and so does my frie⌐
moved away. But I'⌐
California

THE BASKETB⌐
LEAGU⌐

It was a long wee⌐
take a shower an⌐
After a long kiss,⌐
remind me that he was coming over ⌐
like we had planned a week before. Fuck, I thought to myself. I
forgot all about that.

Just after she told me this, I jumped into the shower so I could
be out before Grant got there. I wasn't in the shower fifteen minutes when, out the corner of my eye, I caught a glimpse of Grant
using the toilet. My wife must be in the front bathroom, I
thought to myself. I was trying to figure out why he'd come all the
way to the back of the house just to take a leak.

I thought nothing more of it and continued to wash myself.
When Grant finished, I looked out the curtain to see if he was
leaving, and to my surprise he was watching me with his cock in
his hand.

"What the hell are you doing, you crazy loon?"

He didn't say a word. He just winked at me and started taking
off all his clothes. In ten seconds flat he was completely nude. I
shut the shower door and kept showering. Grant opened the door
and joined me. At first I didn't know what to think as he began
to soap up my body, working his way down to my cock. He looked
up at me to see if I would stop him. Not sure why, I let him continue. He took my dick in his hand, stroking it with expertise. It
was a nice surprise, I have to admit.

When he rinsed all the ⌐
tonished me. He took m⌐
the way down to the ⌐
sucked before (or ⌐
spots, and then ⌐
into his mouth⌐
saw that m⌐
Not o⌐
her p⌐
lick⌐

soap off my cock, he completely as-
nine-inch member into his mouth all
base. He sucked like I have never been
nce, male or female). He hit all the right
e started licking my balls, sucking them each
. My eyes were closed, and when I opened them I
wife was watching him suck me.

ly was she watching, but she was buck naked, rubbing
nk clit. Pussy juice was running down her fingers. She
ed the juices off. Grant, who had resumed sucking my shaft,
et it pop out and suggested that we move to the bed. She ran out
before he saw her and hid outside the bedroom door so she could
hear and watch what was happening. Grant and I climbed on the
bed and no more words were said. He grabbed his dick like he
wanted me to give him a blowjob. His back was to the door behind which Angela hid. I looked at her through the crack in the
door. She knew what he wanted and she gave me her look of approval.

She and I had, at one time, talked about a fantasy we both
shared, and this was it! We share many fantasies, but we always
felt that this one was going to come true for us. Staring at his
seven inches of thick cock, I became so horny I didn't waste any
time. I felt his hard cock hit the back of my throat and I was able
to gently kiss his balls with my lips. I sucked so hard that pre-
come oozed into my mouth. Licking every inch, I sucked up and
down, licking his balls and sucking his head. He moaned with
pleasure. I found myself actually enjoying the idea of sucking
dick, like my wife does to me. A few minutes passed. I looked up
at him and told him I wanted it in my ass.

"I want to feel what my wife feels during anal sex," I explained.
He said, "Rock and roll."

I rolled onto my stomach and he began spreading my cheeks
apart. I felt his finger go inside me. The feeling was unreal! After
only a few seconds, I was ready and relaxed. I gave him a tube of
K-Y jelly from my wife's drawer and told him to be easy because

this was a first-time thing for me and my virgin ass would need it slow. I could feel the head of his cock slowly enter my ass. He let it sit for a few seconds, then with long, steady, slow strokes, his cock was bottoming out in my ass. All the movement made his balls slap against mine. I was so turned on that I wanted it harder and faster.

About this time, my wife had apparently had enough, and she joined us on the bed.

"You guys just keep on going. I'm going to bring myself off just watching you."

My wife sprawled out next to us and started diddling her clit. She looked great as her cunt juice started dripping out of her sex. She could see how much I was enjoying getting fucked. It felt just like she had described it while I reamed her asshole.

Words, however, are not enough. Every thrust of his cock made my cock twitch. I could see him fucking me in the mirrored closet doors, my ass up in the air and his hard cock ramming inside me. I found myself yelling for him to come in my ass.

"I want your hot load deep in my asshole." With the next thrust I could feel his hot goo—five spurts deep in my ass.

My wife was so hot and wet, she had covered her rock-hard nipples with her own pussy juice. She screamed out, "I want both of you."

Grant pulled out of me and stuck his face in Angela's wet cunt. She teased him with orgasms and began lifting her legs around his head. I sucked her rock-hard nipples as she grabbed my rock-hard dick. She knew I wanted to come inside of her. She lay me on my back and straddled my waist, taking my rod deep in her wet cunt. Every thrust made juice run down my balls.

Grant, whose dick was ready to go again, moved toward Angela and eased his throbbing cock into her mouth. My wife looked so sexy, bouncing up and down on my pole as another pole completely filled her mouth. I started bucking wildly, and within seconds I was depositing my seed deep into my wife's abdomen.

She was yelling like a banshee, popping up and down on my cock so wildly that I feared she would hit her head on the ceiling.

When I was spent, she yelled, "Okay, Grant, add your two cents worth."

Getting behind my wife, he spread her cheeks apart and, with one smooth stroke, slid easily inside her.

"Oh, I thought you only did assholes," my wife said.

"Is that where you want it?" Grant asked her.

"You know it, baby."

So fast you couldn't even see it, Grant moved from one sweet hole to the other, and my wife let out an ecstatic "Ohhhh!"

The look on her face almost made me lose my load again.

"Have you got more, my darling?"

"I think so," I said.

With that, she leaned toward me and took me in her mouth.

"Yes," I whimpered, "oh, God, yes."

Right about this time, Grant's dick started throbbing, and I could tell by the look on his face that he was coming.

Then I could tell by my wife's muffled moans that she was coming, and I figured I better get on the ball.

Pumping my dick into her mouth, I released a load to end all loads. There was come everywhere—up my honey's butt, in her mouth and dribbling down her legs.

I was paralyzed. Angela crawled up to me and we shared my come in a passionate kiss. Then we hugged.

After we were all rested, Grant said he had to go.

"What about the game?" I asked.

"That's the only game I was interested in."

I looked at my wife. "Did you guys plan this?" I asked her.

"Who, us?" she asked innocently, and then the two of them burst out laughing.

After Grant left, the two of us lay together in bliss.

That was the night that our main fantasy came true. I felt what it would be like to be a woman.—*W.P., Reno, Nevada*

SURPRISE VISIT LEADS TO SURPRISE ENCOUNTER
WITH SURPRISE GUEST

It was late Friday afternoon and I was driving to my condo. The music on the radio was interrupted by a warning of severe winds and thunderstorms. My girlfriend was away visiting her parents, so I wasn't looking forward to an exciting weekend. I stopped by a liquor store on the way home.

As I was putting my things away the telephone rang. It was a friend of mine, but one that I don't really know very well and who shall remain nameless. We met at the Y and we've played tennis several times and had drinks afterward. He's about my age, twenty-eight, tall, slim and a very competitive athlete. He called to arrange a tennis match for Sunday, then he asked about my plans for the evening. I told him that, because of the approaching storm, I expected to stay at home. Boldly, he asked if he could come over for a drink.

With nothing better to do, I said, "Sure, come on."

I pulled off my coat and tie, drank a beer and relaxed watching the news. At about seven o'clock I decided to take a shower. While I was undressing, the doorbell rang. I put on a robe and let the guy in. I told him I was about to shower, showed him the bar and asked him to make us drinks. I would only be a few minutes. When I stepped dripping from the shower, he was standing in the doorway. He handed me my drink. I took a big swallow and dried off. He followed me into the bedroom and examined some books as I put on running shorts. "I see you have a collection of classic porn novels, " he said.

"Yeah," I replied. "And some tapes also. Want to take a look at some?"

"Sure," he said.

The storm was getting much worse as we went into the living room. Our glasses were empty so I mixed another round. I started the tape and sprawled on the couch. He sat at the other end.

The opening scene was of a male stripper at a girl's party. He danced around and peeled off his clothes to the encouragement of the women. He was soon down to just a pouch and that was soon removed, leaving the guy naked, displaying the beginning of a huge erection. It must have been eleven inches. "Where do they find these guys?" I said aloud. "Mine is only about eight inches."

"I'm sure yours is fine," my guest said.

The girls undressed and attacked the young man. They pulled him to the floor and were all over him. One sucked on his monster as another sat on his face. Then another rode him like a bucking bronco as the others cheered. The guy plugged another girl from the rear. Then two girls were licking his tool. The action was hot, and I was getting hot. My dick was twitching. I glanced over at Rick (oops!) and saw that he had his hands covering his crotch.

On the screen more guys had arrived at the party and the orgy really got going. The storm was getting much worse. I suggested to Rick that he stay and eat with me because of the weather. Also, we were getting too drunk for either of us to drive. He accepted. I asked him to fix drinks while I took a casserole from the fridge. My erection was very obvious when I stood up and so was his, but we'd both had enough to drink to eliminate our embarrassment.

I put the food in the oven, took my drink, and we sat back down to continue watching the movie. The couples paired off and were screwing in every conceivable position. The girls were climaxing and the boys were shooting off big loads of come. My dick was throbbing. Rick was squirming and rubbing his cock through his pants. Our glasses were soon empty again.

I got up, checked on the food and poured fresh drinks. I was obviously getting pretty drunk. Rick wasn't too sober either. I managed to serve supper on trays, and we ate while watching the last part of the tape.

Suddenly there was a very bright lightning bolt, followed by a loud clap of thunder. The lights flickered and went out. I found and lit a candle. Rick turned to me and said, "Since we can't watch the movie, tell me about your first sexual experience."

"Masturbation or the real thing?" I asked.

"Both," he replied.

"Well, one night, when I was eighteen, I was camping out with a buddy. He began to beat his meat and so I tried it too. I'd never done it before. When he saw my inexperience he offered to jerk me off and I let him."

"You were eighteen when you first jerked off."

"Yep."

"Wow."

"My first time with a girl," I continued, "was only a couple months earlier. It was my eighteenth birthday and her parents were out. She wouldn't let me put it in, that came later, but she sucked me off. What about you?"

"I found a sex book in my dad's closet," replied Rick, and he went on to tell how he showed it to a friend and they jerked each other off.

Rick took my glass and fixed drinks. I was getting drowsy and stretched out on the couch. Rick returned and sat down, placing my feet in his lap. He rubbed my ankles as he told me how he first fucked a girl while at a beach-house party. He moved my feet against his stiff dick and ran his hands slightly up my legs. "Have you ever had a guy suck you off?" he asked. His hand moved farther up my leg.

I nodded.

"Did you enjoy it?"

"Sure," I murmured.

He placed his hand on my crotch and nervously asked, "Will you let me blow you?" He grasped my cock. I was horny as hell. I did not say no. He removed my shorts and exposed my raging hard-on. Then he stood up and quickly undressed.

"God, what a dick," he said, as he leaned over me and began to rub my chest and stomach. He pinched and rubbed my nipples and then moved me around so that he could get between my legs. His breath was warm as he blew on my balls and gently massaged them with his hand. His other hand guided my prick to his lips and he licked around the head. Damn, it felt good. I was panting. He teased the full length with his tongue before sucking on the crown. I pushed his head down, hoping he'd get the message and take more into his mouth.

My hips were moving up and down, furiously fucking his face. Finally, he managed to take it all, his face buried in my pubic hair.

"I'm coming," I moaned. "Take it, eat it, drink it all, suck it all out."

My balls tightened and I shot my load deep down his throat. Rick kept on sucking until I became limp, then pulled away. I was about to pass out. Rick stood and pumped his cock, shooting big globs of come on my belly. I awoke late the next morning, naked, with a hard-on. Rick was sitting on the edge of the couch wearing only his briefs, gazing at me. "You feel like talking about what happened last night, or do you just want to forget it?" he asked. "I'm bisexual, as you now know, and I've wanted this to happen ever since I first saw you at the gym. You're probably confused right now."

"No, no, Rick. I'm fine."

Rick dressed, leaned over and patted my dick. "Hope to see you later, big boy. Don't forget our tennis match tomorrow," he said as he left.

I turned over and went back to sleep, trying to get over my hangover.—A.S., *Jekyll Island, Georgia*

LOVING BOYS SPOIL THEMSELVES WITH SPARE ROD

I met Tony two months ago. He is nineteen, blond and cute. I get a hard-on just looking at his face, but with his loose-fitting clothes it was hard to tell what his body was like. We got to know each other after a couple of weeks, and I started to believe that he liked me. On Friday he asked me to come over after work to drink some beer in the hot sun. I put on my worn-out jean shorts, the ones with a few holes in the ass. I didn't wear a shirt.

When I got there he was washing his car. When he walked around the car to greet me, I was shocked to see his nearly naked body for the first time. He was awesome, standing there in his skimpy swim trunks. He got me a beer and started washing his car some more. Watching his tall, lean, muscular body scrub his car was giving me a hard-on. I started to help him dry the car off— he did the sides and I did the roof. He was squatting next to me by the door when he grabbed my ass and pushed me over, telling me to move. He kept drying, moving over towards me as I worked on the trunk.

When he stood up, he brushed his ass against my leg. Then I felt his finger through the holes in my shorts, feeling my ass. I grabbed his hard-on and looked him in the eyes. He smiled and so did I. He said we should go in the house and cool off. We sat on the couch and he turned to me and started rubbing my muscular chest and shoulders. I started feeling his awesome chest and smooth nipples. Suddenly we started kissing like crazy. Then Tony said, "Let's get naked."

We went into his bedroom, stripped and jumped into his bed. I felt his smooth ass-cheeks and almost came. He started feeling my ass and said he wanted a closer look. He crawled around so we were in a 69 position and took my thick seven-inch cock in his mouth.

I got between his legs and started sucking his long, eight-inch cock. It tasted great. His blond pubic hair and tight balls drove me over the edge. I started shooting my wad into his mouth. Almost instantly he blew his load into my mouth, and we sucked each other's pulsing cocks dry.

Then we went downstairs to drink some more beer. After a couple of beers, Tony wanted to take a shower with me. We hugged and kissed while getting wet. He said I was going to force the air out of him, I was hugging and squeezing him so hard. So I loosened up my embrace. We decided to wash each other. While he washed his hair, I did the rest.

It was great washing his chest and nipples, but when I washed his firm smooth buns I almost came. Then he turned around and I washed his blond pubic hairs and long hard cock and balls. Then I did my hair and Tony washed every place on my body, not missing anything. We got out and dried each other off, then back to his bed we went. It wasn't long before he had my cock down his throat and I had his down mine. I asked him if he'd ever fucked anybody up the ass before. He said no, and asked me the same. I told him he was my first taste of male meat.

"I wonder if it feels good," he mused. "Taking it up the ass, I mean."

I told him to get some lubricant, and when he came back he lay on his stomach, his muscular back and cute little buns making my cock rock-hard. I got down and started to lick between his ass-cheeks. He moaned as I licked his asshole. Then I got the lube and started rubbing it into his asshole and onto my cock. I rubbed my cock up and down his crack, then found his opening and started pushing.

After the head slid into his ass, I paused. He moaned as I worked my cock into his incredibly tight ass. I lay down on top of him, hooked my arms under his, grabbed his shoulders and started fucking him hard up the ass. He said it felt great and told me to go deeper. I tried to pick up the pace, but I blew my load up his ass after only five minutes of pumping.

He turned over and his come was all over the bed, his cock and his stomach. I licked him clean. Then we started kissing. It was great rubbing our sweaty chests together, trying to line my nipples up with his, while at the same time rubbing our cocks together. It wasn't long before we were rock-hard again.

We rolled over so that Tony was on top. He started licking his way down my chest and stomach to my belly button. He then took my cock and started to deep-throat it. I almost came again, but he pulled his mouth away just in time. He licked my balls, then grabbed my firm ass-cheeks. I spread and lifted my legs and he buried his face between my buns, licking my asshole. Then he grabbed the lube off the headboard and started greasing my asshole and his cock. He pushed my legs back and put a pillow under my ass. I took his cock and guided it in. He pushed the head of his cock in, then buried it in one push.

He started fucking my ass nice and slow at first, but soon he was pounding away. The sensation of having Tony's hot, smooth cock up my ass was so intense I started shooting my wad all over my chest and stomach. My asshole must have been contracting with each squirt, because Tony moaned louder and pounded my ass faster. Then I felt his cock coming deep up my ass. It was great.

Both of our assholes were sore the next day, so we resorted to blowing each other for the rest of the weekend.—*Name and address withheld*

HAPPY WITH HIS GIRL BUT ALWAYS READY FOR THE RIGHT GUY

I am a twenty-eight-year-old single male who used to consider himself strictly heterosexual. I realize now that during adolescence I was attracted to certain boys because of their looks, personalities and physical abilities.

I was involved in mutual masturbation sessions with a couple of neighborhood friends in high school, but that was when girls were the sole object of my desires and wet dreams.

In college I had a steady girlfriend; we fucked like rabbits for a year and I was devastated when she transferred to a school on the west coast. All through high school and college I seemed to attract the attention of gays, primarily because of my interest in dance and theater, but I ignored them and sought the company of the females in the drama department and elsewhere.

There was only one guy who really stuck out in my mind as someone for whom I felt more than the usual feelings I had about guys who were my friends. His name was Mark.

Mark and I met when we were seniors. He had transferred from another school. He was tall, dark and handsome—built like an Olympic swimmer.

We had summer jobs at a beach resort and shared a room in a cottage nearby. We would work until well after eleven in the evening, and we usually came home exhausted. I often had a date on my nights off and when I returned to the cottage Mark would be lying on the bed reading, usually just wearing his underpants. He would greet me with a hearty, "Well, did you get laid?"

My answer was "No" more often than it was "Yes." One night I staggered in so drunk that I tripped over the breakfast table and fell on the floor. Mark laughed and said, "We'd better put you to bed before you break the furniture."

Even drunk I realized that he was feeling me up as he removed my shirt, shoes and pants. It felt good. I didn't resist when he pulled off my briefs. He put me into my bed and turned off the lights. During the night I woke up to find that Mark had crawled in bed with me. His body was pressed against my back; his arm was draped over my waist and I could feel his hard cock against my buttocks.

I pretended to be asleep as he stroked my cock to its full size. I could feel his hot breath on the back of my neck. "Paul, Paul," he whispered in my ear. "Let me suck you off." I couldn't speak, but moaned and turned onto my back as an invitation for him to grant me some sexual release.

Mark caressed my torso from neck to crotch; he nibbled my nipples and tongued my navel, then sucked on my cockhead. It seemed like only a minute before I shot my load into his mouth. Drained, I drifted into sleep.

As we got out of bed in the morning Mark asked, "Are you upset about what happened last night? Want to talk about it?"

"I wanted it to happen," I said. "You must know that I'm attracted to you. What took you so long to make a move?"

"I was afraid of making you mad," he answered.

I was sitting naked on the side of the bed. "Come here a minute," I said.

He stood in front of me wearing only boxer shorts. Without hesitation I pulled his briefs down and fondled his dick and balls, making him hard as a bat. Then I pumped his cock until he spurted wads of come onto the floor.

We had sex fairly often after that. I finally gave him a blowjob as the summer ended and we parted ways.

I didn't have another gay experience until I met John years later.

We worked in different departments of the same large company and even though I had a steady girlfriend at the time, I was sexually attracted to him almost immediately. When I first saw him in the cafeteria, I couldn't take my eyes off him.

He was six feet tall, slim, black-haired, a very outdoors-type and masculine-looking guy. I finally met him when we were selected to attend a brief training course together in Toronto.

John picked me up the following Sunday morning. The drive was long and would have been boring except for the conversation. We talked of our education, work and interests and found we had much in common.

We checked into the hotel and as we unpacked, John suggested that we go swimming before supper. We grabbed our swimsuits and found we had the pool and dressing room to ourselves. John stripped and put on a tiny bikini. It was hard to keep from staring at his handsome body.

He had long swimmer's muscles without an ounce of fat. I swam fifteen laps but John swam about thirty without even tiring.

As we sat resting on the edge of the pool, the shape of his cock was clearly defined by the stretched fabric of his bikini, and I had an almost irresistible urge to reach out and touch it.

We swam a while longer and then went to the showers. Watching him soap his big cock made my dick swell. He noticed my staring and the effect it was having.

"Getting a hard-on, huh?" he said, amiably. "We'll have to take care of that later." I'm sure I blushed but I couldn't think of a word to say.

After a couple of drinks and a light supper in the grill, I suggested that we take in a movie. John said that he'd rather relax in the room and watch TV. We stripped to our underwear and stretched out on the beds. There was nothing of interest on the regular channels so we turned on an adult movie on pay-per-view.

It was one of those fun-in-the-sun films showing two sexy couples playing on the beach. The action got hotter when they moved into the nearby house.

They were soon naked and engaged in serious foreplay. John said that there was a glare on the screen from where he was lying and asked if he could move over with me.

"Sure," I replied. "And I'll turn off this lamp." John lay back on the pillow beside me. By this time the couples on the screen were engaged in some serious raw sex. One guy was getting a blowjob and the other was giving his girl a tongue lashing. Overwhelmed by the action on the screen and presence of the handsome, nearly naked man lying next to me, I began to get a throbbing, amazingly hard log in the crotch of my underpants.

I glanced over at John and saw that his shorts were poking up also. Shivers ran through my body when John's leg brushed against mine. "What's wrong?" he asked, "Are you cold? Let me warm you up."

His hand moved between my splayed legs and felt my firm cock. "Don't be embarrassed, I've got a hard-on, too. Here, do you want to feel it?"

He put my hand on his erection. "Don't try to tell me you've never had sex with a guy," he said. "You're too pretty and spry. With all those guys wanting to fuck you, I know you must have given it a try. Did you like it?"

His fingers ran under my T-shirt and explored my chest. I trembled at his touch, but I didn't try to stop him. He became bolder and put his hand under the waistband of my shorts and gripped my dick.

God, it felt good. I moaned, "Yes, yes," and that was all the encouragement he needed. He pulled down my shorts and exposed my pulsating prick. John got up and removed his T-shirt and shorts.

His body was beautiful in the dim light. He leaned over and kissed the tip of my cock. "Get out of your clothes," he whispered pleadingly. I threw them aside and lay naked awaiting his next move. John spread my legs and sitting over me he pumped my rod with one hand and his own hard cock with the other. Leaning over, he rubbed our dicks together and scraped my chest and stomach with his fingernails.

My every nerve was on fire. "Now I'm going to suck you. You've been wanting me to, haven't you?" he whispered again, this time with more confidence in his voice.

It was a blowjob I'll never forget. He licked and nibbled on my shaft until it ached for release. He teased the knob with his tongue until I thought I'd go crazy, then stopped and began to lick and suck again. Finally he deep-throated me, burying his nose in my pubic hair as the big wad of my staff bulged his cheeks.

When I yelled that I was about to come, he wormed a long finger into my pliable asshole. My hot juice shot deep into his throat.

I was drained, of course, but he was raring to go. He crawled on top of me and straddled my chest. He held his dick and wiped the pre-come over my face. I refused to take it in my mouth. "Okay, then will you give me a handjob?" he asked.

I teased, tickled and stroked his cock until he tensed and

squirted big globs of come, which he proceeded to smear all over my chest.

Sometime during the night he went back to his bed. I awoke when John turned on the shower. He walked out of the bathroom as I crawled naked out of bed. He stood there drying off, staring at me and grinning like he knew something I didn't. There was silence before he asked, "You didn't know I was gay, did you?"

"No," I replied. I honestly had no idea.

"Surprised?"

"Not really."

"Are you upset because we had sex?"

"No. I wanted it too, but I was afraid to let you know. I spotted you in the cafeteria several weeks before we met. Once in a while a guy attracts me the way you do."

I moved toward the bathroom but John stopped and embraced me. Our cocks rubbed together and he nuzzled my neck.

"We'll be together the rest of the week. I won't force you, but I can teach you a lot about gay sex if you'll allow me to," he said.

I was a willing student. Every night we eagerly stripped as soon as we were alone. We couldn't keep our hands off each other. The education was exciting. Our bodies joined in every possible way and position. John especially like being fucked in the ass, and I learned how to give an expert blowjob. I think we each came at least twice each night and were ready for more the next day.

The week was over too quickly. John and I see each other occasionally at work, where we continue to be flirtatious and sexy around each other in a very unassuming and subtle way.

For example, if I was bending over at the water fountain drinking water, and if no one was around, John would ease up to my backside and rub his tailored trousers against me, nudging me with a bulge I could feel between his legs.

One Friday afternoon, in a playful mood, I sent him an E-mail message on the computer system at work, asking him to meet me in the men's room, back stall, corner wall, for the treat of his life.

I sat on the toilet with my feet resting on the paper dispensers as John eased into the stall. Without a word being said, he whipped out his cock and let me suck him dry right there in the stale, dry atmosphere of the corporate world. I often wonder what would have happened if the CEO had been in the next stall, but luckily everyone had pretty much left for the day when we rendezvoused.

It was a risky deal, nevertheless, and we haven't done a thing since the restroom episode. Not that it might not happen again in the future, but I am very happy right now with my lady friend.

I realize now that I've always been bisexual and wouldn't change back to being purely straight even if I thought I could. —C.B., *Chicago, Illinois*

STRAIGHT MAN LOSES IT AT THE MOVIES

Here's an experience that you might find worthy of inclusion in your "Boys-Boys" section.

I'm a straight, thirty-five-year-old, average-looking businessman. I'm married to a beautiful gal who is equally straight, and we enjoy a super sex life.

Gay sex has always been in the category of "fine for them, but not us." In other words, live and let live.

That changed about six weeks ago when I found myself out of town on a business trip and had the entire afternoon and evening to myself. About two blocks away from the headquarters of my client, there was a porno-movie house.

I haven't seen much porn so I paid my five bucks and went inside. It was an old classic movie palace, big, dank and dark. Downstairs were the hetero-sex films on a very large screen, while upstairs, on a walled-off portion of the old balcony, was a smaller theater for gay films.

I watched the straight films for a while until I was quite turned on. Since the theater was nearly empty, I rubbed my erect cock through my pants, and although I was dripping, I didn't come. I took my hands quickly out of my lap when a guy sat down right next to me.

In an almost empty theater, he picked the seat next to mine, which I assumed was some kind of strategy on his part. I figured I would sit there a couple of minutes, and then move to another more private seat where I could continue my self-indulgence. I didn't want to appear too obvious about it, however.

Before I got up to leave, this guy suddenly reached over and touched my softening penis. Startled by this violation, I pushed his hand away, and moved to get up. I don't remember saying anything to him, except for maybe an angry grunt. Instead, without saying a word, this guy got up and moved some distance from me.

I went back to watching the picture and, as a well-endowed guy filled a gal's mouth with come, I let my hand busy itself with my prick.

Now, I had never in my entire life ever had any sexual contact with another man, but watching the picture I got horny enough to think that maybe I should have let the guy play with me. It was fantasy watching the movie anyway; I could always pretend it was the woman on the screen doing me instead of this rank stranger.

I looked over and I could just barely see that he was still sitting where he had moved. I said to myself, What the hell, and I went over and sat down next to him.

As I sat down, he whispered, "Change your mind?" I nodded. As I looked around to be sure there was no one watching, he unzipped my fly.

I was surprised how soft his hands were on my cock. It was a few nervous minutes, though, before it began to feel good. I looked at him. He was good-looking, probably early twenties, with short hair, a clean shave and nice preppy-looking attire.

Like me, the stranger watched the movie, jacking me off slowly while his eyes feasted on the lusty action on the big screen.

He stopped long enough to pull out his own cock, and while he stroked me, he also masturbated with slow, deliberate strokes.

Once, when I was about to come, I grabbed his hand, as I was sure I was about to ejaculate all over myself, but my signal was understood. He squeezed the tip of my prick between two fingers, cutting off the imminent flow of spermy glue. It certainly kept me from coming completely, but I did drip a little onto his fingers.

When he released his grip, a small amount of semen squirted out and I notice him lick the stuff off with his tongue. He looked over at me and smiled.

Without really being conscious of my action, I reached over and began to play with his cock, keeping my eyes peeled on the screen.

His boner was larger than mine, and I was surprised at how hot and moist it was. I realized it was pulsing with his blood and lathered with his saliva.

I stroked him slowly and cautiously, and by now I was enjoying playing with him and being played with. The action on the screen drove my passion.

I don't remember exactly how it came about, but suddenly he was on his knees, on the floor between the seats, with my cock in his mouth.

My wife sucks on my cock beautifully, but this guy was just as good, and at the same time, there was something even a little better about it.

He was holding the base of my cock with one hand, and had reached into my fly and was playing with my balls with the other. His mouth was up and down on my entire shaft. I started to come a couple of times, but he sensed it and I was able to hold off.

After the second time, he said, "Go ahead and come." But I had another idea.

He got back into his seat, and I told him that if I came, I might not be too horny, and before that happened, I wanted to suck him.

Now remember, I had never even had fantasies about sucking

another guy, but here I was, really wanting to put my lips around that hard, hot, wet thing he'd been fondling while sucking me off.

I kneeled between his legs and sucked his cock. I was really enjoying it too. Like I said, he was hung, and I couldn't suck as deeply on him as he had been able to on me.

A couple of times I felt him tense up, like he was going to come, and I backed off. Pretty soon, I wanted him to come in my mouth, and I speeded up the action, allowing him to gyrate in his seat, fucking my mouth.

He came, and I was again surprised because I didn't find the taste or the texture unpleasant one bit. My only surprise was the hotness of his come—like motor oil on a summer afternoon.

I swallowed as much as I could, but he ejaculated so much that some of his jism came back out of my mouth and down his cock. I licked it up, and almost frantically we swapped places and I found myself draining into his mouth the biggest load of come I'd had for a long time.

Now with my wife, when I come, I'm usually finished—no longer that interested in sex, but with this guy, I had just finished a huge orgasm and I was still ready for more.

My prick started to get soft in his mouth, but he kept sucking and, in what seemed like a short time, I was hard again.

He zipped up his pants, I did the same, and he took me to the men's room. In the light, he was not a bad-looking guy. As we both took a leak he asked me if I wanted to continue. I told him yes, and that I was surprised to find that I was eager to suck him again.

We went upstairs to the gay theater. There were five guys sitting in a group and we joined them. This guy I was with told them I had just lost my virginity, and wanted to get it on with anyone willing. One of the guys volunteered to "watch the door," and in the back corner of this small theater, me, Mr. Straight—with wife, kiddies, job, etc.—sat comfortably in a theater seat and sucked and swallowed five guys.

One guy, the youngest, sucked me through two more climaxes, while I watched these two beautiful boys butt-fucking on the big screen.

I told my wife in pretty graphic detail of my "initiation," and it turned her on so much that she had an orgasm the second I penetrated her pussy.

She confessed for the first time that during high school she had bisexual activities with another girl, and that about three years ago, she had met the same girl for lunch. They went to a motel and made love to each other.

I hope to meet some other guys in the future. My wife wants to watch and, if they wish, take them on in a wild gangbang. —C.M., *Charlotte, North Carolina*

FISHING BUDDIES ENJOY LIFE IN THE GREAT OUTDOORS

I'd like to share the experiences I've been having with two buddies of mine, Roger and Jim. We spend a lot of time fishing, often camping out on weekends.

Roger, Jim and I have become very close, not only from our fishing adventures, but because of our sexual recreation. Roger started it all three years ago when we were younger and a lot more experimental.

We had been fishing about two hours when he suggested that we stash our fishing rods and take a nude swim in a deepest portion of the river.

We played around a bit in the currents, then Roger swam to the shore and emerged, sporting a truly beautiful hard-on. Jim and I swam up and emerged beside him. We all laughed and then Roger began stroking his dick and moving his hips in a rotating fashion.

This immediately caused Jim and me to get throbbing hard-ons. We all stood together in a small circle pumping our glistening cocks in a mutual jack-off session.

All of a sudden Roger put his arm around my shoulder and grabbed my cock. I decided to do the same with Jim, who then took over Roger's prick. We had a glorious time stroking one another's shafts in an almost musical rhythm.

All three of us were moaning and thumping our asses to increase the pleasure of this wildly incredible experience. Believe me, we really had three raging erections all going at once toward one goal.

Jim gasped and said he was about to come. I immediately let go of his cock, dropped down on my knees and took his shaft deep into my mouth. I will never forget the feeling I got the first time I swallowed dick—buzzed!

Jim sighed with delight and began moving my head back and forth. It was a fantastic experience when he unloaded three huge wads of warm come into my mouth.

I lay down on the grass with my spent cock still unbelievably pointed to the sky. Roger quickly mounted me in a 69 position. It was great fun using Jim's come in my mouth as a lubricant on Roger's huge dong.

Then Jim said he wanted to join the party. He took over my prick and Roger began sucking Jim's penis, a homo orgy of glorious proportions.

After about five minutes of mutual sucking, Roger gasped and moaned that he was ready to come. He moved his prick faster and faster and deeper and deeper in my mouth. When he unloaded his silky wad, I greedily swallowed it in three gulps. I couldn't hold on any longer. I delivered my load in Jim's mouth and, at just about the same moment, Jim dumped his wad in Roger's mouth.

We stood up, laughed and kissed one another, letting the come drip all over our lips and chins.

Then we all jumped into the river pool and had fun diving down and playing with our cocks.

I still fish as often as possible with Roger and Jim, and we always look forward to our private jack-off party. We have made it a ritual.

Sometimes we even catch a few fish to take home.—*K.B., Roanoke, Virginia*

EMPLOYEE BLOWS OFF COMPANY PICNIC
TO PARTY WITH HIS BOSS'S WIFE

I want to tell you about a recent experience that I can't believe actually happened to me. A few months ago, the company I work for held its annual picnic for employees and their families. My boss, who was responsible for the picnic, spent the day of the outing making sure that everything went smoothly. I found myself talking to my boss's wife Kathy, who was left to herself as her husband took care of the details.

When my boss finally returned to his wife, it was obvious that he had been drinking. Kathy was upset over being deserted by her husband and then finally having him return drunk. She asked me if I would take her home. I said it wouldn't be a problem.

When we arrived at her house, I walked Kathy to the front door. I had turned to leave when she asked if I wanted a drink. Never one to refuse a drink, especially from such an attractive woman, I accepted the invitation. Kathy is in her late twenties, five feet, eight inches tall, with auburn hair and emerald eyes. Her perpetually erect nipples sit atop small but perfectly formed 34B breasts. She has the longest pair of legs I have ever seen. I'm thirty-five and good-looking, partly due to my love of biking and hiking and partly due to favorable genes.

With the drinks came conversation, and we soon discovered that she and I had more in common than her husband. Our conversation eventually turned to sex. I began to get an erection, and soon Kathy noticed the bulge in my shorts. Looking directly at my crotch, she asked if I was comfortable. I replied that I was as comfortable as I was going to get with my boss's wife. Smiling, she said, "We'll see about that." She softly began to run her red fingernails along the outline that my erection made under my shorts. In response, I cupped her breasts in my hands and rubbed her nipples with my thumbs through her blouse.

Kathy pulled off her top and reached behind her back to unclasp her bra. She sat there looking at me, her breasts unencumbered, waiting for me to make the next move.

Her erect, pink nipples begged for attention. I positioned her on my lap so that I had easier access to her beasts. I softly pulled and twisted her left nipple and sucked on her right nipple. Kathy's nipples stood out at least half an inch. She whimpered, "Don't stop, don't stop. Please don't stop!" I continued to play with her nipples until she pulled my head back and kissed me hard on the mouth. She jabbed her tongue into my mouth, plunging it as deep as it would go. My cock seemed to grow another inch as a result of her efforts. In a breathless voice, she said, "I want you now." I told her to stand up and take the rest of her clothes off. I wanted to see all of her body.

She took off her shorts and stood in front of me in a pair of skimpy panties. Then she began to rub herself through her panties while looking directly at me, with nothing but lust in those emerald eyes. Slowly, she pushed her panties past her hips and I saw the thin swatch of red pubic hair covering her pussy, which was oozing with her sex juices.

Her hands moved down to her cunt. She rubbed her clit with one hand, and with the other she spread her labia open so I could see the deep coral color of her hole. She stood in front of me with her legs bent and head thrown back in the throes of pleasure as she masturbated. Kathy leaned forward and I took her right nipple in my mouth and twiddled her left. With a moan, she crouched down on her knees between my legs and yanked off my shorts. My cock stuck out above the waistband of my underwear. She painstakingly licked up and down the outline of my cock under my underwear, never touching my cockhead. Soon I was leaking drops of come.

Kathy looked up at me, her face a mask of lust, and she moaned, "Give me your cock. I want to suck that big cock now!" I stood up, and Kathy nearly ripped off my underwear. My cock sprang out and a drop of come dripped on her breasts. Kathy rubbed it into her erect nipples, making them shine. Then she lowered her head and licked the precious fluid off her nipples.

She moved closer to my cock, wetting her lips in anticipation. She was totally unrecognizable as the woman I had met at the picnic. She licked along the underside of my cock until she got to the head, then slowly took it in her mouth, running her tongue around the head. I grabbed my cock and rubbed it over her face, smearing the mixture of her saliva and my semen from her forehead to her chin. Looking down at Kathy, I told her she was the most beautiful woman I had ever known. She asked me, looking directly into my eyes, if I wanted her to play with my balls while she continued to suck on my cock. I could only groan in response. She smiled and resumed rubbing and sucking.

She rubbed my nipples when she was through with my balls. All I could do was moan and come in her mouth. My second blast of come went down her throat, the third splashed across her face and the fourth splattered her nose and dripped off her chin. I fell to my knees, drained and holding onto her for support. She licked some of my spattered come off her nipples.

After resting for a few minutes, I regained my erection. I laid Kathy on the floor and rubbed my cock up and down the slit of her cunt. Kathy arched her back and tried to impale herself on my cock, but I pulled away. I wiped up some of the come on her face with my fingers and offered my dripping fingers to her. She raised her head and sucked my fingers into her mouth. When she had cleaned my fingers, she moaned, "Fuck me."

I inserted my cockhead into her slit and then withdrew, running it up and over her clit. I probed her slit from the bottom to the top for several minutes before I inserted my cockhead into her cunt.

The sight of my thick cock penetrating her pussy beneath the small tuft of red pubic hair almost made me blast another load, but I continued to gently fuck her with just the head of my cock. Kathy's breathing became heavy and rapid. Her erect nipples darkened to a deep color and her stomach muscles undulated to a rhythm I had to struggle to match. She pulled her nipples and tickled them, trying to bring on the orgasm she so desperately needed. As I withdrew my cock and continued to tease her slit, she reared up, grabbed my shoulders and screamed, "Do it! Fuck me! Bury your cock inside me until it comes out of my mouth!"

I pulled her legs up until her knees pressed against her breasts and drove my cock all the way into her pussy with one stroke. Her back arched and she opened her mouth wide as if she were screaming, but no sound emerged. The muscles of her body quivered. Her eyes became glassy and she was covered in a sheen of sweat. Then Kathy went rigid, letting out a scream of release. Her juices ran out of her cunt and dribbled down the crack of her ass, soaking the rug under us.

When she started to recover, I rubbed her slit with two fingers and offered them to her. She sucked her juices from my fingers and tried to catch her breath.

Knowing that her husband would be coming home, I got dressed. Kathy walked me to the door and kissed me hard on the mouth while rubbing my crotch. We promised each other that we would get together again.—S.G., *Des Moines, Iowa*

HE BUMPS AND GRINDS FOR HIS BIG, BOUNCY BABE

I have an older client, a generously proportioned lady, who is young in spirit, if not in years. Sarah wears lacy push-up bras under low-cut blouses that she leaves half-buttoned. At first I was sure she wasn't interested in me at all. We had a couple of meetings in my office and she had been businesslike and formal.

One day I went to her apartment to review her financial file. I no longer entertained romantic expectations, but I still enjoyed her company and was only too glad to go out of my way for her. During a break in our work Sarah leaned over the table to hand me some iced tea. I resisted the urge to look at her cleavage (which was significant). Instead I noticed her eyes dropping to my crotch. I was certain she could tell I wasn't wearing undershorts, and that she could see my pecker through my thin, white slacks. But when we finished our meeting she didn't ask me to stay, and she didn't ask when we would need to meet again. I pretty much gave up hope of ever getting more intimate with her.

The next day, to my surprise, Sarah came to my office after lunch, dressed in a long skirt and designer sweater. She asked me if she had offended me in some way, and wanted to know why I had left her home so abruptly. I explained that I had thought she had been uncomfortable with my presence. Laughing, Sarah said that she had actually been trying to entice me to stay, and that she had long been intrigued by the possibility of spending some time with me.

I apologized profusely for misreading her signals and asked how I could make up for my mistake. As I waited for her answer, I reached for her hand and squeezed it gently. She stood up and drew me to her for a warm hug that blessed me with the feel of soft breasts unencumbered by a bra. She said she would let me know how I could make up for my error later. Before letting me go, she ground her hips against me and allowed me to lift her face and kiss her lightly on the lips.

I kissed her again, but this time more deeply, letting my tongue run over her lips until I felt the tip of her tongue searching for mine. I felt her left hand on my butt as her right hand held the back of my neck and fingered my hair. When we broke for air, I whispered in her ear that we should continue our conference at her apartment. We arranged to meet at three the next afternoon. After another lingering kiss she departed.

The next day I arrived at her place at the appointed time. She met me at the door, and we kissed lightly before she ushered me into her sitting room and told me she was not in the mood to work. She wore a white blouse and a short, black, pleated skirt. Sarah seated me on a large lounge chair and I watched her jiggle and bounce as she made her way to the kitchen to get wine.

When she returned I couldn't keep my eyes off her large, soft, jiggling breasts. She sat beside me on the settee, and leaned toward me in such a way as to reveal even more of her voluptuous figure. We sipped her fine French wine and made small talk till the bottle was empty. Then she offered to give me a tour of her spacious apartment. I put my arm around her waist as we walked from room to room. Once again, her hand found its way to my buns. I slowly moved my hand up her side until I could feel her boob through the thin material of her blouse. When we arrived at her bedroom she told me that once I entered I would be expected to stay there until she decided it was time for me to leave.

I could tell that all this was in good humor, and that she had no harm in mind, so I readily agreed, asking what she had planned.

"I want you to do a striptease for me," she said, "and you have to keep doing it until you get it right." I failed to notice the fancy stereo by the bed until she turned on some loud music with a distinct bump and grind beat.

I started to tap a foot in time to the music, at the same time slowly unbuttoning my shirt. Sarah sat in the middle of the bed with her knees lifted, showing that she wasn't wearing panties. When my shirt was off I turned my back, undid my belt and turned gracefully back around while I unzipped. My trousers fell to the floor and my pecker stood straight out at attention. All in all, I thought I'd performed rather well.

The lady, however, hardly smiled. She said my technique was very poor and that I needed to do more twisting and hip movement. Also, she said, she wanted more ass action and that if I couldn't do better next time she would have no choice but to show me herself.

I put my clothes back on and started over—this time trying to move more slowly and sensuously. She seemed to like it better, because I could see her cupping her breasts in her hands and licking her lips. As I stepped out of my pants I turned my back to her and leaned over. While leaning over, I reached between my legs, pulled my ass-cheeks apart and showed off my bunghole. This takes great balance, and I could only hold the pose for a few seconds. When I turned around, she was smiling approvingly. I went to the bed, reached for her face and kissed her deeply. My hand grazed her bosom and detected a hard nipple beneath her thin blouse. But she stopped me and asked me to dance one more time.

This time, however, she said she wanted my dangling penis closer to her face. She kissed it lightly, then turned me around and asked me to lean over. She got some lotion and rubbed it all over my buttocks, subtly bringing her fingers closer and closer to my asshole until one pressed against it and popped inside. She pulled out her finger, put a large amount of lotion on me and reinserted it, rubbing the insides of my ass and softly telling me to relax.

I could feel her finger well up inside me. I sensed that she was doing something that she hoped I would later do to her. I began to think about how it would feel to have my tongue inside each of her holes. She interrupted these thoughts by getting up and starting her own striptease.

She danced to the music, exciting me immensely, until eventually she was naked, showing me her asshole as she leaned over to touch her toes. Then she rubbed her boobs against my face as she turned around. After that we tumbled onto the bed. I licked and sucked her erect nipples and smooth breasts. Then I rolled onto my back and she pressed herself against me. Soon she was crouching over me and carefully placing my rigid pecker into her love-hole. Her strong muscles pulled me up farther and farther into her slick hole. We fucked gently, with her jiggling jugs bouncing up and down above me. After a good, long fuck we exploded in powerful, nearly simultaneous orgasms.

After a brief kiss, I asked her if she was as nice from the rear as she was from the front. She assured me that she was, and eagerly suggested that I judge for myself. I got the cream and greased up my pole, while she got onto her hands and knees with a pillow under her chin. I slowly pressed my middle finger against her dimple until it slowly slid in. When it was in as far as it could go, I pulled it out and put my member against her. It, too, slowly disappeared inside her. Soon it was all the way in, and I fucked her big behind till she screamed with pleasure.

I was about to blast off when she said she wanted to drink my come. I pulled out and fed my penis into her mouth. She finished me off gloriously, swallowing everything I could give. As I rested beside her, feeling her heaving breasts against my chest, I realized I had just had one of my greatest sexual experiences—at least so far. We have plans to meet again very soon and I may have to write in again. I can't wait.—*E.B.W., Fall River, Massachusetts*

HE MISSED A CHANCE TO GET IN HER PANTS, BUT THE DREAM LIVES ON

While in college, I once had a chance to have sex with my good friend, Allison. I didn't go through with it. However, I still think about how it could have been.

Allison and I have been friends since our first year at college. We lived in the same dormitories all through college. I was attracted to her from the beginning. She has luxurious brown hair, big, beautiful brown eyes, firm, grapefruit-sized breasts and an ass you want to grab with both hands and squeeze. Since she came to college with a fiancé from her high-school days, I didn't think we'd ever be more than friends. We did, in fact, become very close friends.

Eventually Allison and her fiancé broke up. By this time, her ex-fiancé was also a good friend of mine, and I wasn't ready to pick and choose between friends. Dating Allison would have been a quick (but certainly not easy) way to throw away a good friendship. That loss might have been doubled if Allison and I didn't work out romantically. Besides, Allison had never shown any sexual interest in me, so it wasn't as if I was turning down a real likely option.

Time marched on. Allison dated a few losers. I felt lousy when she started dating another friend of mine, a guy called Randy whom she had previously found very annoying. As luck would have it, they made a wonderful couple and I had to feel happy for them.

One weekend, Allison and I made plans to take a trip together. I was going to visit a girlfriend and Allison was going to visit her brother. We discussed the details Friday at lunch and decided to leave early Saturday morning. Allison then asked me what I had planned for that evening. Apparently, she was feeling sore and thought that a good friend like me would make the time to give her a back rub. I agreed demurely, but my mind was swimming with lewd thoughts.

Later that night, I went to her room prepared to work my hands off. Allison was working at her desk when I came in, and her desk lamp provided the only light in the room. She was wearing spandex leggings and a sweatshirt. She looked great! We sat around and talked for a while. Then she got up, pulled a bottle of baby oil out of her dresser drawer and asked me if I was ready.

While my mind started working out the implications of the baby oil, Allison turned her back to me, pulled off her sweatshirt and lay down on the blanket on the floor. Her back was totally bare.

After my heart started beating again, I kneeled on the floor above Allison, straddling her ass. I had a raging hard-on. I rubbed, squeezed and pulled at Allison's lovely skin for over a half hour. As the time passed, I bravely made my way closer and closer to her ass, as well as around her sides toward her breasts. I was just getting ready to push my luck when there was a knock at the door.

Shit! A friend of Randy's walked into the room. He immediately flashed a suspicious look at us. I continued rubbing Allison's back in a very reserved way. We tried to act like it was just an innocent back rub. Nevertheless, our friend stuck around for a chat and didn't appear to be willing to leave before me. I told Allison that I hoped I had done some good for her aching muscles and that I'd see her in the morning. Then our friend and I got up and left.

After I left, I couldn't take my mind off Allison and what could have happened. I had to masturbate to two orgasms before I could get to sleep. It was a shame that we were staying at different places for the weekend. There was almost no chance of picking up where we had left off.

The next morning I knocked on Allison's door bright and early. She was already up and waiting for me. I helped carry her bags to the car and we took off. Allison spent the weekend with her brother and I spent the weekend with my friend Diane. Allison and I didn't get to see each other much but (fortunately for my sanity) I spent a wonderful night having sex with Diane.

On Sunday I picked up Allison at her brother's house a little after noon. In the car, Allison and I made small talk for about three minutes before she asked about my Saturday night. She wanted the unexpurgated version, so I gave her all the details. I had a lot of fun describing it all to her. Then came the part I'll never forget.

"I'm jealous," Allison said.

"Huh? What do you mean?" I asked. "Jealous of what?"

"Jealous of Diane," she replied. I couldn't believe my ears. Allison was staring at me, and I couldn't think of what to say next. This was the pivotal point in a day that I believe could have turned out differently. Maybe it was because I had had such a sexually satisfying weekend. Or maybe I have a gallant streak I never knew about. I don't know. All I know is that I told Allison that if we acted on our feelings we would probably mess up a lifetime of choices for an afternoon of pleasure. I sometimes wish I had listened to my instincts rather than my reason.

When I think back to that day, I usually imagine it happening like this:

"I'm jealous," Allison said.

"Huh? What do you mean?" I asked. "Jealous of what?"

"Jealous of Diane," she replied.

Long pause. "Would you like to stay at a motel with me tonight?" I asked. Allison nodded.

I took the next ramp with a hotel sign, and soon we were pulling up to our room. After dropping our bags in the room, Allison said she wanted to take a shower. I headed out for champagne and rubbers.

When I got back, Allison was blowdrying her hair in front of the mirror, wearing a nightshirt that came halfway up her thighs. I grabbed the ice bucket and told her I'd be right back. After filling the bucket I went back and iced the champagne. I walked up to Allison and hugged her from behind.

"Mmmmm, you smell good," I said. "I think I'd better take a shower myself."

"I'll help," she said.

"I'm not sure I'm quite ready for that."

"It'll be all right," she said, taking my hand and leading me toward the bathroom. "It will be easier, and a lot more fun, if I give you a bath."

Allison walked around me and started the bath water. Then

she told me to sit on the stool. She took off my shoes and socks. "Stand," she said. Turning me so I faced away from her, she hugged me from behind, burying her face in my back. Then she ran her hands up my chest and rubbed my pecs for just a moment before starting her hands back down my body. By that time my dick was throbbing and straining against my pants. She avoided it as she ran her hands down the inside of my thighs to my knees. She started back up my thighs and ran her fingers over the bulge in my pants on her way to my belt buckle. Next, she undid my buckle and unbuttoned my pants.

"Be right back," she whispered, and for a moment those wonderful fingers were gone. Apparently she was checking the temperature and turning off the water. "I missed you," she said as she picked up where she left off. She unzipped my pants and pulled them down to the floor. Next she started on my shirt, unbuttoning it slowly, starting at the top and then sliding it off my back.

Allison gave me a little kiss on the back, wrapped her arms around me and started rubbing my chest. Then she ran her hands down my sides, hooking her fingers in my shorts as she went, and pulling my underwear down and off.

As she straightened up, she gave me a little slap on the ass and said, "All right. Get in the tub."

So I did. As I climbed into the tub, Allison slipped out the door. She reappeared almost immediately with the champagne in one hand and plastic cups in the other. She popped the cork and poured a cup for each of us. We both sipped from our cups, and then put them aside. I watched as Allison pinned her hair up. "I don't want to get my hair wet," she said. "And I don't want to get this wet, either," she added, taking off her nightshirt.

Her body was even better looking than I imagined. Her neck looked long and lovely, especially with her hair up. Her breasts were larger than I thought they would be. Her nipples were bright pink and they poked out about a quarter of an inch. My eyes wandered farther down, focusing on her curvaceous waist and hips.

Her bush was trimmed close and I could clearly see her pussy lips. Her legs were fabulous and they were moving closer.

Allison put a towel on the edge of the bathtub and sat down with her feet in the water. She then soaped up a wash towel and started scrubbing my back. Over the course of the next half hour, we sipped our champagne as Allison methodically washed every inch of my body. I was loving every minute of it, but I finally got to the point where I couldn't help myself any longer. I cupped a handful of water in my hand and poured it down her stomach onto her pussy. "I'm sorry," I said. "I think I got you wet down there. Let me get that for you."

With that, I dove for the promised land.

Allison gasped as my mouth started working on her cunt. "Not yet," she said.

"I'm sorry, but I have to have you," I said, getting back to it. Allison grabbed my head and held it for a moment. Then she started running her hands through my hair. I really love that.

I was also really loving her cunt. My tongue teased her lips, up and down, left and right. Occasionally, I pushed my tongue as far up her pussy as I could. After a while she let go of my head and leaned back, with her hands on the bathroom tiles, so that I could get even deeper into her cunt. I put a finger up her pussy as my mouth started working on her clit. Allison started rolling her hips and gyrating her pussy; I could barely keep my mouth on her.

"Now!" she grunted as she shoved her cunt hard against my face. I used both arms to hold her legs and ass for extra support and to keep her cunt in reach. Then I stuck my tongue out and shook my head from side to side. Allison started shaking all over. I just left my mouth on her cunt and rode out her orgasm.

After she settled down, I took her hand and helped her sit up. She immediately leaned over and kissed me full on the mouth. Our tongues danced for a few moments; then she pulled away a little and gave me some quick pecks around my lips.

"Interesting," she said.

"What's that?" I asked.

"I think that's the first time I ever tasted myself. No wonder you really got into it," she commented.

She paused to regain her breath. "Thanks," she added. "That was really nice. Now let's get you out of that tub. You're probably shriveling up like a raisin."

"You might be surprised," I said. When I stood up my dick was stiffer than ever. After quickly drying off, I headed to the bed with Allison right on my tail.

Once in bed, Allison climbed on top of me. She wanted to take it slowly, and I wasn't about to argue.

First she kissed my chest. Next she kissed my stomach. Then she kissed my waist. Then—big gasp—she kissed my cock right on the head. She trailed her tongue down the underside of the shaft, teasing the skin with her breath. Allison and I had had frank discussions about her oral abilities before, and now I was getting first hand proof that she hadn't exaggerated. She sucked my balls while her hand massaged my dick. Then she licked her way back up the shaft until she got to the head, which she sucked into her mouth. She lingered there for just a moment before plunging the length of my cock down her throat.

I was just lying back and enjoying the sensations when Allison stopped cold. "Aren't you watching?" Allison asked.

"I wasn't," I said, "but I will, now that you mention it."

She made quite a show of it, always trying to give me a good view of what she was up to. Watching Allison lick and suck my cock and balls, it didn't take very long for me to get that feeling.

"I'm getting close," I warned, but this only increased her fervor. She pumped her head up and down on my dick like a piston. While watching her lips sliding over me, I came hard and heavy. Allison swallowed every drop.

"Oh God, that was great," I whispered. "Thank you."

"Turnabout is fair play," Allison replied. "Now let's get a rubber on you."

"Sounds great," I said. Allison did the honors, which actually made the act of putting on a condom kind of fun. Then she climbed on top of me and lowered herself onto my dick. I really love this position. I hadn't tasted her tits yet, so I sat up and started kissing her breasts. Breasts always amaze me—mounds of soft flesh tipped with rock-hard nipples. I grabbed Allison's ass with both hands and hoisted her higher to get a better angle on her tits. Then, on a whim, I stood up. Still holding Allison on my cock, with my hands on her ass, I walked over to the wall and propped Allison against it. Making slow, deliberate movements, I pumped my dick into her all the way to the hilt.

After a few minutes of this, my arms started to get tired. I moved her over to the sink and set her down. I turned her away from me and bent her over the counter. Allison spread her legs and I shoved my dick into her from behind. Looking in the mirror behind the sink, I watched Allison's tits bounce while I held her hips and pounded my dick home. After a little while of this, Allison started moaning and thrusting her hips back while I thrust forward. I reached around her and rubbed her clit while I continued banging her pussy. She started moaning even louder, and then she came again. Her sticky juices squirted out and ran down my legs. I stood her up, hugged her and kissed her neck.

I led her back to the bed where I laid her down and mounted her missionary style. I kissed her and fondled her breasts while I achieved my second orgasm of the evening. Then she wrapped her arms around me and hugged me tight.

We spent the rest of the night getting very little sleep. We talked for a while. We snacked a little. We had sex on the floor and in the bathtub. We even gave each other massages before the sun rose again. After showering together, we checked out of the room and headed back to campus so we wouldn't miss our Monday classes.

Randy and Allison have been happily married for nearly three years now, and are considering having kids soon. I didn't get Allison, but I do have my memories of one of the best nights of my life.—*T.R., Ann Arbor, Michigan*

SHE'S SHIFTING INTO HIGH GEAR
WHEN SHE SHOULD BE PARKING

I was living in Northern California and attending college when I met Debra. I had gotten a late start on my academic life at thirty-five years old. Debra was ten years my junior, and was everything I dreamed of in a woman. She was tall, athletic and adventurous. She also had a curvaceous body, slim-waisted with proudly jutting tits, and had a truly delightful pussy, with the fleshiest lips I had ever seen.

We were in a couple of classes together, and soon discovered that we lived near each other. When she asked me if she could catch rides with me to class, I thought it was a great idea. It wasn't long before our mutual interests led us to share an occasional glass of wine or a joint, and we finally hustled each other into my bed one rainy night, when my girlfriend was away in San Francisco.

Debra loved to fuck and to suck cock, and considered it a worthy challenge to take a big dick all the way down her throat.

She was extremely enthusiastic about sex, sometimes begging me to come on her face or do her in the ass. Although she lived with roommates, and I with my girlfriend, we arranged plenty of opportunities to get it on under the pretense of studying. At times we interrupted study sessions in the college library to sneak off to an empty classroom for a quick fuck, or into the stacks for a blowjob. On the way home from school we occasionally stopped at the beach, or in a deserted area, for a moonlight tumble of outrageous sex.

The backseat of my Ford Mustang had never seen this type of action. Once in a while Debra and I would whisper our fantasies to each other over the phone while we both masturbated. It was a great affair, with lots of memorable moments, but one truly amazing event occurred on a Saturday morning study date.

It was a rainy, foggy day. We drove to the campus parking lot in my car. On the way to campus I played with Debra's nipples while she unzipped my pants and lightly sucked on my hardening dick. By the time we got to school we were pretty horny, and we thought that, with help from the thick fog, we might be able to help ourselves to a piece of tail right there in the parking lot.

I drove to a deserted corner of the lot, and we started going at it—kissing open-mouthed and fondling each other's genitals. After a few minutes the car window steamed up and increased our cover. Before long, Debra had slipped her pants off and straddled my lap, facing me, with her feet on the back of my seat. It was easy to slide my cock into her tight, wet cunt. I grabbed her ass to keep it from blowing the car's horn, and Debra slowly rode up and down on my stiff pole.

We fucked for a few minutes, reveling in the glorious sensations. My balls were drawn up tight, and her rising and falling literally had me on the edge of my seat. I thought I'd blow my load at any moment. I was deliriously happy, but Debra, being inventive and curious, was restless. She mumbled something about "putting things into high gear," while carefully assaying the cramped front seats of my Mustang.

Debra slowly lifted herself off my cock, then moved sideways, so she wound up with a foot on each of the two front bucket seats. She was still facing the back of the car and squatting down, but what she did next totally amazed me. She reached down between her two legs where her purse was wedged against the seat, and pulled out a short, gold-colored vibrator. When she flicked it on its battery-powered buzz seemed to fill the whole car. She'd often talked about the "secret friend" who cared for her when we couldn't get together, but I'd never seen it, and was surprised at how loud it seemed to be.

"Hey, what if all that noise draws a crowd?" I whispered.

"The more the merrier," she responded, and touched the vibrating tip to her clit, which was protruding, round and ripe, from between her fleshy cunt lips. The sound of the motor was immediately drowned out by her responsive moans.

I didn't know what to say. At first I felt a little left out, but as I watched her masturbate I became incredibly excited. My expression seemed to encourage Debra more, because before I knew it she was burying the whole golden shaft of the dildo between those gorgeous pussy lips of hers until her juices ran down over her fist.

Her face contorted with pleasure and excitement as her juices ran down the knob at the base of the vibrator. The sight of her squirming was awesome. My motor was revving, to say the least. Debra pumped her hips a few times, then pulled the vibrator out again and ran it around her juicy pussy lips, as if it was a cock and she hadn't had any in months. She plunged it inside her pussy again, pumped away furiously, then suddenly stopped and sighed.

Her juices covered her fingers so that she could barely hold the humming shaft. I was amazed. By the slight tremble of her body and the way Debra's eyes were closed, I knew she had climaxed. I know this sounds weird, but I had never seen a girl getting herself off before. Everyone I'd gone out with always got embarrassed and said that was a really private thing.

Debra settled back down on the passenger seat with a very satisfied smile. She turned to me with a languid smile, then slid sinuously down to the floor. After asking me if she could go down on me, she proceeded to suck my cock. Could she, I thought to myself. I would have surely felt left out if she hadn't.

It didn't take long before I came, and just before I did she teasingly took my cock out of her mouth and rubbed it all over her face. One jet of come hit her square in the corner of her closed mouth, so she tilted her head sideways to let my come run across her full lips. She then sucked my come into her mouth and swallowed it. Then we got dressed and went into the library to study.

After that parking experience, I found myself fondly daydreaming about Debra's lovely wet pussy impaled on her golden wand. My only regret is that we never got the opportunity to shift into overdrive before the fog lifted!—M.V., *Redwood, CA*

SOMETIMES THE BEST LAID PLANS JUST LEAD TO THE BEST LAYS

I'm a twenty-four-year-old woman married to a thirty-three-year-old man who really knows how to fuck. I mean, he's incredible in bed and, being older and more experienced, he has taught me many pleasurable things.

He's six-feet-one-inch tall and weighs about a hundred and forty pounds, trim and muscular with an eight-inch cock. I'm five-foot-five, about one-thirty with 34C tits and shapely legs and ass. I'm going to tell you about the night I blew his mind.

Having been at home all day, I had plenty of time for horny fantasies, and they gradually evolved into a little scheme. Knowing that he loves black lingerie and having his cock sucked, I planned accordingly.

I dressed in a tight, black, crotchless lace outfit, stockings and heels. I finished the look with a tank top and a miniskirt that showed off my curves but hid the surprise. My cunt was hot and wet with excitement by the time I finished dressing up. It got a lot wetter driving to pick him up from work.

When Sidney got into the car and saw my outfit, his eyes widened with surprise and I saw his cock spring to attention. When he was settled I pulled up my skirt and flashed him a peek at my crotchless outfit and hot, pink pussy. He kept glancing over, and before long he had started fingering my cunt. Pretty soon he jokingly suggested we stop somewhere and fuck. He assumed I wouldn't, knowing that I'm shy and reserved, and have always resisted his suggestions about fucking in the open. He certainly didn't expect me to pull off on a side road and pull out his hard cock for a quick suck, but he made no move to stop me when I did.

One thing that invariably gets him going is if I stick my tongue out as far as it will go and swirl it around and around his penis. Every time it passes the underside of his dickhead he jumps, and he usually doesn't jump more than a couple of times before he starts spraying. That's what I did to him on this occasion, and when he started moaning like he was going to come I stopped and told him to save it until we got home. He was surprised at the sudden turn of events, but decided to be patient.

After we got back on the road, I kept reaching over every once in a while to make sure he was still good and hard. I was never disappointed, either by Sid's stiffness or the response I got. He sighed and humped his hips every time I touched the outline of his dick. Instead of rubbing him more, I'd just pat his thigh and say, "Just checking."

At home, Sidney went straight to our room, while I stripped off my outer clothes, leaving my sexy outfit and heels on. Sidney was lying on the bed, all six feet plus of him, naked, with his full hard eight-inch rod waving in the air. This man is a real treat to look at. He could have been a model if he'd been a little more vain.

My mother had told us of a little game her boyfriend plays with her called *Around the World*. It's an anything goes kind of game, except for one important rule: The recipient isn't allowed to touch the giver.

Straddling his body and kissing his neck, I informed him that he was not allowed to touch me. After being sucked so close to orgasm in the car, and watching me in my sexy outfit, he let out a groan and said, "I don't know whether I can do that."

"Try. For me," I requested with a coo. He didn't reply, but I saw his cock leap in anticipation, and that was enough of an answer for me.

Starting with his hard little nipples, I kissed, licked and nibbled my way down his love trail, purposely avoiding his thrusting, purple-headed cock. Knowing his stomach, inner thighs and balls are extremely sensitive, I centered my careful and lingering attention there. I licked slowly from his knee to his tight sac and nibbled on his balls, tongued his tight ass and kissed the smooth skin under his nuts.

Sidney was moaning and gripping the headboard, constantly directing his swollen cock toward my mouth and begging me to suck him. His hot rod was oozing onto his stomach, and I carefully and thoroughly licked up every stray drop. Then, sensing that he was as hot as he was ever going to get, I suddenly deep-throated as much of his huge prick as I could. He groaned loudly and came straight up off the bed, rolling me onto my back. Without any help from me, as I was giggling at the look of intense excitement on his face, he began jamming his pulsing rod at my midsection. I spread my legs and he found my soaked opening and began slamming into me for all he was worth.

Sidney stopped and asked me to get on my knees. With my rounded ass sticking up in the air, he shoved his cock into my slippery hole to the hilt. He was banging away so hard that his balls slapped against my clit with every thrust.

Getting close to coming, and wanting to do something spectacular to finish off this special event, I stopped him and asked him if he wanted to fuck my asshole. He immediately said that he did. I grabbed the K-Y off the nightstand and rubbed some on his cock and my virgin hole. I reached under and behind me and ran his cockhead up and down my crack, finally centering his head right at my tight opening. Slowly he shoved his cock into my tight asshole. He reached around to finger my cunt and clit as he sank his cock in my quivering hole.

When I started to moan and push against him he grasped my hips and started working in and out of me. I fingered my clit while his balls slapped my swollen lips. As we climaxed, I watched him pounding into me in the mirror beside the bed. Still connected, we slumped to the mattress. His cock kept pumping come into my ass and twitching. I could feel the streams pouring out of him so much more clearly than I can in my pussy.

Afterward he admitted it was the best fuck of his life. Then he started patting my breast. Looking at him with a satisfied grin, I informed him that he had touched me, and "Now we have to start all over."—R.B., *Tucson, Arizona*

LIFE IN PRISON LOOKS A LOT BETTER WHEN YOUR COUNSELOR IS A SEXY BLONDE LADY

I am a convicted felon, currently incarcerated for one to seven years in a state penitentiary. Feeling miserable because I no longer had the freedom to enjoy my favorite hobbies (sex, sex and more sex), I began my imprisonment by keeping to myself and not allowing too many inmates or prison officials to get near me. The one question constantly on my mind was, What will I do now that I can't have pussy six or seven times a day? Each time I would think of Debbi, Sara, Lynn, Bette and Kim, the girls I used to entertain every day, I would feel my fat black eleven-inch dick begin to throb in my brown jailhouse uniform. Then I would go to my cell and hang up a curtain so that no one could see me as I feverishly masturbated myself to climax.

I was indulging in this substitute pleasure one day when, just as I was about to reach orgasm, I was disturbed by a soft tapping on my cell door. With cock in hand I went over and pulled aside the curtain enough to see Rhonda, my prison counselor, standing there with my file folder.

Rhonda was a very petite but extremely sexy blonde lady, about five feet two and one hundred ten pounds. Her tits were small, and even though she wore somewhat loose-fitting pants, it was evident that she had a very shapely ass, and hips that flared enough to please any man.

I knew Rhonda could see the lustful expression on my face as I looked her body up and down, pausing at her breasts before meeting her eyes. Still, she gave me a friendly smile as she asked if I could come to her office to go over my programming schedule.

I asked her if she needed me to come right away and she replied, still smiling, "Yes, if you're not too busy." I wondered if she knew what I'd been doing. Deciding to test her out, I took down the top part of the curtain, showing her my naked chest and torso. When my cute and sexy counselor said nothing, but just stood there and looked at me, I boldly turned and walked over to my bunk, knowing she could see my strong hairy ass over the lower half of the curtain. When Rhonda still said nothing, I spun around quickly to expose my solid, meaty, still half-erect shaft to her gaze. I smiled to myself as I saw her swallow and lick her lips. Then she collected herself and turned away, telling me she would wait for me in her office.

After getting dressed (not bothering with my boxers or T-shirt) I walked across the unit, passing inmates playing cards, chess and dominos. I knocked on the office door just as my counselor was putting up a removable blind over her window. She motioned for me to come in, and I took a seat in a soft office chair in front of her cluttered desk.

I noticed that Rhonda had taken down her blonde hair, letting it fall to her shoulders. When she began to speak, her voice sounded kind of nervous. She cleared her throat and started again.

"Is there anything in particular you'd like to do or accomplish while you're here?" she asked me.

Immediately I said, "Do you mean in this office, or in the prison?"

She smiled nervously. "I mean what would you like to do here in this jail during your term of incarceration?"

I knew what she wanted to hear, so I said I wanted to do anything and everything that was necessary in order to make parole when the time came—adding that that included doing whatever pleased my counselor. Rhonda said she was working on my program plan, which included deciding which job details I would be working on. She then informed me that one of my jobs would be to clean her office every day.

"When do you want me to start?" I said.

"Now!" Rhonda replied quickly.

I rose to leave, intending to find some cleaning supplies, but Rhonda stopped me at her door, then got up and walked over to where I stood. Standing close and looking me straight in the eye, she asked, "Did you just get out of the showers when I came to your cell?"

"No," I said.

She took a deep breath.

"You are a very . . . healthy man," she said softly. "I've never imagined a cock the size of yours. I hope I didn't embarrass you by looking at you that way, but I was in shock."

"You didn't embarrass me," I replied. "You just reminded me of my favorite hobby."

Rhonda looked confused. "What does your hobby have to do with your—with you being naked?"

I smiled, looking straight into her eyes as I said, "My hobby is fucking beautiful women. Fucking them and sucking them and bringing them to orgasm."

My gorgeous counselor stared for a moment, licking her soft lips. Then she took my hand and brought it to her mouth, placing my forefinger on her bottom lip. Her tongue reached out to caress it, and I slid it into her mouth. She took it eagerly, closing her lips around it as if it were a little cock.

I liked what she was doing. I liked it so much I felt a stirring in my loins, and I automatically reached out to caress her face. She closed her eyes, still sucking on my finger, and I thought I saw her nipples becoming hard and rigid under her blouse. Feeling confident now, I placed my hand between her breasts and found that she wasn't wearing a bra. I slid the hand onto her breast, caressing its softness and moving my palm in small circles around the hard nipple.

Rhonda was moaning around the finger still lodged in her slurping mouth. My own desire was mounting rapidly. I unbuttoned her blouse to expose her firm, creamy-white mounds, with nipples that stood out like little pinkies. After caressing both of them, I bowed my head to her chest, where my wanton lips and mouth eagerly enveloped her soft tits and hard nipples.

Rhonda threw her head back, moaning softly as I sucked and

licked at her tits. She then reached for my throbbing dick, un-buttoning my fly and freeing my swiftly stiffening cock. Rhonda's hand glided up and down over the thick shaft, both of us moaning now with pleasure. With my free hand I reached down to rub at her pussy through the thin material of her dark blue skirt, and as I did she started grinding her crotch against my fingers. I quickly reached beneath her skirt and pulled the fabric of her lacy panties to one side, exposing her swollen clit to my touch. My middle finger slid into my counselor's tight slit as with my fore-finger I started stroking the little man in the boat, feeling it respond by swelling and stiffening even further. She was so wet that her juices covered my palm. Sliding another finger deep inside her clutching pussy, I continued stroking her clit, rubbing it harder, and not stopping even when I heard Rhonda cry out as she approached her climax. Then she started bucking and twist-ing, grabbing my dick with both hands as she gasped out her or-gasm.

As her climax subsided I moved her to the chair I had been sit-ting in, placing her with her knees on the seat and her arms rest-ing on the back. I moved behind her and kissed her firm ass-cheeks as her juices ran down her inner thighs. My lips and tongue explored her smooth buttocks, and then I moved my mouth to her slick and shaven pussy.

I heard Rhonda moan as she felt my hot breath caress her wet-ness, and as soon as my tongue licked at her opening she cried out, "Eat me! Eat me!" The erotic effect of her words made my large black dick stiffen even further. I licked Rhonda's pussy gen-tly, wetting the creamy flesh between her thighs as I murmured, "Do you like this?"

"Ooooo, yesss!" Rhonda moaned. "Suck on my pussy, oh, God, suck it good!"

I sucked and licked that sweet love-hole until I felt I couldn't wait any longer to fuck her. I stood up, resting my hard throbbing cock on her ass. Rhonda caught her breath.

"I've never had a cock half the size of yours," she gasped out.

"So take it easy, please. We could both get busted if I make too much noise!"

"Don't worry," I said. But even as she was saying that I noticed how she raised her ass and moved it back, trying to urge the head of my dick into her cunt. I aimed my eager tool at that waiting pussy, and Rhonda reached down with both hands to spread her lips as wide as they would go. I placed my dickhead at her entrance and let her ease it inside herself by moving her ass back and down. I couldn't believe how tight she was as she took more of my pole inside. I felt her pussy muscles expand to accept more and more of my eleven inches of black meat.

I let her take it at her own speed at first, but when I realized that she wasn't going to stop, that she wanted it all, I began to thrust deeper into her. The smooth snug flesh of her pussy gripped me so tightly that sweat broke out on my body. I put my hands on her tits and braced myself by holding on to them, and soon I was hammering my rigid tool into my counselor's writhing, twisting cunt.

Rhonda was going crazy with pleasure as I put all I had into fucking her, and when she managed to take the whole of my eleven inches inside her soaking wet pussy, she screamed out, "Yes! Yes! I'm there! I'm coming! I feel it! I feel your big dick all the way deep inside me! Oh, yes! It's sooo right! Sooo damn good! I never want it to stop! Never!"

And then she was coming, exploding over and over in a series of orgasms that she told me later were the most intense she had ever had. My cock seemed to expand and then burst open as the first spasm of my eruption shook the complete length of my rod. The warm hot cream gushed out into her spasming channel, pumping so hard and deep it would probably never come out. Even before I was finishing coming Rhonda experienced yet another orgasm, which rocked her body from head to toe.

As we recovered our breath I was thinking that it was lucky no one had come along to find out why we'd been in Rhonda's office alone for the last half-hour. But a minute later there was a knock on the office door. I looked through the blinds and saw another inmate standing there with a folder in his hand. It was Rhonda's next appointment. She called out for him to wait a moment, and hastily put on her panties and straightened herself out. When I finally let him in, he looked around with a puzzled expression and said, "I smell something!"

Rhonda and I just looked at each other and tried to keep from laughing.

Now I have a regular appointment to see Rhonda every Tuesday and Friday, in addition to cleaning her office every day. On the days I clean her office, she cleans my cock, and I do the same for her pussy. On Tuesdays and Fridays we have more time, so we try out every position and variation we can think of. In the intervals between fucking and sucking each other, we are working very hard to make me eligible for parole when the time comes, so that I can enjoy my special hobby with her on the outside too.

Not to mention with Debbi, Sara, Lynn, Bette and Kim!
—*Name and address withheld*

SHE LIKES THE LOOK OF HIS TRUCK, AND SHE LIKES WHEN HE GIVES HER A FUCK

It all started one evening when my friend Brad stopped by and asked me to go shopping with him. My wife and I had just had a fight, so I was happy to get away for awhile.

After doing a little shopping Brad and I decided to have a drink to relieve the stress of the day. We stopped by a liquor store and picked up some beer, then went cruising through town.

As we passed a local singles hangout I noticed this beautiful brunette waving at us. Naturally we stopped. The girl's name was Norma, and she said she really loved my four-wheel drive truck, and wanted to know if she could have a ride in it sometime. I told her there was no time like the present, and invited her in.

She sat between Brad and me as we rode around town. Soon Brad was ready to go home, and asked if I could drop him off at his car. The problem was that his car was at my house, and I could only hope my wife wouldn't see me dropping him off with this girl in my truck. When Brad got out I took off again down the street. I noticed that Norma didn't move over into the passenger seat, but kept sitting close beside me.

She asked me if I had a girlfriend. I told her I was married, but it didn't seem to put her off. She told me she was eighteen and had a boyfriend. She still sat close to me, so at the next stop sign I decided to seize the opportunity, and I turned to her and started to kiss her. We French-kissed for about two minutes. She was very cooperative, but it must have scared her a little, because after that she said she wanted to go home.

Well, I figured I would never have to worry about her again, but I was wrong. One night while I was working around the yard I happened to see her drive by my house. She was driving slowly, as if looking to see if I was home, and when I waved to her she stopped.

She was driving a Nissan Pathfinder and was smiling as I walked up to her. We said hi, and she told me she didn't have much to do because her boyfriend was out of town for the night, and she wanted to know if I could get away for awhile. I jumped into her car and said, "Let's go."

She drove a little way out of town and parked in a secluded area under some trees. A little surprised, I asked her why she had to leave so quickly the night I kissed her. She told me that what happened had scared her a little, because she was afraid of what it might lead to. My next question was, why did she come back? Her reply was that she had been so turned on by our kissing that she figured she wanted to try again.

Well, that was definitely the sign I was looking for, so I moved closer to her and began to kiss her. Her tongue responded to mine, and soon her breathing was getting heavier and we were French-kissing with great enthusiasm.

I moved my mouth to her ear and then to her neck, kissing and licking, and was rewarded with soft moans of pleasure. We played around for some time before I placed my hand on her breast. Oh my God, she had the greatest tits I've ever had the pleasure of fondling! But after a minute she moved my hand away. I looked her straight in the eyes and immediately pulled her sweater and bra up over her tits, then began to kiss and suck on her wonderful nipples. Any initial inhibitions on her part were soon swept away by her desire, which she expressed with murmured comments of pure satisfaction.

I was so hot and hard I was ready to explode, and I couldn't control myself any longer. I began to place soft, wet kisses from her tits down her stomach to the waistband of the shorts she was wearing. But when I tried to open the shorts she grabbed my hand, saying that no one but her boyfriend was allowed to touch her there. So I simply placed my hand on her crotch and started to rub very gently. Norma was too worked up to resist, and she spread her legs to give me better access as she began to squirm with pleasure. She was so hot I could feel her pussy juices soaking through her shorts. I asked her to remove her shorts so I could lick her pussy, but at that point she drew the line and told me she had to go home.

I was very disappointed, and tried to get her to give me a blowjob, or at least a handjob, because I needed to get off so badly. But she wouldn't. So I sighed and told her that I really wanted to make love to her, and that if she ever wanted to go that far she should let me know.

A few weeks went by, and then, to my delight, Norma called me and asked if she could see me again that night. I suggested she stop by my office after work, and then I called my wife and made up some excuse for being out that evening.

Norma arrived at my office right on time. I met her at the front door and invited her to see our new showroom area. As we walked around the showroom looking at all the products, I asked her if she was sure about her decision. I mean this girl was a total knockout, and as excited as I was, I didn't want her to do anything she'd regret. Norma stared into my eyes and told me she hadn't been able to think about anything else since I made that offer a few weeks ago.

She looked absolutely radiant, and I couldn't wait any longer. I moved close to her and our lips touched. Her body pressed close to mine, and I knew without a shadow of a doubt that this was going to be a night to remember. I slowly kissed her neck and gently nibbled her earlobes, and the low soft moans that I remembered began to escape her mouth.

After a few moments I unbuttoned her blouse and opened her bra to unleash her 36D tits from their confines. I held these breasts in my hands and buried my face in them. Norma seemed to be in a trance of pleasure as I sucked and licked her nipples. I slowly kissed her stomach and inched my way down to her shorts. She made no resistance as I unbuttoned the shorts and slid them down around her ankles. I slipped off her shoes and pulled her shorts off over her feet. After another kiss or two on her stomach I slowly removed her panties. Then I just knelt there looking at her perfectly manicured bush. My heart was pounding so hard I could barely hear myself think.

Norma just stood there waiting for my next move. Still kneeling in front of her, I looked up into her eyes and asked her if she would like me to lick her pussy. She told me that her boyfriend had never done that for her, and that she had always wanted to know what it was like. So who was I to disappoint her?

Moving her legs apart, I placed my tongue on her wonderfully wet pussy and began to lick up her juices. Norma's knees almost buckled when my tongue touched her clit, and she moaned loudly with approval. I licked and sucked her for quite a while, until she told me gasping that she wanted to lie down. She positioned herself on the floor on her back, and I knelt down in front of her. I spread her legs, bending them at the knee to allow me perfect access to her dripping pussy. Leaning forward I began to eat that sweet twat once again. I couldn't get enough of the way she tasted.

Finally I had to satisfy the raging desire in my loins. I positioned myself above her and French-kissed her, allowing her a taste of her own juices. At this point Norma was going wild. She looked at me and told me how much she needed to be fucked. "Please," she begged, "please take off your pants and fuck me hard and fast." I couldn't get my pants off fast enough. I lay on top of her and asked her again if she wanted to be fucked. She said "I don't just *want* to be fucked. I *need* to be fucked!" And she grabbed on to my hard dick and positioned it at the entrance to her soaking wet pussy. "Please," she said. "I need to feel this hard thing inside me."

I rubbed the head of my dick against her opening, teasing her just a little bit more, until she was practically begging me to put it in.

Slowly I inched my way into her, feeling the warmth of her so tightly wrapped around me. I pumped slowly at the beginning, enjoying every second of pleasure, but Norma asked if I could go faster. Immediately I began to speed up my rhythm and she shook her head from side to side, moaning, "That's it, fuck me. Oh God, fuck me. Oh yes, that's it, fuck me harder!"

At one point Norma asked me to suck her tits, but I was so into fucking her hard and fast that I couldn't position myself to give her breasts the attention they needed. So she began to massage them herself. Soon her moans and gasps changed to short, deep groans, and I knew she was about to have an orgasm. I continued my rapid, steady pace, and within seconds she put her hands on my shoulders and cried out that she was coming. Her fingers dug deeply into my skin, her groaning loud and irregular. I knew she was right at the edge, and I pushed extra hard to help heighten her explosion. Suddenly I felt her pussy tighten, and she came with so much force that it was all I could do to stay inside her.

I looked into her eyes and she smiled at me as her orgasm subsided. I moved down to her come-soaked crotch to get a taste of her juices. I ran my tongue upward from her asshole to her pussy to lick up her come. It was wonderful. She tasted so good! I continued to lick her opening until she asked if I could please fuck her some more.

I got into position and buried my hard dick inside her again, and this time she raised her head and began to suck on my nipples. At that point I think my dick grew another inch. My sensations intensified still more, and I knew my own orgasm was approaching fast. Norma placed her hands on my chest and began to rub my nipples between her index finger and thumb. I couldn't take it anymore. When I told her I was going to come, she rubbed my nipples harder and said she wanted to feel my jism deep inside her. Oh what a feeling! My heart was pounding a mile a minute, and my dick was pumping in and out of her pussy, and still I was trying to hold back in order to savor the moment as long as possible.

"Wait," Norma said. "Don't come yet. I want to make you come in a very special way." So I stopped, exerting all my control, with my hard dick buried deep inside her. She then began to contract and relax her pussy muscles. I felt a pulling sensation, as though my dick was being sucked in and out of her tight hole. It was absolutely fantastic! Within seconds my orgasm had peaked and I exploded into her. It felt like I was coming harder than I ever had before. Finally I collapsed on top of her with a feeling of total satisfaction.

After awhile we sat up and caressed each other, expressing our appreciation of this tremendous mutual experience. Norma told me that it was the first time she had ever had an orgasm, and also the first time she had tasted her own come. She said her boyfriend never took the time to let her really enjoy sex. She wanted to know if we could see each other again real soon. I told her I couldn't wait to see her again. Then she lowered her head to my still hard and dripping dick and stuck it into her mouth. She licked me clean and then said, with a grin, "How about right now?"

I had to remind her that I was a married man, and needed to get home before my wife got suspicious. We finally got dressed and passionately kissed again before saying good night.

Norma and I have made love several times since that night, even though she recently got married to her boyfriend. She says he has his good qualities and she loves him very much. It's true that he isn't as sensitive to her sexual needs as she'd like, but she says as long as she can go on having great sex with me, she doesn't really mind a bit.—Y.B., *Amarillo, Texas*

HE WAS NEW ON THE JOB BUT A REDHEADED COWORKER BROKE HIM IN REAL GOOD

My wife and I have been married for twenty years and have two children. My wife is a very attractive lady, but is pretty straightforward when it comes to sex. She's not big on experimentation in the bedroom. But recently I did get the opportunity to expand my sexual horizons, though not with my wife.

It began when I took a position with a new company. One of the women working there was a petite redhead named Ronnie, who had a personality that overwhelmed me. Over the course of several months Ronnie began to spend more and more time in the department I was in charge of. Usually our conversations would start out with small talk, such as what we did over the weekend, but almost always they eventually veered toward sex. We were both married, but Ronnie seemed to be struggling with her marriage, and she confided in me enough to let me know that she no longer enjoyed having sex with her husband. In fact, she made it quite clear that her life was in need of some excitement, and a few times she came close to asking straight out if I would like to fuck her.

There was definitely an attraction between us, and since we were both unsatisfied with our current partners, it seemed obvious that what we both needed was some raw untamed sex to help soothe the frustrations we were experiencing.

One Thursday evening I stayed late at the office in order to try and get caught up on a few projects. I thought I would be the only one there, but around eight o'clock I heard the office door open and footsteps approaching the entrance to my department. I looked up, and to my surprise there was Ronnie. She held up a four-pack of wine coolers and asked if I was thirsty.

We sat and talked for awhile, and Ronnie told me she was supposed to be out on the town with her girlfriends, but had decided to cancel at the last minute. She asked me when I was expected home, and I told her not until later. Ronnie looked at me with her beautiful green eyes and asked me if I wanted to go for a drive and talk. It sounded like a great chance for us to be alone, so I agreed.

We took my car, and it wasn't long till we were driving along an old quiet road, just talking about everything. Suddenly Ronnie asked me to stop the car. I stopped in the middle of the road and looked over at her.

Ronnie took a breath and then asked me if I had ever cheated on my wife. I told her that I had given it some thought a few times, but up to that point I never had. Then she looked at me and asked me to kiss her. I was so excited I could hardly breathe. I leaned over and pressed my lips to hers, feeling a bolt of electricity shoot down my body and into my dick. I pulled away and looked at her. She asked me to do it again, and this time our tongues went wild and my heart was beating like a racehorse. The next thing I knew there were headlights coming up behind us, and I hastily put the car in gear and drove off.

Ronnie looked at me and told me that she'd had two orgasms

while we were kissing. I couldn't believe what I was hearing. She went on to say that she was so incredibly horny that if I didn't pull over and fuck her, she was going to remove her pants and finger-fuck herself right there in the car. Before I could find a place to pull over, she had her pants and panties off, with her feet propped up on the dashboard and her legs spread wide apart. She placed her hand between her legs and inserted her index finger into her pussy. In a moment she was moaning and panting.

I couldn't stand any more of this. I pulled the car onto the shoulder of the road and shut off the engine. In a flash I was totally naked.

Ronnie pulled her soaking wet fingers from her pussy and boldly stuck them in my mouth. The taste and smell of her juices almost made me shoot my load on the car seat. Then she leaned down to my crotch and began licking and sucking on my throbbing cock. She paused to look up at me with a smile and tell me how much she loved to suck cock, and how horny it made her.

After about ten minutes of what had to be the best mouth job I've ever had, Ronnie repositioned herself in her seat and told me it was her turn to be satisfied. I moved over and began kissing her full moist lips, then slid my mouth slowly down her neck. She quickly unbuttoned her blouse and unhooked her bra to expose two small but wonderful breasts. Her nipples were hard and ready to be sucked, but to my delight she pushed my mouth away from her tits and down toward her wet and waiting pussy. I slowly spread her legs and touched my tongue to her opening. "Oh my," she moaned. "Oh my, oh, that feels so good!" And after a few more licks she was coming again.

As soon as she caught her breath, Ronnie said she needed my hard cock in her pussy. I lay down on my back on the seat and she straddled me, reaching between her legs to grab my cock and shove it into her pussy. I could feel every inch of my prick being consumed by that hungry hole as she began to ride up and down on my shaft.

Then suddenly she pulled away and moved to lean over the

back of the seat, legs wide apart and ass sticking out. This was a fucking dream come true. I assumed a position behind her and began to fuck her doggie-style with everything I had in me. Several times I was on the verge of coming, but I stopped to put my tongue in her dripping pussy before entering her love channel again. I couldn't get enough of her.

Finally Ronnie placed her fingers on her clit and began bucking like crazy, coming with a force that I had never experienced. She drove me right over the edge, and I came so hard that I thought my balls were coming out through my penis. After I shot my load deep inside her pussy she slid down to my crotch and licked my cock clean.

Since that night we have helped each other with our sexual frustrations many times. For example, one night when we were in my car again, fucking doggie-style, I removed my dick from her pussy and began licking her asshole. Ronnie went crazy, telling me how good it felt, and how she had always wondered why her husband wouldn't lick her there.

I put my cock back in her cunt and began a slow rhythmic in-and-out motion, and then I surprised her again. I licked my finger to get it nice and wet and began probing her ass with it at the same time that I was pumping her pussy full of dick. She gasped and moaned, and was soon begging me to stick my cock into her ass. I wondered if she had ever had anal sex before. I knew damn well I hadn't, but I'd always wanted to try it out. Now was the time.

I pulled my cock out of her cunt and bent down to lick her asshole again in order to get it all lubed up. Finally I placed my throbbing dick at the entrance to her anal cavity and slowly began to slide it in. It was slow going, and it took almost twenty minutes to get all of my meat into her, but all the time she was begging me to put it in deeper. As soon as I got it all in she pleaded with me to fuck her hard and fast. After five minutes of slamming my meat into her ass we both came so hard that we collapsed on the car seat, holding onto each other until we had regained our composure.

Wouldn't you know that after I got home, took a shower and went to bed, my wife wanted to ride the pony. Actually it didn't take long for me to get hard again, as I was still thinking of the fabulous sex I had had with Ronnie only an hour earlier.

Ronnie and I no longer see each other, because we felt it wasn't worth the risk of our spouses finding us out and turning a great sexual experience into a nightmare. But I'll always be grateful to her for opening up my sexual horizons, and I believe she feels the same.—G.F., Charleston, South Carolina

ONE MAN'S BOXER REBELLION IS PROOF THAT PANTIES ARE DANDY

There's nothing I like more than the feeling of female flesh surrounding my cock. A nice warm, tight pussy, a hot mouth or a pair of firm tits are my dick's idea of a dream vacation. But I have my special tastes too, my favorite of which is the wonderful world of women's panties. As a matter of fact, I'm writing this letter wearing a fabulous pair of snug, red lace bikini panties that cradle my cock like a second skin.

Since the life-changing evening two years ago when I first tried on a pair of my wife Betty's panties, they are all I've worn under my slacks, jeans and shorts. Whether at work, shopping or out partying with the boys, no matter what I'm wearing on the outside, beneath the surface my life has been one continuous panty party. The only time I don't wear them is when I'm bodybuilding or jogging—and that's only because I don't want to get my silky, frilly undergarments all sweaty.

I thought my wife would be reluctant to fulfill my desire to slip into a pair of her panties, but I was wrong. She must've read my mind that night when I looked longingly inside her underwear drawer, wishing I could slip into some of her finery. I'd worn panties quite often in my earlier days, but gave it up when I met Betty. I hadn't realized how much I missed the delicious feeling until that night when I peered into her drawer. I'd never told her of my earlier affection for panties, so I was surprised when she asked if I wanted to model a pair of hers. I'll never forget them. They were simple pink satin ones with tiny embroidered roses, and putting them on was thrilling.

Once Betty saw the raging hard-on I popped when she helped me slip out of my boxers and into her panties, a smile came to her face. From her lingerie drawer she pulled out pair after pair of silk, cotton and lace panties and laid them out on the bed for me to try on.

I think she was planning to have me give her a private fashion show, but it didn't exactly work out that way. My cock was night-stick hard from the moment Betty slid that very first pair of satiny pinks up my leg and into place. Betty saw the advantages of this right away. She asked me to turn around so she could see my ass in the panties. When I completed the turn, she knelt down and began to fondle my behind without removing the panties. She happened to be wearing panties too, and there was no mistaking the wet spot in the crotch of the pair she had on. Betty nibbled at my cock through the satin, getting the fabric all wet with a combination of her saliva and my precome. She freed my cock and took it into her mouth, bathing me with her warm tongue. I creamed almost instantly, soaking her gums with a helping of batter so huge it took her several gulps to swallow it all.

My hard-on didn't go away after I came. If anything, my dick was even more rigid than before. I lay back on the bed and Betty sat astride me. We were still both wearing our panties, which we pulled aside just enough to allow my cock to sink into her sopping well. She rode me hard, grunting and playing with her clitoris. I could feel her cunt muscles clenching my prick, just as I could feel the satin panties clinging to the skin of my thighs and ass. I erupted into her like Old Faithful, and kept drilling upward until I'd brought her to an explosive orgasm as well.

And still my erection would not quit! We fucked all night, with me trying on a new pair of panties after each climax. By the time morning arrived we were exhausted, but more satisfied than we ever thought possible. Needless to say, I haven't worn boxers since.

It's amazing how much more intensely erotic our lives have become since that night. Before we got married, Betty had no idea that I once wore panties. But now they're a very big part of our fun. We both wear the same size, so we can shop together and pick out pairs we know we'll both enjoy wearing. I feel very comfortable going into a department store, with or without her, and taking my time to find just the right style and size. Often I'll even ask one of the pretty sales clerks for help. When she realizes the panties are for me, she smiles and helps me pick out just the sort of thing she knows I'll like.

Once a week Betty shaves the hair on my balls and trims the rest of my bristly pubes so that the panties fit just right. She says that nothing turns her on more than the sight of my stiff log outlined in the smooth panty fabric. Over the past few months I've also started to wear sheer-to-the-waist panty hose. At first I just bought a pair on a lark, but I suspect that soon they'll be as big a turn-on for us as the panties.—B.R., *San Diego, California*

Part Two

~

Letters to
Penthouse X

A HUBBY LEARNS THE HARD WAY:
IT'S ALL IN THE DETAILS, DEARIE

I am writing you this letter to tell you about a very beautiful sexy lady: my wife, Norma. She and I have been together for just short of eleven years, and married for eight. Norma stands five feet seven inches tall and weighs one hundred seventeen pounds. She is thirty-two years old, and her body measures a stunning 34B-24-33. She is lean and firm and has always had a voracious appetite for sex.

My beautiful bride turns heads everywhere with her hot body, long auburn hair, radiant smile and dazzling brown eyes.

When Norma and I first met we quickly learned that we both loved to suck and fuck a lot. We spent the next two years trying to ride each other to a standstill. Then Norma got pregnant, and our son was born. There went our red-hot sex life. Eventually, we came out of our slump and we began to discuss our fantasies. Norma had had sexual relationships with a fairly large number of men before we met, and it never failed to send me over the edge of horniness when she whispered all the sordid details in my ear while we were fucking.

And when I say details, believe me, I mean just that. Norma was quite explicit when she told me how she had sucked some guy's cock and swallowed his load, or how she let another guy fuck her repeatedly, just because his cock felt so good. My two personal favorite stories were the one about the married man she fucked and sucked in the backseat in his driveway, while his wife was asleep in the house, and the one about the day she fucked and blew two different guys just a few hours apart. These and other stories about her pick-ups and boyfriends never failed to fuel me to mind-bending orgasms.

So it seemed only natural to suggest that she help me act out my favorite fantasy—watching her fuck and suck another man's cock right in front of me. She consented, and we took out an ad in a swingers' magazine. We received quite a large response. It turned out that there were many men out there who wanted to bang my hot little wife. Every time we got a letter from a guy with a photo showing his hard cock, we would fuck like crazy. We'd talk about that guy fucking her, or how she would suck that cock like a Popsicle.

Norma decided on a young guy named Dirk for our little fuck party. Dirk was twenty-five years old. He turned out to be a handsome fellow with a thick, eight-inch schlong. Just looking at a picture of it made Norma drool. My own cock measures nine inches, but it is not nearly as thick as Dirk's. We contacted him and arranged a meeting at our place. We all got better acquainted over drinks on a Friday evening, and of course the conversation turned to sex. We explained to Dirk that watching was my fantasy and that we had chosen him to help us fulfill it.

Dirk said he was more than willing to help out. I said, "Well, all right. Let's get this party started." I took Norma in my arms and kissed her deeply. I paused only to reassure her that I loved her very much and that I was very proud of what she was about to do.

At this point, Norma took off her blouse and her bra to display those lovely firm tits and large nipples of hers. This took place on our sun deck in the backyard, where any of our neighbors could have seen her. She sat back down in her chair, freed my throbbing cock from my jeans and deep-throated the entire length. Upon seeing this, Dirk took out his cock and grabbed Norma's tits. When he did this, she turned her attention to him. She swallowed his prick and stroked mine.

Norma alternated between our cocks out on the deck for about ten minutes. Then she announced that she needed some good, hard fucking. We all retired to the privacy of the bedroom. Norma lay down on the bed and spread her luscious thighs to expose her extremely wet pussy. Even though I knew how badly Norma needed to be fucked, I could not resist diving between her legs and licking her to orgasm. When I had done that, I stood up and told Dirk, "You're the guest. By all means, fuck Norma first!" He was more than willing to comply. He could not get his cock into Norma's cunt fast enough for his tastes—or hers.

I watched in awed fascination as, inch by inch, he slid his fat prick into my wife's lovely pussy. After only a few strokes she was whimpering and begging him to fuck her harder. Dirk responded by placing Norma's legs over his shoulders and slamming his prong in and out of her at a frenzied pace. After a few minutes of this, Norma came with a shriek that could have wakened the dead. When she had settled down, she got on her hands and knees, turned her head over her shoulder, and told Dirk, "Give it to me doggie-style." Doggie-style is Norma's favorite position, and Dirk seemed to like it too. He fed her a lot of cock from behind, and in no time at all she screamed in ecstasy as yet another orgasm ripped through her body.

This electrified Dirk. He stiffened and growled like a bulldog as he pumped a steaming load of semen into Norma's throbbing, gushing twat. After Norma caught her breath, and as Dirk lay panting alongside her, she rolled onto her back and opened her legs. "Come on, hubby," she said. "Give me some of that home cookin'."

I had been overcome with lust at the sight of my wife on her back with another man's load dripping from her gaping pussy. I could not get my cock in her cunt fast enough. I grabbed her ass and raised it as I plunged my massive hard-on into her tight, slick pussy. I fucked her slowly at first, savoring the feel of sloppy seconds.

"Did you like watching me come all over Dirk's cock?" Norma asked.

"Yes," I said, and I began fucking harder.

"Can you feel his come in my pussy, baby? Does it feel good?" she cooed.

I moaned, "Yes," again, and started a series of deep, hard lunges. Norma's pussy was so wet she handled my deepest thrusts with no problem at all. As she built up to another orgasm, she returned my thrusts. Then wave after wave of pleasure washed over her and she again wailed out her climax. That triggered my own climax, and I shot a torrent of white come into her overflowing pussy.

After that, the three of us had another beer as we rested for what we knew would be another round. But soon we were hard at it again. Over the next four hours we fucked and sucked in every combination we could think of. By the time it was over, Norma had been fucked eleven times. Both she and our guest were exhausted. But Norma is a trooper. Somehow, she found the energy to do me one more time after Dirk left. Our sex life got better and wilder from that night on, but that's another story.—*J.J., Plymouth, Massachusetts*

ONLY THE WALL OF HER PUSSY
SEPARATED THEIR COCKS

In my thirty years I have enjoyed two threesomes that included me and two women, as well as one semi-orgy involving three couples. But the most memorable threesomes I ever experienced involved my best friend and his wife.

For many years, Malcolm had the hots for Ellen, whom he eventually married. But it was I who first went with Ellen—for about a year, when we were going to the university. She was an enthusiastic and enjoyable fuck, but for various reasons we broke up. And when we parted, I told her that my buddy Malcolm was really attracted to her, and I told Malcolm to go ahead and call her. Within weeks they were a couple, and within a year I was best man at their wedding. After we all graduated from the university, I started a career in government. Malcolm and Ellen, however, decided to see the world.

They were in London when I got a call from them asking if I could visit them for New Year's Day. Something in their tone of voice told me that this was a trip I would not want to miss. So that New Year's Eve I found myself in a jet high over the Atlantic on my way to London.

When I arrived at Heathrow I was met by both of them. As Malcolm shook my hand, Ellen gave me a passionate French-kiss. With what seemed whirlwind speed I found myself in the back seat of Malcolm's car with Ellen, and quite pleased to have her swabbing my tonsils and groping me. I slipped my hand down her pants and discovered that she wore no panties, and that her pussy was soaking wet. By the time we got to their apartment, Ellen and I were half-naked. Fortunately it was dark, so no one noticed as we stumbled from the car into their ground-floor flat. As I dropped my luggage on the floor I was finally able to catch my breath and ask, "What gives?"

Malcolm was grinning from ear to ear as he explained that several months earlier he had lost a bet. The penalty, he said, was that he became obliged to fulfill any fantasy that Ellen requested. This had turned out to be taking on two guys at the same time. "So who better to ask than my best man?" Malcolm asked.

I couldn't argue with his logic, especially with the fair Ellen now lying spread-eagled on their bed, madly finger-fucking herself.

"Are you guys going to talk all night? Or is someone going to fuck me?" she asked as she licked her fingers. I quickly stripped off the rest of my clothes and buried my face in her sopping-wet pussy. As I did this, Malcolm also undressed and stuck his cock in his wife's mouth. He groaned as she began feverishly sucking it.

In a few minutes my face was covered with pussy juice and my cock was dripping pre-come. I couldn't wait any longer, and Ellen was shouting for some cock. So with one smooth stroke I buried my prick in that familiar twat. As I thrust into her honey-pot, Malcolm fucked her mouth. This continued until I felt her pussy convulse. Ellen came with shouts of relief. Her excitement triggered my own orgasm, as well as Malcolm's. But that first orgasm barely took the edge off our lust. With come dripping from both her pussy and her mouth, Ellen got on all fours and asked me to slide around for a blowjob. This time, she sucked me off while Malcolm enjoyed sloppy seconds. She came several more times before she pushed my prick away from her mouth. I remained on my back as she pulled her pussy off Malcolm's twitching cock and impaled herself on mine.

Malcolm wasted no time. He grabbed some lubricant and began buttering up Ellen's tight, puckered asshole. She moaned in delight. Then, as my cock was buried deep in her pussy, I felt the weirdest sensation ever. It took me a second to realize that it was Malcolm fucking her up the ass! Only the wall between her pussy and anus separated our cocks as she rode both of them to another series of mind-blowing orgasms.

Ellen took us every way she could think of that night, as well as every night for the entire two weeks of my vacation with them. When it was all over and I was due to head home, Ellen admitted that she only had one regret—that there hadn't been a third guy, so she could have had all three love holes full of cock at once!—R.W., Detroit, Michigan

COOL WHIP IN THE TENT HELPED THEM
HEAT UP THE WHOLE NEIGHBORHOOD

My boyfriend George and I had been living together for almost a year when we put up a tent in the backyard so that we could have some privacy from my two teenage sons. I can't tell you how many times I came in that tent. George was sure I woke up the neighborhood now and then, screaming with delight. But hell, it was hard to be quiet when George was munching away on my pussy. Lord, did he know what he was doing.

Our neighbor Christine had an eighteen-year-old daughter, Meredith. When Christine had to go into the hospital for surgery, she asked me to keep an eye on Meredith for a week, until she came home. Meredith wasn't your average eighteen-year-old. She had grown up quickly after her dad died of AIDS. She had a body that I would die for. Her perky tits were firm, and it was easy to see through her small lacy tops that her nipples were as hard as pebbles. I tried to think of her as a kid, but when she bent over in those tight little shorts of hers, you could see her dark bush hairs straggling out.

I had always had as much a thing for brunettes as George, and I know George had nasty thoughts about Meredith from time to time. She was really affectionate, and she would always wrap her arms around George's neck. More than once I noticed his cock bulge through his Levi's. At first I was jealous, but what could I say? She made me hot too. She was a sexy little thing. She definitely was a tease. She knew how people looked her up and down. She enjoyed wearing tight bell bottoms so we could see her sexy ass.

One night George had to work late, and Meredith decided to take a shower. Since I don't have any locks on my bathroom doors and have two teenage sons, she asked if I would come into the bathroom to keep her company. I didn't mind. We lit the candles and turned up the boom box, and Meredith turned on the water. I tried not to stare as she undressed, but with two mirrors in there it was hard to avoid ogling her hot body. Unexpectedly, after she got in and pulled the shower curtain, George came in the bathroom. I signaled him to be quiet. He glanced over to see what I was staring at, and saw Meredith's sexy silhouette through the curtain. He took off his clothes, and I stripped in a hurry.

Meredith asked, "Could you wash my back? I have soap in my eyes."

I whispered to George to be patient. He sat on the can and watched as I entered the shower. I washed Meredith's back, and let my hands linger on her ass. I was waiting for her to pull away, but she didn't. She just purred, "Please don't stop, that feels so good." I pulled her closer. I liked the way my wet titties felt against her young body. Meredith didn't notice when George climbed in with us—possibly because by then I was sliding my hands down to her tiny waist and lowering my other hand to her furry hot snatch. I felt George's boner as he pulled me closer. I turned Meredith around and kissed her sexy full lips. I had never kissed a woman before, and I was nervous. To my surprise she not only didn't push me away; she wrapped her arms around me and pulled me closer. Only then did she feel George's hairy strong body behind me. She seemed startled at first, but soon was grinning ear to ear. I knew this was going to be an experience for the three of us.

Meredith got out of the shower. I turned and grabbed George's pulsating cock. It got bigger as I stroked it. He asked me if I was sure I knew what I wanted. "Oh yes," I said. Tonight I was gonna have it all! The three of us dressed, and went out to the tent. I made Meredith comfortable and I thought of some things that would make the evening fun. I went in the house and to the refrigerator, and got out some Cool Whip, a can of pineapple rings and a few surprises. George was again naked when I got to the tent, smoking a cigarette and watching Meredith play with herself. She had her nightie on but I could see by her moist pussy hairs that she had forgotten her panties. I quietly removed the nightie, and placed a pineapple ring on each of her titties, and Cool Whip on each nipple. I asked George if he was ready for a snack. He reminded me that he disliked Cool Whip. I knew that! I leaned over and sucked all the Cool Whip off of her nipples. I loved feeling the nipples stiffen and grow in my mouth. I lay back and let him enjoy the full, beautiful titties. I got off watching my man satisfy this hot little tease. (George loves pineapple.) I knew she had already let some immature little boys screw her, but I didn't think she'd ever fucked a man as experienced as George.

Many a night when George was going down on me, I had longed to have someone watch him make me come. Now I asked George if he could teach Meredith how to eat pussy by example. He didn't hesitate. He spread her legs wide and gave me a good view. How he ate and licked her! She squirmed, and as I saw her eyes roll back in her head, I knew she was satisfied. I knew the level she had reached—I had been there dozens of times.

It was hot watching my man make a woman climax over and over again. He was good at it, and I was proud of him. After a while, I lay next to Meredith's trembling body, and George placed the pineapples on my 42DD tits. He put Cool Whip on my nipples and my belly button and clit as well.

This all excited Meredith greatly. "Honey," George cooed in her ear, "let's see if you can make my old lady come!" Meredith sucked lasciviously at my breasts. As she chewed the pineapple, the juice dripped on my tender nipples. George licked the sweet juice off. Meredith ran her tongue down my body and lapped up the Cool Whip. When I felt her warm breath close to my snatch, I watched George beat his meat. His juices flowed onto her sexy belly. I licked every drop of come off her quivering body.

I knew now that this would be one of my very favorite weeks. I would teach Meredith how to suck cock. I loved the taste of my man's come, and I was looking forward to licking his come out of her gorgeous snatch. I could have the best of two worlds—her juices mixed with George's hot sperm. But right now, I was full of wild passion. I wanted to fuck. I pulled George on top of me and pointed my legs to the ceiling. George fucked me slowly and occasionally pulled his pecker out of my wet cunt to stroke it over my clit. Meredith came close and licked first his cock, then my clit, back and forth. George and I both got off watching her show. She learned so quickly that it occurred to me that she might soon teach me a few tricks.

I bet the old man who lived in back was busting his nuts, listening to the three of us moaning and groaning, naked in the tent. May his wife get lucky for a change and get some dick! We like to think we help our neighbors' sex lives.—*D.C., Plainview, Texas*

A GOOD WOMAN IS HARD TO FIND,
BUT TWO ARE EVEN BETTER!

I'm one of those women who find the female form attractive. I'd never investigated whether I was bisexual or not, but I've always known that I liked looking at women and wondered how it would be to make love to one. I also wanted to give my husband a treat by realizing his fantasy of being in bed with two women at once. So I became a woman with a mission, subtly looking for that one woman who would do the right thing.

Well, I found her. Her name was Barbie, and she was perfect. Both my husband and I like women who look like women— women with nice, full breasts and great, wide nipples; women with nice little asses; women who are pretty and sexy; women who smell good and like to fuck. I found all this in Barbie. I'd known her for six months. I had to work closely with her and I was in a good position to become quite aware of how attractive she was. She was my assistant, and I was training her. She was gorgeous, about five-two, with a honey-colored complexion, lips that looked like they were ever-ready to suck anything that came along, the nicest pair of breasts I'd seen in a long time and a cute little ass that she showed off in tight, short skirts. Barbie wore the kind of bra that made her look like she wasn't wearing a damn thing. How often I had wanted to reach out and fondle her tits. But I didn't want to lose a good assistant by making a pass at her.

I knew she was single and lived alone. She didn't have a

boyfriend and she didn't mind working late. It was on one of those late nights at the office that I found out some delightful things about Barbie. She was working on a layout at the desk, and I was leaning over her shoulder, explaining how I wanted it to look. My breasts were level with her face, and as she turned around to ask me a question, her lips grazed a nipple. The touch thrilled me, but I pretended to take it in stride. I answered Barbie's questions as if nothing had happened. Then I went back to my desk, trying not to think about Barbie's mouth on my nipple. I was getting wet just thinking about it. I could not keep my mind on my work.

At last I told Barbie to call it a night. I stood up, stretching the kinks out of my back. As I did so, I felt two hands cupping my breasts. To my surprise and delight, Barbie was rubbing, pinching, and tugging on my nipples. I could feel her breasts pushing themselves into my back, and before I knew it I was rubbing my ass against her pussy. Damn, she felt good! Neither of us said a word, but our actions were loud and clear. I felt one hand leave my hardened nipple as she pushed my skirt up over my hips and started rubbing my outthrust bottom. She breathed hard into my ear, and moaned about how good I felt and how wet she was going to make me. And wet I was—squishy wet. In a trance, I lay forward over my desk, and she sat in my chair. Her flushed face was level with my bare bottom and hot, wet pussy.

And then she gave me a sensation I'd never had before. She started licking and kissing my ass all over, nibbling on it, stroking it with her tongue. She was driving me wild! She spread my asscheeks with her hands and licked the crease, as well as my rosebud asshole. She stuck her tongue where I'd never felt a tongue before. While she reamed me with her tongue, her fingers were all over my pussy. Her thumb was inside me and her middle finger was stroking my clit.

By this time I was begging her to eat me but she kept right on fingering my pussy and licking my ass. I knew she was going to make me come. She felt so good! I kept rubbing my ass on her face and it seemed that the more I did that, the more she liked it. I was loving it! Never before had someone licked me like she was licking me, with her tongue in my ass and her fingers in my pussy. It felt so, so good. "Oh Barbie, do it! I love it, please make me come!" I cried.

She lengthened her tongue strokes and began licking me from slit to asshole, all the while moaning and sucking up the juice flowing from my pussy. "I knew you'd taste good," she panted. "I've wanted a taste of you for weeks!"

Barbie started licking up the juices that had started to run down my legs. Every time she'd lick my inner thigh, she'd dart her tongue between the lips of my juicy pussy, scooping up my wetness. I could hear her making these sucking and licking sounds. Just listening to her was making me hot! Her fingers were rubbing and stroking my clit. Then she rolled my clit between them. I felt my legs quiver. I knew I was going to come any second.

That was some of the best oral sex I'd ever had, and I wanted Barbie to know it. I had to find out if she would be the one I would invite over to my house. I wanted her to come over and play with my husband and me. I knew I had to say something. This woman had just devoured me. How did she know I'd be receptive to that kind of thing? I turned around to ask just that, but all I could say was, "Ohh." Barbie was sitting in my chair, short skirt hiked up around her waist, one hand going to town between her legs. Speechless, I watched mesmerized as Barbie toyed with her pussy. I could see the glistening come on her fingers. Barbie watched me as I watched her. I was getting more turned on by the minute, and I could feel myself getting weak in the knees. I wanted to push my fingers inside her. I wanted to fuck her and suck on her clit at the same time.

Before I realized what I was doing, I had reached over and put my hand between the hot moist lips of her pussy. I slid my fingers all over her velvety softness, feeling the heat of her body. I slid my fingers slowly back and forth within her pussy. I wanted to feel her come on my fingers, and I knew just what would do it. As I fucked her with one hand, I used the fingers of the other to stroke Barbie's clit. She sat with her legs wide open, offering me every bit of herself. She wanted it as much as I wanted to give it to her. I put my fingers inside her, spreading all the sweet love juice between her ass-cheeks and around the dusky rose winking at me. I wanted her well lubricated for what I was going to do. I buried my face in that juicy pussy, sucking and licking and rolling my tongue all over her clit as I pumped my finger in and out of her nice, puckered tight asshole.

Barbie went wild, grinding her pussy in my face. The position was perfect. I'd stretch out my tongue and her love button would be right on it. Then I'd stroke her clit, ending up with my tongue right at the opening of her pussy. I began licking and stroking and fucking her with my tongue and finger. She tasted so good! I had pussy all over my face. The taste and scent of her was driving me crazy! I sucked her clit into my mouth, flicking her clit with my tongue. Barbie's body tensed. I stuck my tongue deep into her pussy, and she trembled with pleasure as she came in my mouth. Then I held her until the trembling stopped.

Barbie agreed to come home with me. As I drove, I told her what I wanted us to do with my husband. A slow smile spread across her face as she looked at me. "Well?" I said, "what do you say?"

"As long as I can have more of you, let's do it!"

We pulled into the driveway and got out of the car. I watched Barbie as she walked up the driveway. I liked the way her ass moved, and I knew that Tony wouldn't be able to take his eyes off of her.

We heard music as we walked in. "Tony, I'm home!" I called. "Come downstairs, there's someone here I'd like you to meet." I watched Tony as he came down the stairs. He is tall and good-looking, with brown hair, nice eyes and a quick smile. He and Barbie would get along just fine.

Barbie asked to use the bathroom and as she passed me she

squeezed my breast. Tony was sitting on the sofa, sipping his drink. "Where'd you find her?" he asked.

"She's my new assistant," I answered. "I told you about her." Barbie came into the room and we sat down on either side of my turned-on husband. "Tony, close your eyes," I said. "I've got a surprise for you. Keep them closed, you can only open them when I tell you." I motioned for Barbie to take off her clothes. "Okay Tony, you can open your eyes now!"

When he opened his eyes, they had something to bulge out about. Barbie had placed her pussy just inches from his face. Surprise! "What's going on?" he asked.

"You'll see," I said. I grabbed one of his hands and Barbie grabbed the other. I led the way to the bedroom. By the time we got there, Tony's cock was straining his jeans. I unzipped them, made sure I had a firm grip on his briefs and pulled them off. Then I took off his T-shirt. His cock was standing straight out. Barbie crawled over and gave the head of his cock a wet lick. Then she sucked it. Tony was mesmerized. I helped out, pushing more cock into her mouth. Watching me feed Barbie his cock really turned Tony on. Barbie slowly sucked on the head of Tony's cock while he caressed her face and her hair. I put my hands between my legs, playing with my pussy as I watched. I looked up and saw that Tony was watching me. I spread my legs wider. He stuck out his tongue and wiggled it as if he were licking my pussy.

"First you can watch me lick your pre-come from Barbie," I said. "Then she's going to sit on your face so she can feed you that pussy-juice you like so well. You know I've always wanted to watch you eat pussy, and I'm going to fuck you while you're licking and sucking her off!"

Tony grinned from ear to ear. I knew how much my husband loved eating pussy, especially a juicy one. The juicier the better. Tony sucked and licked up come like it was nectar of the gods! I couldn't wait for him to get his first taste of Barbie's honeyed come. Barbie crawled across the bed and began to kiss me. I could taste Tony's pre-come on her tongue and lips. Tony watched as I sucked Barbie's tongue. I reached down and stroked her clit while I kissed her mouth. Her pussy was wet; the lips and clit were swollen and satiny soft. I put my index and middle fingers inside her hot cunt, using my fingers to fuck her ever so slowly. I moved my fingers in and out, coating them with Barbie's juices, and then put them in my mouth. Tony moaned as he watched me suck the juice from my fingers. I smiled up at him and I did it again, scooping up her wetness and giving him my fingers to suck. Tony sucked greedily, using his tongue as he did so.

"Come here, Tony. Let me feed you, baby," I said as I fingered Barbie's pussy once more. I fed her hot, gooey love juice to my husband, and watched him lap it up.

"She tastes so good, and I like it when you feed it to me," he said. "Feed me some more, honey."

Barbie and I were leaning against the headboard as Tony crawled into position. Barbie straddled his head with her knees on the pillows. Tony was stroking his cock as he watched Barbie lower that juicy pussy over his face. I straddled his hips and lowered my fat wet pussy toward his stiff cock. Watching Barbie feed my husband her pussy made me come all over myself. His dick was rock-hard. Pre-come oozed out the tip. I ducked my head and licked it up.

"I'm coming!" Barbie suddenly cried. "Suck it, Tony. Suck up every last drop!"

Tony went wild. His tongue was everywhere. Barbie arched her back, jamming her pussy on Tony's mouth. They were lip to lip, and I could hear Tony sucking up her come. Both Barbie and I exploded all over my husband. Barbie sank back into the pillows and I lay down beside her. Tony kissed us both, telling us how good we were.

"I'll go make us something to drink," he said and went down the hall to the kitchen.

"Well, Barbie, did you like it?" I asked.

"Loved it!" she said. "But I want you to eat me too. Don't you want me to feed you? Tell me that you want me to feed you. I love to hear you talk dirty to me. Go on, tell me."

I reached over and stuck my fingers into her gooey pussy. I pulled her close and kissed her as I moved my fingers around inside her. Then I pulled them out and licked off her come. "Mmm, tastes good," I told her. I felt the bed move, and knew that Tony was behind me. Ever so gently, he guided my head between Barbie's wide-open legs. "I want to watch you eat her pussy, I want to see you lick up every last drop," he said.

"Sure, baby, you can watch her feed me," I said. I was on my knees with my head buried in her pussy, licking and sucking that sweet pussy, when I felt my husband's cock slide into my pussy. It felt fine. That dick was rock-hard, thick and pulsating! I was making all kinds of slurping noises as Barbie rubbed her pussy in my face. Tony was really turned on watching me and Barbie was getting turned on watching him. Barbie came all over my face as Tony came in my pussy.

Suddenly he pulled his cock out and shot hot come all over my ass. When Barbie saw what Tony had done, I saw a gleam in her eyes. I knew what she wanted, and I made sure she was going to get it. She crawled behind me and started to lick up all Tony's jism. She wanted every last drop. As she licked the come from my ass, Tony stuck his cock into her pussy. He fucked her as she reamed me with her tongue. We ended up having the biggest, best orgasms we'd ever experienced.

Needless to say, Barbie, Tony and I are the best of fucking friends. We share everything. I not only gained a great assistant, but Tony and I made a brand-new friend.—K.M., *Seattle, Washington*

SCHOLARSHIP CAN WAIT; THESE THREE WANT
TO CONDUCT A SEXUAL TUTORIAL

I had been sitting at the computer for hours, with only a buttered roll for lunch. My paper was due the next day and I had put it off until the last minute.

I was concentrating so hard that I didn't hear Thor open the apartment door. The first clue I had that I was no longer alone was when his hands began to massage my aching shoulders. God, that felt good! To hell with the paper. I barely had the sense to hit the Save key before I closed my eyes, leaned back and abandoned myself to his warm, strong hands. I soon began to melt under his ministrations. And I was not surprised when the rubbing started to go lower on my body. With eyes still closed, I sighed in contentment as I felt warm hands cup my breasts through the fabric of my bra and blouse. Soon I felt the buttons of the blouse being opened one by one. He slid the straps of my slip and bra down my right shoulder, pulling down the cup and exposing my nipple. My breast was engulfed in warmth as Thor's hand covered it, squeezing, massaging my nipple between his fingers.

What bliss! I was being rescued from the drudgery of study! Oh, shit. Yeah, I'd fail the course, but so what? What did I care for the topic of women's oppression in the eighteenth and nineteenth centuries, when I could take comfort anticipating the latest onslaught of Thor's mighty meat wagon at the dawn of the twenty-first? Soon the sturdy computer chair swung around on its swivel and my boob was blanketed in warmth as a wet tongue caressed my nipple. I softly murmured, "More, more. It feels so good."

Then I felt the straps descend my left shoulder and expose my other boob, which was soon suffused with a similar warm and wet feeling. It was wonderful, but even amidst my growing pleasure I could pause and ask myself how each of my nipples could be sucked at the same time. I might even have to open my eyes in an attempt to figure that one out. So my eyelids snapped open, and I beheld not one but two naked men kneeling on either side of me. There was Thor, of course, my beloved husband, my Viking warrior—but I had not expected to see his friend Janos.

I was bemused, but it felt so good to have those two wonderful men sucking on my breasts that I simply closed my eyes again and let them have their way with me. Just think, I thought, not two minutes before this I was thinking I was starving myself in every way to try to turn out a paper I wasn't interested in for a course I hated, and now I have the prospect of getting double-fucked. Well I ask you, would you have gone back to the keyboard if you were in my shoes, which I was pretty sure I'd soon be out of, along with my blouse, slip, and any other item of clothing on my hot body? Well, horny reader, I don't think so!

Of the latter eventuality I was sure, because after a delightful interval of sucking and licking I felt hands at the buttons of my skirt. Lifting my ass slightly off the computer chair, I permitted my skirt to come off, and soon my panties and hose joined it on the floor. Strong but gentle hands spread my knees apart and the central outpost of my femininity was exposed to the two randy Biblical men, one of whom—Janos—was hairy; and Thor, smooth.

Fingers brushed across my damp bush, slowly working their way toward my interested vagina. Wishing to be the soul of co-operation, I wriggled toward that hand and gave myself totally to the excitement that was building in my crotch. I assumed it was Thor's hand, for didn't a husband have first right of entry? Soon, one gentle finger slid into my snatch. Shock waves of pleasure spread from my cunt to the nipple that Janos was still sucking. I opened my eyes again to see that it was indeed my mighty Thor who was frigging me, and doing a great job of it. Between his middle finger on my clit and Janos's tongue on my nipple, I began to feel the result of these tender ministrations. My orgasm was imminent. It came ever so slowly, from somewhere deep inside me, building with each suck on my nipple and plunge of finger into my cunt. I rode it, felt it and finally cried a shuddering cry as it overwhelmed me. I soared and burst on high like an Independence Day firecracker. My eyes were closed again and I saw the fireworks burst and shower my inner vision with sparks of delight. And before I could start to descend from this peak I felt myself filled with a massive cock.

Have you ever been fucked in a computer chair? It's perfect. I'll explain: press the handle and the height is just right to align cock and cunt. I felt myself being brought to the right level, and then the wheeled chair slid back and forth as I was impaled by a wonderful length of masculinity I readily recognized. It was the redoubtable hammer of my Thor!

Again, I didn't want to look, I just wanted to enjoy. In and out that massive dong drove, filling me with flesh and then pulling out. I brought my legs up and leaned back as far as I could in the chair, opening my eyes long enough to see a sight that was well worth getting wide-eyed about.

It was Janos's rod, standing long and firm and looking delicious. Oh yes, that meat was being offered to my mouth. And I was hungry! So I lolled my head to one side and let my tongue drop over my lower lip. And I moaned, long and low. I licked my lips and let a little spit drool. I made a slurping noise. Janos and Thor both laughed. Then Janos fed the hungry pleasure-taker.

The lower part of his large dickhead touched my tongue. With greedy eagerness, I moved my lips along the shaft, closer to his clump of pubic hair. Janos gasped in appreciation. I immediately sucked even more deeply, making a loud, sloppy noise that drew happy laughter from the two men. Another strong suck, though, and Janos's laughter turned to a long buzz of appreciation. I'd never given him head before—I'd never so much as touched his hand!—but now I worked on him as if I were making up for lost time. And that low moan indicated he was getting a similar feeling toward me.

A rivalry seemed to commence. Thor was apparently determined to show he could fuck my cunt better than Janos could fuck my mouth. He lifted my legs to a higher level and worked in a rhythm designed to increase my pleasure further, something I wouldn't have thought possible till my marvelous husband made the effort.

I wondered if I would be able to stand up to such roaring delight, but I was damn determined to accept the challenge! And I had to be, since, to add to Thor's effort, Janos was fucking my face, employing his own unique skills admirably.

"Easy . . . easy, lover," he said, trying to temper the excitement I was exerting as I sucked, sucked, sucked on his majestic Magyar meat. O Turkish hordes storming across the plains of Hungary, I fantasized (my mind momentarily returning to my history studies), thy fury was no greater than mine!

I tried to gauge the progress I was making on these two strategic fronts, to feel the tension in each penis. My lips and tongue could detect the slightest nuance in the pulse within Janos's phallus while my lower lips tried to sense how close to climax was my Thor's thrusting piston. That way, my sucking and the throwing of my hips could move in rhythm toward the unspeakably good moment when both my warriors would gush!

I could feel that moment was approaching, and I could hear the coming of their coming in the groans that were arising, seemingly unwillingly, from the throats of each man. My own throat was feeling the loving pressure of Janos's rod, which also told me the climactic orgasmic cannonade could not be very far off.

So here it was: my opportunity to make that moment explode! Emitting a throaty growl of my own, I snapped my pelvis and drew long suction simultaneously. The noises in their throats grew louder. Another thrust, another suck and—they blew!

"Aahhgghh!" the two stout fellows cried in unison, and immediately I felt what I'd fomented. Each phallus swelled. Then each gushed a heroic discharge. The pleasure in my loins was intense, and in my mouth I had to handle a pulsation of semen so strong that much of it gushed back out on my lips before I could drink it. I heard a riot of climactic cries, a duet of Thor's helden-tenor and Janos's basso profundo. And my body thundered with a crescendo that, had I been able to express it, would have featured my own high C.

In a little while the three of us were enjoying the afterglow. We lay on the floor; I laid kisses on their bodies and they kissed and caressed mine. I'd get an explanation later of this gorgeous surprise, of which I had never detected the slightest hint from those two devilish boys! Also, with my good sense returning, I'd have to get back to the paper, the current blankness of which mocked me from my computer screen.

"Oh, we'll help you, darling," Thor said, smiling and kissing my breast.

"We'll be your ghost writers," Janos said, caressing my face.

After such fucking, we felt we could do anything!—G.L., *Provo, Utah*

SHE TOOK THEM FROM THE THREESOMES YOU TALK ABOUT TO THE ONES YOU PERFORM

Last year, my wife Cindy and I took a vacation down in the Florida Keys. Our thought was to stay at bed-and-board places whenever possible, in order to savor the feel of the Keys.

On the second night of our journey, we stayed at a small, de-lightful place that consisted of about eight rooms circled around a beautiful patio. We spent the morning snorkeling, and I must say that Cindy attracted plenty of attention on the dive boat be-cause of her great figure and skimpy bikini bathing suit.

I know that more than one guy developed a pronounced bulge in his suit as my wife sauntered around on the deck. It was almost frightening to see, but when I thought, "And she's mine!" then fear was replaced by unadulterated pride—and I proceeded to get a little hard myself!

After snorkeling, my wife decided she wanted to do some shopping. It struck me that she was perfectly capable of doing that without my help, so I opted to return to our room to take a midday nap. The swimming and sun had left me pleasantly relaxed and groggy.

Back at our room, I slipped into a cotton waist towel and headed for bed. At the window, I looked out to take in the lovely patio, loaded with semi-tropical plants and flowers. As I gazed, I noticed that the room on the far side of the patio had its window open and curtains drawn apart, probably to let the breeze in, I thought. Suddenly I realized that I was able to see a riveting reflection in the dresser mirror. It was the figure of a naked woman!

Owing to the size and location of the Victorian mirror I was able to see the figure only from the waist down, but what a figure it was! Remembering the binoculars that we've always taken on our trips, I quickly fished them out of our suitcase. Carefully, I focused in the seven-power, fifty-objective glasses to the point where the figure was virtually in my room. I could make out the neatly-trimmed pussy so well that the individual hairs were visible. The woman, "Madame X," had a deep suntan and it was apparent from the tan lines that she, like Cindy, wore a very sparse bikini when out in the sun. Her legs were slim and beautifully shaped. I wondered what her face looked like.

As I peered through my binoculars, I saw one hand appear and begin slowly stroking and massaging the area around the mystery woman's cunt. I held my breath and began to feel a great erection developing.

I also propped the glasses on a solid surface, since my hands were trembling with excitement; I drew up a chair and rested them on the back of it.

By now, the woman had slid a finger under her clit and begun to tease it. I marveled at the skill and patience this person had in getting herself off. Her other hand appeared. It held what looked like a battery-operated vibrator. One of the fingers on this hand was adorned by an unusual and beautiful emerald-and-pearl ring shaped in an oriental fashion. Hand number one disappeared and then reappeared with a tube of lubricating jelly. I was tempted to jack off as I watched, but I wanted to save myself for Cindy's return.

"Madame X" continued to play with herself. She used the vibrator and her fingers in a marvelous fashion, plucking, squeezing and spreading her cunt lips. Her juices were really flowing now and she apparently felt herself ready for the insertion of the vibrator. She slid it in slowly, twisting and turning it as she fucked herself. Her hips began to buck up and down and she was in the initial throes of an orgasm. The actual orgasm was volcanic and I was having a difficult time not coming myself. Hands off! was my mental reminder.

Eventually the mystery woman calmed down and disappeared from my view. I went to bed and fell into a deep and erotic sleep. I resisted the temptation to think about that figure in the mirror, since I wanted to restrain myself from exercising my armadillo.

About an hour later, I was awakened by Cindy's return from shopping. She began showing me what she had bought and then noticed the giant hard-on I was sporting.

"Well, well, what's that all about?" she asked.

I told her about what I had seen, in vivid detail. She smiled and told me to stay the way I was, since a hard cock is a terrible thing to waste. She went into the bathroom to freshen up and returned clad only in a large bath towel.

Without any directions, she assumed one of our favorite positions. She lay on her back across the bed with her head hanging over the side. I slipped out of my waist towel and moved to the side of the bed so that my cock could find its way into her mouth. I leaned over her hips and removed her towel. My mouth eagerly sought her cunt and I began sucking and fingering my wife in a delightful frenzy. I was very hard and large, thinking about

Madame X as Cindy sucked my cock. She sensed my urgency and monitored my come by using the squeeze method.

Eventually we moved into the missionary position with my wife's legs draped over my shoulders. She was hot, hotter than hell when I pumped it to her. Her nipples were never harder or larger as I tweaked them during our fucking. We finally exploded together in a mixture of come, sweat and pussy juice.

Later we both commented on each other's performance and admitted that each of us was thinking about my earlier voyeur experience. We fell asleep and were lucky to wake up in time to clean up and dress, for both the happy hour at the inn and the subsequent dinner at a restaurant I had chosen.

We were sipping wine and talking about the dive sites with another couple when she walked in, unescorted.

I knew it was my lady in the mirror, my Madame X, because of the ring on her finger. She was indeed a beautiful woman. Her hair was auburn and the flowing white casual pants suit could in no way disguise a truly marvelous figure.

Cindy hissed, "My God, she is *gorgeous!*" I don't remember previously seeing my wife that taken with another woman's appearance. I was caught in a conversation about snorkeling when I suddenly realized that Cindy had left my side and gone over to talk to my mystery woman. This was unusual, since Cindy never found it easy to strike up conversations with any strangers.

I excused myself from the folks I was talking to and wandered over to Cindy and the mystery woman. Cindy introduced me to Eunice, who was indeed traveling alone. Her husband, it seemed, did not enjoy travel since it detracted from time at his business. What a jerk he must be! I thought, to leave this magnificent woman traveling alone.

We chatted about the area and the shopping and then Cindy offered Eunice an invitation to join us for dinner. Eunice protested at first, saying that she didn't want to interfere with our evening out, but Cindy insisted. I added my influence to the invitation, though I was quite frankly surprised at Cindy's insistence in the matter.

At this point, let me say that Cindy and I have never been involved with anyone else sexually during our marriage. We do enjoy reading *Penthouse Letters* and watching porno films and we do fantasize to each other about threesomes and such, but there's nothing further. So I was wondering where the events of this evening were leading.

The restaurant I had chosen was casual, but had very good seafood. We found Eunice to be a very pleasant conversationalist. She was an interior decorator and widely traveled. As we talked I couldn't help but think of what was beneath her white pants suit and of her two talented hands. Cindy seemed to be entranced by her. We ordered coffee after dinner and Cindy excused herself to visit the ladies' room. Eunice leaned across the table and spoke in a low, sweet, soft voice.

"Did you like what you saw this afternoon?"

I was shocked and must have turned red.

"I know you were watching and it was a real turn-on," she continued. "I could see you in my mirror, after all." She smiled.

Cindy came back to the table at about the same time the coffee arrived. Eunice, without batting an eye, looked at Cindy, saying, "Your husband had quite a treat today. I suppose he told you all about it?"

Cindy smiled sweetly. "He told me everything, and in great detail."

"Are you angry or jealous?" Eunice asked.

"No, I just wish I had been there to watch," Cindy responded. "But—" and she smiled as brightly as I'd ever seen her smile, "I got my reward afterward."

We drank our coffee and I wondered what was next to come (or who, maybe).

Finally Eunice suggested that we go back to her room for an after-dinner drink and some fun and games. I started to say that we weren't into that, but Cindy interrupted to say that it sounded like a great idea.

I was absolutely dumbfounded, but also horny as hell about what might be ahead during this evening. I paid the bill and we headed back to the inn. Needless to say my cock was very ready, willing, and able. But I wondered about Cindy and her ability to handle something like this. But I was to find out that not only could she handle it, she relished the touch of another woman.

When we got to Eunice's room, she begged us to make ourselves comfortable while she poured three small glasses of what she called her liqueur. I sipped it and noticed it had a distinctive licorice flavor. Shortly afterward she asked me to sit in a chair in the corner of the room while she acquainted herself a little better with Cindy. I expected an interesting show.

My wife, I noticed, seemed to be in almost a trance. She watched Eunice through half-closed eyes. I sat in the chair and watched Eunice as she slowly, ever so slowly, began to seduce my wife. She stroked Cindy gently on the shoulders, on the breasts, up and down her legs. As she did, she kept whispering things in Cindy's ear and putting light kisses on Cindy's neck, ears, and lips.

After a few minutes of this foreplay, Eunice began to undress Cindy slowly and seductively. Soon my wife stood before us, clad only in panties and bra. Eunice continued and gently pulled down Cindy's panties and undid her bra. As she did this, Eunice lightly brushed her lips and tongue on my wife's cunt lips. Cindy shuddered in anticipation. Finally Eunice had my wife on her back on the bed. Her legs were splayed, her cunt was open and her eyes were shut. Eunice disrobed and I was treated to one of the most delightful bodies I had ever seen. Her breasts were not large, but were perfectly shaped and firm. The cunt that I had watched earlier in the day was even more beautiful up close. I had the intimation I was going to see the most erotic event of my entire life.

Eunice went to work on Cindy's cunt: licking it, sucking it, gently finger-fucking it. Every so often, she would reach up and tweak Cindy's tits. It didn't take long for my wife to have her first of many orgasms. If I'd been blind I'd have heard and recognized her gasping and climactic cries. Fortunately I could see, and savored the sight of my wife vibrating with erotic pleasure.

Needless to say, I was hard as a rebar and I found some relief in opening my fly to release my stalk from its uncomfortable confinement. Eunice whispered something to Cindy and the next thing I knew they were in a 69 position across the bed. Eunice was on top facing me as they began the session, sucking and licking each other's cunt.

Eunice would look up occasionally and give me an almost lewd smile as she brought my wife off again and again. I noticed the skill and dexterity that she applied with tongue and fingers as she stroked, pulled, spread and fingered Cindy's cunt lips. She had my wife's clit at full attention and fully engorged. I could hear the sounds of my wife's mouth against Eunice's pussy. The two women had brought themselves to a state of sexual frenzy.

Suddenly, Eunice took her mouth off my wife and in a very excited tone said that she, Eunice, wanted to get fucked by me while she, Cindy, licked my cock.

She motioned me over to the bed. My clothes were off in no time and I took a position behind Eunice.

Looking down, I could see Cindy's face looking up from underneath Eunice's pussy. I entered Eunice easily because of Cindy's work on her.

Hers was a heavenly cunt, tight and responsive to my thrusts. I could feel Cindy's tongue along the underside of my shaft as I ran it in and out of Eunice's magnificent love tunnel. Cindy's face was coated with cunt juice that freely flowed from the lovely crater of Eunice's femininity.

Once I had entered Eunice, she returned to her work on my wife. We were in a classic threesome.

Try as I might, I couldn't hold back my orgasm. Eunice sensed it and my wife knew by my throbbing member that I was close. We climaxed together, the three of us.

After we had all calmed down, we disengaged. Eunice looked at us, eyes shining with enthusiasm, and said that the fun had just begun.

The balance of the evening we spent fucking, sucking and fingering in every conceivable manner. I guess the ultimate was Eunice's convincing Cindy to let me fuck her in the ass while Eunice did me with a strap-on dildo. Cindy and I had never done anal, but with a few more glasses of the love elixir and preliminary entry with anal probes, my wife and I were ready for the great adventure—two links in a daisy chain.

The next morning, we joined Eunice for breakfast and she announced, to our dismay, that she was about to be heading up north. At the same time, she asked if we were interested in meeting again at a different location and we readily agreed. After we said goodbye, Cindy and I wondered if she would indeed make contact with us again. Then, last week, we were thrilled to get a letter from Eunice. Now, the two of us are looking forward to meeting her this summer on beautiful old Cape Cod!—*T.L., Toledo, Ohio*

WHEN SHE WANTS HER PORN VIDEO DREAMS TO COME TRUE, SHE HEADS FOR BOB

I'm married to a beautiful woman. Her body is perfect. She works out five days a week and men often stare at her strong legs and firm breasts. This used to bother me because I was jealous, but over time I came to see their attention as a compliment. Eventually I started asking her to dress to attract the stares of other men, and eventually, she too came to enjoy the stares.

There is nothing more exciting to me than watching Trudy's

beautiful body respond to sexual pleasure. Over the years, my quest to please her had brought us up to a number of sexual plateaus.

The first device I introduced to our lovemaking was an egg-shaped vibrator. Trudy was reluctant to try it because she'd had few sexual experiences before she met me and was very conservative in the bedroom. However, she soon came to enjoy the intense sensation the vibrator gave her as I ate her and inserted it into her cunt or pressed it against her asshole.

Over time we experimented with a number of sex aids. Looking for something new to try, I introduced adult films into our lovemaking.

The first tape I rented was awful. On my next trip to the video store, I rented four different movies and copied onto tape only the scenes featuring attractive couples' performing straight sex. After what had happened with the first movie it took some convincing to get my wife to give it another try. We watched the tape with the volume off while I fucked her from behind and rubbed her clit with my thumb.

This time, her eyes didn't leave the television set, and by the end of the second scene she was rocking her hips to an amazing orgasm. Seeing her get off like this had me shooting my load shortly after she shot hers.

As time went on, I learned which videos to rent, based on the producer or the actors. One thing I noticed when Trudy watched, she really got a thrill from the well-built, good-looking guys in the videos. One night I rented a film and was fingering and fucking her from behind as we enjoyed the first scene. Trudy's eyes were like golf balls watching the second scene, where a beautiful girl ended up in bed with two good-looking guys. Halfway through the scene, the girl ended up on all fours, blowing one guy while getting fucked from behind by the other. Trudy went crazy, really apeshit! She started grinding against me wildly while taking two of my fingers into her mouth as if she were giving them a blowjob, the whole time not taking her eyes from the video.

As I said, nothing makes me happier than seeing my wife get off. This started to give me further ideas.

One night, before we started to have sex, I asked her what her fantasies were. She said something about sex on the beach, a typical answer. She then asked me what my fantasy was. I told her that it was to watch her get a hot oil massage from a handsome, well-built man who would masturbate her until orgasm.

She was amazed and a little upset by this. She wanted to know how I could stand to let her be with another man. I explained to her that I was not jealous and that allowing another man to turn her on would not be any different from using a vibrator or X-rated video to get herself, or myself, off. She said she couldn't understand, but the lovemaking that immediately followed was glorious.

From time to time I brought up the subject of another partner while we were fucking. I would say, "I would love to fuck you while you blow some hot guy," and this would always make her hotter, but beyond moaning, she would never say anything in return. Whenever we would talk about it outside of our lovemaking she would always say she would never be able to do it.

I was just about to give up on the idea when I noticed she kept mentioning a guy who worked in the same office building. She kept saying there was a dentist named Bob who worked on the next floor up from her private office, and that he was always checking her out. I wasn't sure if she was hinting at something or if he was just some slob who kept bothering her, so I asked her if he was.

Her reply was, "No, he's not bothering me. Actually, he's real good-looking. He definitely works out."

During our next lovemaking session I told her that I wanted to fuck her while she sucked Bob's cock. Trudy came so hard she almost passed out. I kept repeating my wish to her through her orgasm.

The next night I told her that I really wanted it to happen, that I wanted to pleasure her with another man. Again I assured her that I wouldn't be any more jealous than I would be of her getting off on a vibrator or a man in an X-rated movie. I told her that if she said no, I wouldn't bother her with it again (though I wondered if I could keep that promise).

Trudy replied that she would be too nervous, especially with me present. I then told her that to ease into it, she could experiment with another man without me present, but that I didn't want her to fuck or blow him. After a little more coaxing she said that since I wanted so much for her to do so, she would try it for me.

With that, we decided it would be Bob from her office building and that she would tell me all about it when she got home the next evening. So the next morning, Trudy went to her office dressed in a short but not slutty black skirt, tight zipped sweater and black three-inch heels that accentuated her cute ass. Her tan legs are flawless, so she didn't need stockings.

That evening, she lay naked next to me and told me what had happened. As she told me, I fingered her pussy, which was wetter and more slippery than I'd ever remembered its being.

Trudy said that she timed her entrance into the building so she would walk in with Bob. As Bob and she walked in, he was trying not to be obvious about checking her out, but couldn't conceal his curiosity. As she entered her office on the first floor she asked him if he could change a fluorescent bulb that building maintenance hadn't gotten to in a week. He said he could, but that he had to open up his office. He'd be back in about two hours. Trudy said that she was so turned on by the anticipation that her underpants got wet.

When Bob came in she was bent over, pretending to be getting something out of a closet. When she turned around he was actually blushing. Bob then pulled a chair beneath the light and stood on it to open the fixture. As he did, Trudy stood just inches from him and put her hands on the outside of his thighs as if to make sure he wouldn't fall. When she did this, she took a sly look at his crotch and saw that a bulge was forming thereunder. She then looked up and saw Bob was looking down at her, hopeful that this was going to turn out to be more than an embarrassing situation for him.

Trudy, still staring him in the eyes, moved her hand to the swell in his pants and felt his cock through the fabric. Bob let out a groan of pleasure. She said at this point her knees were actually weak as she felt the outline of another man's penis in her hand. She then turned and told him to follow her from the sitting area to her office. She locked the door behind them.

Trudy told him that she wouldn't fuck or blow him but wanted to jerk him off, and that he could touch her any way he wanted to. Bob then raised her sweater, exposing her tanned, firm tits. Bob sucked each tit in turn, making her nipples long and hard. Trudy has unusually long nipples and when sucked to full length they are a mind-blowing sight. Bob then slowly pulled her skirt and panties down. He then stepped back to admire her perfect ass and long legs as she stood there in only her black heels, her panties at her ankles. Slipping off his clothes, he pressed against her and softly ran his hands along her legs, cupping each ass-cheek as a concluding gesture. He delicately traced his fingertips down her neck to her arms, breasts and belly, then lingered on her smooth inner thighs.

She said the sensations were incredible as she stood in the middle of her office exposed, legs slightly spread. She was covered with goose bumps from Bob's erotic touch. Her nipples became so full of blood they went from pink to brick-colored—and were, incidentally, hard as brick. The desire to have her cunt pleasured— she knew her labia must be swollen with blood also—was overwhelming.

Bob then lifted her onto her work table, gently pulled her knees up, and buried his face in her cunt. His tongue left no part of her sex unexplored. It swirled and darted before finding a perfect rhythm on her clit. Trudy's wetness and Bob's saliva trickled and dripped to form a puddle on her work table. He brought her to three powerful orgasms with his expert tongue.

Trudy told Bob to stand up. She proceeded to rub her sweaty body against his. She rubbed her tits over his muscular chest, belly and thighs, savoring the gorgeous contours of his body, which looked as if it had been chiseled by a great Greek sculptor.

Then she turned and, using her hot ass, rubbed his cock and balls a couple of times. His dick slipped between her ass cheeks and glided along her silky pussy lips, the soft head of his cock massaging her clit. On the verge of fucking him, she pulled away. Unable to resist taking his hard-on in her mouth, she turned, got down on her knees and, in a frenzy, sucked and licked his cock.

She said the feel of her new lover's shaft on her tongue and lips and poking into her throat made her delirious. Bob quickly started to moan and buck as Trudy flattened her tongue out on the bottom of his penis and bobbed steadily, using long, deep back-and-forth strokes.

Feeling his cock on the verge of orgasm, she maintained a firm but gentle hand on his balls while sliding the fingers of her other hand between the firm cheeks of his ass. Bob then let out a long, deep moan as Trudy pressed her finger against his asshole.

Thick jets of jism came coursing out of a body that could restrain orgasm no longer. She told me she had to swallow furiously lest his pearly fluid back up and spill from her mouth. She also said she wished I could have been there to see it.

After Trudy told me all that, we had the best sex we'd had in years. After she came, she kept whispering to me, over and over, "I can't wait until you fuck me while I'm sucking Bob's cock!"

The wait won't be long!—K.L., Florissant, Missouri

FIRST THE FAST FOOD, THEN THEY SPREAD
THE SPECIAL SAUCE ON THEIR MEAT

I have a great story. Hell, I have a great existence, one that's bound up with the story. Permit me to explain.

Several years ago, my wife and I built a new home in an exclusive development, one where the minimum building lot is an acre. The houses are well secluded, so much so that no one can see who is pulling in or out of a neighbor's driveway.

I went into semi-retirement at age thirty-nine. I was extremely lucky, since I was able to start my own business and then sell it for a great deal of money while remaining a highly-paid consultant there. I am now forty-five, and it appears I'll never have to work again.

My wife, even though she doesn't need to, still teaches. Our marriage is effectively over, but we remain together for the sake of the children. I believe she desires to work for her own pension, both of us knowing very well that once our last child enters college, we'll probably get a divorce and go our separate ways.

Anyway, on to the juicy parts. In our development, we've become involved with a social group that meets at a different house once a week, and a different restaurant, also weekly. The conversations are sometimes deep, mostly entertaining, but always safe. Most of the people in the group are older than we are, though not all of them.

There are two absolute knockouts in our group. The first, Pia, is a voluptuous thirty-nine-year-old, a hard-bodied, divorced breathtaker. She and her ex never had children and she vowed she would remain childless. What they did have together was a chain of very successful businesses, of which she got half, and a huge house with a great view of the lake.

There is another woman, Inez, forty-four and married. Though a mother of three, you'd better believe she has a phenomenally good body. I have always thought Inez might be a happily married woman, even though I have trouble believing there can be such a thing as a person who is happily married.

There were a few times when I was with either Inez or Pia, or sometimes with both, when we would throw little sexual innuendoes about, but only among us three, never when anyone else was around. I fantasized about both of them sometimes, but never actually thought there was any possibility of fulfillment.

Once in a blue moon, I will treat myself to a short-order lunch. This particular day, I walked in our local burger joint, got in line, then heard someone call my name. I looked up and saw a grinning Inez. I said hello, and she went on to explain that she was just returning from morning aerobics. I made a joke about her doing things backwards—that she should have stopped at the burger joint first, then gone to aerobics to burn off the calories. Just then, we both heard Pia call our names. She was smiling broadly and looking brilliantly sexy as she came over to us. We all hugged. After getting our meals, we decided to sit outside together so we could, according to Pia, talk more freely.

As we were eating, the conversation took a turn toward much less safe topics than we had ever broached as a group. We had a great time. We traded a few filthy jokes, a few slanderous comments and a few sexual words like *fuck*, *pussy*, *cock*, *blowjobs*, and *cunt-licking*. Inez then announced that she was very envious of Pia, who, she fancied, was divorced and free to experience whatever and whomever she pleased. Pia and I, both believing Inez to be happy, asked as concerned friends if anything was wrong. Inez went on to explain that she was just very unhappy being married to the guy she had indeed married.

"My husband and I haven't slept together in years," she told us. She added, "I've had a few meaningless affairs to fill the void, but what kind of fulfillment and pleasure do you get from just—filling the void? The very phrase depresses me.

"I have to say it—I simply *hate* being married."

Pia looked at me and asked about my wife. I told her the two of us had over the years become distant from each other and were thoroughly unhappy. I commented that I was in the same boat as Inez, who leaned forward, placed an elbow on the table, put her face between her hands and very seductively asked if I meant in the same boat as she in respect to the marriage, or to the affairs.

"Both," I said.

At this point, we discovered many others had come outside also, so our frank but risky conversation had to turn safe again. Pia then asked us to come over to her place to visit and continue the discussion.

"I think there's a lot we could say to each other," she said. She looked at one or another of the tables, where perhaps other stories like ours might be heard.

We all drove to Pia's place in our own cars. I was anticipating more than conversation, but couldn't be sure such a feeling would be in common with theirs.

My first indication that something was definitely going to happen occurred to me when Pia opened her spare garage doors and motioned for us both to drive in and park inside. When we parked our cars and emerged on the driveway, she mentioned that putting the cars away was only to keep rumors from circulating in the neighborhood. Even the true ones!

When we got inside, Pia turned on some smooth jazz and we resumed our talk. After a while, our conversation turned to sexual techniques.

Pia and Inez both described the ways they liked to be fucked. Inez went first, saying that she is always irritated by men who don't like to eat pussy. Then she stated that men who would not kiss her after they come in her mouth also pissed her off.

Pia jumped in and said that she loved the pearl necklace and was greatly turned on by a man who liked to have his jism spread like cream all over each partner's body.

They both asked me if I liked eating pussy. My eyes widened and I let out a short laugh. I leaned forward.

"Ladies," I said, "I love giving face—I mean, more than *anything*!"

I also said that I loved women who were uninhibited and not afraid to swim around, so to speak, in jism; also, that I thought the sexiest odor on earth was the aroma of pussy juice mixed with jism.

Pia, very excited, leaned forward herself and asked, "Have you done a threesome, either of you? How about it? We're safe, only we will know, we'll all keep our mouths shut about it."

Without answering, Inez immediately whipped off her top to expose two of the most beautiful breasts I have ever seen. With that, I stripped off my clothes in a matter of seconds. I looked over at Pia, and saw another set of absolutely gorgeous boobs, and a thick and beautiful, brownish-red muff. Looking down on the couch, I saw Inez's almost clean-shaven pussy was wet and dripping. We were ready!

For the first few minutes, it was a kissing frenzy, from Pia to Inez, then back to Pia. Inez pushed me back on the couch, straddled my face, and lowered her cunt, shaved down to the bristles, onto my mouth. It was sweet tasting, with hardly any odor, and the stubble tickled. Then I could feel Pia going down on me. I had to hope Pia would not suck too powerfully, since I come quickly when the suction is strong. Inez looked down at me and smiled. I lapped her lovingly and drew groans and writhing. It was an overwhelming pleasure to have my face and dick treated simultaneously.

My worries about Pia were groundless. She sucked cock with artistry, bringing my come along at a leisurely pace. My mouth had comparable skill, and I could feel Inez twitch as I prolonged her pleasure with just the right pressure from my tongue. When the great moment came, she and I were quaking with orgasm and her cries bounced off the walls of the house stereophonically. When I came, Pia pulled back and let my jism gush from me in a warm, sticky fountain, which she gathered in her hands and began spreading on all three of us.

That first incident happened three years ago and the three of

us have been in a threesome ever since, or so to speak, anyway.
—R.N., *Lake Forest, Illinois*

SHE MEASURED UP TO THE HEALTH CLUB'S
HIGHEST EXPECTATIONS

Although I am an avid reader of your magazine, my wife is completely against your type of literature. So I keep my collection at work and indulge my taste for sexy reading materials while I'm traveling.

I joke frequently with my wife, Margaret, about her making out with my best friend. She is really an abandoned, sexy woman but she had an old-fashioned upbringing and seems to think it is proper to act like a prude. Even though she gratifies her full, voluptuous appetites when we go to bed—and even though she demonstrates a great and filthy imagination while we are fucking—she seems to feel obliged to play goody-two-shoes at all other times, and especially in public.

For that reason, even though we had often discussed the fantasy of her fucking and sucking with another man while I watched, I had resigned myself to the probability that it would never happen.

However, hope springs eternal, and it was encouraging that Margaret began working out at a gym two or three times a week to relieve stress and stay fit—even though at thirty-four she's quite fit and has a great body. Every couple of months she checks her measurements to check on her progress. This had never been a big deal until recently, and the reason for that is one of the new instructors—a shy and quiet young man named Trevor who is in his early twenties. Margaret and the other women at the gym tease Trevor about being a young stud and a slut, and this makes him blush and stammer.

Before long, Margaret and I were talking about a fantasy in which she seduces Trevor and fucks and sucks him in every imaginable way. This turned Margaret on immensely, and our sex life improved to no end. But, I told her repeatedly, our sex life would be enhanced tenfold if she ever lost her inhibitions and actually seduced Trevor.

"Oh," she protested, "I couldn't do that. I'm much too shy." With that, just to show her how wrong she was, I stuck my index finger into her twat and wiggled it while I sucked her erect and still stiffening nipple. "Yes," she sighed, trembling with passion, "I might do it at that, with proper stimulus."

I was further encouraged when Margaret proudly told me after her last measurement session that the other girls teased Trevor about trying to cop a feel. She laughed wickedly when she described how the poor guy made it worse for himself by protesting his innocence. Margaret told me later, again with a certain amount of gratification, that his hands had seemed to linger on her upper thighs and under her breasts while he took those measurements.

I told her that she should give the kid an experience to remember next time—let him cop a real feel. She laughed and blushed a bit, and when I pressed her she admitted that she had shifted her weight a bit while Trevor's hand was on her ribs and he had brushed against a stiffening nipple. And when he was checking her legs, she said, she had felt the back of his hand brush against her crotch.

"We could really have a great threesome or something with this guy," I said. "Or I could just watch the two of you, if you'd like that better."

Margaret actually blushed when she told me, "I'd really like to, but I think I'd have to be extra horny to take the first step." She was thoughtful for a while, then said, "You can help me by turning me on, you know." I promised I would, and that night, while we were engaged in foreplay, I ran my hand from her stomach up onto her tit. I squeezed the nipple and told her that was what she should let Trevor do the next time. Then I moved my hand up her leg and stroked her thigh a few times before placing it on her pussy. As she parted her legs, I told her that when Trevor measured her legs, she should bend her knees slightly so that his hands would slide right up to her hot-spot. I did just that to demonstrate, and when she ground her hot, wet pussy onto my knuckles I told her she should do that to Trevor's hand too. Margaret immediately moaned, climbed on top of me and engulfed my hard rod in her dripping cunt for an extended and heated fuck session.

For the next month, every time we made love I would tease Margaret's nipples and rub my hand against her pussy while telling her that she should have Trevor do this the next time he measured her. That always got her quite hot, and she would fuck like crazy. In the three days before Margaret was due for her measurements, we agreed not to fuck, so that Margaret would be in a good mood to make her move on Trevor. It was hard for me to pass up all that great pussy, but Margaret assured me that once she nailed Trevor, we'd really expand our sexual horizons. And I was all for that.

Margaret called me at work on the day for her next measuring session. "Come on home for lunch, and get me as horny as you can," she said. "I really want to lose my inhibitions and get it on with Trevor."

Needless to say, I was on my way immediately. We talked dirty, and both got turned on over lunch. Then we went into the bedroom to prepare Margaret for the big event. Margaret stripped and had a leisurely, steaming shower, emerging a virginal pink that was belied by the way she swung her ass and tits as she walked around, selecting her outfit. With no ceremony, I started playing with her nipples. Margaret moaned her excitement, and I caressed her pussy and rubbed my finger up and down the slit. Her moans increased, and she rotated her hips, ready for a farewell fuck. But I pointed out she'd be late if we did that. I gave her a flimsy set of silk underwear and told her to wear them instead of her sports undies. "Trevor will appreciate them," I said, and left the room so she could get dressed. When she came to kiss me goodbye, I tweaked her nipples until they were visible through her top and rubbed her pussy. She moaned again.

"I'm ready for Trevor now," she told me. "Ready for anybody." I was inclined to agree she must be pretty well primed for an extramarital adventure. Then I told her to have fun and be nice to Trevor. Her face was flushed as she left. I figured Trevor was going to get lucky that day.

When Margaret came home a few hours later, she headed straight for the shower, as usual. Afterward, she came out into the living room in her robe. I could tell she was wearing only her panties underneath. She had little to say when I asked her how her session went. I coaxed her for details. She sat on the couch beside me, and sighed deeply. "It went just fine," she said.

"How's Trevor?" I asked. She blushed, and said nothing. I put my arm around her and squeezed her tit. "Look," I said, "whatever happened with Trevor is okay with me. I was the one who egged you on, remember that? So you can tell me about it. That was supposed to be part of the fun, wasn't it?" I could feel her relax then, and as she told me what had happened, her nipples hardened under my fingers.

Margaret said that Trevor was busy with some other people when she arrived at the gym. She started to work out on the equipment. The silk bra rubbed against her nipples and made them harden—so much so that she knew they were visible to anyone who might happen to look at her. This thought, and the fact that her flimsy, lacy panties were riding up into her pussy slit, made her start to lubricate. Margaret was heading for another piece of equipment when she noticed Trevor watching her, extra-close. She smiled at him as she climbed onto an exercise bike. The increased movement of her tits within the bra made the nipples even harder, which she knew was a step in the right direction, and to help things along she rubbed her pussy into the seat, trying to get some pressure onto her clit. Just then, Trevor called

to her to come and get measured. As she walked over to the side
of the room where the measuring took place, she told me, she felt
Trevor's eyes on her swaying tits and stiffening nipples. The two
of them made small talk as Trevor started taking her measurements.

At this point in her story, I was really pulling on Margaret's
tits. She threw her robe open and pulled my head to her breasts
and their engorged nipples. I sucked on each of them as my
wife—heating up again now—continued her story.

Once Trevor was done with the preliminaries, he began to
measure the dimensions that required him to touch the spots he
had been teased about previously. He reached around Margaret
from the back to measure her, and in doing so he brushed a trembling hand against a stiff nipple. Margaret said she sighed just
enough so that Trevor could hear, and pushed her tit forward,
into his hand. Trevor then put his other hand around her, ostensibly to retrieve the other end of the measuring tape. As he did
so, he pinched Margaret's nipple. Then he quickly squeezed the
entire tit. Then, she said, as Trevor pulled his hands away, he
"sort of accidentally" slid them down her sides and along her
hips. Trevor then knelt beside Margaret to measure her legs. Margaret remembered what I had told her. When his hand was high
on her leg measuring her inseam, Margaret buckled her knees
slightly, so that his hand pressed lightly against her pussy. When
he looked up at her inquiringly, she closed her eyes and dropped
further onto his knuckles. She softly moaned as he made contact
with her slit. Trevor pushed his hand back at her and rubbed it
harder against her stiff love bud.

Margaret was ready for some shameless action now, and she
began to grind her hips on his hand. Trevor whispered to her,
"Don't go anywhere. I'll be back." Then he rose and went over to
see off the few women who were still exercising. Margaret pretended to do her cool-off stretches for about five minutes. Then,
when the last woman left, Trevor locked the door and came over
to where Margaret was standing. He came up behind her and ca-

ressed her ass, then ran one hand up between her legs to rub her pussy. She moaned her appreciation, and that got results. He pulled her sweatpants down to her ankles and started kissing the backs of her thighs. Margaret spread her legs farther apart and leaned forward, over the stool in front of her. Then Trevor kissed his way to Margaret's pussy, and tried to lick it through the panties.

Margaret got very horny as she related all this, and she pushed my head down from her tits to her lower body. I urged her to go on with her story, pulled her panties down her legs and dived into her pussy. She continued the story as I lapped away.

She said Trevor pulled her panties down to her ankles, and licked both her pussy and her thighs. She kicked the panties off and spread her legs to give him ready access. Trevor lay on his back and pulled her over him so that she straddled his head. Margaret said her pussy dripped on Trevor's face as he stuck his tongue up into her slit. At the same time, he slid his hands beneath her top, raised her bra above her tits and played with her extended nipples. She ground her pussy as she came on his tongue. When my horny darling caught her breath, she saw that the head of Trevor's cock was pushing out from under his sweatpants. She pulled the pants down below his balls, leaned over and licked the hard shaft as she played with his balls. Trevor renewed his tongue action on her clit. Margaret said she wanted him to come first, so she rubbed his cock with her hands as she licked the head. When he moaned and bucked, she tightened her grip and increased her speed until he grunted loudly and shot hot seed that she gulped down as she came with him. When they caught their breaths, Margaret wiped them both off with a towel, and they dressed and parted. They agreed that this should not happen again, Margaret said, but we both knew that with my help, it would.

As she told me the story, Margaret had been stroking my cock. I had two fingers diddling her hot pussy while my thumb rubbed her clit. She started to tremble, and suddenly she pushed me onto my back. She dropped herself onto my hard cock, and ran her pussy fully down on it in one motion. I sucked her hanging nipples as she rode me fiercely. Then she shouted loudly as she orgasmed. I shot come deep into her hungry snatch. While she recovered her calm, I told her that next time I wanted to watch her and Trevor. She gave me a long, deep kiss.—*T.L.*, *Petoskey*, *Michigan*

"YOU SQUEAMISH PEOPLE JUST DON'T KNOW WHAT YOU'RE MISSING!"

For years now, my wife and I have been addicted to *Penthouse Letters*. The letters get hotter and juicier with each issue. We really lick our chops reading about sensuous threesomes and erotic gang bangs. I don't think anything gets our blood going more than reading aloud about a wanton housewife who is getting banged by two studs while her husband jerks off to the action.

Well, I shouldn't say there's *nothing* sexier. Penny and I have become obsessed with afterplay—licking and sucking up come after a torrid love scene. I think that's what gets us horniest— reading about some slutty housewife lapping it up like a lioness in heat. We especially like the hot stories where the spouse joins in the fun, slurping up cunt cream and stringy sperm right alongside his wife.

It's taken us a few years to realize our full sexual potential, but now there's no going back. We get hungrier all the time. Sometimes we make love just to feed our sexual appetites for come, slurping up gobs of pussy juice and hot semen like there's no tomorrow. I've grown accustomed to going down on Penny after we've had intercourse and licking our combined love juices from her tasty love hole. Then we usually share a wet French kiss for a few minutes before resuming come-slurping and tongue-swapping.

Penny often licks her fingers after she finger-fucks herself. Her twat juice is so damn enticing, the smell and taste drive us both wild. We can never get enough of this action.

Penny loves it when I shoot my entire ejaculate into her mouth. Sometimes she won't share it with me, but usually we find a happy medium and each samples part of the load in a meeting of our mouths and tongues. There's nothing like the taste of come after sex. It's the most intimate and sexy thing a couple can share. Hell, you squeamish people out there just don't know what you're missing!

You probably think we're pretty kinky, but what I've told you so far is only part of our story. I'll share some more of our sexual escapades with all you readers. It may convince you to open up and try a few naughty things in your own bedrooms.

One day, I got home about five-thirty, a little beat but not too tired for some fun if Penny was in the mood. Boy, let me tell you, she was definitely in the mood. I found her in the dining room, all decked out in her most sultry black lace teddy and her most seductive black raspberry lipstick. Her bedroom eyes said, "Fuck me now!"

She was smoking a cigarette, and one arm was rhythmically moving back and forth. Obviously, she was playing with herself under the table. "Hi, honey," I greeted her. She replied with a long, drawn-out moan and smiled seductively, lazily exhaling smoke and gently grabbing my prick, already standing at attention. She rolled her cigarette in her pouting, wet lips as if it were a small, erect cock, and she sucked the cigarette like she was coaxing it to climax.

Then she slowly raised her hand from under the table. I almost came then and there! She held out a half-peeled banana, slick with pussy come, with which she obviously had been fucking herself.

"I couldn't wait for you so I started to have my fun a bit early," she said. "Hope you don't mind." She added, "I have to watch my figure, so I thought I'd have some fruit for supper. The only thing is, I can't find any low-fat whipped cream for a topping. Think you can help me, babe?"

My dick was rock-hard and I knew it wouldn't be too long before I provided my horny little wife with a hefty load of fresh cream for her banana split. What a sight it was when she brought that squishy banana up to her nose for a whiff and snaked her tongue down it to taste her own come. "Mmm, this tastes good," she said. "But it needs a nice coating of something white and gooey. C'mon honey, help me out."

I had my cock in my hand by then, and I was feverishly pumping away. Her eyes grew wider as my prick grew thicker and longer. As my breathing quickened, she held the banana close to my prick and coaxed me to aim my jets at it. In a moment I felt that familiar sensation in my loins and I growled, "Oh baby, I'm gonna come for you now. You're the sexiest woman in the world. Oh God, here it comes!" I shot a humongous load of fresh, sticky semen all over her hand, as well as the banana. I covered Chiquita with sperm.

Penny wasted no time in licking and sucking up the jism from her hands. Then she gave me a look of pure passion as she brought her freshly coated dessert to her mouth. She engulfed half the come-decorated banana with one greedy lunge, then devoured it like a come-crazed whore of Babylon. She moaned in delight as she grabbed her gooey reward. I wondered, What have I done to deserve such a randy little vixen?

Penny burst into her own magnificent climax as she licked, sucked and nibbled her sex fruit. Her orgasm was violent and quick. She raised a glistening finger up to my lips for a tiny taste. That gesture got me hungry for her wet snatch. I dropped to my knees and began to slurp up all her oozing come, darting my tongue deep into her folds for all I was worth. Her fluid filled my happy mouth completely. I swallowed it greedily, slobbering all over her thighs and legs in order to get every tasty drop.

We locked our moist lips passionately and twirled our tongues together, tasting every flavor with such erotic delight that we both moaned in appreciation. I got rock-hard again as I tasted her pussy juice and my sperm, overlaid with the distinct flavors of banana and menthol cigarette smoke. It was so damn sensuous and exhilarating that I knew I would need more, much more before the night was done.

"What do you want, honey? Do you want something more?" Penny cooed as she gulped down the last gooey bits of banana. "I know I'm still hungry. I definitely need to suck more down. Looks like that scrumptious dick of yours could explode again. Mmm! I hope you have another big load for me. God, I think I could drink down a whole big glass of sperm tonight!"

My mind was still crazed with lust, and she was right. My cock could probably explode several times more before I used up my supply of semen. "You're such a greedy girl," I said. "What do you want me to squirt on next? You want it in a glass, in your palm, or maybe right into that pretty mouth of yours? I'm gonna give you more come than even you can swallow, baby doll!"

"Oh, I doubt that, honey, my thirst is insatiable tonight," she replied. "Too bad you couldn't have some of your stud friends over and give me a circle jerk. Mmm, I can just picture their swollen pricks spurting wad after wad of hot creamy spunk into my hungry mouth. Just imagine me swallowing a quart of jism from all those guys, honey. Pretty sexy, huh?"

It definitely was. Now my dick was close to coming without me even stroking it. Penny sensed this and hurried to the wet bar. She returned with a bottle of red wine and a glass that she poured two-thirds full. "Remember that porn flick we saw, when a couple of guys jerked off in a woman's glass of red wine, and she swallowed it all in one gulp?" she asked. "I've never forgotten it, and now I want to do the same thing. C'mon baby, fill my glass with sperm so I can drink it all up—color my wine with white globs of semen. It'll be sexy, floating and swimming around in my wine. Then I'll throw my head back and chugalug it." She continued: "I want your come so bad, honey. Feed me. Give me all your spunk now. Oh, I need it, I want to eat it now!"

With that, I spurted a rope of jism across the top of the glass and onto her red fingernails. That gush was followed by several forceful squirts that hit the wine in the glass. Penny raised the glass and engulfed the head of my cock in the wine. As I spurted, she licked her lips and savored the come. She watched, fascinated, as I smeared the red wine with about a shot-glass of semen.

"That's it, Penny baby, clean off those sultry lips of yours," I said as the last few drops of sperm dribbled out of my cock into the glass. "Now get ready for a wine you'll never forget. Drink it down, baby, drink it all down like you said you would."

"You don't mind if I have a smoke, do you, and enjoy the bouquet first?" she asked. She lit a fresh cigarette as she took the glass away from my limp dick. She shook it to mix my come with the wine, brought it to her nose and inhaled luxuriantly. "Oh, that's simply heavenly," she said. "What a nice combination. I'm so lucky to have a man who gives me what I want."

I think I'd ejaculated more jism than there was wine in the glass. The two liquids looked quite separate, with their contrasting colors and textures. Penny's eyes were fixed on that glass as she took a drag and then announced, "Well, here's looking at you, sweetie. Bottoms up!" With no hesitation at all, she raised the glass to her mouth, locked her eyes to mine and tipped the glass. The wine and semen oozed into her eager mouth, and she slowly swallowed them. I couldn't believe the eroticism she created as the fluids disappeared into her throat. She took one gulp after another until it was all gone. What a performance! What a gal! I was excited and proud.

"Delicious, honey, just like I knew it would be," she said. She came close and found my lips with hers. Her mouth opened and her tongue darted into mine. I tasted myself again. The flavors of semen and cigarettes were prominent, along with lingering flavors of banana and pussy juice. We kissed passionately for some time, her semi-clad body against my growing prick.

We rested for an hour or so, snuggling and chuckling over our newest afterplay adventures. Penny looked absolutely radiant with her hair pinned back, her rosy cheeks and her heaving, exposed breasts. Her lips still showed dried sperm and banana. After a bit she turned to me and said, "It's your turn now, Tony, what do you say?"

I nodded and held onto my prick, which was getting even stiffer. What delights lay ahead for me now?

"I'll be back in about fifteen minutes, honey. Just think of me with about twenty guys standing all around my nude body, jerking off their fat thick schlongs as my wet tongue hangs out begging to be fed. That oughta keep you hard for a bit. See you soon." Penny kissed me on the cheek and left the room.

And I did think of the mental picture she'd given me, but my mind raced ahead to the part where they all come in buckets and splatter her mouth with gallons of steamy, gushing semen. I envisioned her splashing in sperm and pictured spunk running out of the corners of her mouth. I imagined her gulping and swallowing as fast as she could the mixture of jism from several well-hung studs. Right then and there I had the ultimate picture of my wife as the complete come-queen. Nothing could be kinkier or nastier as every guy jerked off and shot huge streamers of sperm between her sexy lips. Just knowing she would not think of missing one drop of come from all those guys almost made me come then and there. But I knew I had a treat coming in a couple of minutes and might find better use for the sperm.

Finally Penny returned to the bedroom where I was dreaming about her. She was carrying a hidden treat for me, a tray or something covered with a small towel. "My big hungry guy needs to satisfy his appetite too," she said. "So I fixed you another favorite: My *Penthouse Letters* special. Can you guess what this is?" she asked.

"No, I can't imagine. Why don't you indulge me, let me see what it is. I can't wait," I said, with urgency.

With one swipe of the towel she revealed my prize—a fresh stack of hot, steaming pancakes. But not merely pancakes. No, these were dark chocolate ones with puffy, porous little holes just like they'd whip up in a diner. My dick lurched forward as my sweet wife brought the plate down near my aching loins. The heat from the pancakes danced around my cock like a trade wind from the tropics. My manly flesh grew as rigid as granite.

"Oh, damn it," she said, "I forgot to get some pancake syrup. Jesus, now what can we do? And you so hungry, too." She took my hand in hers and placed it on my throbbing cock. She gave it a few jerks, as if to prod me on—as if I needed prodding! "C'mon, baby. Show me how much prick syrup you can make so these hot-cakes can be all rich 'n' gooey to eat!" she said in her sexiest voice. "Mmm, I bet your sloppy white sperm will look absolutely delicious against their dark color."

Two minutes later, I was shooting streamers of fresh spunk all over her hand and onto those pancakes, erupting in an even more powerful climax than I'd had all night. I must have built up a nice supply of come very quickly. Those flapjacks were saturated with my hot jism, even to the point where it oozed down the sides just like real syrup would. A final gasp erupted from my throat that signified to Penny that I was done coming. She squeezed my dick to get the last few drops, milking me like a cow.

"Now open up, honey, let me feed you—you look so depleted and hungry," she said as she took a fork and cut a big portion from the stack of hotcakes. She even moved it to the top of the stack and made sure to smear even more jism into my first bite, satu-rating it with sticky white sperm. Like a good little come boy, I parted my lips and let her feed me my sexy little treat. It was gooey and different, and I would not have changed a thing. The sheer eroticism of the moment—as well as the recollections of the earlier ones—made my heart race as I chewed and chomped on the kinkiest and sexiest breakfast I'd ever imagined.

"Let me see if I cooked these things well," Penny said. She brought a big sloppy forkful of sperm-cakes up to her mouth to sample it. "Mmm. Oh man, that's good. Real gooey and tangy. Baby, you're gonna have to bottle that syrup, that's really special stuff!" she giggled. For the next few minutes we both savored those come-cakes until they were all gone. We topped it off with another wet, deep French kiss, swirling tiny bits of come-soaked pancake between our horny mouths and moaning in ecstasy. I must say, it was quite an eye-opening experience, and I fantasized ahead to our next nasty adventure—what could we devise next time to top this kinky fun?

In the months that followed, we tried out more things than even I thought were possible to think up. We also got back into a more normal love life, enjoying intimate foreplay and inter-course more regularly. But as always, we would indulge in our fa-vorite afterplay sex sessions. If I wasn't sucking our come juices from out of her twat or from around her sexy butthole, she would be slurping them from off her fingers or her favorite dildo after we'd climaxed from intercourse. One time she even had me clean off her ten-inch black dildo with my tongue after she'd mastur-bated to orgasm with it. Then I jerked off and shot all my semen onto it. She told me I looked as slutty as she does as I licked and sucked every drop of come off that fake dark phallus like a cock-sucking pro.

Sometimes when we go out for the night, I can't get but a mile or two down the road before Penny has my fly open and my cock stiff in her sexy mouth. It takes me only a couple of minutes be-fore I'm filling her hungry mouth with all my gooey seed, and it keeps me on my toes to avoid hitting another car or going into a ditch. One time after she'd sucked my cock that way and I had blown my wad into her mouth as I drove down the highway, she zipped my fly back up and sat up without saying one word for about twenty minutes, when we arrived at our destination. It was there that she grabbed me in a lip-lock as I stopped the car. The little vixen actually had held my load of spunk in her mouth the whole time we were driving and now was giving it back to me in a juicy kiss! It was the most incredible "snowball" I'd ever gotten, and Penny admitted that holding a mouthful of my warm sperm for so long turned her on so much that she had several small or-gasms.

Another time, when we'd just had sex and had come powerfully together, she informed me we were late for a dinner engagement and must rush to get there! Hell, my dick was still wet, and her pussy was dripping and squishy as we rushed off in the car. That was a night to remember. My little darling made sure to lick my dick clean and dry with her adoring tongue as I drove the car as best I could. She didn't miss a fold in my uncircumcised cock, and she sucked every drop of come off my still-pulsating rod. When she announced that she also had to get her pussy completely clean, I just sat back, stumped. "Even your finger-licking talents couldn't totally clean out your luscious cunt, with all that come," I said.

"Oh, I brought a glass from the bar for this. Did I forget to mention that?" she asked. And without any hesitation my little come-eater raised her skirt, shoved her moist panties out of the way and brought that glass down to her dripping crotch. As she leaned back on the seat and arched herself up, she looked at me with a totally lust-filled stare and said, "Wow, I can't wait to have my first cocktail of the night, I bet it's gonna be real rewarding and tasty, don't you think?"

After three or four minutes she lowered her spectacular ass back down to the seat and brought the shot glass up from below. She proudly showed me that it was filled almost to the top with come. "I can't believe I never thought of this before," she muttered as she slowly raised her fresh, new cocktail to her waiting lips. My heart raced, and the car swerved slightly as my honey stuck her tongue into her gooey drink for a taste. "I want it all, honey, I'm gonna chugalug it all down now like the sexpot I am!" she murmured. Once again, she locked her eyes onto mine as she tipped the glass back, and with an open mouth and wagging tongue poured the mixture of pussy come and semen between those sexy lips.

She actually accentuated the gulping sounds with her naughty throat as she sucked down every bit of come juice from that shot glass. I watched in fascination as she snaked her gooey tongue into the glass and all around the sides to get every little residue of cunt cream and spunk from the walls and bottom. She moaned a hushed, mesmerized moan. "Simply heavenly, delicious! I love to eat come, honey, I just love it!" she announced quite boldly and proudly. She gave me a quick peck on the lips to share the moment (and a little taste of what she knew turned me on as much as it did her).

I know: You readers think this is some fabricated story, or at best the work of a couple of perverts. Well, let me tell you, unless you really let yourself go in this world of sensuality and lovemaking, you'll never fully know what you're missing and capable of enjoying. Be bold, try new things. Hey, not everything is for everyone, I know that. But I bet as your inhibitions fade and your love for that special someone grows every day, you'll feel obliged to try some fantasies here and there. Believe me when I say that foreplay is exquisitely dreamy, lovemaking is passionately erotic, but afterplay is enticingly sensual and heart-pounding! A man and a woman can't share a more intimate act. The kinkier the better! So let your hair down, guys, and try some juicy stuff; I bet you'll want to incorporate some of it into your love life on a regular basis!—*T.K.*, *Key Biscayne, Florida*

THESE PHONE-LOVING COMPUTER GEEKS FINGERED MORE THAN THEIR KEYBOARDS

It all started one night when I first got hooked up on the Internet. I found myself playing on the computer for hours and hours. I was quite surprised when I found the world of cybersex in a chat room, and at how explicit women could be when masked by the computer. Not that I am complaining. I met my cyberlover that night, and she was fantastic.

We made love over the computer, and I was surprised at how

hard my cock became as I typed and read the messages she typed to me. At one point she asked me to take my cock out of my pants and jack off for her while she told me what she was doing. She said she was fingering herself to orgasm.

Well, it took me only two minutes to spurt come all over my keyboard as I typed my response: "I'm coming!"

My cybersex sessions with her went on for about a month. Silky Satin was her screen name, and she was so hot I wished I could have had her for real. However, she lived clear across the country.

Well, soon I asked Silky Satin if she wanted to take it one step further. Silky Satin typed back, "What do you have in mind?" I told her I wanted to make love to her over the phone. Silky Satin agreed and I typed my telephone number. She called me collect, and after the introductions, which were minor since we already had been chatting on the computer for over a month, it started— the hottest, most passionate sex I have ever experienced. After she gave me her phone number we could not get enough of each other. My cock and my phone bill really shot up! Silky Satin was not only a moaner, but a loud, hot screamer. I started playing games with her, telling her all about the pleasure I got as I licked her body. Over the next six months she fucked herself at my request with makeup brushes and ice cubes, finger-fucked her asshole, licked the pussy juice from her fingers and sucked her own nipples. We had incredible phone sex.

After I graduated from cybersex to phone sex, I realized I was hooked on phone sex. That was fortunate since women have often told me that I have an extremely sexy voice on the phone—a voice that makes them instantly hot and uncontrollably horny! I have a total of about twelve women that I talk long distance to and make love to over the phone. Each one is unique and passionate and willing to do as I ask during our lovemaking.

Then one night, my wife and I were making love and I decided to make a call and my wife agreed. I called Silky Satin and, not knowing how she would handle it, I told her that I had a woman giving me a blowjob while we talked. Silky Satin went wild with desire and passion. Silky Satin told me to tell my wife to finger my ass fast and hard. My wife did with pleasure as she sucked my cock. I described every delicious detail to Silky Satin and could hear her fingering herself as I moaned with pleasure. I laid my wife down and crawled between her legs and ate her pussy so Silky Satin could hear it. I then started to finger my wife and Silky Satin could hear my fingers sloshing in and out of her pussy. Silky Satin screamed her way to four orgasms. It was truly the wildest time any of us had ever spent together.

About a week later, I decided to try it with this twenty-year-old girl named Angela I had met over the computer and had enjoyed phone sex with twice. Angela had the hottest voice you ever heard. My wife said she would love to do it again. So I called Angela as my wife lay there and started playing with my cock—I talked to her and felt her out about this new adventure. She asked me if the other woman was with me now. I told her yes and that she was sucking my cock. Angela moaned, "Oh wow! This is so hot, tell me about what she is doing to you."

I described everything in detail to Angela as my wife gave me the best blowjob ever. Angela then told me to turn the woman I was with on her back and finger-fuck her. I got down between her legs and fingered her pussy fast and hard. Angela was moaning loudly as she listened to my fingers going in and out of my wife's pussy. After Angela came twice, my wife told me to fuck her hard. She told me to lie down for the fuck of my life!

My wife climbed onto my cock and rode like there was no to-morrow. Angela kept on telling me to moan louder as she fingered herself listening to me. Angela told me she wanted to be there licking the other woman's pussy. I asked her if she would really like that. Angela said yes and asked me to give the phone to the woman. My wife took the phone and Angela begged my wife to let her lick her pussy as I fucked her.

That sent my wife over the edge. My wife admitted to Angela, "God! Yes! That would be so nice to have you lick my pussy!"

She then handed the phone back to me. Angela told me she wanted to lick her pussy and my cock as it slid in and out of her. This drove me wild and I told Angela over the phone that I was going to come! I let loose and screamed and grunted into the phone like a wild man. Angela started moaning that she too was coming. I shot my spunk deep and hard into my wife's pussy as I heard Angela and my wife coming together.

I got an e-mail from Angela the following day telling me how wonderful that was and that she had called her girlfriend, Lucy, and together they made love in the afternoon. Angela said she kept on hearing my voice as her lover, Lucy, sucked her clit and brought her to orgasm.

I am now working on another woman who is a forty-one-year-old divorcee. She has agreed to be my Pleasure Unit. When we talk over the computer chat room she calls me Svengali. This is all I want her to call me. She has told me that this is so out of her character that it excites her to no end! She is loyal and does as I request. She lives in Utah. I have spoken to her once over the phone and listened to her masturbate to two orgasms. I vividly told her what I would do for her if she imagined that her hands, which stroked her clit, were actually mine. Later she told me, "Svengali, you are an incredible lover. I am here to pleasure you!"

She had grown as a lover through me. She had never read a sex magazine until I urged her to purchase a copy of *Penthouse Letters*. Now she is a subscriber. She also ordered her first dildo and vibrator through an ad in the magazine. I was with her the first time she used it on her pussy. She had her hardest orgasm ever when she imagined that her eight-inch dildo was really my throbbing cock.

When they say that a long-distance call is the next best thing to being there, they are not kidding. Through the computer and the phone I have had the most amazing sex ever and have never had to actually stick my cock into another woman.

Sex is all in the mind. The fact that my wife lets me fuck around in cyberspace and over long-distance lines tells me that she understands the natural urge men have to fuck around and fantasize. Fantasies make our sex life better. I lust in my heart and I don't even need a condom to enjoy it!—C.G., *Dayton, Ohio*

THEY PROVE THAT JAMAICA IS FOR LOVERS— EVEN IF THEY ARE MARRIED

Vacations to Jamaica are very few and far between. My wife, Shannon, and I wanted to make the best of it. Now that our two sons were in college and sneered at the thought of vacationing with their folks, we saw this as a long overdue second honeymoon.

We arrived at our all-inclusive resort tired and ready for a week of relaxing, ocean and sex. I was looking for a pay-off of wild and reckless lovemaking with Shannon all week long.

After five days of tanned bodies and thong bikinis and two very normal love sessions I was getting depressed. I wanted something to remember this vacation by, so I wrote a note for Shannon and left it on the dresser and went for my morning run on the beach.

The note read, "I dare you to come with me for drinks at midnight. But you must wear your black halter top and long black semi-transparent skirt with no underwear and a shaved pussy."

I waited all day for a response, only to find out that she never noticed the note. I'm sure housekeeping got a kick out of it!

I showed Shannon the note about nine-thirty p.m. and did not get the eager response I hoped for. I was afraid my fantasy was dashed, so I left the room and went for a walk. I stopped for a Long Island iced tea and continued my walk. Then before going back to the room I stopped back at the bar for a second drink. I'm a guy that gets very sexual when I have a drink and when I got back to the room I was ready for some action.

Still holding onto the slim hope that I would return to a smooth-shaven sex machine, I entered the room to find her watching TV. We sat in silence for about twenty minutes and suddenly Shannon pulled off her blouse, turned off the TV and rolled over close to me. This forty-three-year-old mother of two still has one fine set of tits and I wasted no time in sucking those pert nipples to attention. After a little while my foxy wife whispered in my ear that she wanted to be blindfolded and put to bed!

I came on this vacation prepared for anything so I quickly went to my suitcase and brought out a silk scarf. She was stretched out on the bed, wearing nothing but her panties. I went over to her and lifted her head and tied the scarf around her eyes. Then I kissed her deeply, and I licked my way down to her perfect breasts, her stomach and finally rested between her legs. I kissed her hairy mound and immediately sank my tongue deep into her pussy. She squealed in delight, as I have always taken my time with pussy eating. Tonight I wasn't wasting any time. Shannon liked the way I fucked her pussy with my tongue. Her juices tasted sweet and her scent was as stimulating as the ocean breeze. I always loved the way my wife tasted and smelled and tonight was no exception.

After a few minutes of tongue-fucking my wife's breathing was getting heavier. She placed her hands on the side of my head and lifted my chin. I stared at her beautiful face over a tanned, gorgeous spread of pussy, tits, and hair. "I want something in me but not your fingers or cock yet," Shannon whispered. "Any ideas?"

As I said, I came prepared for sex on this vacation so I went to my suitcase again and came back with a fourteen-inch, double-ended black dildo. Jamaican customs agents didn't check this bag going into the country, but they would certainly check it when I left. I wondered what they would say when they saw my assortment of sex toys and novelties.

Shannon pulled up her blindfold and looked at the giant black dick. "Holy shit! That is the biggest dildo I ever saw!" she said.

"Yes, it is big," I said. "But you are supposed to be blindfolded. So put it back on and let me do as I please!"

I knelt between her spread legs and swabbed the giant rubber penis with a tube of lubricant. I placed the tip of the greased black monster in her pussy. Little by little I slid it in, then pulled it out, going deeper each time until nearly all of it was buried in her drenched cunt. I fucked her with it for a good while until I brought her to her first orgasm of the night. The pleasure seemed intense, and after a little rest I slid the cock out at her request so she could go to the bathroom. I took off her blindfold and stretched out on the bed, stroking my cock, waiting for her return.

My eyes lit up as Shannon came out of the bathroom wearing the black outfit that I had asked her to wear. I could see she was wearing a black thong under her skirt, which did look very sexy. I had to ask, "Are you shaved smooth?"

"I guess you'll just have to wait and see when we get to the beach!" she said. "But first we are going down to the bar for some drinks." I didn't tell her I had already had two Long Island iced teas but I wasn't about to throw any wrench in this plan. I put my clothes back on. We went down to the bar.

We walked into the open-air bar and I loved the looks my wife was getting in her black outfit. I ordered a glass of wine for each of us. Shannon wanted to walk to the beach so I walked behind her, watching her beautiful black-thonged ass sway back and forth.

We came to a bench and my hot-looking wife sat on the top of the bench back with her feet on the seat. We sipped wine, talked, and began kissing. My hand found its way to Shannon's perfectly shaped breasts. I was enjoying the feel of her hardening nipples under the black, ribbed knit halter top. As I ran my fingers over them my wife was moaning and licking my ear. We finished our drinks and I held both glasses as I watched my wife reach under her flowing skirt and wiggle out of her panties. She held that thong up to my nose and I inhaled an evening's worth of wet pussy. I could also feel a very damp spot as my tongue reached out and licked the creamy satin crotch. Shannon then folded the thong and put it in my pants pocket and told me to go get us more wine.

It was getting hard to walk straight but I managed to get to the bar and order two more drinks. As I waited for the wine my hand was in my pocket, rubbing over that wet satin crotch. If only the people at the bar knew my hand was touching a soaked pair of panties.

I made it back to the beach without spilling too much wine. When I arrived I spotted Shannon standing knee-deep in the ocean. She was holding her skirt up to keep the bottom from getting wet. As I approached her she turned toward me and flashed me a shot of her shaved pussy.

"Did I see what I think I saw?" I asked.

"Take another look and see," she said, as she pulled that skirt up again. Yup. She had a perfectly smooth cunny in full view on the beach.

I sat down on a beach chair because I was drunk, and horny. Shannon came over and straddled the chair and I reached up to touch a dripping wet, sweet-smelling mound and two of my fingers slipped right in. I worked her pussy like magic and brought my wife to her second climax of the night. I knew her ass was probably showing and I saw three guys walking our way on the beach. I started to pull her skirt down but her hand stopped me.

"Let them look if they want to look," she said.

As they walked past I continued to finger-fuck this steaming hot lady and they all gave me the thumbs-up sign as they slowly walked past. By now I was ready to get to our room for a good second honeymoon fuck.

As we walked from the beach, Shannon asked for her thong since we had to go through the resort lobby to get to the elevators.

"I think you'll have to walk through the lobby without it," I said. I was hot just thinking about that wet, smooth V between her legs, strolling through the lobby with people getting faint glimpses of the woman I was going to fuck.

We got on the elevator and had it all to ourselves. As soon as the door shut I was on my knees and under her skirt. I had nine floors to go and I slipped my tongue between those smooth, puffy lips that I wanted so badly. I heard a "bing." Shit!

The elevator stopped and I got to my feet quickly and just in time for the door to open. Two very nice-looking women got on and we tried to look relaxed. I did a good job except for the pussy juice running down my chin. The ladies were with us until we got off at the ninth floor.

As we were getting out one said, "Now go finish the job properly."

All I could do was laugh and say, "I sure will."

We hurried down the hall and put the key in the door. As we stepped inside I said, "Just strip all your clothes off, quick."

I did the same and I grabbed Shannon's hand and pulled her into the shower. I pressed her up against the wall, kissing her deeply, and put my leg between her spread legs. Using just my kneecap I rubbed her pussy like my knee was a giant dick and made her come.

Exhausted, I threw myself flat on the bed. My ass was sticking up in the air like a baby. My hard cock was pressing against the sheets. My sizzling hot wife came to bed and straddled my legs and started giving me a great back rub. As she crept closer and closer to my always sensitive ass I was really enjoying her soft touch. I nearly shot off into the sheets when she said, "Sometimes I wish I had a cock so I could fuck you the way you fuck me."

"I wish you had a cock, too," I said. The idea of my wife with a big, hard cock was very exciting to me. But I knew it was impossible. First, I was not a homosexual. Second, what if I liked it? Would that make me queer—or just a bit odd?

Shannon provided the answer by moving down on my legs and massaging my ass-cheeks. Then I felt a warm squirt of lubricant dripping down between my ass-cheeks. Soon her fingers were massaging my asshole, making me feel all relaxed and peaceful.

"Cupcakes," my wife said. "I am the man now, so you just spread your legs and relax those jailhouse pussy muscles!"

She received no argument from me. I felt a finger slide deep inside me, and before long that finger was joined by another. The feel of her sliding in and out of me was wonderful but suddenly the fingers disappeared. I heard her fumbling a bit. When I looked over my shoulder I could see from the corner of my eye that she was holding the Big Daddy black dildo like a Louisville Slugger.

"Do you like my big, black dick?" Shannon asked. "How would you like it if your wife shoved this big black dick up your white ass?"

As I said before, I was no homosexual, but I did want that dick up my ass! I nodded like crazy. She smiled and started to swab it up and down with lubricant. Then she held it like a battering ram and pressed the head against my butthole. She was shocked to see that the first six inches entered rather smoothly.

"Cupcakes, you haven't done this before, have you?" she asked.

Like I said, I am no pansy-tailed faggot, but sometimes when my wife is not home I like to stick my fingers up my ass and think about Brad Pitt. One time I got a carrot up there thinking about Mike Tyson.

"No," I answered, "I'm just real relaxed."

I was really enjoying her rhythm, when suddenly there was a slight pause. There was a weight shift on the bed. What I saw next as I turned was the sexiest thing I ever saw!

One end of that dildo was still sliding in and out of me but the other end was now buried deep inside my wife's cunt. She was fucking both of us. I nearly lost my load but I managed to hold back because I wanted so much to fill her pussy with my hot lava. After five minutes more my wife whispered in my ear that she was ready to be the woman again.

Always happy to please, I reached back and pulled the dildo

out of my ass nice and slow. I rolled over and pulled her end of the dildo out of her pussy. It was ready for me, wide and wet and hot! I positioned myself and slid my rock-hard cock in as far as I could. If you have never pierced a freshly shaven pussy before, you are missing a real treat! The feel of your balls slapping against those warm, wet, hairless cunt lips is incredible. I managed to hold on until Shannon had one more orgasm and I let it go. Hot come spurted from my cock for a long, satisfying time.

My wife wants to come back to the island next year. Jamaica? No problem!—*D.H., Lenexa, Kansas*

IF YOU ARE YOUNG AT HEART AND TAKE YOUR VITAMIN E SEX BEGINS AT SIXTY

I had thought I was reasonably experienced sexually until I started dating Gertrude. We are both divorced with grown children. We are in our late sixties, retired, in better than average shape, and crazy about each other. After our first night together, very rushed, on the couch in her living room after a party—she warned me that after five years of celibacy, she was ready to give me all the fucking I could stand!

For the first few days at my house, we were all over each other, fucking, sucking and ass-fucking hour after hour. Gertrude was the first woman I ever had that was enthusiastic about butt-fucking. I could get her shivering with excitement just by talking about bending her over, working my spit against her asshole, and working my cock in. By the time we left for a vacation in Miami Beach, we were really loose with each other, grabbing pussy or cock or tit whenever we felt like it.

In the car, I had her kneel down in the front seat, pull my wrinkled, stiff dick out, and suck it. She was extremely enthusiastic. Since she had double-knit slacks on, I couldn't get to her cunt. I settled for playing with her erect nipples. They stick out really hard from her somewhat firm tits when she's hot.

We were just getting to the boat dock to go sailing when she started coming all over the place. Her eyes rolled back and she started making some very nasty grunting sounds as I told her what a nasty cock-sucking slut she was. When I told her to make more noise while I rubbed her cunt, she went really crazy. On the sailboat, we cooled it, except when I pulled my dick out of my swim trunks and she sucked it! Don't know where she learned such excellent breath control, but it seems like she never needs to breathe.

Things got much hotter on the way to lunch later; when we pulled out of the lot, she lit a reefer, and we got wasted. Soon she was back on the floor with my extremely hard six inches deep in her throat. Gertrude makes the loudest slurping and sucking sounds when she swallows cock. Since she had a short bathing suit skirt on, I immediately yanked the bottom portion over her butt so I could play with her asshole and cunt.

Her cunt was extremely wet. I started fucking her with two fingers while she went crazy on my cock, almost standing on her head to get my balls in her mouth. I started telling her that her willingness to take it in the ass was a dream come true. Ever since I was in the Korean War I had always wanted an ass-fucking woman to please me.

This is the kind of language that makes this Bible Belt babe go insane! But now, we were in heavy traffic at a red light. As a truck pulled up next to us, I said I hoped the driver was watching (he was!) and slid a finger up her ass. The very thought of the driver watching her suck me as I worked a finger up her pussy got us close to climax. As we turned left into the restaurant lot I started moving my fingers back and forth, rubbing them together and pressing on her very obvious G-spot. I told her if she didn't come really hard before I parked, we would park in front of the door and I would jerk her off with people being able to see her as they went in or out. She pulled my dick from her mouth and started screaming and humping up and down. It was great!

She was exhausted during lunch, barely eating. She kept talking about never having been so hot or wild. When I went to the restroom, my cock was drooling pre-come. I saved some on my finger and rubbed it under her nose when I returned. She got off on the smell and said it was time to go fuck in the hotel.

On the way to the hotel, we played around again. Instead of walking to our room, I pointed out a sign that said "gazebo." When I started in that direction, she got a really slutty smile on her face and said nothing. Even though the sun had just gone down, there was no one there. I sat her down, unzipped my shorts, and started fucking her mouth. She acted like there was no thought in her but to be used, as she said later, as my come receptacle. Since I hadn't spurted all afternoon I was soon jamming her mouth hard. I exposed her tits so I could rub my come all over her nipples. When I was ready to shoot my load she leaned back, opened her mouth, held her tits up and told me to spray wherever I wanted. I soaked her cute nipples. She licked me clean and I returned the favor, sucking her tits until she came quietly.

This wasn't the end; back in the room, we started fucking again immediately. I still hadn't been in her cunt or ass since the morning. As we screwed, we talked about how we liked to fuck in public—Gertrude enjoys being told what a bad girl she is for running the risk of being caught with a cock in her mouth by strangers. Suddenly, I pulled my cock out, pulled her up off the bed, and headed to the balcony. Without any words or hesitation, I turned her around, bent her over until her hands were on the ground, and in one smooth motion fucked her pretty ass with all I had. The noises she made were incredible—with all our previous practice and effort, I don't think I'd ever gotten so deep into her ass. It felt great to be screwing her butt while looking down at the people entering and leaving the hotel. She pulled off my dick and moaned, "Fuck me in the bathroom, on the marble floor!" Fine with me. In no time I was on top of her, shoving my cock in her mouth while my hand fucked her ass and cunt.

Gertrude was coming every few minutes, harder and harder. Finally, in a frantic voice she begged me to really stretch her ass. I bent her over the tub, put one finger from each hand in her ass, and stretched it in every direction. I told her to make a lot of noise—so that everyone would hear that she was a proud ass-fucking babe. She came so loudly and hard I had to help her to the bed.

This was not the end of the fun for that trip. We learned more about each other. We realized our fantasies overlapped quite a bit. Maybe I'll write about the weekend that she made love to an old man at a nearby nursing home. Thanks to Gertrude, he's now known as the Man of Steel!—*J.P., Parma, Ohio*

HOW TRUE IT IS: "SEX DOESN'T END WHEN A WOMAN TURNS FIFTY"

I am a fifty-six-year-old woman, widowed five years ago. I married at twenty—a virgin—and enjoyed a wonderful sex life all my married years. I have been healthy all my life, and only weigh eight pounds more than I did the day I was married. I swim every day and eat healthy food.

A few weeks ago the house next to mine caught fire. The remains had to be torn down and a new house built. The work crew asked if they could store drinking water in my refrigerator, the weather being very warm. This I readily agreed to.

I spend a lot of time in my flower garden and yard, dressed in shorts and a halter top. Several days after work started on the new house, I was sitting at my desk in the den, and through the open window I could hear a conversation between several of the workers who were having a coffee break. They were talking about me and my lovely figure. One commented on my beautiful legs, saying, "I'd like to kiss them from her toes to her beaver. Then I want to get my tongue in that beaver and suck on her clit."

His remarks stayed in my head for days. I soon figured out which one had spoken those words. He was an attractive man, husky, and always seemed happy. I watched him every day, and one night as I slept I dreamed of him kissing my legs, which ended in a climax for me. I awoke to a surprisingly wet vagina, the first one I ever remember having from a dream. I touched myself, enjoying the feeling of rubbing my own soft flesh. I was really getting into what I was doing, and soon went over the top in a shattering orgasm.

I could not get this man out of my mind, so I spent a lot of time in the yard and garden, hoping I would be seen and that I would see him. The day came when he came into the garden and asked if he could put a container of water in my fridge. Of course I said yes, and invited him in with me. My heart was beating fast. I wanted him.

I asked him if he would help me move a desk in the rec room, as I wanted to clean behind it. He readily agreed. We moved the desk, but in the process I bumped my thigh. He was sorry I was hurt, and put his hand on my thigh. His touch drove me wild. I pulled his head toward me. Instead of kissing my lips, he dropped to his knees and was kissing my legs and holding my bum.

Lust drove me to pull this man's head into my crotch. He picked me up and laid me flat on my back on the floor, pulling my shorts down, along with my panties.

He spread my legs and began licking my vagina. I was wild with desire from his licking me when he stood up, undid his belt and pulled his pants and shorts down. An overwhelming wave of lust washed over me, and I craved the cock he exposed to me. He lowered himself gently on top of me, and I felt his glorious cock enter me. I couldn't stop squirming as I felt the release of all my pent-up desire.

I exploded. When I came back to reality that cock was still in me, and I still wanted to feel it probing me. I was aware that all the time I'd been recovering from my orgasm he had been thrusting in and out of my vagina, and I loved every minute of it. His movements became faster. Suddenly he broke out in a small sweat, pushed all the way into me, and I felt the spurt of his sperm, which sent me all the way.

When reality returned the second time he was standing over me, looking down at me tenderly. He kissed me, and told me I was wonderful. He shyly asked if we would be able to do it all again later. I told him it was a good idea.

He withdrew his cock, then bent down and played with my clit. Straightening up, he said he would be back later in the afternoon.

The men left the new house at five o'clock, and I was disappointed when I didn't see my man. Fifteen minutes later there was a knock on my back door. There stood my heart's desire. In no time, I was naked on my bed and being fucked. Two months later I'm getting laid regularly and feeling like a bride. All my friends comment on how well I look. Sex doesn't end when a woman passes fifty.—R.S., *Selma, Alabama*

HIS NEW SWEETIE SHOWS HIM WHAT'S SWEETER
THAN ICE CREAM: THEIR CREAM

I had a book of Bukowski's poems on my lap and Coltrane blowing his own poetry thru his sax on the CD player. I wondered why women go for assholes, guys who just want what's between their legs, with no respect at all.

My year-and-a-half relationship had ended several months ago. I had drowned myself in work and reading, controlling carnal desires by masturbating at least three times a week. I'm not unattractive, or too shy to meet people. I didn't know where to find the *right* women.

The bookstore offered nice sights, but they all seemed to have boyfriends. Bars were filled with horny assholes and drunk women who just played games. I wanted to meet someone special, someone I could have a *conversation* with after a night of love-making.

I had about given up when one night I went to the snowball stand near me. Ahead of me in line was a brunette with a firm ass and heavenly legs. I begged the gods to get her to turn around. At that moment she glanced back, right into my eyes.

I couldn't help but fall in love with this green-eyed goddess. Her face was like silk. Her lips were just right for savoring and sensually sucking. Her eyes said she might be interested in this lonely poet gazing at her.

While she ordered, I told myself I had to say *something*. I couldn't pass this up. What did I have to lose? But what to say to this beauty?

"I'll take a large sky-blue with marshmallow," she told the clerk in a silky voice.

And I blurted out, "You know, ice cream would go better with that snowball."

I regretted it immediately. But I do like ice cream with snow-balls, and anyway I couldn't think of anything else to say. I was astonished when she turned to me and said, "I can think of tastier places to put ice cream than the bottom of a snowball."

In her eyes I saw a look of total sexual desire. She had signaled me to grab her and whisk her away to my place to find out what was really tastier. I had a pretty good idea that *she* would be.

"My name is Terry," I said, "and I couldn't help but notice how beautiful you are."

"Well, I'm Elizabeth, and all I needed was your smile to tell me you want me."

By now her snowball was done. I ordered mine, cherry with vanilla ice cream on the bottom. She waited next to me, dipping her spoon into the gooey marshmallow and bringing it to her mouth, licking the white mess off with a pink tongue that whispered, "I want this to be you."

After paying, I turned and asked Elizabeth if she'd like to come back to my place.

"Sure, we can find out which is more fun to lick off our hot bodies, my marshmallow or your ice cream."

I wanted to grab her hand and run home, but I didn't want to screw this up. It had been too long for me to scare off a willing woman when I needed her the most.

We reached my place. I fired up the CD player, and sensual jazz came through the speakers. Elizabeth came up behind me, placed her hand on my chest and traced circles down to the top of my pants. "Let's get these clothes off, shall we?"

I turned around and drew her to me. We stood there with our mouths dancing and our hands exploring every curve of each other's body. Elizabeth pulled my shirt up over my head and sucked on my nipples. This had never happened to me. Despite the tickle, orgasmic tingles ran up my spine.

Thinking had yielded to pure desire. I lifted Elizabeth's T-shirt to find firm breasts hiding behind a black see-through bra. The nipples were as hard as my love member. I undid the clasp and bared those milky breasts. My mouth plunged to the half-dollar-size nipples. She moaned as my tongue traced around each nipple, then swallowed it whole.

Her magic fingers unbuttoned my pants. She lowered my pants and boxers, then applied her mouth to the place right under the head of my cock where the Garden of Eden became man's again. Pulling back from my swollen shaft, she reached for her snowball and spooned marshmallow all over my penis.

"This will be sticky," I thought, "but it'll be worth it."

She dove back to my rod and sucked the marshmallow off with such vigor that I didn't think I could hold on any longer. She wrapped her lips around the cockhead and got her tongue beneath my penis, then slid down and back, down and back.

Eyes closed, she bobbed all the way down to the tuft of my pubic hair and back up, almost but not quite lifting completely off. Her rocking head pulled me to the edge of climax. I moaned. A growl emanated from me. It was the most amazing experience I'd had.

By now all the marshmallow was gone from my penis. As she withdrew to the head, I knew I was about to come and screamed out, "Please, please don't stop." She glanced up, smiled and dove slowly down my shaft one last time, all the way to my pubic hair, swallowing everything male about me.

I exploded. She enjoyed it more than the marshmallow!

As waves of ecstasy rippled through me, she stood up and said, "It's your turn to show me how good that ice cream really is."

I nudged her gently to the floor and removed the rest of her clothes. She spread her legs wide. Her clit peeked out of her folds, gleaming with desire. I ran my fingertips over her hard nipples and traced figures all over her body, skipping only her most private area. I fingered the inside of her thighs. Her back arched and her butt scooted closer.

My fingers had done their job. It was time for the ice cream. I poured the snowball ice into a cup sitting on a table, then spooned some ice cream out. It was cold, but she wanted it. Her eyes cried out pleas for me to give her pussy and clit complete attention.

I lowered the spoon between her legs and smeared ice cream on her hard clit. She bucked at first. Goose bumps popped up all over her beautiful skin. I smeared more over the outer folds of her pussy. It melted right away. I lowered my head into her love zone and lapped up every last bit.

Her body rocked back and forth, up and down. At times it was hard to keep up with her writhing orgasms, but I managed to keep my tongue stuck to her cunt, because I wanted her so much. I enjoyed every moan she let out as I ate her out.

When the ice cream was gone, I kissed her clit, then unleashed my tongue on the erotic spot. As I worked on it with my lips and tongue she had another orgasm, yelling, "Oh my God, oh my God, you are my fucking soul."

When her body turned to mush, I worked my way up to her mouth with kisses and Frenched her for a while.

"That was the best experience I've had," she said. "You are a wonderful lover."

I looked down at the rug and saw drops of our come. Elizabeth noticed them too. "Looks like you found something tastier than your ice cream, huh?"—*T.F., Oklahoma City, Oklahoma*

LATE NIGHT SPEEDING GETS HER
A TICKET TO PARADISE

About five years ago I worked nights from about eight till four in the morning. I liked it; the commute wasn't bumper to bumper and most of the time the sunrises were out of sight.

Anyway, the hour of freeway driving through pretty countryside was calming, and gave me a chance to daydream.

One morning I was daydreaming too much. I was snapped out of it by a cop's flashing red lights and his siren telling me to pull over. I remember fumbling for my license as I tried to figure out if I had been speeding or had done something else worthy of attention from this man in blue.

Actually, I couldn't tell whether he was in blue or black or what, because the sun wasn't up. The side mirror gave me a view of a very tall figure silhouetted against the spotlight. His gait was very slow and deliberate. He stepped heavily on the stones of the road's shoulder. I wondered what was behind the uniform—man or beast? Could I talk my way out of this, or was I going to get stuck with another ticket I couldn't pay?

I was expecting "driver's license and registration please!" from a bent figure looking into my window. I got those words, but they seemed to come from a torso in a starched, black-belted, accessory-clad uniform on a nicely muscled body.

As my outstretched arm handed him the papers I accidentally brushed his belt. That's how close he was to the car. He didn't move back, as I'd assumed he would. Instead he stood very still and did his paperwork.

He didn't say a word, but I could hear his breathing. And it was faster than I would have guessed it would be. Could he be turned on, I wondered.

I extended my arm out the window and "accidentally" let it touch his belt again. He didn't move, much to my delight. I did it again, this time brushing his crotch. This time he moved, but not back. His crotch got tighter than it already was.

I began caressing his crotch, and he got even more excited. By this time so was I. Unzipping his pants was a risk, but a risk worth taking, as I wanted to see how far this dude in blue was ready to go with me.

I hardly got him fully unzipped when out sprang a fine cock. It wasn't the biggest I'd ever seen, but a real work of art—straight, veiny and perfectly cut, making the proud mushroom cap even more proud.

Still he hadn't moved. I wasted no time. First I applied a timid kiss, then sucked the mushroom between my moist lips. Then I went the whole nine yards—in and out and swirling around—everything I could think of. Still he didn't move. What is this guy, I wondered, a rock?

I increased the depth of my throating. I quickened the pace. He didn't flinch, but his breathing became faster and louder. I then used my hands to caress him, alternating lips and fingers. This must have been the magic, because he began to thrust his hips. The thrusting was followed by three streams of his juice, filling my mouth to the rim before I could withdraw and swallow. Damn, I thought. He looks good, he smells good and he even tastes good.

I licked his dick clean and put it back in his pants. When I'd zipped him up he still hadn't moved, except to hand me a ticket and walk back to his car. I could see more of him now. The sun had begun to rise.

He was indeed tall. I just wish he'd been more generous, considering what had taken place. Oh well, I thought. You don't always get what you want, but you may get what you need. Yes, I wanted to blow a studly cop this morning—but I'd have preferred not getting a ticket.

The next morning I saw the ticket on my dresser. It was blank, except for a name and phone number.—*K.L.*, *Blytheville*, *Arkansas*

MOM AND DAUGHTER BOTH
LIKE IT DOGGIE-STYLE

What an incredible couple of weekends! My parents have a friend named Georgette, who was planning a week's vacation in Miami with her kids. I met her last year for a quick five minutes and she seemed like a nice enough woman. My folks told me she would be in Florida and that it would be nice of me to visit her. You know parents.

I was going to say no, but my dad was going to make a big thing out of it. She was a family friend, it was only a ninety-minute drive and what else was I doing anyway? I agreed to meet them at the condo that she time-shared on the beach. Good call.

Talking with my parents about her, I found out she'd been divorced for three years and only recently started dating again. They told me I should show her a good time. My father added that she was looking forward to spending time alone with me, away from her daughters, and we should make plans to spend one day of her vacation here in Pembroke Pines. I've been single for about six months, so I figured what the hell. If she wanted a good time, I would oblige.

A few weeks later I decided I would definitely go see her. My dad hinted something to the effect that she was expecting something sexual to happen when she came down. It was all set up for me, all I had to do was drive down the following weekend.

Georgette called me the day before her plane was to land, and we talked for maybe half an hour. It was just small talk, getting to know each other better and finalizing directions on how to get to her condo. Then she started talking about how great it would be if her daughter and I hit it off. That's when I discovered that her oldest daughter was eighteen (I'm twenty-four), and Georgette just couldn't stand the loser that her daughter was dating.

I wasn't sure what to expect when I got to Miami the next day. Was the woman interested in me for herself, or in getting me together with her daughter? I'd never imagined being in a situation quite like this.

I arrived at seven in the evening, and met her two daughters, Kathi and Pam. We all sat around and made conversation for a few hours, killing time until the dance clubs got rolling at around ten. Pam was quite a looker: a very petite five-four, with a twenty-three-inch waist. She couldn't have weighed more than ninety-five pounds.

We were getting along fine, and we all headed to the club. Pam and I immediately hit the dance floor. Her boyfriend said he just wanted to soak up the atmosphere and watch for a while. We danced a few songs, then broke for refreshments.

I told her she was a fabulous dancer, and she shocked me by saying, "I should hope so, I only do it for a living. It's different dancing and not taking off my clothes, though." I should have guessed that little secret from the way she was gyrating her hips. Boy, was she sweet! I wasn't sure what to do. Her man was there, so I tried to keep my distance from Pam. At the same time, I still wanted to let her know I was interested. And then I was also flirting with Georgette. It was a difficult task, and it got harder to keep my hands to myself the more I had to drink.

We would be going back to the condo soon. Pam danced up close and said to me, "I know a great way we can cool off later. How would you like to go skinny-dipping in the ocean when we get back?" Would I ever! I almost grabbed her right there.

The sleeping arrangements pretty much sucked. Pam's sister was in the bedroom, so the rest of us were sleeping in the living room. Pam and her mother settled down on the sofa sleeper, and I took the cushions on the floor. Both of them fell asleep right away. I guess it was the fatigue of flying all day. I wanted to ask Pam about that dip, but I decided not to, as I might wake her mom.

In the morning I woke up horny, as usual, and decided to shake Pam and see if she still wanted to go for a swim. She did, so we snuck out and headed for the ocean.

There was nobody out there but us, and after only ten minutes she stripped her suit off and handed it to me. I put it in my pocket and swam around with her for at least an hour, enjoying the sight of those perfect breasts of hers bobbing around in the water.

We threw each other around a bit, playing in the surf and talking about everything. We didn't start kissing for quite a while, and by then there were kids starting to swim in our vicinity, so she replaced her suit and we went back up to the condo.

At the condo her mom was up, and told me she was going out to the pool to check on Kathi. A few minutes later, Pam came out of the bathroom, where she had been changing, and asked where her mom was. I told her, and she fixed me with a lustful stare that could melt steel.

She sauntered up to me and gave me the hottest kiss I'd had in a long time. She pulled up her shirt, exposing one of her nipples for me to go to work on. I swirled my tongue around the hardening nipple, then sucked for all I was worth. She started shaking after a few minutes of this and told me she was about to come. Talk about your sensitive breasts!

She pushed me onto my knees and told me how horny I had made her. She unzipped her jean shorts, revealing a pair of silky red underwear. I grabbed the waist band and had just started pulling them down when we heard the doorknob turning. She zipped up quickly, whispering that we would have to continue this some other time.

I asked her if she and her mom wanted to come to Pembroke Pines with me. She said no, but her mom said yes. Georgette told me that she wanted to spend some more time alone with me, and she followed me back north in her rental car.

All I could think about on the drive back was her daughter, but I knew what Georgette was expecting also. She wasn't bad looking for a forty-year-old. She was in good shape. Obviously she made an effort to take care of herself.

We got to my apartment around three in the afternoon. We went for a swim in the pool, then lay out in the sun for a little while. She looked all right in a bathing suit, and I flirted with her on and off all afternoon, still trying to decide what to do.

After dinner, Georgette and I went to listen to a jazz band and have a few drinks. She took my hand and asked if we could go back to the apartment. There was no question what she was thinking about. When I said okay I was committed, there was no turning back. Her daughter had made me extremely horny in the morning, and I was still in the mood.

Georgette put on a silk nightgown and climbed into bed. I stripped to my underwear, shut off the lights and crawled in next to her. I put my arm around her and started kissing.

She told me she was very nervous, but I told her we would go slow, and she didn't have to do anything except relax. I kissed her gently, finding her tongue a willing recipient of my attentions.

My hand glided down the smooth material to her rear, which was surprisingly firm. She sat up and removed her nightie, and in the darkness I could see the outline of her breasts, which were a little bigger than her daughter's and not quite as perky. I kissed them just the same, as I had done to Pam's that morning, and continued downward with my tongue until I reached the top of her panties.

She stopped me long enough to remove the barrier to my efforts, and I got down to my favorite job: eating a woman out. I was very methodical, wanting her to get maximum pleasure from my attentions. I licked her up and down for several minutes, stopping each time to tease her clit with a swirl at the top. She was bucking her hips and moving around so much I didn't think sometimes I was going to be able to maintain contact.

Panting heavily, Georgette pulled me up to her and had me lie on my back while she removed my briefs. I'll admit I was looking forward to this. I had heard so many good things about how experienced older women were at giving head that I decided I was just going to lie back and enjoy it.

She spent a lot of time licking the underside of my shaft, then moved on to the head and finally took my whole shaft in her warm mouth. She continued swirling her tongue around my glans while I rubbed her shoulders and told her how good it felt.

She crawled up beside me sooner than I would have liked, but she was ready to move on to bigger and better things. I positioned myself at the entrance to her sex, and slowly tried to enter her. I tried several times, but she was as tight as a virgin.

She apologized, saying she just needed to relax some more. I told her I knew what would help, and happily went down on her one more time. This time I ate her with verve, pushing her legs up to her chest to give me complete access to her slit. I love that position, because a woman's whole vagina down to her asshole is open for examination by my eyes and tongue. I used extra saliva and tongued her hole inside and out, exciting her without bringing her to the point of climax.

When I thought she had squirmed enough, I moved forward and found her tunnel more than ready to receive my tool. I rocked with her back and forth, kissing her as we fucked. Her eyes were rolled back in her head the whole time I was in her. I sat up with her feet on my shoulders, and continued to stroke her. I licked her arches and played with her breasts and then she asked if she could be on top for a while. No problem here! She didn't appear too comfortable up there, however; we just couldn't find a good rhythm.

I crawled out from under her and got behind her. She said that was her favorite position, and it's mine too. She pushed back against me, meeting me stroke for stroke.

What a tight squeeze she was from this angle! I'd swear I was doing it with a teenager, it was so tight. We had fucked for an hour before moving to this position, and I only lasted another ten minutes, before emptying my load deep inside her. This was a first for me, as I have always pulled out. But it was at her request, and it was the most powerful orgasm I've ever had.

She thanked me, then went to the bathroom to wash up. We dozed off together, but my internal sex mechanism was thinking of anything but sleep!

I woke at four, and found I was spooning her. I slid my hand up to her breast and gently kissed the back of Georgette's neck, slowly waking her. She rolled onto her back, and I took my tongue on another tour of her body, stopping at each breast before diving back into her sweet pussy. She was moaning more than the night before. I guess by that point she was done with the nervousness.

We did a long, slow missionary fuck this time around, changing pace near the end when I couldn't hold my enthusiasm back any longer. I waited for her to come before I exploded again inside her. She said it was better than she'd ever imagined sex could be, and I told her I didn't want to disappoint her, as it was pretty clear it had been a while since anyone had treated her right.

It was time to get up when we finished, as I had to make it to work—with a smile on my face! I told her I would try to make it down the following Friday if I could get off, and she said she and Pam were looking forward to my coming down again.

All week I thought about how I could get with the daughter and not have her mother find out. I didn't know what kind of jealousy would be generated by that move, but I was willing to take the risk.

When I called later that week to confirm that I would be able to come, Georgette told me that Pam was looking forward to going dancing again, and added that Pam would be wearing a skin-tight dress and looking very hot for my visit. She knew exactly what I was after!

When I arrived, I sat down on the couch next to Pam, and we talked to her mom while we watched the tube for a bit. I took her feet in my lap and started giving her a foot massage. That led to a calf rub, and I had to stop myself several times from going any further. From the moment I got there we couldn't keep our hands off each other.

I got dressed to go out, and Pam did the same. I asked Georgette what she was wearing, and she said she was going to stay home. Then she told us to have a good time.

I couldn't have been happier. I didn't have to worry about behaving myself. And neither did Pam—when we got in the car she hiked up her dress and told me she'd worn her favorite black G-string just for me. I was in for a wild night.

We got drinks and found a seat. There was hardly anybody there, as it was early, but those who were just kept staring. She sat down on my lap and started tonguing my ear, then grabbed my hand and tried to put it up her dress.

I'm not one for a public show, so I put a stop to that. I told her we should dance a bit, and work off some of the sexual energy we were storing up.

We began just dancing normally, then we got a little closer and were dirty dancing the rest of the night. I'm sure the bouncers were enjoying the show. There were five of the big lugs forming a wall near us.

Then she said, quite coyly, "How far do you think we could get before they threw us out?" I told her I thought we'd better leave instead of finding out, and she happily followed me to the parking lot. This girl was anything but shy—she gave me the choice of going to a cheap motel or doing it on the beach. Of course I picked the latter, and we headed back toward the condo.

I took some towels out of my trunk, and we scurried down to the ocean. We laid them in a semi-secluded spot. Before I could even get my shirt off she was already lying down naked, waiting for me to join her. I kissed her passionately, but when I looked up there was a pair of people headed down the beach toward us. I told her, and all she said, before giving me another lip-lock was, "So, let 'em watch."

After they passed, my bravery was restored and I went straight for her perky breasts. She didn't let me stay there long, pushing me down to her finely trimmed bush.

She had a narrow strip of hair running from her tan line to her twat, making a perfect runway for my tongue. I took all the time in the world to enjoy that sweet meat, sliding up and down between the folds of skin, sucking the juices into my mouth and teasing her clit with my thumb. I let her come three times before moving up beside her and letting her get a taste of her own sex on my lips as I Frenched her. I almost got whiplash when she threw me back on the towel and moved to engulf my rod.

She had the most eager mouth I'd ever had on my prick. As she took the full length in her mouth, her tongue was doing a number on the underside, where it's most sensitive. She stroked me while she sucked and fondled my balls with her free hand.

I was really getting into it when she stopped and pulled me on top of her. I entered her slowly, making her squirm all over, because I knew she just wanted me to give it to her. She was having none of that nonsense, and thrust her hips up to meet mine, burying my member in her moist heat.

What an incredible feeling! Her pussy muscles were doing a major squeeze number on me. We tried all variations of the missionary before she climbed on top. She made herself comfortable and got to work, gyrating her hips in a circular motion and pounding me for all she was worth!

She got tired pretty fast (three orgasms can do that to you), so we switched to the doggie-style, which, she informed me, was her favorite way. Like mother, like daughter, I guess!

Then I got the surprise of the evening. She pulled me out and lay spread-eagled in front of me. Turning her head over her shoulder, she said, "You know where I want it now, don't you?" She didn't have to ask twice! I bent down and ran my tongue down the crack of her ass, darting it in and out of her puckered hole. It was already pretty wet from her own cunt juices running into it, and it didn't take long before I was deep in her tender young ass. I couldn't get enough of this! All too soon I blasted her ass with my sticky come.

When we were done, we had sand sticking to us everywhere. We swam in the ocean to wash it off. Then Pam suggested we go for a walk in the buff. We went maybe a quarter mile before turning back, and almost immediately there was a man heading for us from inland with a walkie-talkie.

He said, "Don't worry, I won't turn you in. I do it myself sometimes. But my friend is shore patrol, and he'll be by in about fifteen minutes, so you might want to be gone by then." We thanked him for the warning and beat feet out of there.

What a fantastic night! The next day they all flew back north, and I drove back to Pembroke Pines. On the way I found a note in my car from Pam, thanking me for a very memorable vacation, complete with her address, phone number and her black G-string.—L.F., *Pembroke Pines, Florida*

A LUST-CRAZED FAN, A SEXY CELEB, A CAMERA: WHAT MORE COULD YOU ASK?

I keep telling Carrie she should be the one writing this, but she's such a space cadet, I know she'll never get around to it. So here's the scoop: Carrie and I are roomies at a college where it can snow until May, so we made plans to spend spring break in the Bahamas. Soon after our arrival, Carrie heard that a certain movie star was vacationing at a nearby resort. I won't say who, as I learned all about libel stuff in a journalism class last semester and don't want to end up in court. Mr. X is blond and hunky, and Carrie has one of his posters tacked to the ceiling above her dorm bed. Since she has the top bunk, that puts her pretty close to him every night.

Carrie likes this leading man a lot. When one of my classes was canceled because the prof was sick, I got back to the dorm earlier than usual and found Carrie in her bunk, naked, with her legs spread wide. She was tugging her left nipple. It was an inch long and so stiff it looked like a pinkie sticking up. She was rubbing her pussy with the other hand. She didn't hear me come in because she was wearing headphones. The volume was so high that I recognized the CD as the soundtrack from Mr. X's latest movie. She kept saying his name over and over like a mantra, lost in her own little world.

Any guy on campus would have died to be in my shoes then. Carrie is really pretty, with dark hair and big brown eyes. What the boys like best, though, is that she has exceedingly large breasts for so petite a girl. The first time we got undressed in front of each other, I kidded that if law school didn't pan out, she could always work as a lingerie model. Her nipples also drew attention. I once told her that no matter what type of bra she wore, they stuck out like thimbles.

"I don't think any guy I've talked to since puberty has looked me in the eye," she said.

Considering how prominent her nipples were in "neutral," it shouldn't have come as a surprise that they were even more impressive when excited, as they certainly were now. She wasn't exactly being dainty with them, either. Seeing that alone would have got anybody going, but what was going on south of the border was even hotter.

Carrie and I talk about everything, and early on we compared notes about pussy grooming. She said she was lucky because she never got razor stubble when she shaved her bikini line. Judging by what I saw that day, her shaving went a lot further than a little "edging." Her legs were wide open. She had two fingertips pressed against her mound above the slit of her pussy, making quick circles, so that most of her cunt was visible. I didn't see a single hair on it. Her pussy lips were shiny with juice and gaping open. She dipped a finger into her pussy opening, wormed it around a little, then went back to rubbing her mound.

She opened her eyes, and I thought she'd spot me. But she stared straight up at her poster without glancing left or right, straight into the clear blue eyes of her dream man. She kept whispering his name. She bucked her bare crotch, climaxed, then rolled over, gasping for air. I hurried out of the room, stayed away for a half-hour, and never mentioned what I had seen. Until now, that is. That's what Carrie gets for making me write this letter! Anyhow, to get back to the story:

We're in the Bahamas, and Carrie hears that Mr. X is staying down the road from us. She tried getting into the place, but security was too tight. So she took her camera and staked the place out, hoping he would eventually leave the resort to see more of the island. I thought she was nuts, so I hung out with friends from school while she played spy. Two days later she spotted him and his girlfriend leaving the resort. She managed to follow them on a rented motorbike. When they parked near a sign that read "Private Beach" and got out, she ditched the bike and threaded her way through the undergrowth to get some photos.

That night Carrie wore a dazed grin when she described the scene. "At first I saw them playing in the water, which was about waist high. Nobody else was around. His girlfriend was topless, but I didn't think that was any big deal, since that's cool at a lot of beaches. But when they walked back to their towels, I saw that both of them were totally naked. Totally!"

"Well, come on, what's he got?" I asked.

Carrie all but swooned. "You wouldn't believe. You just

wouldn't believe! His body was like a Greek statue, all toned and muscular and smooth, and his dick looked like it was a foot long. I know it probably wasn't, but it looked huge!"

"Circumcised?"

"Oh, yeah. With a big, smooth head. His balls were drawn up tight against his body, which made his dick look even bigger. I wanted to run out of the bushes and offer to be his love slave for life."

"So why didn't you?"

Carrie rolled her eyes. "Well, his girlfriend started sucking his dick. I didn't think he'd appreciate being disturbed."

My mouth practically dropped open. "And you've got pictures of this?"

"That's not all. After she blew him—and she did one hell of a job, taking the whole thing down her throat—she lay down and he fucked her. I got so wet watching them that I was dripping."

She said Mr. X alternated fucking the girl and pulling out to eat her pussy every few minutes. Carrie admitted that she was so turned on watching Mr. X make his lover cry out and come that she reached inside her khaki shorts to finger-fuck herself. "I couldn't help it," she said. "If you could have seen the way his tight butt flexed when he pumped in and out of her body, you would have done the same thing."

I smiled, but I didn't mention the time that I had seen Carrie fiddling with herself in our dorm room. If his poster alone had been enough to work her into that frenzy, I could imagine how overwhelming the sight of him in the flesh—and only the flesh— must have been.

"The last part nearly made me pass out," Carrie said. "When he was ready to come, he pulled out of her pussy and held his big, beautiful dick in one hand. He was up to his knees in the sand. The girl scrambled around to suck him, jerking her hand up and down the length of his prick the whole time. He groaned so loud I could hear him from twenty feet away. She tried to swallow his come, but a lot of it dribbled out of her mouth. God, it was so sexy I could have died."

"I'm surprised you could keep on taking pictures!"

She waved her camera in the air. "It's all right here. My God, can you imagine what this film is worth?"

I told her she should keep the roll in a safe place until she could get it developed. She agreed that was a good idea, and opened the back of the camera.

Did I mention that Carrie is a scatterbrain? Tears formed in her eyes when she looked down at the camera. She had forgotten to load it! Just then, we heard a jet pass over our hotel. Somehow, we both knew who was on it.—*T.P., Fort Collins, Colorado*

A HORNY HONEY WHO IS SCORNED GOES FROM FORLORN TO REBORN

I was supposed to be meeting my boyfriend Chad at a club. Other guys hit on me for more than an hour before I admitted to myself that the son of a bitch had stood me up. It wasn't the first time. Chad was a workaholic whose job came first, last and always. I was so pissed, I felt like fucking the next man who asked me to dance. I had had a shitty day at work and I was horny as a cat in heat. I needed to get off really bad.

I felt a tap on my shoulder. This is it, I thought, putting on a smile before I turned around. This was going to be somebody's lucky night. With any luck, he wouldn't look anything like Chad.

That turned out not to be a problem.

"Hi, I'm Ashley," said a petite girl with huge eyes and a short, gamine haircut. "I wondered if you might want to dance."

This was a new one. I had never been approached by a girl—not one like this. She didn't have a necklace that spelled out "dyke" or a lambda tattoo, but it was obvious she was interested in more than just dancing. She was really pretty, and not at all butch. Her top was shiny purple velvet, held up by two thin spaghetti straps. Her breasts were small, but with plump protruding nipples. Her black jeans were tight on her slender legs. An image flashed into my mind—of this girl on her back in bed, naked, with another woman's face between her legs, licking her pussy, tasting it.

"I'm sorry, I don't—" I began.

She cut me off. "I noticed you turned down all the guys who asked you, so I thought, you know." She nudged me with a bare shoulder and gave me a conspiratorial grin. I looked around. I hadn't spotted anyone I recognized at this club since getting here. No one I knew would be the wiser.

"Come on." Ashley took my hand and led me to the dance floor. I swallowed the rest of my drink and put my glass back down on the bar. The thought that kept going through my head as we danced was, "Why not?" I was sick to death of Chad. Maybe it was time to expand my horizons. I liked the way Ashley's velvet top moved against her little breast-buds as she danced. When she turned around, her ass looked so firm that I wanted to grab it. Until that night, I never believed the line about how everybody is a little bit bisexual. I'd had lots of girlfriends, but none I wanted to kiss. With Ashley, it was all I could do to keep my hands off her.

"You're good," Ashley said, coming close. She rested her hands on my hips and swayed with the music. I could tell that people around us were staring. I didn't care. Let them look.

I rested my own arms on Ashley's shoulders and said, "So are you."

She cupped a hand over my ear. "Do you want to get out of here?"

I nodded emphatically. We took her car. As soon as we were inside her apartment, she said, "I'm all sweaty," and pulled her top over her head. She fanned her bare chest with her hand and turned up the air-conditioning. Her nipples had no distinct central points or halos. She saw me looking at them.

"You like?" she asked. She tugged at them with her thumbs and index fingers. "They're not very big."

"They're perfect." I put my palms against them and kissed Ashley's tiny mouth. Her hands went around my waist and found the zipper of my skirt. She unzipped me and pushed the skirt down my hips. It dropped to the floor.

Then she was grabbing my ass through my pantyhose and pulling my crotch against hers. I thought that girls who liked other girls would take things slow and gentle. Was I wrong! Ashley and I were going at each other like nobody's business. When she squatted and tugged my pantyhose and panties down, all I thought was, "What took you so long?"

On her knees, Ashley held my cunt lips apart so she could lick my clit. I ran my fingers through her short, silky hair while she ate me. I tilted my crotch forward. Her tongue felt wonderful. I wanted her to suck my tits. I wanted to suck hers, too, and lick her pussy the way she was licking mine. I started unbuttoning my blouse. It was like a dream—the really dirty kind of sex dream that is erotic as hell while it is taking place, but makes you feel confused when you wake up. I had never so much as kissed another girl, but at that moment the thing I wanted most in the world was to get Ashley in a 69 so we could eat each other's cunt at the same time.

"Fuck, you taste good," she said, staring at my crotch. She slid a finger back and forth in my slit, then glanced up at me. "I'm glad I was right about you back at the club."

"Let's go to bed," I said. My voice was low and husky. I couldn't help it.

Ashley skinned down her black jeans. I thought it was wonderful that she wore no panties. It made me feel sexy to think of her going out with nothing between her pussy and her jeans. Her pubic hair was pale and fine, almost invisible. We pushed down the covers and climbed onto the mattress. Ashley played with my tits. She alternated sucking them and giving them gentle love bites. She sensed precisely how much pressure excited me. She kept two fingers working on my pussy while she tongued and teased my nipples. I heard the wet sound of those fingers fucking in and out of my cunt, driving me crazy.

"Let me eat you," I moaned. "I want to eat you while you eat me."

Ashley turned, and we lay on our sides with our crotches in each other's face. She lifted a leg, showing me her little treasure. Her pink asshole was just an inch away from her pussy. I had never seen a woman's private parts this close in my life. I could smell Ashley's cunt, with a perfume that was bitter and sweet at the same time. Ashley licked back and forth in my slit. I gave her pussy a little kiss, then another. I spread her cunt lips as she had done mine earlier. Her clit was a pink, hooded nub. I flicked it with the tip of my tongue.

"Oh yeah, oh yeah," Ashley said. "Keep doing that. It feels wonderful." I swirled my tongue all around her clit, then let it travel down farther. Ashley was very creamy at her pussy's opening. I probed into that tight little hole. I felt daring and lapped across the bridge of skin between her vulva and anus. She squealed when I circled her asshole with my tongue. I knew she'd like that. It was one of my favorite things Chad did for me, when he wasn't too tired to fuck.

Ashley licked my ass the same way. Then she went back to sucking my clit, really going at it. "Come in my face," she said. "I want you to come. I want to make your beautiful cunt come." She kept two fingers deep in my fuckhole as she sucked harder, taking me past the point of no return. I groaned and spasmed, squeezing her fingers tight with my pussy. I wanted to give her a climax as good as the one she had given me. I took another tip from my unreliable boyfriend. I wormed my middle finger into her slippery pussy, then pushed the finger, now well-lubricated, up her ass. With my finger buried in her backside and the thumb of the same hand up her cunt, I sucked her clit hard.

"Yes, yes, *yes!*" Ashley cried, trembling through her orgasm. If she was sweaty earlier, it was nothing compared to this. Her body shone as if dipped in oil. She turned around so we could kiss while we caressed each other.

"That was fabulous," she said. "I knew you would be good the minute I saw you at the club. You're wonderful."

I decided not to tell Ashley that she had been my first girl, or that I had learned a lot of my technique from a man. Earlier that night, I had thought that I wanted to forget all about Chad. But I had to admit that a few things about him would be useful to remember.—G.T., *Biloxi, Mississippi*

GIRLS LIKE THIS COME ALONG
ONLY ONCE IN A BLEW MOON

I have a theory that most women hate TV sports because they don't like anything that distracts men's attention from them. But while most women just bitch and moan about the situation, my one-and-only used a different strategy.

I have to admit that I spend a lot of time glued to the tube. The final straw for my girlfriend Krissy came when a crucial game was airing the night that she got back from a two-week business trip. She was horny as hell when she showed up at my apartment.

"If I don't get fucked right now," she said, "I'm going to explode."

I explained how important the game was, but she ignored me. She sat on the edge of my bed and started undoing my pants. I glanced at my clock radio. It was kick-off time. The silent television set at the foot of my bed mocked me. I like screwing as well as the next guy, but a division title was at stake!

I saw that my best choice was to throw Krissy as quick a fuck as possible and hope she would be satisfied. I whipped off my clothes. After all, two weeks was a long time to go without pussy. My dick stiffened as I watched Krissy unbutton her blouse, un-snap the front clasp of her bra, and reveal her sweet tits. She wasn't kidding about being charged up. Her nipples were stand-ing out stiff and pink.

I almost forgot about the game I was missing when Krissy took off her skirt. She wasn't wearing anything under her pantyhose. I saw that she had done some special grooming down there. Her pussy was bare. I imagined her sitting in a hotel room before her flight home, shaving her pretty cunt especially for me. When she peeled off her pantyhose and I got a clearer look at her smooth, bald lips, I got hungry in a hurry.

She saw where I was looking. "You like that, huh?" she asked. She put her hands on her hips and pushed her crotch forward to give me a better look at her immaculate cunt.

"I'll bet it tastes as good as it looks," I replied.

"You tell me." Krissy climbed on top of me in bed, straddling my face.

I grabbed the cheeks of her ass and covered her hairless pussy with my open mouth. I knew that she liked being eaten with long, flat strokes. I licked her from asshole to clit and back again, over and over. I detected the scent of soap on her skin. The thought of her lathering up her crotch and shaving was so erotic that I hoped she would let me watch the next time she did it.

"Mmm," she sighed. "I didn't know if I would have time to make myself pretty for you down there, but now I'm glad I did." Why did she say "have time"? It sounded too much like "half-time." My dick stopped throbbing and went half-soft.

I looked Krissy sincerely in the eyes. "Honey, please," I said. "Just let me have the game on in the background. This is one that I can't miss."

She rolled her eyes and crossed her arms under her big tits. "Go ahead," she said. "I don't mind." Obviously, she had some-thing up her sleeve—or somewhere. I knee-walked down the bed, not wanting to make any sudden moves. I was just about to lean over and grab the remote when Krissy did some grabbing of her own. She reached between my legs from behind and got hold of my prick. She had moved around in bed so that her face was between my thighs. She took the head of my dick between her lips and sucked it. I'd never had a backward blowjob before. It felt good. Damned good. My cock stiffened again, but Krissy kept a good grip on it and went on sucking. Because my prick could not spring up like it wanted to, I had to keep bending over farther and farther. Soon my shoulders were pressed against the mattress and my ass was sticking high in the air. Krissy's tongue was all over the head of my straining prick as she sucked. Her fingers were wrapped around my shaft as tight as a vise.

It was a delicious, fantastic sensation—especially when she probed my asshole with a finger. Because of my undignified position, my ass-cheeks were spread wide enough to give her easy access. Soon she was massaging my prostate like an expert, just enough to make my eyes roll up in my head, but not enough to make me spurt my load. I felt like I had died and gone to heaven. Finally, though, I gasped, "Baby, let my dick go. I've got to come, and I can't do it in this position."

Krissy took her mouth off my prick, but kept a firm grip with the non-massaging hand. "Swear you won't turn on that goddamned football game?"

Sweat dripped from my face. "I swear, Krissy. I swear!"

"Well . . . okay." She let go of my dick. It sprang up against my belly. But not for long. I was between Krissy's legs in a nanosecond, fucking her smoothly shaved pussy. I must have shot two quarts of come into that tight, pink hole.

I forgot about the other ball game. We spent the next three hours sucking and fucking. Sometime after midnight, Krissy fell asleep. It was then that I quietly phoned the local sports hotline. My team had lost. Ah well, I thought, it's only a game. I ran my tongue over my lips and tasted once more the flavor of Krissy's cunt. My dick rose. I scooted down under the covers, spread

Krissy's legs and licked her creamy pussy again. It never hurts to go for extra points.—*I.T., Louisville, Kentucky*

WHEN A WEATHER GIRL GETS WET, A HIGH-PRESSURE SYSTEM MOVES IN

My job as an intern at a small TV station last summer consisted of "gofer" duties and running errands for the bitchy general manager. You can imagine how thrilled I was driving around town at her command, buying her tampons and picking up her dry cleaning. But hey, anything to get that college credit.

The one good thing about the job was that it put me in proximity to Wendy the weather girl. One look at Wendy—with her honey-blonde hair, oversized tits and miniskirt-perfect legs—made it obvious why she was on TV, with or without meteorology skills. She had to be the best-looking female in the tri-state area. Seriously, she couldn't walk through a room without causing every man with a heartbeat to stare.

Phil, one of the reporters, saw me gawking at Wendy that first day. He took me aside and told me that all the weather girls in the country had one thing in common. "They're the best pieces of ass you'll ever fuck," he said, his voice gruff from years of cigarettes. "Take it from me," he added. "Even in a rinky-dink burg like this, you can bet that the weather girl only got where she is by using her mouth, her tits, her pussy and her ass."

"But our general manager is a woman," I said.

He cocked an eyebrow. "Like I said," he muttered, "they're the best. They'll fuck anything."

I thought Phil was just playing the cynical, hard-bitten newshound. But later that day I saw Wendy go into the general manager's office and close the door. She was in there a long time. I eased up beside the door and quickly deduced that the moans and groans I heard were not inspired by a discussion about an impending storm front.

Wendy's hair was disheveled and her clothes in disorder when she emerged, and that made her look sexier than ever. I felt my dick start to get hard. Even though I knew the general manager was a bitch, I had to admit that she was damned good-looking for a woman in her thirties. So it was definitely a turn-on to think that Wendy just had sex with her. I wondered if she had Wendy eat her pussy, or if she ate Wendy's. Hell, maybe they ate each other out.

Wendy seemed surprised to see me standing there in the hall. "Oh, hi," she said, distracted. "Um, I've got to get ready for the show."

She walked past me. Nobody else was within sight, so I decided to take my shot. I caught up with Wendy and said, "Look, would you like to go out sometime? A movie or something?"

She stopped and looked at me again. This time she really looked, like she was seeing me for the first time. "You're one of the new guys, right?"

That was close enough to the truth—for my purposes, anyway. I said, "Yeah. My name's Marty."

Wendy stepped closer to me, far enough into my "personal space" to make my cock throb. Her lipstick was slightly smeared. I pictured her mouth on the GM's pussy, licking and sucking it, pushing her tongue up inside.

"Marty, I'm horny as hell now," Wendy said, keeping her voice low. "D'you know what I was just doing in that office?"

Her breasts were almost touching my chest, and I could smell her hair. I could not have lied if I wanted to. "I think so."

"And what exactly do you think?" Her lips were full and pillowy, and her eyes half-closed. She couldn't have gotten my prick any harder if she had dropped to her knees and blown me.

"I think you were having sex."

She leaned in even closer. "That's right. The boss sat me on her desk and ate my pussy. Now I'm all charged up and need some cock. Are you man enough to help me out?" This was like something out of a wet dream. I thought sluts like this only existed in porn movies. Compared to the low-libido girls I knew on campus, Wendy was like a species from another planet.

She didn't wait for an answer. She knew that no man would turn down that kind of request. She led me to the office that doubled as her dressing room. I grabbed her and stuck my tongue in her mouth. Her big tits felt firm against my chest. I knew she could feel my hard dick on her belly. She unzipped my pants, reached inside them and into my boxers and pulled out my stiff hard-on.

I loved the feel of her soft hand on my cock. After a few strokes she got up on her desk, pulled her skirt up around her waist and spread her legs. She wore pantyhose with an open crotch. The short curls of her golden pubic hair were still wet and plastered against her skin, from her session with the boss.

She asked me, "Have you got a rubber on you?"

I felt like a prize jerk. "No," I admitted weakly. I hoped I hadn't just blown what promised to be the best piece of ass I'd ever had just because I'd ignored the Boy Scout slogan, "Be Prepared." I don't get lucky all that often, so I wasn't in the habit of carrying condoms.

"Then get one out of my top left drawer," she said, patiently. One of her hands was at her crotch, rubbing her pussy. Was she so eager to get off that she was starting without me?

There must have been three dozen rubbers in the drawer, in various packages. I picked one at random. When I unwrapped it and rolled it down onto my dick, I realized it was the kind with concentric rings of raised ridges.

"Stick it in me," Wendy said. "I need a dick in my pussy before I can come. A nice, hard dick."

I put my cockhead at the lips of her cunt and eased it in a few millimeters. Her pussy was slick, tight and hot. She kept rubbing her mound while I gradually gained more and more depth.

"Fuck, yeah, yeah," she said, furiously massaging her clit. "I'm going to do it. I'm going to come!"

She threw her head back and panted as she climaxed. Her pussy opened and shut powerfully, pulling on my prick and milking it. I pumped what felt like a pint of come into the rubber's reservoir tip.

When Wendy's breathing returned to normal, she patted me on the shoulder and said dismissively, "Good man, What's-Your-Name. That was great." Then she pushed me aside and said, "But now I really do have to get ready." My cock slipped out of her snatch. I was so dazed that I tucked it in my pants and zipped up without removing the rubber.

Wendy was as ditzy and delicious as ever on that night's newscast. No one would have guessed that she had spent the hour before airtime getting eaten by her boss and fucked by an intern whose name she couldn't remember.

Well, maybe one person could have guessed. Phil the reporter saw me come out of Wendy's office that day. The front of my pants was soaked, my dick was still hard enough to be very obvious, and the ridges of the rubber made me look like I was smuggling a Slinky. I remember him shaking his head and muttering, "Like I said, they'll fuck anything."—M.C., *Spokane, Washington*

SOME DAYS YOU EAT THE BEAR,
AND SOME DAYS THE BEAR EATS YOU

It's hard not to stop and stare when you see a bear walking down the sidewalk with its head under one arm. The blonde girl whose head was sticking out of the top of the costume looked thoroughly miserable.

I rolled down the window of my car and called out, "Do you need a ride?"

She smiled and hurried to the door. "I sure do. Are you heading downtown?"

I wasn't, but she was pretty enough so that I didn't mind going out of my way. "Wherever you say. Hop in. You must be smothering in that outfit."

"Tell me about it." She tossed the bear's head into the backseat. She had a hard time fastening the shoulder belt over her bulky bear costume, but finally got it latched.

After she told me her name—Toni—and her address, I said, "Do you always go around dressed like that?"

"I was at a kid's birthday party, but the jerk from the agency who was supposed to come pick me up afterward never showed. I got tired of waiting on the curb."

"Couldn't you have called a cab?"

She gave a funny smile. "I was sort of told to leave early. The kid's parents weren't in the mood by then to do me any favors."

"How come?"

She looked at me like she was assessing whether I was the kind of guy who would appreciate the story. I must have passed the test. "These gigs only last an hour," she said. "But about halfway through, I really had to use the bathroom. The kid's mom showed me where it was. Once I was inside, I had to take off my whole outfit before I could, you know, do my thing. And I don't wear anything underneath except underwear, because the costume gets so hot."

Like any guy, I couldn't help screening a mental movie of her stripping down to her bra and panties. I could see from the shape of her face and her slender neck that Toni was skinny and girlish—just my type. Watching this pale-skinned Goldilocks emerge from a bulky bear costume would be a real treat.

"So, okay, I did what I was there for," she continued. "But before I could get back in costume, the bathroom door opens. No knock, it just swings open, and there is the kid's dad, staring at me standing there in nothing but panties."

The fact that she didn't say anything about a bra did not slip past me. My opinion of her went up another notch. I envied the hell out of the guy who got to see her topless. I took a sideways glance at her chest. Even through the furry bear costume, I could see that she was packing a nice pair in there.

"I don't get it," I said. "I can see where the guy would have felt awkward, but it sounds like you're the one who should have been mad, not him."

"Well, I wasn't exactly thrilled. But before I could say anything, he said he recognized me! He was more embarrassed about that than about walking in on me. That's because he knew me from my . . . other job."

"I don't get it," I said.

"I make most of my money doing bachelor parties. Dancing, stripping, the whole thing. You know."

I knew all right. I had been to two bachelor parties in the past two months. Each had a stripper, and they did a hell of a lot more than strip. At one party, the girl picked up dollar bills with her pussy, then gave blowjobs in the bedroom to three guys for twenty bucks a pop.

At the other party, a girl did a naked squat-and-grind on the groom-to-be's face. She said that if he didn't fuck her, she would feel like he didn't have a good time. I remember wondering how much extra the best man had paid her to say that. The groom ended up fucking her, all right—on the couch, in front of everyone. While he was doing it, he asked her if he could bone her backside.

"My fiancée won't let me fuck her in the ass, so she shouldn't mind," he said.

The stripper told him that would cost an extra fifty. Several of us got out our wallets and contributed to the pot. Our buddy deserved whatever he wanted.

The girl found a tube of lube in her purse and greased up his cock. "Put some on me, too," she said, getting on all fours and sticking her bare ass in the air. I wasn't the only onlooker who had to adjust his cock as we watched our buddy squirt lube onto the stripper's pink asshole, wedge his dickhead into that little ring, and push it inside.

The stripper let out a throaty groan as he fucked in and out of her asshole. The bridegroom was as unperturbed as a porn star about having an audience. He was thoroughly into what he was doing, pumping his hard-on in and out of the stripper's anus. Then he grimaced and shot his load right up her ass.

"Fuck, that was good," he said afterward. "Would somebody please remind me why the hell I'm getting married?" Somebody did, and he got hitched the next morning, right on schedule. But I know he has to think about that stripper a lot. I sure do.

If the girl sitting beside me in the car was that kind of stripper, I could see why the birthday boy's father was upset. But I played innocent and said, "So he saw you at a bachelor party? So what?"

Toni said, "He did more than just see me. I kind of sucked his cock." She giggled at the memory. "He said his wife never gave him any head. He was pretty pathetic, really, but he was a great tipper."

Toni seemed to remember that she was talking to someone she had met only five minutes ago. "I guess this all sounds kind of shocking," she said.

"Oh, no, I hear this kind of thing every day," I joked. "So then the dad kicked you out?"

"First he got all holier-than-thou. While I got in my costume, he said it was disgusting that I did both kinds of jobs, and that I would have to leave. But right in the middle of this lecture, his wife appeared behind him. She asked what was going on. So I told her."

"Ouch," I said.

"I had gotten paid in advance, what did I care?" Toni said. "Sanctimonious asshole. Anyway, I'm really glad you picked me up. That's my place, right up there on the left. You want to come in?"

"Only if you'll put on a show for me."

She smiled. "I assume you don't mean the kind in the costume."

Inside, she let me watch her go from bear to bare. Her tits were as big as silicone jobs, but looked one hundred percent natural. Her nipples were as big around as beer coasters. I couldn't believe she was wasting her time doing bachelor parties instead of dancing at strip clubs for real money. It was no wonder the guy that afternoon had recognized her. She was the kind of girl who left a lasting impression.

She lowered her skimpy panties. Most of her crotch was shaved, except for a little tuft of golden hair above her pussy. It pointed to the split between her puffy cunt lips like an arrow.

Her whole body was shiny with sweat from being in the hot costume for so long. She asked if I wanted to take a shower with her. I said, "I like you just fine this way." She seemed to like that answer. She led me to her bed and lay back against the pillows, keeping her legs discreetly crossed while I stripped.

I licked sweat from her neck, her tits and her armpits. She rolled me onto my back and started sucking my dick. I was worried that she would try to make me come in a hurry. A girl in her line of work was probably an expert at getting guys off as quickly as possible.

What I didn't expect was that she also knew how to make a guy last a long, long time. Each time I was ready to come, she backed off and squeezed the base of my cock with her fingertips. When my urge to shoot had passed, she would go back to licking and sucking my prick.

I returned the favor by eating her pussy for all I was worth. I speared my tongue as deep in her hole as I could. I sucked her clit and nibbled on the big, soft lips of her cunt. She responded by grinding her pussy against my face until she came. She cried out with release. Then she put her mouth back on my dick. I knew that the next time I started coming, she wouldn't stop me.

My balls were hard. My whole dick was throbbing, forcing my come up its length and shooting it into Toni's mouth. She sucked even harder, wanting it all, and I gave her everything I had. It was sweet. And I didn't even have to tip her.—M.C., *Roanoke, Virginia*

A HELPING HAND—GOOD NEIGHBOR POLICY
PAYS OFF BIG-TIME

I'm one of those men who like to see their wives get fucked by other men. My wife Heather is a natural auburn-haired beauty with a shapely body and highly sensitive 38D titties. Her pussy hairs are thick and curly and she has the most beautiful long legs in the neighborhood.

Heather had not been fucked by anyone else for quite awhile, and she agreed she was ready for some action. She knows how I like to watch. If her lover does not know this, all the better.

Heather is twenty-six years old and she has the hots for Bill, our black nineteen-year-old neighbor. Bill likes to help Heather with the yard work, and she loves to cock-tease him. She gets a charge out of watching him try to hide the bulge in his pants. She likes to work in a slim G-string and skimpy halter top. She keeps the G-string pulled up tight into the crack of her cunt, exposing her thick cunt lips and glimpses of auburn pussy hair. I felt good about all this. The time had come for me once again to watch my wife get fucked by another man.

I was hiding in our spacious walk-in clothes closet. The door, ajar, gave me a full view of our bedroom and TV room. Heather had invited Bill over to watch the ball game. She was wearing white see-through bikini panties that showed her luxuriant growth of pussy hairs. Her stiff clit was swollen and red. Her transparent bra fully exposed her firm round breasts. Heather and Bill sat on the couch, laughing and talking. Then she took the bull by the horns, so to speak. She pulled Bill's face to her own, then kissed him fully on the mouth and obviously ran her tongue down his throat. This had the desired effect. As Heather steered him toward our bedroom, Bill put his arms around her. When Heather held her mouth open against his, Bill was obviously running his tongue down *her* throat, and she just as obviously was liking it. My cock was as hard as a rock and I could hardly breathe.

Standing by our king-size bed, Heather helped Bill off with his shirt. He reached around and unhooked her bra. As her tits spilled out, she grasped his head again, and moved his mouth tight onto one of her large nipples. He fondled the other with both of his large hands. Her breast looked like a cream puff, cupped in his black fingers.

As Heather knelt to slip Bill's khakis down and off, I could see his monstrous rod sticking up over his jockey shorts. When Heather rose to her feet she assessed the goodies and realized what a large cock she was getting ready to take on and in. She took a step back to admire it fully. She slowly reached out and placed both hands on that broad shaft, feeling it, trying to take its measure. Then Heather pulled the boy next door down on the coverlet next to her.

Bill's mouth found Heather's tit again as he slipped off her damp panties. She pulled his shorts down and pressed his huge salami to her legs and then to her mound of Venus. By then, my cock was jerking so hard I thought for sure I was going to come. But I held out for even hornier inspiration. Heather lay back with a pillow under her hips, and spread her legs good and wide. She grasped Bill's prick and rubbed the plum-size cock-head on the distended labia at the entrance to her pussy. Then she tilted her pelvis to give that thickening rod better access to her eager, dripping cunt.

After what seemed like an age, Bill took his penis in one hand and guided it into my wife's welcoming pussy. I could almost feel the tightness and the heat as I watched Bill feeding Heather all that black cock, seeing how much she liked it. Then Bill pumped his ass forward just as Heather hunched herself forward on that huge salami of his and ran it in several final inches, to the hilt.

Heather came almost immediately. Bill must have come at the same time. I don't know how long his body kept quivering before he finally pulled back. There was an audible "pop" as his cock left that happy but grasping cunt. I stifled a gasp and came in my pants. Then Heather had Bill stand in front of her. She played with his cock and balls and gradually jacked him up to a full a spectacular erection again.

I heard her tell him she wanted him to fuck her like a horse. He was all for it. Heather got on her hands and knees, and he easily entered her love-tube from the rear in what for anyone else would have been doggie-fashion. Bill was gentle in his fucking after Heather told him she had never taken a cock that big. But she joyfully shouted, "I love it!" when he got the monster all the way in, and he pumped her deeper and faster. When Bill reached around and grasped Heather's pendulous tits, I thought she would go crazy. She yelled about how good it felt. "Harder, Billy," she shouted. "Pull my nipples. Squeeze me!" I came again as I watched that stallion drill my wife while she hollered for more.

Since that first afternoon, I've arranged to watch those two fucking several more times. After each visit, when Bill has gone home and Heather has rested, she sucks my cock to full erection, then fucks me until I can't get it up anymore.

Some day I'll invite Bill to watch me fuck Heather. But I want to watch them a few more times before I let him in on our secret.—*J.L., Rochester, New York*

TWO MAY BE COMPANY,
BUT FOUR'S AN ADULT BIRTHDAY PARTY

This letter is to share with your readers the wonderful birthday present I gave my wife. Caroline had often fantasized about how wonderful it would be to have two lovers at the same time. Little did she know that I would arrange that for her, and also hang around to watch the show.

My beautiful wife was preparing to turn forty. Although she looks much younger and has a figure any woman would be proud of, she was feeling down about it. Over the years, she's often told me of how every woman dreams of having two men in bed at the same time. I'm sure she never thought she'd live out those fantasies.

As a regular reader of *Penthouse Letters*, I'd been fascinated by the letters from men who like to watch their wives with other men. The idea was a little daunting, but it also got me very excited. I finally decided Caroline deserved the opportunity, and that I would arrange for two friends to be of "service" to her. My plan included watching them at first and joining them later. Dave and Larry, the lucky friends I chose to help, were at first shocked, then interested. They both agreed that my wife is a very sexy lady.

Caroline and I went out to dinner the weekend of the big four-oh. I had arranged for Dave and Larry to "accidentally" meet us after dinner, when we were having drinks. They joined us at our table, and the four of us spent the evening drinking and dancing. The evening advanced, and I had fewer dances with Caroline as the two of them competed for her attention. During one slow dance, Dave kept his hands firmly on Caroline's shapely rear. The music ended, and he kissed her before returning to the table.

The combination of her male admirers and the alcohol made Caroline lose her inhibitions. Even the gentlemanly Larry got into the spirit of the evening. As Dave and Caroline held each other in another slow dance, Larry snuggled up against Caroline from behind. His cock was obviously straining against his trousers as he pressed it up against Caroline's ass. She wiggled appreciation, and he nuzzled her neck as the three of them moved to the music. It was at that point that I realized it was time to adjourn the party to our house.

I told the guys that Caroline and I needed to head home while I could still drive. Caroline protested, until I suggested that Dave and Larry follow us home for a nightcap. Luckily the drive was a short one.

I had arranged for another friend to leave a message on our answering machine requiring me to drive to the office and deal with a systems security problem. This would give Dave and Larry the opportunity to fulfill Caroline's fantasy and for her to feel she was safely alone to enjoy herself. I told Caroline that I was leaving her in good hands, drove the car around the corner, then walked home. I went around back, to watch the action through a sliding glass door.

I had left the drapes open for a full view of the living room and the three heated, horny participants. Not even Dave and Larry knew that I was going to watch from the deck, which also provided a view of the bedroom.

The first thing I saw was Larry and Caroline slow-dancing. I still don't know if there was music. Their lips locked together for what must have been a tongue-probing kiss. After a few minutes, Dave got up from the sofa and joined them. Caroline turned her head for a passionate kiss.

While this was happening, the two men explored Caroline's curves. At first she half-heartedly brushed them away, but she soon relaxed and enjoyed it. Then things happened quickly. As Dave kissed Caroline, Larry started undressing my horny birthday girl. First her skirt fell to the floor. Then he unbuttoned her blouse, revealing a black lace bra. He caressed each breast in turn. Caroline showed no direct reaction to this, but concentrated on her passionate kiss with Dave. Larry unfastened her bra. He somehow got his head between Caroline and Dave, and took her rosy left nipple into his mouth. That got a reaction. Caroline grasped the back of Larry's head, as if to be sure he kept sucking her tit. By this time, Dave realized she was wearing only a half slip and panties, and as Larry kept up his attentions on the top half of Caroline, Dave moved his hand down her stomach until he found her cunt and the wetness between her legs.

I could tell when he slid his fingers inside her pussy. That was when she broke off the embrace and spread her legs. Dave and Larry were enjoying my wife's body right before my eyes in my own living room, and I sat there watching and rubbing my cock as I enjoyed the sight of it.

Dave removed the last of Caroline's clothing and I saw her glistening love juices run down her slim legs. Larry continued sucking her tits. Dave began licking her pussy. Caroline stood erect the whole time. Then she broke off a kiss to tell the guys, "Time to come up for air, studs, and let's get horizontal—fast." She was triumphant as the two men carried her to the plush rug in front of the fireplace. Dave placed a pillow beneath her head as she reached up, unzipped Larry's slacks and liberated his rock-hard cock. It was the size of my own—about seven inches long. She popped it right into her mouth.

As she hungrily sucked Larry's cock, which I could see from her bobbing Adam's apple was down her throat, she went for Dave's love-stick. It must have been ten inches long, and thick as my wrist. I wondered if she could handle a prick of that size.

Meanwhile, my two friends were devouring my wife's body, both with their hands and with their mouths. It was only a matter of time, of course, until Caroline got a rampant cock stuck into the apex of her long, shapely legs. Caroline knows a lot about giving head, and Larry was getting the blowjob of his life. Meantime, Dave made good use of his time, making sure Caroline got well lubricated to accommodate his big salami. He also placed a large down pillow under Caroline's ass. Obviously, he was arranging for a good angle from which to angle that horse-cock of his for easy and painless penetration.

Caroline was hitting on all cylinders, and never missed a beat. She raised her legs, spread them wide, and flung her ankles over Dave's shoulders, avidly sucking Larry's smaller prick as Dave gently eased his nobler steed into her honey-pot. She was indeed well lubricated, and wide open. Dave's cock-head easily lodged in her pussy, and in a few easy strokes his prick was buried in her sweet pussy.

Now, encouraged by the way Caroline moved her pelvis into his, Dave started some healthy thrusting in and out. That felt so good that Caroline lost track of Larry's cock. She let it slip out of her mouth. She was in seventh heaven. I could see Dave's muscles tense up as he shot wads of jism into her pussy. He collapsed, and she held him tight for several minutes before he rolled off. The three of them lay there, satiated. I thought the evening was over—then Larry picked up Caroline and carried her into the bedroom.

It took me a few moments to move to the bedroom window to catch the late show. By the time I was in place, Larry had Caroline on her side, at the edge of our bed. He was holding her left leg straight up in the air while he stood alongside the bed with his rod sliding easily in and out of her sopping-wet hole. Dave was licking and sucking her nipples. I knew it wouldn't be long before she sucked his pussy-soaked cock between her lips for a superb second helping of prick. This, I decided, was a good time for me to join the party.

I jogged back to the car and drove it into the garage. When I reentered the house, I went straight to the bedroom. The scene hadn't changed much since I'd left the deck. As I had expected, Dave was enjoying one of Caroline's marvelous blowjobs while Larry pumped his prick in and out of Caroline's appreciative pussy. She had rolled over onto her back by then, so that Larry could hold both her long legs up in the air to penetrate her love-hole more deeply. I was hotter than a two-dollar pistol at that stage, and as Larry pulled his prick out of Caroline, I quickly moved in and replaced him.

Caroline looked up to see me between her legs. She smiled and said, "Welcome home, and thank you." Her cunt had never been so well lubricated. It didn't take me long to add my come to the two loads already deposited there. The party was far from over, as far as Caroline was concerned. "I can take all three of you on at once," she said, and got busy on our limp dicks with both hands and lips. I'll never forget the sight of my beautiful wife working on three cocks as her own love juices ran down the crack of her pretty ass and down her legs.

"Okay," she said. "I want some more of Dave's monster." He got between her legs and slipped his huge cock into her with one thrust. She sighed happily, then grabbed Larry's prick and slipped her lips around it. At the same time, she gripped my own rod and jerked me off. In fifteen minutes, we had all come. I sprayed jism that Caroline rubbed into her titties. She swallowed all Larry had, and she milked Dave's prick dry with her muscular pussy. We spent the next several hours trying new positions. We plan a repeat performance in a few weeks. Watch this space!—*T.R., San Jose, California*

HARD REALITY SURPASSES FUCKING FANTASY

My husband and I have enjoyed your publication since you first started. We are a liberated couple, but because of our position in the community we must be careful. My husband Roger is a successful business professional who's quite attractive. He's thirty-eight years old, six feet tall, weighs one-seventy, and has a nice tan and an eight-inch prick. I am twenty-eight and a natural blonde. I'm five-ten, one hundred thirty-five pounds, and have 36D breasts and a permanent tan. And I love to fuck.

After reading your last issue, we decided we should write you about one of our own experiences. One night, after a bottle of wine and some great sex, Roger was talking about fantasies. He had been married before and was quite the ladies' man long before I met him. I wanted to know if he ever fantasized about sex with one of his previous partners. He said no, but I kept prodding him about what his fantasy would be if he had a choice. He finally told me that I wouldn't want to know because it was pretty kinky. I immediately thought, Oh my God, he's gay, or a cross-dresser, or he wants to watch me have sex with another woman. It turned out to be none of the above, but I felt I had a right to an answer. When we first started seeing each other, Roger would ask me about some of my ex-lovers—usually after a long, hot session of sex. Each time, he'd ask for more intimate details. He was especially fascinated with details of cock sizes, how big a load they shot, whether I ever picked someone up at a bar and took him home to fuck.

And when I told Roger about my past, he would get a rock hard-on and fuck me like a wild man. It never failed. Many times when I told him about one particular ex-boyfriend, the one who shot the biggest load, Roger got so turned on that he'd lick his own come out of my pussy. I thought that was a little kinky, but what the hey! A good pussy licking is a good pussy licking.

Roger finally 'fessed up to his fantasy. He wanted me to fuck someone else and tell him all about it. Better yet, he wanted me to fuck someone while he watched. Now I saw the connection between his interest in my past and his fantasy. I was a little shocked at first, since Roger is very jealous. But I went along with his fantasy for awhile, not actually fucking anyone, but making up stories. Roger travels a lot on business, and when he came home from a trip I made sure to leave a couple of condoms on the nightstand. I'd stretch the rubbers with a dildo and put a lot of K-Y jelly on them. He enjoyed my little games immensely, and I actually started getting turned on to the idea of fucking someone for real. But I was a bit concerned about how Roger would react if I went through with it. I enjoyed the game, though, and it always gave him a huge homecoming hard-on. For the next three days I'd get the fucking and the eating of my life.

Then Jenny, my best friend in the whole world, called to tell me that her little brother was getting married and invited Roger and me down to Houston for the wedding and the partying. Roger had scheduled a national seminar for his salespeople that weekend, so I was up against a stone wall. But I figured out a way. I asked Roger if I'd ever told him about Joey. He said no. As I started my story, I unzipped Roger's pants and pulled out his big dick. I told him that Joey was the first guy I ever tried to fuck. But I said I couldn't, because of the size of his prick. That got Roger's cock hard as a rock. I told him that Joey had dated me for about a month before we started to get down to business. I was on the pill for medical reasons, I said, so I didn't have to worry about getting pregnant. I had decided this was the man I wanted to take my cherry.

Joey was about six-foot-three and strong as steel, I continued. What I had not anticipated was the size of his cock. We went to his house when his parents were away for the night. We started kissing in the living room. When Joey ran his hand up my skirt and found no underwear, he started fingering my pussy. I rubbed his cock through his jeans. I had done this many times before with guys, I told Roger, but had never taken the next step. I pulled his zipper open, unbuckled his pants and pulled them off. I had never seen a cock in the raw before, so I assumed they were *all* that big. I later measured it. The thing was nine and a half inches long and seven inches around. I started jacking it off with two hands, and after just a couple of minutes I was rewarded with the biggest load of come I ever imagined could exist.

I definitely had Roger's attention now, and I continued. So, I told him, I did Joey. He kept finger-fucking me. I told him I was ready, and he rubbed Vaseline on his dick. It had never softened, I told Roger. Then, I related as I stroked Roger's prick, Joey slowly rubbed his horsecock on my pussy. That got me so hot I couldn't wait to get fucked. I had been anticipating this moment for months, I said, but try as we might, Joey never could get that rod into my cunt. After about five minutes, he deposited a huge creamy load all over my pussy. This continued for about two weeks, I told Roger, who by now was a bit red in the face and breathing hard. I jacked Joey off, and he rubbed his big dick on my mound till we both came. Before I could lose my virginity, Joey moved away. We never got to fuck!

Then, I told Roger, I started dating Wayne, a guy I went to school with. Within a week we were into heavy petting. He would finger my clit while I jacked his meat. I had been pleased to find, I told Roger, that Wayne had a nice dick that was only six inches long—nowhere near as thick as Joey's. Now I was certain that it was time to get fucked. I was tired of finger-fucking! One night we were down at the boat dock, playing around. After he slipped my panties down from under my skirt, I sat on his lap, grabbed his cute cock and rubbed it all over my pussy.

When I was all hot, and lubricating like mad, I guided his prick into my virgin pussy. I slowly sank down on his cockhead. Joey must have broken me in well, I told Roger, because getting it all the way in was easy. I bobbed up and down on Wayne's cock for a few minutes. Then I jumped off and flipped over onto my back, and Wayne started power fucking. This lasted about three or four minutes, and then he shot his wad. I didn't come the first time, but it felt fucking unbelievable. I fucked Wayne for awhile, then fucked five or six other guys before I moved to Atlanta. None of the guys had anything close to Joey's dick, I assured Roger, and I was sure Joey would be in Houston for the wedding, since his mother and father were the grandparents of Rick, the bridegroom.

Sure enough, Roger changed the dates of his sales meeting. For the next six weeks our sex was unbelievable. All I had to do was hint about fucking Joey on our weekend away, and I'd get the best balling of my life. Then Roger would suck my pussy until I shouted for joy. The weekend finally arrived. We were all packed and ready to go when the call came from one of Roger's factories: major problems. Roger had to go troubleshooting. I was desolate; I was going to miss Rick's wedding. Then Roger told me to go without him; he would catch a flight the next day.

I was a bit disappointed, since I'd bought some really sexy lingerie to wear for him on the trip, but I headed for the airport. I got into Houston about one-thirty in the afternoon, checked into the hotel and found my way to the pool. I went back to my room about four, to get ready for the wedding. On a wild impulse, I decided to shave my pussy. Roger had been after me to shave it for a long time. I left just a little triangle of short hair above my pussy. I didn't know what I would do if I saw some of my old boyfriends, but I wanted to be ready.

I wore a conservative dress to the wedding, pale blue, off the shoulder, and about six inches above the knee. I put on white suspender hose (Roger loves them) with a pair of see-through silk panties. (I almost went with no panties at all.) I think I looked hot but not completely like a slut.

The wedding went well. I caught up with several people I hadn't seen in years. I went from the wedding to the reception without incident. I was missing Roger, since he is so good with the public and with family, and I wanted to show him off to my old friends.

But this all changed in a matter of moments. Joey came up behind me while I was talking to some friends and said, "If you didn't come down here with your husband, it's his fault and not ours." The next two hours flew by. We talked about old times, old friends and what could have been, what might have been. Joey told me that the one regret he had was that he never fucked me. We danced a lot closer than we should have, since everyone knew that I was married. When the party started winding down, Joey asked if he could drive me to my hotel. I told him, "Yes," and before we left the reception I phoned Roger's beeper and left the hotel number. I wanted urgently to speak to him. On the way to the hotel, Joey made it quite obvious what his intentions were.

He kept running his hand up my skirt and trying to get it into my panties. I kept telling him to be a good boy. I saw no reason to lead him on unless I got the okay from Roger.

Once we got to the hotel bar I told Joey that I had to go up to the room to see what was happening with Roger. There was a message to call him at home. I called and asked him how things had gone at the plant. He said he had gotten everything cleared up and would catch a flight out the next day. He asked why I had phoned his beeper. I told him, "If you really want that fantasy to happen, tonight's the night. I've got the guy downstairs, and he's raring to go." When I told him it was Joey, "the guy with the monster cock," he went silent. I told him if he didn't want it to happen, just say the word and I would blow the whole thing off. If he wanted it to happen—for real, no fantasy—I would take Joey up to our room and fuck him all night long. I told Roger if he said yes, not to change his mind. I told him once I left the room to go down to the bar there was no turning back. Roger told me to call him in the morning—after Joey left.

I decided to change out of my wedding garb. Roger had bought me a really sharp outfit for the weekend. It was a short plaid skirt with a solid blouse that was way too small. The blouse showed off my tits, and it had a vest that did the same. I kept my suspender panty hose on, but took off my panties. I got hot just thinking about that big log I was going to try and fit into my pussy.

I went back down to the bar and copped a seat beside Joey. He said I looked great and asked if it was a special occasion. I told him he'd have to wait and see for himself. We danced to a couple of tunes before he asked me what was going on that night. I took him by the arm and led him out of the bar to the elevator. I couldn't wait any longer to get my hands around his dick.

In the elevator, he pulled my skirt up and started fingering my pussy. I rubbed that great prick of his through his dress pants. I could see the crown of his cock through his pants and he wore no underwear at all. Touché.

When we got to the room, we hopped into bed—no preliminaries. I unzipped Joey and unleashed that monster I'd been thinking about since I'd left home. I had no doubt now that I could fit that big prick into my pussy, and soon. I was sucking his humongous cockhead before my skirt hit the floor, and I jacked the throbbing boner as I sucked it. My first reward was an eruption of come that I gulped down my throat like a baby sucking on her bottle.

Joey was sucking my clit when I had my first orgasm of the night. As soon as I calmed down, I urged him to lie supine, and I pounced upon his prize prick. I lowered myself slowly onto the shaft. I felt my now-experienced pussy expand to accommodate its girth. I was about halfway down on it after about fifteen strokes. That was all Joey needed. He grabbed my hips and plunged the monster up into me. His balls slapped against my ass as he pumped his prick. I immediately realized the advantages of a big cock. He filled me and touched me in places I'd never been touched. I had come only rarely during intercourse, but his big dick massaged my clit, and I felt a tidal wave of orgasm. I shouted, "Come on, big boy, gimme that load of come!" Immediately, I felt the first of his five eruptions of cream shoot into me. And he didn't stop fucking. The golden rod stayed stiff, and he kept pumping it into my cunt. When I started to come again, he slipped the big pecker out, raised me by the ass-cheeks he held so firmly, and sucked my pussy. That gave me a multiple orgasm that lasted for over sixty seconds. We lay quietly on the bed for a few moments. Then he reached for my pussy again. I nibbled his nipples, then worked my way down to that fabulous prick, where I tasted love juices and Vaseline. I slid my hands up and down the shaft and licked the knob as he got hard once more. I got as much of that swollen magic wand into my mouth as possible, and after I sucked what I could and jacked the rest for a few minutes, I felt his nuts tighten. I slipped the cock out of my mouth and licked it luxuriously, up and down. Then I took one of his giant nuts in my mouth and sucked it. He moaned in pleasure. I changed to the other ball. Then I swooped lower and licked his asshole.

That action drives Roger wild, and Joey loved it too. In a few seconds, he moaned that he was about to come. I was never one to let a good load go to waste. I got my mouth around his cockhead, ready for some hot cream. I bobbed my head up and down as I swallowed it all. Then I got up and fixed us a couple of drinks from the mini-bar.

We surfed the TV a while. I was still horny and wanted to fuck again, and I was looking forward to telling Roger all about the sex orgy I'd had with Joey. No doubt he'd want to fuck all day tomorrow, and that was fine with me.

I went to the bathroom, and when I got back Joey's jolly giant was hard again. I kissed him passionately and asked what he wanted to do. "I'm yours for the night," I told him, "and I'll do anything you want me to do. Whatever you want, baby." Joey looked thoughtful but said nothing as he got up and went into the bathroom. There, I heard him start the shower going. Then he called out for me to join him. It looked like I was going to get some more action right now. I got into the shower with him, and we started soaping each other up. Joey lathered up my big tits, playing with my nipples.

I was getting hot again. I was looking forward to about another mile of that cock of his, in satisfyingly large installments. He soaped the little patch of hair I'd left on my mound and fingerfucked both my pussy and my rosy asshole. Joey couldn't know it, but I'd learned to love getting fucked in the ass. I wondered if we could get that monumental prick of his up my fundament, and I rather looked forward to his trying. Joey picked up my razor and shaved my pussy all over again. Surely, I thought, I couldn't already have five o'clock shadow. This shave did not leave any hair on my snatch at all, and Joey shaved all around my pussy and asshole, making both of them smooth as silk. When he finished, I soaped up his dick and started jacking it. Hallelujah! It was rockhard once more! Then I knelt down and licked it a few times before I grabbed the razor. Joey seemed quite shocked when I started shaving his dick, then his gigantic balls. "Turnabout's fair play," I told him as I rinsed the gear off. "Let's go back to bed."

Joey's prick looked even bigger when we got into the other room. We jumped into bed, kissing each other and running our hands over each other's body. I asked Joey how he wanted to fuck me this time. "Doggie-fashion," he said. I got on my hands and knees, with my ass high in the air and my head against the headboard. Joey took his time and caressed me with that big hunk of meat. He rubbed the head on my bald pussy, then ran it between my pussy lips and tickled my asshole with it. I remembered then how it was when I was still a virgin, unable to fuck him and wanting to so bad.

Finally, I told Joey, "That's enough lovemaking. Let's fuck." I reached back, grabbed his joystick and guided it to my soaking pussy. But Joey had his own definition of "doggie-fashion." He got hold of his prick and placed his cockhead at the entry to my tiny asshole. "Do you think we can get that big thing in there?" I asked.

"All it takes is a little love and understanding," he said. "And Vaseline." He scooped some out of the jar on the nightstand and rubbed it into my anus, and all over his prick. Then he pressed forward, and I felt the knob nudge in a fraction of an inch. "We'll get it done," he said. "Play with your pussy. That'll get you hot." I happily diddled myself as he rubbed his dick on my clit and my asshole.

Occasionally Joey put the tip of his dick into my cunt, only to pull it out. The guy was good; he set my pussy on fire. He got the Vaseline out again and asked me to rub it into his dick. It felt nice, all smooth and throbbing. Next, he asked me to finger-fuck my asshole. I was happy doing this—and preparing the way for the monster—when he suggested I frig my cunt with one finger and my asshole with another. Both holes accepted the fingers easily, and I loved it. All the while, Joey rubbed my ass with his rod, telling me how gentle he was going to be when he slipped me his big cock.

I was hotter than a firecracker by the time he asked me if I wanted him to fuck me in the ass. "You're damn right, sweetie," I said. "Go for it!" He suggested I put a second finger in my asshole against the one in my pussy. That felt marvelous. I was impatient at that point to get down to some serious buggery. I explored both holes fully, both to prepare the way and to enjoy the thrills it gave me. It was marvelous! I started coming immediately.

Joey now pumped his dick in and out of my pussy, up to the balls, and I orgasmed again. Then he placed that prong of his at the entrance to my asshole. "Just a little bit at a time," he said. I gently rocked back against his dick, and I felt success! I felt it penetrate my tiny but well-lubricated hole. The head slipped into my ass up to the crown, and it felt marvelous. I wanted more. Joey sensed my relaxation, and gently pushed the head in and out, preparing for the main event. I kept rubbing my clit, getting a heavenly charge, and I called out to him, "Give me some more cock!" I hunched back on that prick of his harder now, until at last I felt the head going forward, followed by the main body of the schlong.

Joey was in! We both heaved deep sighs of contentment and anticipation. He fucked me slowly, still gently, in and out. When he had his dick all the way out, he would wait for me to plunge myself back on that prick of his. Soon we settled into a nice rhythm. Actually, he told me later, he never put more than three-quarters of his dick in. I felt my next orgasm close upon me, and I reached down between my legs and grabbed hold of his bald nuts. I stroked them as I shouted, "Come in my ass, Joey! Come with me!"

Joey did just that. Roger had fucked me in the ass countless times, but I don't remember actually feeling him discharge in me. It felt as if Joey had a squirt-gun in my fundament. I felt jolt after jolt of jism exploding in my butt, and I came again.

I went to the bathroom to clean up. When I came back, Joey was sleeping. I crawled into bed with him and quickly fell asleep. I couldn't wait to tell Roger.

I'm too horny to write any more right now, but I'll tell in another letter what happened when Roger arrived the next day.
—*Name and address withheld*

SLUTTY SECRETARY GETS EVERYTHING
BUT FUCKED BY HER NEW BOSS

Betty just turned twenty a few months ago, and has been working as a secretary for about a year. She's an Italian girl who just has fuck me written across her forehead.

I got a job this summer as an intern in the same building. The other day I overheard a discussion between a black businessman and one of the cleaning guys. The gist of it was he'd just gotten this really hot secretary a couple weeks ago, and she'd been teasing him like crazy.

The janitor said, Yeah, one night after hours he had heard her behind a closed door in the office moaning while some buzzing noise droned up and down. He figured she was vibrating herself. It turned out they'd both asked her out, but she'd said she wasn't into black guys.

As the guy in the suit got up with his tray, he told the janitor to come around to his office the next day, 'cause he was planning something special for her.

Hearing him mention Betty's last name dispelled any doubt I might have had as to who the young lady was. And after hearing that discussion, my curiosity was up to see what was going to happen.

The next day I called in sick but went to the building early. I waited until the businessman from lunch walked in, and I discreetly followed him upstairs to his office. I waited for him to go back out for coffee, then I snuck into his office and frantically looked for a good hiding spot. There was a deep coat closet, with sliding wooden doors. I got in there and closed the doors enough so I was concealed but could still see and hear everything in the office perfectly.

It was a couple of hours before Betty made her appearance in the boss's office. She was wearing a white stretch dress that stuck to her like glue, and a light gray jacket. The focal point of this girl has always been her great ass. She's about five foot seven, and generally very trim, but has really wide hips and a sweet, round tail that jiggles and shakes with every high-heeled step. Moving up from there, and that's tough to do, I noticed her nipples poking at the front of her dress. It looked like she probably was not wearing a bra. Her brown hair rested on her shoulders and outlined her pretty face, with its big eyes and full lips. She has a large mouth that always seems to be asking for somebody's dick to wrap itself around.

Come to think of it, *she* always seems to be asking for that too. She's the kind of slut who sucks off the boyfriends of girls who have pissed her off in some way, just to get revenge. She knows the effect her fat ass and long legs and high heels and lips have on men.

She strutted in to give her boss some papers he had asked for and then, on the way out, dropped her pen near a side table. Instead of kneeling down to get it like a lady, she got down on her hands and knees to look for it, with her wide ass facing the boss and her panties just peeking out from the hem of her short skirt.

Her boss sat there staring into space and shaking his head for a while after she left. About twenty minutes later he picked up the phone and called her in to take dictation.

Betty walked into the office expectantly. Her boss started laying down the law. He said that her provocative behavior was driving him crazy, and that if she really wasn't attracted to him she shouldn't act like that. If she couldn't get it under control, he added, he would ask to have her transferred back to her old position.

She stood there blushing. "Don't do that," she said.

"Why not?" he asked.

Betty took a deep breath. "It's embarrassing to admit this, but I only told you that I wasn't interested because I was. Does that make sense?"

"Not really," he responded.

"It's a girl thing," she informed him. "I wanted to make sure you really wanted me, and weren't just playing around with me."

"Oh, I'm serious," he told her in a soft voice. He motioned for her to come over to his chair. He spun his legs out from under the desk, leaned back and shut his eyes like he was hoping for a kiss.

Instead she strutted over and, still standing, unzipped his pants and whipped out his black sausage. It was long, but kind of thin. Betty bent over at the waist, with her legs still straight, and gave the crown of his dick a few kisses while holding it in her hand. She then put the knob between her lips and tugged and suckled on it until he got really hard. She swirled her tongue around the pink ridge at the top of his meat and then slipped down to her knees at his feet. She teased him by only moving the very tip of his cock in her lips for a while. Then she dove down on his pole until his balls were against her chin and her feet were kicking off the ground to keep her balance.

She obviously really did have a lot of cocksucking experience. She got him going with her slow and steady pulls on his rod and her slurping noises. When he started to come he suddenly pulled out and spurted his jism all over the place. She tried to catch the come in her mouth, but a lot got away. I must admit I had to suppress a huge boner from seeing her there on her knees with that pouty look and come flying everywhere.

Once the boss's cock was spent he just said, "My, my, my. You certainly do have a talent."

She said, "I love my work," and asked if she might please have another try. Her boss told her in a minute she could, but asked her first to dance for him. He grabbed his remote control and turned on a stereo to some song from the Spice Girls and told her to take her dress off and dance.

Smiling, she got up from her knees and peeled her dress off. My suspicion that she was braless was confirmed as her lovely boobs shivered with exposure to the open air. She began to shake and dance. She really got into dancing, her creamy white ass shimmying wildly. She swung her head and hair all around, her body jumping wildly around the room.

A couple rap tunes came on, and she kept right on grinding to the heavy bass rhythms. She got up right in front of him and started swinging her hips and shaking her ass right in the boss's face. He told her to crawl under the desk because his dick was ready again. I was pleased at this, because I knew this would give me a good show.

Betty danced over to the other side of the desk and got down on her hands and knees. She stared into her boss's eyes as she crawled catlike under his desk. From his angle, I think he could only see her ankles and high heels on the floor opposite him. she pulled his pants down to his ankles as he begged her to lick his black balls. Her head started to move. She held his dick up and off to the side with one hand while supporting herself with the other. I shifted my position in the closet to get a better view. She looked hotter than hell on her hands and knees like that, her fat ass sticking out from under the desk all lonely and begging to be played with.

She started sucking on his dick again, and from my new view-point I could see that dark form moving in and out of her mouth. Her eyes were closed and her cheeks were sunken in as she dreamily bobbed her head up and down. Every once in a while she'd let his cock fall out of her mouth and she'd hotly kiss the head before drawing him back in with a loud, wet vacuuming sound.

She had crossed her ankles, slipping one shoe off her heel and making little circles in the air with the toe. A few times, she'd go to what I've heard she calls "the famous Betty suction-cup method," both feet coming off the ground for balance, while the boss's dick disappeared completely into her mouth and his face contorted in pleasure.

Her little panties had gotten an obvious wet spot in back. They had ridden way up her ample ass, and were splitting the swollen pink lips of her dripping pussy. At one point she reached her foot up and tried to pull her panties out of her slit with the spiked heel, but she couldn't quite reach.

Her boss still had the music on, and I noticed she was casually wagging her awesome tail back and forth to the beat of the tunes. She was still dancing.

Her boss was clearly holding out on her this time, because this activity had gone on for eight or nine songs without him coming. That's exactly the kind of thing she takes pride in never happening when she's blowing a guy. Sometimes she plays games with herself, like saying she'll make a guy come in three minutes or something. That's how into it she is. She was pulling every trick she knew. She was drooling and making big, sloppy slurp sounds. She was gently kneading and tickling his heavy balls with her painted fingernails. She was even trying to talk to him with his wang in her mouth, telling him how much she loved to suck his cock and thanking him for this opportunity to please him. I saw the boss make a motion with his hand, but I couldn't see why or what he was looking at.

Then that janitor walked into my view, staring at Betty's shapely legs and snow-white tail, wagging in time to the music under the desk. I'd forgotten all about the guy until this point.

The boss smiled at him and flashed him a thumbs-up. The janitor quietly got on his knees behind Betty and slipped a finger past her wet panties and into her pussy. She gave a muffled yelp of surprise and her head bumped against the desk.

When she saw who it was, she reached back and slipped her panties off, giving him easy access to her pretty pussy. Meanwhile, the janitor had pulled his cock out, and he was a different story from the boss. He was rock hard from the moment he got in the room, and he was packing a hell of a load. It was as big as my fore-arm. It was amazing to see that much dick on just one guy.

The janitor beamed a big grin at her fat white ass, just quiver-ing there on display in front of him.

Betty went back to trying her best to get her boss to squirt in her mouth. The janitor ran his hand along her upper thighs and pussy to get some of her juices. He stroked his mammoth dick with his hands to lube it up, then spread her wetness around her asshole.

Betty's big, soft ass is like a magnet for hard-ons. Her sexy tail and slutty nature beg you to do it, but from what I'd heard, she'd never let anybody so much as rest the tip of his cock there. So I was highly intrigued as the janitor put one hand on her hip and started slowly pushing his Wiffle bat into her ass. She squirmed, but did not try to stop him.

The janitor eventually got in to the hilt. His dick was com-pletely up her ass, and his balls rested heavily against her burning box. That sac was so achingly full it looked like he carried around a couple of tennis balls in there.

He just held himself there for a minute, laughing with pure joy, then began fingering her pretty pussy. She started these real deep moans of pleasure as he did that, and I was real surprised. The janitor slowly began moving back and forth in her tight asshole, tickling her fleshy cheeks with one hand and massaging her cli-toris with the other.

She had loosened up, and he suddenly started slamming into her, his overfed balls clanging on her pussy like a door knocker every time he thrust in. He was swinging his hips like a piston and fucking her enormous shaking butt like he was a cowboy rid-ing a horse. After only a dozen or so pumps of that big bone up her sweet little asshole, I could see her calves tense up, and she started shuddering in a really hard, strange orgasm.

Just then her boss started to come again. She reached her hand up to try to hold his tool in her mouth this time, but Mr. Big was still slamming into her from behind, and the come once more flew in all directions.

Betty said to the janitor, "I don't know your name, and it's a little late for introductions, but whoever you are, please fuck my pussy. I need that big thing in my puss so bad." The janitor eased his thick log out of her big, pillowy ass and told her to get up on top of the desk so he could help her out. The boss was just leaning back in his chair and recovering. Betty edged back out from under the desk, her ass leading the way.

She likes nothing better in this world than big dicks. I've heard her swap big dick stories with her friends. They talk with reverence about the hugest ones they've seen. Her eyes were focused on his wang as she stood up.

She crawled up onto the desk and lay on her back, with her head hanging down near the boss and her hips at the edge on the other side. Her legs were dangling off the side, and she said, "All right, Hammer. Get me with that whale-dick. Please. Please fuck me. I need it so bad."

The boss slid away from the desk and let the other guy move in. She was still begging when the janitor put one leg on either side of her head and dropped his balls right in her mouth. Her head was hanging down below desk level and her tits were gently swaying as she started tonguing his balls.

The janitor reached down and massaged her breasts, teasing her hard brown nipples while feeding her his meaty balls. He told her to suck, and she happily reached up and tried to steer his ridiculously bloated dick into her mouth. She admiringly whispered, "Damn, you sure got a biggie."

She was able to sneak about a third of it past her lips. She couldn't even move her head with that, much less suck up and down, so she ended up just sucking on it, and slurping and drooling all over herself. The janitor apparently found this sufficiently stimulating.

Betty pulled her knees up and put both feet on the desk for leverage. She was tickling his balls (which were now resting on her eyes!) with one hand, and playing with her pussy with the other, when the boss moved her hand away. He then stood between her spread knees and put the knob of his cock right between her puffy cunt lips.

The janitor was leaning over her and playing with her tits while his cock continued to stretch her gaping jaws and his heavy balls rested on her face. She was squirming and wiggling her hips big time, trying to get the boss's cock inside her just a little bit. But he was teasing her with it.

After a few minutes of this, the boss asked her to roll over on her stomach. She pulled the janitor's dork from her mouth with a pop, and a string of saliva ran from her lower lip to it as she sat up and shifted.

One of her shoes fell off as she moved around on the desk. The other slipped off her heel and was dangling from the front of her foot as she lay on her stomach. Her legs were sticking straight out, horizontal to the floor, and she was up on her elbows to resume her work. Her gorgeous, wide ass shook as she moved around, and came to a jiggling rest as she lay on her stomach.

The whole time she was moving, her eyes were locked on the janitor's humongous, fat dork. He held her chin and guided that huge sucker into her open mouth.

She moaned contentedly on his big black dick and twirled her feet like a schoolgirl. She bobbed slowly up and down on it and gazed into his eyes while she blew him, one of her best tricks. The boss grabbed her back so she was standing on one high heel and the toes of her bare foot, while her stomach was still flat on the desk.

She continued sucking and talking through the entire thing. She slurped something that sounded like, "Peas fuck be dow," and the boss said sure, anything she wanted. Then he proceeded to grab a fistful of each ass-cheek in his hands, spread them wide apart, lubed up her asshole again, and explored that tunnel himself. Betty moaned that her aching, hot pussy was never going to get filled with all their black meat.

The boss reamed out her no-longer-virgin tailpipe, and she kept on sucking for all she was worth. Her ass was rippling like milk each time her boss plunged into her. He gave her creamy pillows a few triumphant squeezes, then pulled out with a shout of "Yes!" and came again—this time all over her butt.

He looked down at her, bent over at a ninety-degree angle and, laughing heartily, said, "Your pretty white pussy is dripping all over my office." Then he laughed some more.

The janitor was coming at that point too. His dick was like a stopper in her mouth, and her full, red lips were clamped around it as he came. Her lips twitched as powerful spasms of come lurched through his horse meat. She gulped and gulped, her eyes getting wider and wider as she kept swallowing. Finally he was empty, and Betty was able to close her eyes and rest her head on the desk with his bloated, freakish wang still stuffed between her lips.

She was breathing tiredly through her nostrils. Her back was covered with shimmering pools of come, and her big, white butt still looked unreal at the front of the desk. Her own juices, as well as some of the men's come, glistened all the way down her soft thighs and deliciously long legs.

The janitor's cock started to shrink as last, and she was able to slip it out of her mouth. She sighed lovingly as she continued to stare at it. With a few pussycat cleaning-licks of its knobby head, she said, "Well, boss, I did it. I swallowed every tasty drop. Now will somebody please have a heart and fuck me right? Make a white girl happy."

But no, the janitor suddenly remembered the vibrator he'd heard her using one night, and went out to the other room to get it. He laughed as he came back in and handed her the vibrator. "You've worn us both out," he admitted. "You'll have to make do with this little toy."

She was in such desperate need of satisfaction at that point that she had no choice. She went and sat on the floor, not five feet from where I was hiding, kissed her humming friend, then slipped it quite easily into her soaked pussy. She moaned deeply and happily, and began writhing sluttily on the rug.

The two black men stood there watching. In two minutes she had a tremendous, shuddering orgasm. She was holding and thrusting the big vibrator with both hands and shouting, "God, yes!" and all kinds of other less coherent exclamations.

Then her whole body kind of went limp, and she was sprawled out on the floor, legs spread, her eyes closed and a contented little smile on her face.

The janitor picked up her stray shoe, wet panties, dress and jacket and set them next to her in a pile. The boss lifted her to her feet and said, "That will be all for now," and patted her bare butt as he ushered her—totally naked, one high heel on, vibrator and clothes in her hand and a startled look on her face—out his office door and back to her own office. He closed the door behind her. Then the janitor and her boss shook hands, said, "See ya tomorrow," and started giggling like a pair of loons.

Fortunately for me, soon afterward everybody cleared out, and I was able to sneak off. I know it's tough to believe, but I swear I witnessed this entire episode just as I've reported it. I only wish I could have found some way to participate.—*K.R.*, *Detroit, Michigan*

SHE COMES WITH HUB'S FRIEND
WHILE HE LOOKS ON AND JACKS OFF

When Carter introduced me to his new girlfriend, I was awestruck. She was the most beautiful girl I'd ever laid eyes on. She was a gorgeous five-foot-six-inch redhead. She had a beautiful face, a creamy-smooth complexion and big, beautiful brown eyes. She was twenty years old, three years younger than Carter and I, but she had an air of maturity about her.

She may have been dating Carter, but for me it was love at first sight. I didn't say anything to my friend, but I knew the second I met her that she was the one I wanted someday to be my wife.

I hoped that if I bided my time I might get a chance with Candy. Seeing a gorgeous girl on Carter's arm was nothing new. He was tall, well-built, quite handsome and a natural charmer.

I'm five inches shorter than Carter, weigh at least fifty pounds less and am not what you would call handsome. I was always shy around girls, and I never had much luck with them. I knew I could never compete with Carter for a fabulous fox like Candy, but I also knew that none of his relationships ever lasted that long.

I made it a point to see Carter more often, in order to see Candy. The more I got to know her, the more impressed I was. She was not some empty-headed bimbo, like many of Carter's girls. She was smart, sweet, caring and just plain fun. She and I became good friends, and I found myself falling harder and harder for her.

Sure enough, three months after he introduced me to her, Carter broke up with Candy.

I wasted no time. I called Candy up and asked her out that very day. We began dating, and I was in hog heaven. Carter was occupied with some new gal, and I didn't see much of him.

Candy and I had been going out for about a month when I ran into Carter. The first thing he asked me was how I liked dating a hot number like Candy. He made some remark about her being a real woman in bed.

I got mad. I knew Carter normally bedded every girl he dated, but I was certain it had been different with Candy. Candy was actually very straitlaced. She didn't drink, she didn't smoke and I could not imagine her using a four-letter word. We had talked about sex, and I believed Candy when she told me she was a virgin. I didn't believe a word of Carter's macho bragging.

Carter looked at me like I'd just fallen off the turnip truck, laughed and said, "You're just as naive as ever. You go ahead and marry Candy if you want to, that's your business, not mine. But I can't believe you actually believe Candy is a virgin."

I was really mad then. Candy and I were married six months later, and I was so put out that I didn't even invite Carter to our wedding. She and I hadn't had sex, and I hadn't bothered to tell Candy the awful things Carter had said about her.

On our wedding night, I was prepared to take it slow and gentle with my new bride. I was not very experienced, but I knew enough to understand that a woman's first time can be painful.

After lengthy foreplay I rolled on a rubber, added lubricant to it and entered her. I expected to encounter a barrier, or a least a very tight, difficult entry. Instead I slid right in. She wasn't loose, but Candy was clearly no virgin.

It didn't change my feelings for her, though. Candy wasn't a virgin, but being inside her was sheer heaven. In fact it felt too good: I didn't last three minutes. Poor Candy barely had time to start to get into it when I filled the rubber with come.

I could tell it had been a letdown to her, but she tried to pretend it had been fine. After recovering, I rolled on another condom and made love to her again. I lasted longer my second time, but I still didn't get her off.

After we showered the next morning, my new bride showed me she wasn't lacking in experience in another way also. She took me in her mouth and nearly made my eyeballs pop out from the incredible sensations she gave me. In nothing flat I came, and Candy expertly swallowed every drop.

We got along fabulously as a married couple. She was definitely the wonderful wife I thought she would be. In our time together we've never had a single argument.

Carter had told me, though, that Candy was multi-orgasmic, and she would come so hard she would nearly black out at times. Try as I might I could not get her to climax. I used my tongue on her for hours on end, but I couldn't make her come. Candy always told me it was fine, but I wondered if it really was.

We'd been married just over a year when I decided to approach her with an idea. I'd read in *Penthouse Letters* about men who enjoyed sharing their wives with other men. I wondered if some well-hung stud might be able to sexually satisfy my wife. I wasn't sure I would like it very much, but I was willing to do it for her.

It was awkward bringing the subject up. I finally did, though, telling Candy I had this kinky, perverted fantasy about seeing and hearing her with another man. At first Candy seemed hurt, but I quickly convinced her that I wasn't trying to get rid of her, and that I loved her as much as ever. My wife said I was the only man she needed, but I noticed, when we went into the bedroom, that her panties were sopping wet in the crotch.

I wasn't sure whether to bring up the subject to Candy again or not. But then, two nights later, Candy herself said, "Hinckley, when you brought up the idea of my being with another man were you just talking, or did you actually mean it?" I told her I had meant every word of it. Candy thought for a minute, then she replied, "Okay, if that's what you want, then I'll do it."

Candy told me she already knew who she wanted it to be. I should have realized who, but I didn't see it coming. When she said, "Carter," I froze. I pretended to have no problem with her choice, but I sure wished she'd picked someone else. We talked about which of us would approach him. I insisted I be the one. I didn't relish doing it, but I wanted to talk to him first. We then made love. She was really hot and wet, but I still didn't cause her to climax.

I called Carter, met him for a couple of drinks and finally summoned the courage to tell him what it was about. He smiled and said, "Can't satisfy her, can you, Hinckley? I told you Candy was too much woman for you."

We decided that Candy and I would meet Carter for dinner the next evening. We had a good meal at a nice restaurant. Our conversation was cordial, but it avoided what we all knew would happen later. There was a definite air of sexual tension. Candy and Carter openly flirted, there was a lot of eye contact between them and several times he put his hand on hers.

After dinner we went to a nightclub. Carter and I ordered mixed drinks, Candy a Coke. They headed for the dance floor before the drinks ever came. Things really began heating up as they danced. After their second dance, I watched Carter give Candy a kiss that lasted and lasted and lasted. In the hour and a half we were there they never once returned to the table. When we headed for our house, Candy rode in the front seat with Carter.

Once we were in the house they were ready for action. I'd never seen my wife so hot. She and Carter practically tore each other's clothes off in our bedroom. Once they were naked they fell on the bed together. Candy was sighing and moaning, begging Carter to put his cock in her. She rolled over on her back, Carter on top of her, and he sank his massive cock in her hole. Almost immediately, I saw my wife finally go over the top. She shuddered, oohed and moaned as she climaxed. As she did so, Carter's balls twitched, and his hip muscles clenched. Watching my wife in orgasm as my friend blasted her cunt full of his hot sperm, I filled my undershorts with wet, sticky come. They shuddered, moaned and kissed passionately.

Finally they just lay still. Weak-kneed, I slumped to the floor. I felt jealousy, but I also felt grateful to Carter for satisfying my deserving wife's sexual needs.

After resting briefly, Carter withdrew and dismounted Candy. She snuggled into his arms and they began kissing. Carter was very quickly hard again. He lay on his back, and Candy swung her legs over him and settled her crotch down on his. I could see milky come gush back out of Candy's cunt as she settled down on his massive dick. My wife bit her lower lip and closed her eyes as she settled on Carter's cock. It was easy to see that his cock did things to her that mine could not. She leaned forward and began undulating her hips, stirring Carter's prick around in her mushy cunt. Candy lowered her breasts to Carter's chest, and his hands cupped her gorgeous butt. Soon they were hunching each other madly.

They again reached climax in perfect unison. My wife threw

her head back, moaning loudly as he orgasmed and Carter pumped his second load of hot sperm up into her body. She then relaxed and lay prone on Carter's body.

I wound up sleeping on the couch that night. Carter slept with Candy in our bed. Twice more I heard her cries of ecstasy as Carter serviced her in our bed.

The next morning I heard the shower running, and went to the bathroom. I jacked off as I watched Carter fuck her in the shower. She had a very strong orgasm just as Carter blasted off inside her cunt. I splattered my load in the toilet as I watched my friend plant yet another load of his creamy seed in my wife's belly.

After Carter left, Candy was in a better mood than I'd ever seen her. She's always cheerful, but that morning she was exuberant. It was obvious that Carter had given her just what she needed. She thanked me over and over.

To show her appreciation, she dropped to her knees, unzipped my trousers and fished out my prick. When I felt my wife's warm, sweet mouth envelop my prick, my eyes closed and I was instantly hard. In only seconds I spurted.

Candy stood up, licked her lips, smiled and said, "Delicious, as usual." She then gave me a kiss, my own sperm still very much on her breath.

Carter came over again that night, and the next. In fact, he became a regular visitor to our house. I would watch him fuck my dear, sweet wife. Candy always climaxed in unison with Carter, and I would beat off, timing my orgasm with theirs. I would shoot my wad in a tissue as I watched Carter blast my wife's cunt full of creamy come.

After Carter left, Candy always gave me an unbelievably satisfying blowjob.

Candy admitted she craved the sex he gave her, but said she was sure plenty of men could satisfy her just as well. We discussed it, and she decided to call another guy she'd once dated. Candy said Dave was well-built and good-looking. She'd never slept with him, but she'd heard from a girlfriend of hers that Dave was really hung.

Candy called Dave, and two nights later I watched him fuck my wife. Dave screwed Candy twice, and then left. I had already jacked off, but I got in bed with Candy after he was gone. She felt unusually loose, but the feeling of Dave's slick come on my dick was exquisite. I humped her awhile, and then Candy had me pull out.

When I did, she instantly engulfed my slimy cock with her mouth. She didn't seem to mind at all that the prick was coated with a slimy mixture of her juices and Dave's come. In less than thirty seconds she gulped down my cream load. We then cuddled and fell asleep.

A couple of weeks later Candy added George as a lover. He was another old flame of hers. My wife has had from one to four steady lovers ever since. Sometimes I watch, and other times she tells me about her liaisons later. After her lovers leave she usually sucks me off before we go to sleep. Other times I fuck Candy after she's been with one of her studs. Her pussy always feels exquisitely soft and velvety, all slick with oily come, when I do that.

For the last two months, my wife has been exclusively seeing a very good-looking black man. It's her first experience with a man of another race. Hugh is a big man, standing about six-three and weighing well over two hundred. He has well-toned muscles, and the darkest skin I've ever seen. Candy met him through a mutual friend a little over two months ago, and I could detect a certain twinkle in her eye as she told me about him.

"You want to fuck him, don't you?" I asked.

My wife nodded, but she immediately said, "But I won't if you don't want me to, Hinckley. I admit I want to have sex with Hugh, but you know I'd never do anything without your permission. I'd never run around behind your back, and I'd never sleep with a man you told me you didn't want me to."

I nodded, patted her knee and replied, "You know I would

never refuse you what you wanted, sweetheart. If you want Hugh, then I'm all for it. Whatever makes you happy is what I want."

Candy squealed in delight, threw her arms around my neck and hugged me. Five minutes later she was dialing the phone number Hugh had written on a napkin for her. Twenty minutes later Hugh was at our door.

It was nearly ten o'clock, and the kids were already in bed. If my wife has a man over earlier in the evening, I watch the kids while she entertains her gentleman friend in our bedroom. If it is later, I often watch.

We went to our bedroom, and they began making out. When they had undressed, they stood there admiring each other. Rising to full hardness was a cock that would have put even Carter's to shame. It was not only longer than Carter's, it was much thicker. I wondered if it would even fit inside her.

They got on the bed, made out some more and played with each other's privates with their hands. Candy sucked in a gasp of air as Hugh's mighty cockhead began parting her pussy lips. He managed to split them apart, and nudged the head inside. Then I watched as my wife's vaginal opening slowly dilated and accepted more and more of his prick inside. Even then it would not all fit. There appeared to be a good two inches of his meat left when he bottomed out inside her. My wife moaned and squirmed, and her breathing became rapid and shallow as she got used to him.

Very slowly at first, very gently, Hugh began working it in and out of her pussy. Hugh was a big, powerful man, but he had a slow, gentle nature about him. I saw him gazing down at Candy's face, watching her expression, seeing how she was doing as he began fucking her. Like a powerful locomotive, he slowly and surely began picking up steam. It took him a full ten minutes before he really began putting it to her.

When he finally did, though, Hugh gave it to Candy like she'd never had it before. The other lovers she'd had were just boys compared to Hugh. I watched her wrap her legs around him, her creamy white skin contrasting so strongly with his. Her white fingers clutched his black back. Candy's eyes were shut tightly. Her breath came in snorting puffs.

As her orgasm neared, I saw her feet and legs raking up and down the outside of Hugh's thighs and calves. She was on her back, but she seemed to be riding up at his body as he rode hers.

As Hugh neared his peak he groaned, "I'm about to come, Candy. Let me come."

That set off her own climax. "Yes, do it! Do it!" she cried out in a loud, clear voice. "Come in me, Hugh! Do it, baby! Oh, do it! I want your sperm in me!" she cried out. Hearing my wife begging for her black friend to fill her with his seed had me ready to come also. Candy's butt flew up off the bed and her groin hunched at his cock as she shuddered in orgasm.

Hugh spasmed, and I could see his balls twitching as they delivered their precious load. I saw excess semen gush back out as it overflowed her hole. I whimpered and lost my load also. My prick squirted come as I watched Hugh pump jet after jet of his sperm deep into my wife's body. Candy's eyes flashed open. She gazed back up at him with a wondrous, satisfied look before plastering her mouth on his. Their snow-white and coal-black bodies seemed to meld into one as they groaned, shuddered, shook and finally lay serenely still.

She's been seeing Hugh nearly every night for over two months now, but I feel no fear of losing her to him. Candy also knows she is in no danger of my leaving her. We are a perfect match. Other guys may plant some seeds in my wife's fertile garden, but I know I will reap the fruit in the end.—H.D., *La Salle, Illinois*

RECIPE FOR MARITAL BLISS: WIFE READY FOR INTEGRATION, PLUS PEEPING TOM HUSBAND

I met Glenda back in my deep South hometown, on break from my northern university. She was a student at the local community college, and replied to the note I'd posted at the library looking for work as a physics or math tutor. She was stunning: five-foot-two, with shoulder-length blonde hair, a wonderfully rounded ass and firm, perky breasts. It was love—or at least lust— at first sight.

Glenda's grades improved with my tutoring, but by then we were in an intimate sexual relationship. Soon I returned to school, and for the next three years we exchanged visits, wrote often and phoned each other regularly. We were so horny for each other that when Glenda came to visit, we'd spend the entire weekend in bed. I'd spend hours licking and sucking on her, and she would scream and thrash around with pleasure. I could get it up two and three times a night after not seeing my lovely girlfriend for a month.

After I graduated, I took a job down South, and we were married. Everything was great for the first couple of years, but then our sex life cooled down. We fucked about once a week, but some of the spark was gone. I still loved eating pussy, but Glenda usually grabbed my prick and put it in after she came the first time. Since her tight, slick pussy made me come within a minute or two, our lovemaking was over in ten or fifteen minutes, compared to our former sex marathons. I chalked it up to being in a rut, and I was excited when my company transferred me to a new office. I thought the change would do our marriage good.

By our third anniversary Glenda and I were settling into a new condo in Trenton, New Jersey. Soon Glenda revealed a provincial Southern attitude that worried me. I had never placed any importance on the fact that, except for visits to me at college (which were spent mostly in bed), she'd never been out of the deep South. We were at the condo pool one day when she said, in a shocked tone, "Look! There are two black men here!" She referred to two young fellows, Edward and Vince, who had an apartment in the condo. She was fascinated at the ease with which they were talking with a group of young white women.

"Oh, that's the way things are here up North," I told her. "You'll get used to it. Just give people a chance."

Looking them over, I could see that the guys were well built, young and interested in girls. Edward was a six-footer and had shoulder-length dreadlocks. Vince was even taller, and had short cropped hair. Both glanced admiringly at Glenda from a distance, and I could see she was flattered. That might have been the reason that Glenda that night gave me a pleasant surprise after our usual uninspired fuck. She got into the 69 position, sucked my cock and sat on my face.

Although I didn't get another erection, and she tired of sucking my flaccid pecker, I brought her off a couple more times with my tongue, licking my come out of her.

The next week I had to leave town Friday for a weekend trade show in New York City. I was going to leave from the office, but I got really horny thinking of that session of 69. So I decided to sneak home on my lunch hour and surprise Glenda. Maybe we could have a repeat before I left.

When I got home around one, the place was empty. Glenda's car was in the parking lot. I decided to check the pool, and slipped on my trunks in case she was there. When I approached the pool, I thought I heard Glenda's laugh. I peeked over the wooden fence. It was indeed Glenda's laugh. She was sitting on the edge of the pool with her feet dangling in the water. Vince and Edward sat on either side of her. The pool was otherwise deserted. It took me a moment to realize she was wearing a bikini instead of her usual one-piece. Her firm breasts looked great, with water dripping down the bare inner curve, and her large nipples visible through the damp fabric. She was laughing and pushing her tits together with her upper arms as Edward splashed water onto them.

"I told you the water was cold," Vince said. "Look how hard it's making your nipples." Glenda turned to him, licked her lips and drawled slowly, "How do you know it's the water getting them hard?" Then she stood up, and walked slowly to the lounge where her towel lay. I freaked out when I saw it wasn't a bikini my wife was wearing, but a thong—barely more than a G-string. Her gorgeous ass was there for all to see, with only a thin strip of wet nylon between her ass-cheeks.

Vince and Edward exchanged a brief look that said, "Shit, I can't believe this chick," and followed her.

Glenda lay on her stomach. Edward asked if he could rub some suntan lotion on her back. She agreed, and he began with the back of her legs. He worked up until he was rubbing her practically bare ass. His hands occasionally dipped into her crotch area, and she spread her legs wider to give him a better access. Even from a distance I could see she had shaved her pussy before putting on the tiny thong. I couldn't believe my eyes when he rubbed up her back and casually unhooked her bikini top as he rubbed in the lotion.

"Why don't you roll over, let me do the other side?" he asked. Without a pause, Glenda rolled onto her back and exposed her naked tits to the two men. I gasped, just as they did. Her breasts jutted upward. She gazed seductively at Edward as he rubbed them. Then she moaned and wriggled her hips.

"Damn, you're hot," muttered Vince. He bent down and removed her thong. She raised her ass and legs to make it easy for him. Before long my wife was lying back, naked in the sun, as one black man sucked her tits and another ate her bald pussy. She moaned and gasped and ground her crotch into Vince's face while Edward sucked and licked her nipples. I was so horny that I pulled down my bathing suit and jerked off my five-inch dick.

After Glenda came, Edward raised his head and dropped his trunks, revealing a huge, hard, black cock. Vince didn't lift his head from his work on her pussy. Glenda grabbed Edward's prick. It was easily eight inches long and much, much thicker than mine.

"I've never even touched a black cock before," said Glenda as she stroked his monstrous meat. Edward laughed as she stuffed it into her greedy mouth. Glenda sucked it as best she could. She took the head and the first several inches in and pumped the rest of the shaft with her fist. She took the prick out of her mouth and rubbed the fat, gleaming head as she ducked her head down to lick his balls. At this point another orgasm shook her body. She convulsed and cried out, still hanging onto that monster cock. She went back to sucking as soon as her orgasm subsided, and she actually fucked him with her mouth, enthusiastically jabbing six or seven inches of prick down her throat.

After what seemed like an eternity, Edward pulled out of my wife's mouth and jacked himself off onto her tits. She sat up for this, pushing Vince away for the moment. She rubbed her boobs all over Edward's squirting dick, then rubbed the come into her tits like suntan lotion.

Meanwhile, Vince had unleashed his cock and was eagerly fisting an even longer prick than Edward's. It wasn't as thick, but I am sure its length was in double digits—ten or eleven inches, at least. Once Edward stopped coming, Glenda reclined on the chair. She grabbed Vince's prick and guided it to her pussy. Edward raised her legs to give Vince unobstructed access. After Glenda gently put the head in, Vince began slowly to rock into her. She started coming instantly.

"Keep going. Further, baby," she begged breathlessly. By the time he had half of it in, she had had three orgasms. "Do you think you can get more of it in, honey?" she asked Vince.

"You can take a lot more, baby," he said. "You just gotta loosen up. You haven't had black dick before, that's all." Five minutes later, Glenda was grunting through another orgasm as Vince poured in all of his salami. Edward was holding her legs up for her, as well as fondling her breasts.

I was jerking my dick furiously when I heard the giggles. I whirled around, and saw two young women in their bathing suits, watching me. They said nothing, but they were far from shocked. In a moment, one of them was beating my little woody for me while the other licked my balls. They brought me off in seconds. I pulled up my pants, and they waved me good-bye. They quickly went to the fence, to see the show I'd been watching.

By the time I got to my car, I was horny again. I pulled my suit down around my ankles and furiously beat off. I squirted all over myself. Then I realized I had nothing to wear but a bathing suit, and nothing to wipe my hands off with. Instead of getting come all over the upholstery, I licked it carefully off my fingers. After that, I sneaked into the house to retrieve my clothes, headed back to work, and left on my trip.

I tried to call Glenda that night, but got no answer. I gave up at midnight, and tried to sleep. Images of Glenda with her two lovers kept me up in more ways than one. I was a wreck all day Saturday. I had planned to fly home Sunday morning, but the thought of catching Glenda in the act again got me on a late Saturday afternoon flight. I didn't call Glenda to let her know I'd be home early.

When I got to the condominium, I looked up at our place and saw that the lights were out. I figured Glenda had gone out for the evening. I went to our patio to see if there was any way I could set it up to spy on my wife again. As I was peeking through the back window, I suddenly heard voices and then the living room light went on. Glenda was home—along with Edward, Vince and Rosita, a gorgeous brunette whom I had met at the pool earlier. She was Hispanic, and she had flashing dark eyes and a great body.

Glenda wore a short, tight dress, fishnet hose and high heels. Her face was flushed. She laughed a lot, and moved as if she might be drunk. Rosita wore a tight blouse that showed off her flat belly and her full breasts, as well as black hot pants and ankle boots. Rosita had full, sensuous lips and a mane of black hair.

The guys broke out some more booze from my liquor cabinet, and Glenda put on some rap music (which she had formerly hated). She and Rosita danced. The guys settled on the couch with their drinks and watched my wife and her friend dance. It was a suggestive dance, and soon Rosita pulled off her top, showing off those magnificent tits of hers. They were very large and firm, the color of milky coffee, and tipped with large brown nipples. Not to be outdone, Glenda removed her dress. Soon they were both naked, except for Glenda's garter belt, hose and high heels. Then the two girls started dancing even closer to each other. At Vince's suggestion they began to bump and grind. Soon they were French-kissing and grabbing each other's crotch.

The two fellows lapped this up. They whipped out their dicks and started jerking off. But not for long. Both girls dropped to their knees and lunged for the black pricks, licking and sucking them for all they were worth. I remembered then that Glenda had never been an enthusiastic cocksucker with me. She would blow me, but only if I begged her, or for my birthday or some other occasion. Anyhow, there I was, on my own back porch, jerking off as these two gorgeous women gave two strangers head in my living room.

It wasn't long before Glenda got off her knees and straddled Vince's erect cock. She grabbed it firmly and rubbed the cock-head along her shaved pussy lips. "Ooh . . ." she moaned and arched her back as she diddled her clit with it. Soon she had the schlong up in into her tight, slick twat. She happily rocked up and down on it. When she had most of it in, Edward moved off the couch so Vince could lie back and Glenda could bounce around all over him. He gripped her hips as she squatted on his ebony pole. Glenda began to raise herself and then drop quickly back on his massive joint.

As if that weren't enough, Vince urged Rosita to sit on his face. She was quick to comply, and straddled his head facing Glenda. I could almost hear Vince's tongue diving in and out of sweet Rosita's tangy pussy as she and Glenda kissed and fondled each other's breasts. Glenda seemed fascinated with Rosita's large boobs. She stroked and licked them, and she hefted them, either estimating their weight or enjoying their texture.

Edward wasn't going to be left out of the action. He approached Glenda and presented his cock for her attention. It was semi-hard and still wet with saliva and pre-come. She rubbed the big head on her cheek, still concentrating on kissing Rosita deeply. But Edward's prick stiffened with this treatment, and soon Glenda had one black cock in her mouth and another up her pussy. Meanwhile, Rosita rubbed her big boobs on Edward's shiny prick as it slipped in and out of Glenda's luscious lips. Soon Edward spewed thick, gooey come. It overflowed from Glenda's mouth onto Rosita's tits as I shot off into the bushes.

I don't think Vince had come yet, but Edward's orgasm had sent both girls over the edge. They both shuddered through intense orgasms. Then they climbed off of Vince, whose prick was still hard as a rock. They ignored both studs, though, and Glenda really shocked the hell out of me when she thrust her face into Rosita's crotch and licked her pretty pussy. Vince made use of his erection, rubbing it all over Rosita's tits while this was going on. Unfortunately, he had his back to me. I'd love to have seen those two melons squishing around his huge black cock.

Now Edward was horny again. He knelt behind Glenda as she ate out Rosita, and gave her pussy a lick. She wiggled it provocatively, and he eased his schlong in. Soon they were hard at it, doggie-style. I jerked off as I watched, wishing I was one of those black dudes getting all that good sex from my suddenly sexy wife and her friend. That exhausted me, and I left. I spent the night in a motel. When I went home the next morning, I woke up a very sleepy Glenda. She was surprised to see me, since I wasn't due until noon. When I asked her what she did over the weekend, she said, "Nothing much." She said she had gone to the movies by herself. Glenda took her shower while I unpacked, and I heard her lock the bathroom behind her.

I was unpacked, still in the bedroom, when Glenda walked in

a half hour later, wearing only a towel. "I want to show you how much I missed you, tiger," she giggled, throwing the towel down with a flourish and letting me see, supposedly for the first time, her shaven pussy. "I thought it would be a nice homecoming surprise, sweetie," she said.

I didn't stop to discuss the matter; I was too horny. I dived for her pretty pussy and ate it out thoroughly, pent up from watching her fucking and sucking all night. She came powerfully, and I rubbed my face all over her wet, bald pussy, licking greedily at it. That was only the beginning. My proper little wife sucked my prick stiff again, then straddled it and sank down on it. I wondered how my puny prick must feel to her after so much hefty cock.

I got my answer right away. The only difference in Glenda now was a lack of inhibitions. Not only had she given me a great blowjob to turn me on, but her sweet little pussy was tighter and slicker than ever. Apparently black cock was good for her. And her enthusiasm for good old-fashioned fucking had a good effect on me as well. In recent months, I would have come in an insipid way after only a few of the powerful hunches she was taking on my prick. Now, though, I was so caught up in the passion we shared that I held out until she raised herself for one last long hard thrust, threw her head back and shouted, then climaxed for a good five trembling minutes. That, and only that, got me off. We came together for the first time in a long time.

Later, as we cuddled contentedly together, I told Glenda about watching her and Rosita and the guys.

"You saw it all?" she asked. "What did you think?"

"You've come a long way, baby," I said.

I also told her how much I admired Rosita's olive skin and big tits. Since then, we've done some threesomes with that lovely girl. Not to mention fivesomes with me and the entire original cast. I no longer have to stand outside and watch—but I still like to watch.

At the same time, Glenda and I have a happier, more honest

life. Apart from our sessions with our friends, we like going to bed with each other. I'll have to close now, because Glenda, across the room, is giving me that look of hers again, and licking her lips in a significant manner.—W.C., *Trenton, New Jersey*

DON'T YOU HAVE TO LOVE A WOMAN WHO COMES TO THE PARTY PREPARED?

Every summer, a group of buddies I've known forever—we grew up together—and I get a beach house down the nearby shore for a week. The shindig is different from year to year. Anywhere from six to fourteen people will come on down for a fabulous week of booze and babes, fun and sun.

Sometimes the crowd includes girlfriends, but this past year none of the guys brought their girls with them. Instead, everyone was hoping to hook up with somebody at the beach.

I didn't invite my girl either, but I did invite someone pretty special. I first met Melissa on the Internet. She said she was nineteen years old, still lived at home and had brown hair and soft brown eyes. She E-mailed me pictures from her prom, and I was surprised to see that no prom date was in evidence. As for me, although she was cute, I didn't find myself all that attracted to her.

Like most of the women I have met on-line, our E-mail exchanges were friendly and flirtatious. Because she is on the young side (I'm twenty-five), we would joke that I was on my way over to pick her up on my Big Wheel and that I promised to have her home before the streetlights came on.

She replied by saying that if she were to get home late, her uncle would surely have something to say about her being a bad girl. It seems she was often a bad girl.

Although as I said, I didn't find her picture all that attractive,

I still enjoyed communicating with her because she could keep up the verbal banter with me. Soon our exchanges were going like—

"So, how's the pussy?"

"Shaved."

"Really?"

"No, not really."

I was a bit disappointed by this particular exchange, but I was still intrigued by Melissa. She kept insisting we meet, but I kept putting it off because I already had a girlfriend. Finally I relented. I said something to her about our shore house, and she agreed to meet me there for the annual shindig.

I was prepared for disappointment. I knew she was coming down to fuck me, but I didn't expect her to be all that good-looking, based on the photos she had E-mailed me. When she showed up, about two days after everyone else, I thought she was presentable, but I still wasn't especially impressed.

Later, when we all went to the beach, Melissa wore a floral-print two-piece bikini. There was no question that she had a nice, tight little body. Still, there was something about her that just put me off. What can I say? She just wasn't my type.

Later that night, however, the lack of feeling I originally had for Melissa turned into something very different.

It was around ten, and she said she was tired, kind of hinting that she didn't want to go to bed alone. I remember thinking then that we were coming up on the moment of truth.

She started kissing me, and I must say that she demonstrated a great deal of skill at it. She told me how much she really liked me. She said that I was really good-looking and that I was the guy she really wanted to fuck her soaking-wet pussy.

As she described some of the preparations she had made, my interest level grew. First off, she said she had brought her own dildo. And condoms. And lotions and creams. And a feather, and, oh yes, grapes.

"Grapes?" I asked. "What are these for? A snack between sessions?"

"You'll see" was her teasing reply.

Faster than a snake can shed its skin, Melissa had her bikini off and heaped in a (very small) pile on the floor. She was spread-eagled wide, and was twirling the fingers of one hand in her pubes. She invited me to join her in playing with her pretty pussy.

"My type" or not, her perky tits and tight ass commanded my well-trained soldier to attention. And you know, there are certain calls to action you just can't easily resist. At any rate, I didn't even try to resist this one. My clothes came off as fast as hers did.

She was already wet as I slid my cock inside her and began to suck her tits. As I pumped her pussy, she told me I was the four-teenth guy she had slept with. She even hinted that she had been with a couple of girls.

"A woman licks pussy better than a guy," she said suddenly, out of the blue. I let that comment pass without comment. Still, for a girl who is supposed to have been with at least thirteen other guys, she was surprisingly tight.

"Sex with you is by far the best I've had," she cooed.

"I bet you say that to all the guys."

"No, really," she said. "You make me feel really good. You're pretty big too."

As I was about to drop my goo, Melissa asked, "Would you mind fucking me in the ass?"

I was taken aback by such a bold request, but she had asked too late, for a stroke later her tight taco was filled with all the love sauce I could give her just then. Her heels were on my ass and she was clenching my cock with her pussy muscles to squeeze every last drop out of me.

But the night was not over, not by any means.

With her knees in the air and her heels to her ass, Melissa stuck two fingers in her pussy and used my jism to wet herself again. She made little circles on her clit, and put her fingers in her pussy again when they began to dry.

I had never seen anything like this. I once had a girlfriend who would masturbate for me, but it was nothing like this. As you might imagine, I got hard again really quickly.

Melissa got on all fours, doggie-style, and I fucked her with the dildo that she had brought along. Her tight little ass looked mighty good to me, but since I am pretty big (about nine inches), I started by fucking her with the dildo while I waited for the right time to inset my cock in her poop chute.

Melissa's rear entrance was tighter than it looked, even after the dildo fucking I had given her. I was only able to put my cock halfway in her ass and got only five strokes before I shot my load again.

I lay almost exhausted, and Melissa went into the bathroom to freshen up. As she was leaving for the bathroom, she rested her come-filled pussy on my cock and said, "Don't go anywhere. I have one more surprise for you."

I thought, What more can there be? Then I must have fallen asleep, because the next thing I knew, Melissa was shaking me, saying, "Wake up, lover boy! Time for round three!"

I'd like to think that I'm as studly as the next guy, but really, *three times* in less than two hours? I honestly didn't think that I would be "up" to it.

I was a bit groggy as Melissa announced, "It's time for the grape game."

"What the hell is the grape game?" I asked.

"Watch," she said.

Again Melissa was sitting spread-eagled. But this time she proceeded to stick about three grapes, one at a time, into her pussy.

"Now," she said, "I want you to suck the grapes out of me, as slowly as you can."

I was wide awake now, and before I knew it my head was between Melissa's legs and my nose was right on top of her pussy. I stuck my tongue down her cunt, and sure enough, I could feel the first grape in there.

I tried my best to remove the little sucker with just my tongue, but I just couldn't get it. After this first failure, I took her pussy lips into my mouth and began to suck like a vacuum. I increased the pressure slowly, and eventually the first grape came out.

When it did, Melissa let out a low moan, like the sound came from the back of her throat. She came something enormous, because I actually felt her pussy quivering in my mouth. I didn't want to stop her pleasure, so I tried to use the same technique to suck the second grape out pretty fast.

The second grape was harder to get. All the while, remember, Melissa's pussy was quaking in my mouth. I kept adding to the stimulation by trying to reach the elusive grape with only my tongue. As I reached and reached, she squirmed and squirmed with pleasure. Her pussy was shaking so hard in my mouth that several times the shaking almost made me bite my tongue.

The third grape was even more elusive than the second. After I finally sucked it out, Melissa got on top of me, with her pussy still in my mouth, and started to fuck my face! I never knew that pussy juice could taste so sweet.

She said, "I gotta do somethin' for you, for that great pussy-lickin'." She seized my cock and gave me the best blowjob of my life. She deep-throated my nine inches and my balls too! She took all of my cock in her mouth eagerly and skillfully, without gagging once. She licked my cock, sucked and squeezed it with her hand, all at the same time.

When I came this time, the eruption wasn't as intensive as it had been the previous two times. And of course by now I just didn't have much spunk left in me to give. Now completely spent, I fell into a deep sleep, from which I woke up feeling really well rested.

Melissa and I still keep in touch via the Internet. She would like to spend more time with me, even though she knows that I already have a girlfriend. She still tells me that I was the best fuck of her life, and that anytime that's convenient for me is okay with her.

My girlfriend Carly has a good personality, but our sex life is nowhere near as intense as what Melissa and I had. I want to be faithful to Carly, but as I hope you can now understand, my mind keeps taking me back to that wonderful night of sex, which climaxed (in both senses) in the mind-blowing blowjob Melissa gave me.

Carly and Melissa live about sixty miles apart from each other, so there is not much chance they will run into each other. So I could have my (pussy) cake and eat it (ha!) too. Should I? —O.S., Wilmington, Delaware

FOR A REALLY GOOD TIME, IT HELPS TO HAVE A STUDLY FRIEND WHO'S FEELING TAXED

Last night I had an experience that I thought might be good enough to share with *Penthouse Letters* readers.

It started very innocently, as most of these things do. I have a married friend who is built better than the average person. He called me at work and asked me if I wanted to have a drink or two with him that evening to relieve the stress of having to get his income tax in on time, since it was the fifteenth of April.

We met at the local pub, and we each had a couple of beers. Mitchell excused himself—to go to the bathroom, I thought. When he came back he told me how he hasn't been getting laid much lately by his wife. He also told me he had just called an old girlfriend of his and she wanted to meet up with him. I finished my beer and started to leave, telling him, with a big smile on my face, to go and have a great time.

That is when the real fun started for both of us. He told me that this old girlfriend of his really got into good sex. He wanted to know if I wanted to come along. Since I hadn't been getting much from my wife lately, I told him, "OK, I'll try something different."

We went to a motel on the other side of town. When we got

there, his girlfriend was already waiting for us in the parking lot. She was wearing a big smile on her face and was very happy to see him. Mitchell went into the office to pay for the room while Suzanne and I got to know each other.

When we got inside the room I told them I had to take a shower. I made it a quick one. When I was finished Mitchell went in and took his shower. While he was in the bathroom I sat on the bed with Suzanne. She put her foot between my legs and started playing with my hardening cock through my underwear.

I reached over and started rubbing her pussy even though she still had her clothes on. After about three minutes she stood up and took all her clothes off and lay back down on the bed. I started fingering her clit and put one, then two fingers in her moist hole. The more I played with her, the wilder she got.

I asked her how she felt about oral sex. She said she loves it, so I got on the bed and started tonguing her clit. She clamped her legs around my head as she had her first orgasm. I then mounted her in the good old missionary position and started slowly fucking her.

After a few moments of this Mitchell came out of the bathroom. I felt him at the bottom of the bed. He reached up between my legs for Suzanne's now very wet cunt.

I couldn't believe this was actually happening to me. (I am just an average guy with an average six-inch cock.) He was trying to spread her cunt out further, and as he did so, his hands would rub against my cock.

Finally Mitchell got up and asked me to switch positions with him. He told me it's a great view from down there. When he stood up I got my first glimpse of his cock. It must have been eight inches long and very thick. He mounted her and started fucking her. She gradually raised her legs until she had her feet up to her head.

By this time Mitchell was pounding her like a stud in heat. At one point his cock slipped out of her hole. He told me to take it and stick it back in her. I reached up and hesitated a second. He took my hand and moved it to his hard cock. I took hold of it and guided it back into her waiting hole. That was new and wild, touching another guy with my hand.

I then started fingering Suzanne's asshole, using her cunt juice as a lubricant. I got two fingers into her bunghole and could feel Mitchell's huge cock on the other side. This seemed to drive her crazy. I could feel her muscles clamp onto his cock and my fingers simultaneously. This was her second climax.

To my surprise, Mitchell then pulled out of Suzanne. He asked her if she could take it up her ass. She said she was so turned on, she was up for anything. He then lay down on his back. She slid down on his rock-hard cock, which was once again buried in her cunt. I moved in behind her. My cock was already slick from my own pre-come, so I rubbed my juice against the crack of her ass to make her asshole slick.

The lady was so turned on that she started fucking Mitchell while we got my cock into her ass. I put the head of my cock next to her hole and let her work herself onto it. Suddenly it seemed just to pop in her to the hilt.

We all kind of stopped for about thirty seconds. Then Mitchell asked if I was all the way in. Suzanne let out a low sensual sound of "Yessss, all the way." Then she started moving very slowly, fucking both of us at once. I could feel my balls slapping Mitchell's.

Suzanne began to have another orgasm. It built very slowly until she started saying, "Fuck me, fuck me, fuck me hard. I want to feel every inch of both of your cocks."

I could take no more. I shoved my cock hard into her ass until I unloaded my come deep in her. I can't remember the last time I had such an intense orgasm.

Mitchell kept fucking Suzanne's pussy for another few minutes. Then he asked her if it would be okay if he fucked her in the ass. She responded, "Yes, yes, anywhere you want to fuck me. I just want your cock in me."

I couldn't believe this woman. She got up on her knees and

Mitchell inserted his massive cock in her asshole. She reached under herself and started playing with her clit. I got behind them and put a couple of fingers in her dripping wet pussy. I felt Mitchell's cock between her pussy wall and her ass.

That was all Suzanne could take. She clamped her pussy and ass muscles around my hand and Mitchell's dick. They both had wild orgasms. Mitchell fell off her and she fell to the bed on her stomach.

After we all recovered we got dressed and Mitchell spent ten minutes doing his taxes. Mitchell said it was the first time Suzanne had let him fuck her in the ass, and thanked me for lubing it up for him. I told him I'd be glad to do it anytime. They both want to make arrangements to do it again.

Mitchell then asked me if I would drop his tax forms off at the post office. I knew it would be a one-hour wait, and it was already nine o'clock. But I gladly mailed his taxes. I figured it was the least I could do to thank him for the fun I just had.—*J.B.*, *Cleveland, Ohio*

WELL, IF YOU'RE SEXUALLY FIXATED ON YOUR OWN ASS, WHAT WOULD YOU CALL IT?

It wasn't until my neighbor asked me to gather in her mail while she was on vacation that I found out that she, too, subscribes to *Penthouse Letters*. Now, she must have realized I would see the magazine. So, with this fact already out in the open, I didn't see any harm in asking Lessie point-blank what kinds of letters really push her buttons.

To appreciate her answer, you need to know that Lessie was born and raised in the Deep South. Her drawl sometimes makes one-syllable words like "boy" come out sounding like "bow-eee," whereas words that ought to have more syllables get knocked down to one or two. Lessie's take on "probably," for example, is something like "prol-ly."

The day I asked which *Penthouse Letters* she likes, Lessie stopped what she was doing at the time and looked at me through a fringe of loopy lashes. She rimmed her lips with her pink, wet tongue.

I tried not to get overly distracted by how hot she looked. Instead of thinking about my soaking panties, I tried to concentrate on her answer.

And what I heard was "autoasphyxiation." I was stunned. Autoasphyxiation? I registered my astonishment, and I must have been very up-front about it.

Lessie was startled.

"Good gracious, no," she insisted. "I never did say autoasphyxiation? Whatever do you take me for? What I said was auto-ass-fixation." (I will spare the reader any attempt to reproduce how either "word" sounded as pronounced by Lessie.)

Relieved as I was by the clarification, I still had no idea on earth what auto-ass-fixation might be. Lessie tried to explain, and this time I tried my darnedest to stay with her.

It seemed that being banged by her boyfriend was never enough to satisfy her. One night she found herself lying in bed thinking about the way the boyfriend fucked her up the ass, and before she knew it she was as wet as the Okefenokee swamp. She was, she said, practically climbing the walls for relief.

She bounced from her bed, fetched some body oil from the medicine chest, took off her panties and plopped back on the bed. Then she lay down on her back and gave the oil a squeeze, carefully directing the trickle of oil past her wanting pussy.

It coursed its way down to her anus, where she met it with her middle finger and traced the letters of her boyfriend's name on her asshole. She then added lubrication to her middle finger, spread her legs as far as they would go and positioned her finger over her anus. She slid it slowly into her rectum as far as it would

go, then traced her index finger over her perineum, over her oozing slit, finally coming to rest on her kernel-hard clit.

From the climaxes that resulted, she knew she was on to something, and for her next auto-ass-fixation session she refined her
technique. This time she equipped herself with a dildo, though
even now she often prefers to let her fingers do the walking.

I muttered something incoherent like "Uh-huh" or "Oh, really?" and bolted. I couldn't wait to get home to try it for myself.
Heaven only knows what Lessie thought of my hasty exit. If by
chance she is reading this now, she will understand what happened that day and know how much I am in her debt.

I have developed an auto-ass-fixation of my own, which has
led me into all manner of experimentation. I would love to tell
everybody I meet what I'm into, but I'm afraid they'd misunder-
stand and think I have some kind of sickness or sexual perver-
sion.—*F.K.*, *Philadelphia, Pennsylvania*

THEY USE A BACKDOOR AID PLUS HIS OWN
EQUIPMENT–AS GOOD AS A THREESOME?

Many of your letters deal with "threesomes." Being in a long-term
monogamous relationship with a very sexy woman, I find it hard
to believe there are so many men who share their partners with
someone else. My wife is even sexier than when we married. Her
long well-shaped legs and great breasts are mine to enjoy. Why
would I want to share?

On the other hand, I have fantasized about giving Désirée new
and bigger pleasures. Among these has been the thought of overwhelming her with multiple cocks—fucking her in the pussy and
ass at the same time. Despite my fantasies, my selfishness and our
conservatism would never allow a threesome in real life.

I should note that Désirée and I have enjoyed a wide range of intimacies such as an assortment of sex toys and anal sex. It's not an exaggeration to say that after appropriate foreplay Désirée loves me to fuck her in the ass. Hence the concept of fucking her in the ass and the pussy is not unthinkable. It's just our mutual desire to be only with each other that rules out a three-way.

Last night we enjoyed a close alternative I'd like to share with your readers.

In the morning I left Désirée a sexually suggestive note, as I often do. I like to give her a sexual thought for the day. This note told her I had a new anal dildo, and described it—hot pink, about three inches long, with the neck-and-bulb shape common to dildos intended for the ass. The note directed Désirée to a dresser drawer where the dildo was displayed on a satin cloth for her inspection. The note said I hoped she'd be teased throughout the day by the thought that after dinner this evening I planned to fill her ass with the dildo—holding it securely in place with the leather harness she had once made for such occasions.

I should note that the harness had been custom-designed and fitted by my wife after I'd shown her something similar in a catalog. It holds a dildo perfectly in her ass but leaves her pussy exposed, making it even better than anything I could have bought. It was a fantastic act of love for her to make it, and we'd enjoyed it many times.

My note concluded by saying that after perhaps an hour of necking on our couch I expected we'd adjourn to the bedroom, where I'd remove the dildo and fill her conditioned ass with my cock. I encouraged her to think about the evening I had planned for her ass throughout the day.

I daydreamed off and on yesterday about the note and hoped Désirée had found it intriguing and exciting. While I leave sexual notes for her frequently, I can never be sure how she will react, nor whether outside forces will spoil whatever sexual mood the note might have initially created. When conditions are right, her sexuality and our mutual lust usually outdo any fantasies I've outlined on paper.

When I arrived home last night I was treated to Désirée wearing a cleavage-revealing top, high heels and a very short skirt. I knew in an instant that my note—or something else—had put her in the mood for intense sex. I told her how delicious she looked as I stared at her breasts and felt my cock begin to harden. It was a great way to be welcomed home.

As I put my arms around and kissed Désirée, I could not help but grab her ass. She felt very soft and sexy through the thin skirt, and after a few seconds I realized her ass-cheeks must be naked under the skirt. My mind enjoyed the thought of her ass in a thong, an obscene concept in panties we'd discovered only a few months ago but had already enjoyed many times.

Perhaps sensing my thoughts about her ass being framed by a thong, Désirée told me seductively that she assumed I didn't mind that instead of panties she'd decided to wear the leather dildo harness. I smiled and assured her that her ass felt great. She said that putting the harness on late in the afternoon had gotten her very excited, so much so that she hadn't exactly stopped there.

I was enjoying the thought of Désirée pulling the harness up between her legs and against her pussy, and expected her to tell me that she'd brought herself off in one way or another—descriptions that I always find hugely exciting. Instead, she surprised me by saying that she had been thinking about the dildo all afternoon and thought we would both enjoy her surprising me by inserting it before I got home. She whispered that she'd almost come as she'd pushed it in.

My mind immediately painted the picture of Désirée lubricating and filling her ass with the harness-held dildo. Needless to say, my cock throbbed at the thought. She said she'd been very tempted to go for an orgasm but had steeled herself to merely prepare her ass for me. As a result she said she was very horny and very ready for anything I might have in mind.

I kissed her and explored her ass with my hands, feeling for and finding the line of the harness through the skirt and being both aroused and amused by the thought that these panty lines gave a whole new meaning to the term. I cupped each cheek in my hands and squeezed, pushing inward somewhere in the middle to move the dildo if I could. Désirée's moan told me I had.

We decided dinner could wait and moved into the bedroom. As we walked, one of my hands stayed on Désirée's ass—fondling, touching and grabbing. Every contact was amplified by the knowledge that she had a dildo buried in her ass and was eager for me to fuck her there.

I stripped my business suit off as we entered the bedroom and thought of how we might best enjoy Désirée's preparation. It struck me that to remove the dildo and replace it with my cock would be great, but would also mark the end of her sexy preparation. How could I prolong all or some of what she'd done?

In seconds I had an answer. I finished undressing myself and removed Désirée's skirt. Her naked ass was framed with the black leather harness and looked every bit as fantastic as I had been imagining. Her great legs looked even longer and sexier than usual, since her naked ass blended into them. Every visual image was further enhanced by my thoughts of the dildo, which I couldn't see but certainly could imagine. I kissed her and fondled her ass some more as I reveled in her sexuality.

Désirée and I then moved over to the side of the room where her sewing cabinet was, and she bent over the cabinet. Previous experience had shown it to be the perfect height to facilitate rear-entry sex.

From experience, Désirée knew immediately how to rest her arms on the cabinet. She moved her ass blatantly for me as she spread her legs and assumed the position she knew I had in mind. When she was bent over, her legs and ass merged even more, and my cock throbbed at the sight of her.

Leaving the dildo in Désirée's ass, I approached her from behind with my cock pointing at the ceiling. I had to use a hand to push it down and guide it between her legs, but soon found her wet pussy and easily slid into her. As I entered her, I could feel my hips pressing against her ass cheeks.

Her groan of pleasure told me I was moving the dildo just as I had hoped would happen. With each forward movement of my hips, the dildo would move in. As my hips came back, the dildo retreated to its at-rest position. The thought that I was fucking Désirée's ass with the dildo as I was filling her pussy with my cock doubled my excitement.

I tried to be gentle at the start. As I fucked her, it became obvious that she was thrashing about with pleasure. Her reaction and the realization that I was fucking my wife in both of her openings was incredible.

I held Désirée's hips and fucked her harder. We were both out of control and loving every minute of it. Violent orgasms soon swept through both of us, reducing my muscles to jelly. Now I *had* to hold onto her hips for support, as we each felt the aftershocks from our own and our lover's orgasms.

Needless to say, I wholeheartedly recommend this kind of threesome. You need a very sexy and cooperative wife, but no one else. In a few weeks I expect to fuck my wife while her ass enjoys a large black dildo I've just ordered.—*D.S., Scranton, Pennsylvania*

THE LETTERS HE LIKES GIVE THIS CLEVER LADY SOME FANTASTIC IDEAS

Every month my wife Judy and I look forward to reading *Penthouse Letters*. We usually stretch out in bed and take turns reading aloud to each other. When I'm reading she is busy sucking and stroking my cock. When she is reading I'm busily sucking and fingering her cunt. Eventually we end up in a great fuck session, our passion fueled by the images conjured by your readers' letters.

Not only does the reading enhance our sex, but it also reveals what scenarios turn each of us on. Judy's cunt seems to really get juicy and hot when she is reading about some woman taking on two or three guys at the same time. My turn-on is reading about women who slide their finger or some appropriate stimulator up their partner's ass while they're getting sucked or fucked.

Well, about six months ago, on a Saturday afternoon, we were both horny as hell and decided to spend a few hours engaged in our favorite pastime. I noticed that Judy had a sort of devilish look in her eyes as we headed for the bedroom. She suggested that we slip into a nice 69 with me on top. Soon we were busily sucking and fingering each other. My head was at the foot of the bed and Judy had her head on her pillow underneath me.

She was doing her usual fine job with her lips and hand when suddenly I heard the unmistakable sound of a glob of K-Y jelly being squeezed from a tube. The next thing I knew I could feel Judy's finger massaging and exploring the area around my asshole. My God, what a turn-on! I wondered if she would go further, and she did! I felt her finger slide inside my butt and move in and out.

My cock felt like concrete, and it felt larger than it has ever been. Judy pulled her mouth away momentarily and told me how gigantic I had become, and then she resumed her sucking and stroking. I warned her that I was going to come if she kept it up. She gave me the squeeze treatment and at the same time removed her finger from my ass, to my great disappointment.

Once again I heard the K-Y. This time I felt a larger item pressed against my anus. I had great difficulty keeping myself from coming. Somehow I managed to hold back, and was rewarded with the sensation of a device being slid up my ass. It went deeper than Judy's finger and it filled me up as well.

Judy took her mouth off my cock and begged me to fuck her with my "monster." We managed to shift positions while keeping the device in my ass. Judy was still on her back, with me now positioned between her legs. She had reached around behind me to keep the device in place. I entered her eagerly, amazed at the size and hardness of my penis. The sensation of my cock in her cunt and my prostate being touched drove me wild.

Then Judy flipped a switch and the device began to vibrate. I came so hard I saw stars. Judy went just about as wild herself. My cock felt thoroughly drained, though still surprisingly hard, when I finally withdrew. Eventually we calmed down, and Judy showed me the anal stimulator that had done the job.

She told me that she noticed how turned on I was when letters were read concerning anal stimulation, and that a girlfriend loaned her a marital-aid catalog so that she could order a stimulator for herself. We got our own catalog and began ordering other items. I bought a very lifelike dildo for Judy which also has a built-in motor that causes the dildo to rotate and vibrate.

She loves to close her eyes and have me fuck her with "Steve" (as we named the dildo) while she sucks my cock. I talk to the imaginary other guy, urging him to fuck my wife while she sucks my cock. Eventually I added Judy's own anal device so she can take on "three guys" at a time. It's amazing what your imagination can do when your eyes are closed.

Thanks, *Penthouse Letters*, for opening the door to new sexual adventures.—*E.M., Regina, Saskatchewan*

AS A BIRTHDAY GIFT, HER HUSBAND GIVES HER ALL THE MEN SHE CAN TAKE

My husband Adam and I have a progressive attitude toward sex. We enjoy all forms of erotica, especially *Penthouse Letters*.

What really gets my juices flowing are letters that involve women having sex with more than one man while their husbands watch. Adam and I have an open marriage—not surprising, as we met through a swingers' club.

For much of the last year, I had to stop having sex due to a high-risk pregnancy, which required plenty of bed rest. I am happy to report that I gave birth to perfect twin girls.

After a three-month recovery period, I was eager to resume our swinging lifestyle. While I was out of commission, Adam offered to stop swinging, but I wouldn't hear of it. I admit that I felt a twinge of jealousy every time he went to a swing party, but I knew it wouldn't be forever.

Once I had recovered, we made love whenever we had the chance, which is not often when taking care of two babies. I began to think I would never have sex with a man besides my husband.

Then last Saturday, Adam suggested we drop the girls off at my mother's so the two of us could celebrate my birthday with a nice romantic dinner. I jumped at the idea, and he gave me a present: new lingerie from Victoria's Secret.

He had bought a black lacy strapless bra, a garter belt, a G-string and silk thigh-high hose. I took a bubble bath to relax, and when I got out, he had *another* package for me. I tore it open and found the most beautiful tight white dress. It was very short, barely covering the tops of my hose. But after all those months, I felt like a sexy woman again.

Adam said I had worked so hard to lose the weight I gained during pregnancy that it was only fitting that I show off my body. My juices were flowing, and I suggested that we stay home and make love. He said I had to be patient.

We had a lovely candlelight dinner at our favorite restaurant and went dancing at a local jazz club. While we danced, Adam ran his hands up and down my ass. After a few songs, I whispered that I wanted to go home and ravish him. Soon we were driving home.

I was so horny, I unzipped Adam and put my head in his lap. He stopped me from sucking his cock, saying I'd have to wait until we got home. I got so frustrated, I hiked up my dress and began to finger myself. I was so wet, my fingers squished in my cunt. I came as we pulled into our driveway.

Adam and I went in the house. When I turned on the light, I was greeted with "Surprise!" I couldn't believe my eyes. There was a banner across our living room: "Wel-*come* back, Karen!" I was still in a state of shock when Adam came up behind me and whispered, "Go unwrap your other presents."

I looked around. Six guys were standing naked except for G-strings and ribbons tied around their crotches.

They had rearranged the furniture and placed a large mattress in the middle. Hank and Noah were there. Last year we often swung with them and their wives Sunny and Megan. Will and Robin were also members of our swing club; we had had encounters with them and their wives. The other guys, Ronnie and Ted, I found out were coworkers of Adam's.

He arranged the men in a line and reviewed the ground rules. The men were at my service for the evening. I had never been gang-banged, but Adam knew it was a favorite fantasy of mine. The largest number of men I had had at once was two.

I dropped on my knees in front of Hank, the first guy in the line, and unwrapped my present. I untied his ribbon and pulled off his G-string. His cock sprang up and hit my chin, so I licked it. While sucking him off, I reached over and unwrapped Noah. I started stroking his cock while continuing to work on Hank's with my mouth.

I shifted positions and took Noah into my mouth while stroking Hank with my left hand and unwrapping Robin's cock with my right. Pretty soon I was stroking Hank and Robin while sucking Noah. I continued moving down the line of men until I tasted each of them. After giving Ted a couple of licks, I noticed that Adam was not in the line. I turned around. He was behind me, naked, taping all the action.

I got up and took off my dress, then lay down spread-eagle on the mattress. I told the guys to come and get it. Ronnie and Ted lay down beside me and started removing my bra while Hank got between my legs and removed my G-string.

After Ronnie had unstrapped my bra, he and Ted sucked my tits. Hank, a surgeon, said that my ob-gyn must have been excellent, as he could barely see the scar from my C-section. I told him to shut up and eat me, which he did with gusto.

I was enjoying it all when I felt something wet on my cheek. Robin had straddled my head, and his cock was just inches from my face. I lifted my head and started licking his shaft. After a couple of licks, he put his cock in my mouth and face-fucked me. These sensations were just too much. I soon cried out in a tremendous orgasm.

I took Robin's cock out of my mouth and begged someone to fuck me. Hank got on top of me and slowly inserted his cock in my pussy. God, it was wonderful. I reached up and pulled Robin's cock back into my mouth and sucked hard.

Ronnie and Ted had gotten on their knees and were rubbing my nipples with the tips of their cocks. I continued sucking on Robin until he came. Ronnie and Ted moved to either side of my head, and I licked their cocks alternately. Hank grunted, shot a load in my pussy and collapsed on top of me. I felt as if I had left my body and was watching it from above.

Someone replaced Hank in my pussy and began to fuck me, exploding just as I came for the third time. I continued to stroke Ronnie's cock with my hand while I sucked on Ted. I was in a blissful trance until Ronnie shot his load down my throat.

I called time and drank a glass of wine. Then I got back on the mattress and asked Noah to eat my pussy, his favorite position. Last year whenever we got together he ate Megan's pussy after he and Adam dumped their loads in there. Noah is so come-crazy, Adam and I wondered if he might be a closet homosexual.

Noah licked my clit and fingered my pussy and asshole until I came again. After resting awhile, I got on all fours while Noah and Will fucked me in my mouth and pussy. The guys came and were replaced by another pair of cocks. Adam, who was taping all of the action, acted as traffic cop, directing any available hard cock to an empty orifice. This continued for several hours, until I was too tired to go on.

I thought the evening was over until Adam mentioned that he hadn't had his turn. I offered him the orifice that hadn't been used, my ass. Adam and I rarely have anal sex, but when we do, it usually is fantastic.

I got on my hands and knees again and sucked Adam until he was really hard. While I sucked him, one of the other guys, probably Noah, ate my pussy and rubbed K-Y jelly up my butt crack, preparing it for my husband's cock.

When Adam was rock-hard, he got behind me and slowly entered my ass. Since I hadn't had a cock there in over a year, he was gentle. After a couple of minutes of steady pushing, he got his entire cock in me and started to fuck me hard. Since he had spent hours watching me take on his six friends, it wasn't long before he shot a load up my butt.

I finally collapsed out of sheer exhaustion. I woke up later that evening with Adam fingering me to another orgasm. I had recovered enough to get him off with my mouth. That was the most intense sexual experience I've had, and I owe it all to my loving husband.

Adam's birthday is next month, and I have already arranged with Sunny, Hank's wife, and Megan, Noah's wife, to make it memorable.—*K.T.*, *Saint Louis, Missouri*

ANOTHER BIRTHDAY: THIS HOT COUPLE DOUBLE-DIPS IN THE FOUNTAIN OF YOUTH

My name is Steph and my wife is Diane. We enjoy reading *Penthouse Letters* every month, and would like to share an erotic encounter we recently experienced while on vacation in Mexico.

A few months ago we decided to celebrate Diane's birthday with a much-needed vacation, and booked a long weekend at a favorite resort of ours. We arrived about ten Friday morning. After we hurriedly checked in, we headed for the pool.

Since it was spring break, the resort was filled to capacity with young couples and college students, and the lounges closest to the pool were filling up fast. As Diane went to look for a good location, I headed to the cabana bar. I picked up our drinks and joined her at the pool.

We had only been seated about twenty minutes when two young men asked if they might squeeze their chairs next to ours. Being the congenial couple we are, we welcomed them and introduced ourselves. Nelson and Stuart were both eighteen, on spring break from school in Southern California. It was their first real vacation on their own, and they hoped to meet some pretty young ladies.

Over the next two hours, the four of us drank, joked and became comfortable. Both guys were not only very good-looking and well-built but well-mannered. As conversation progressed, Diane told them we were here to celebrate her thirty-sixth birthday, the next day. Of course, they couldn't believe I was forty, or that my wife was even close to thirty-six!

We take great pride in our appearance, both of us spending hours at the gym. I am five-ten, one hundred seventy-five pounds, with a flat stomach and a thick eight inches. My wife is absolutely beautiful, five-four, one hundred four pounds, a slender, mouthwatering 33-21-33.

For our vacation and her birthday, I had bought the red thong bikini Diane was wearing. It was barely three small pieces of cloth, held in place by thin straps. When wet, it left little to the imagination. Diane occasionally paraded about in front of us, enjoying the obvious effect she had not only on the guys and me, but on every man in the place.

Once when the guys went for a swim, I joked with Diane that the two eighteen-year-olds would make a great gift for her thirty-sixth birthday. Did she think she could handle three cocks at once?

She said, "I don't know, but it sure would be fun trying."

By all outward appearances Diane and I are your typical urban professional couple. But we have on occasion shared our fantasies—and our bodies—with select friends.

She loves to suck cock, on occasion achieving orgasm while sucking off an attractive male partner. I could just imagine her on her knees pleasing these young men with what would no doubt be the blowjob of their lives.

As the guys swam back toward us, Diane headed to the cabana for a new round of drinks.

As she did, she pulled the tiny string holding her top in place and allowed it to fall to the ground. Nelson and Stuart climbed out of the pool staring in disbelief, watching my gorgeous wife walk away wearing little more than sunglasses!

Nelson said, "Is she really going to the bar topless?"

I smiled proudly and said, "She sure is. Wait till you see the view from the front!"

I told the guys about our special relationship, in which we occasionally invite close friends to party with us. As this was Diane's birthday, we hoped they would join us on the beach that night at eleven to celebrate. They said they would come and bring the champagne.

Just then Stuart spotted Diane headed our way. The three of us watched as she made her way back, proudly exposing her perfect breasts, wearing only the thong bottom, dark glasses and a baseball cap. Giggling, she said the bartender so loved her showing up at the bar topless that the drinks were "on the house for the pretty American lady."

Before Diane and I went back to our room to prepare for dinner, it was agreed we would meet on the beach at eleven. In the room, I told Diane of my chat with Nelson and Stuart and said I had a feeling her hot body would get a workout before the night was done. She kissed me and said, "Honey, I'm going to be a real little slut tonight. I'll do my best to please you."

At eleven sharp we headed over the dunes. The guys, as promised, had brought two bottles of good champagne, as well as their CD player. Diane wore her tiny bikini, while Nelson, Stuart and I had on shorts and sandals. It was a full moon, and we decided to head down the beach half a mile and walk back in the dunes for a little more privacy.

We found a great location—dunes on three sides and a view of the moonlit ocean. I spread out the blanket, Nelson opened the champagne, and Stuart put a good CD on the player.

Diane went over and put her arms around Stuart's neck. She pushed her body against his and said, "Don't I get a birthday kiss?" Stuart responded by pulling her close and sticking his tongue in her mouth. Not to be outdone, Nelson put his arm around her. He pulled her close and placed a hand on her shapely butt. He took over the French-kissing and continued till she moaned and went limp in his arms.

My wife is an excellent dancer and has long wanted to dance, strip and sexually please a group of attractive men. As the champagne flowed and the music played, it was clear that she was about to live out that fantasy.

For the next twenty minutes Nelson, Stuart and I sat on the blanket drinking champagne while she danced, teased, stretched and exposed her luscious body to us. She then urged the guys to their feet and felt their chests and arms, complimenting them on how attractive they were.

When the guys returned the compliment, she asked them to remove her bikini and touch her all over. Nelson looked to me for approval. I asked why he and Stuart weren't honoring the birthday girl's request.

Both guys sported huge hard-ons. They pulled the strings holding Diane's bikini and let it fall to her feet. Nelson licked her left breast, while Stuart hugged her and licked her right breast. I watched my wife give herself to the horny young men. She reached to massage their rigid poles through their shorts. The guys, more and more excited, ran their hands all over her body, licking and kissing and rubbing their bodies against her.

Not wanting to be left out, I removed my shorts, walked over to them and asked my wife if she wanted to blow me while the guys watched. Wanting to put on a good show, she sank to her knees in the sand and massaged my cock to its full eight inches while licking my balls and making whimpering sounds.

She started to lick the shaft. I slid the big head past her lips and in her throat, and she sucked away. I gestured for the guys to remove their shorts and move in so Diane could please them too. As they moved to either side of me, cocks thrusting forth, she took one in each hand and guided them to her mouth.

After a few minutes of her taking turns blowing them, it became evident from the moaning that all three were nearing orgasm. Diane concentrated on Nelson, clutching his ass-cheeks while her mouth moved like a piston on his six-inch cock. He leaned back, yelled, "I'm coming," and emptied his cream in Diane's mouth.

No sooner did Nelson's cock fall from my wife's lips than Stuart slid his seven-incher in. He stood over her fucking her face. Just as she reached orgasm and opened her mouth to scream, Stuart's hard cock slipped out of her mouth and erupted. His thick white come poured onto the sand.

Diane crawled over to me on the blanket. She rolled onto her back, with her arms stretched back over her head, and closed her eyes.

"Mmmm, honey," she said. "See how much come they gave me?"

I kissed her and told her I loved her and it was my turn to please her. I kissed her neck and ears. I caressed her body with hands and lips and worked my way down her firm tummy. I tongued the inside of her thighs on into her pussy. She ran her fingers through my hair, saying how good she felt.

I continued kissing, licking and working my fingers up in her.

The guys lay on either side of her, rubbing her stomach, up her ribs and lightly fondling and licking her nipples. My licking brought her nearer climax.

Stuart continued to lick her nipples and Nelson French-kissed her. The three of us held her through her orgasm. I repositioned myself, lifting her legs over mine and around my waist. I set my cock against her pussy lips and eased it into her.

Fully impaled, she threw her head back and arched her back, pushing her hard-nippled breasts skyward. My wife is so light, I can lift her back and forth on my cock, which is what I did as Nelson and Stuart watched. I set her back on the blanket and climbed on top. I pushed my cock in and fucked her to another climax.

As I finished, I told Stuart to fuck her as vigorously as I had and fill her with come. She lay on her back, legs spread and arms stretched to either side. Stuart got into position, and you could see the action of his back and ass muscles as he moved his strong cock in and out of my wife's pussy. She moaned with each thrust. He gave my baby the fucking of her life, finally announcing that he was about to come.

As Stuart climbed off, Nelson took his place. He guided his cock into Diane's pussy. Again my wife was being fucked by a guy half her age raging with hormones. He seemed to use every muscle in his body as he drove his cock in and out of her. He brought her to another mind-blowing orgasm and still wasn't done.

As he neared his orgasm, in one motion he pulled his cock from her pussy and popped his load in her mouth. Later I found out that Diane had whispered to him to come in her mouth so she could taste his spunk.

This went on for another three hours. We'll remember that birthday for a long time.—S.G., *Salt Lake City, Utah*

THE JOURNEY TO AN ORGY BEGINS WITH
A SINGLE STEP: MEETING A FRIENDLY COUPLE

My wife Morgan and I are regular readers of *Penthouse Letters* and love the exciting stories your readers share.

We have been married for ten years and still have great sex with lots of sucking and fucking in all positions. Morgan has an amazingly sensual body. She has pear-shaped breasts and the nicest ass I've seen. We like to read letters about swinging couples and end up making love as we read them.

In a recent issue we were both extremely worked up over a letter about a poolside orgy. It led to hours of balling as we talked about how much fun it would be to get involved in an orgy.

Unfortunately we didn't have a clue as to how to go about it. We didn't feel comfortable suggesting it to our current friends. We finally decided to try to find another couple to swing with. Morgan suggested that we head downtown for the weekend, hit some of the hot nightclubs and hope for the best.

We both went shopping the week before our lustfest was to occur. My wife bought an extremely short leather miniskirt that showed off her great legs. When she turned around I felt the leather material over her perfectly curved ass and knew she would be a hit. To complement the skirt she bought black crotchless panties.

On the Friday night of the long-awaited weekend we entered one of the more popular dance clubs around midnight. It was packed.

My wife immediately eyed a good-looking man sitting with a blonde near the dance floor. I ordered Morgan a vodka martini and we checked out the couple a little more from a distance. The blonde got up for a moment to adjust her skirt and I nudged Morgan.

We quickly walked over and asked the couple if we could join them. They seemed pleased that we'd approached them, and I had a feeling the night was off to a good start. The guy's name was Jules, and his coy and sexy wife was Lainie. They looked to be around our age, thirty-something, so it was easy to make conversation. They were also down for the weekend looking for a little excitement.

We continued talking until a slow song came on and Jules jumped at the chance to ask Morgan to dance. She readily accepted. Lainie then stood up, affording me another look at her curvaceous body. She smiled naughtily as she asked me to dance.

By the time Lainie and I were in each other's arms on the floor, Jules was already squeezing my wife's perfect ass-cheeks. I couldn't believe how fast things were happening. They were dancing so close together you would have needed a crowbar to separate them.

I pulled Lainie close to me. Her breasts were much larger than my wife's. She asked if I was a jealous husband; I smiled back at her as I shook my head. She pressed her tits against my chest. The feel of them and her narrow waist in my hands gave me an instant hard-on.

Lainie smiled back and wrapped her arms around my neck, pulling me close to her. I got a whiff of her sexy scent and grew excited about the possibilities. I lowered my hands to her ass and began feeling it all over. She just moaned in response and whispered that she wasn't wearing panties.

My throbbing member sprang to attention and pressed against my pants. I was sure Lainie could feel my arousal. When the dance ended, she thanked me and then looked right at my cock. She said she would like to take care of my problems; we should see if the others were ready for some fun.

When we got back to our table Morgan was sitting in Jules's lap, locked in a passionate kiss. Lainie suggested we head back to one of our hotels. As soon as we could settle our bills, the four of us left.

They had a gorgeous suite in one of the more extravagant hotels in town. I felt like I was in a movie. As we entered, Jules asked if anyone wanted a drink. We all said yes, and he popped open an excellent bottle of champagne.

Lainie asked Morgan to come with her into the bedroom and told us guys to relax and enjoy our bubbly. I noticed Jules had a boner in his pants that looked at least as large as my eight-incher.

The women really took their time. Unconsciously, I started rubbing my pole through my pants. Jules quickly unbuckled his pants, and I saw that his cock was in fact *larger* than mine, with a fat purple head.

The idea of him fucking my wife with it made me more excited than anything thus far. Just then the bedroom door opened. The ladies strutted out in see-through teddies, looking good enough to eat, which is what I wanted to do to Lainie's pussy.

Jules took Morgan on his lap and I laid Lainie on the opposite couch. As I expected, Jules buried his face in my wife's cunt. He pulled the material of her teddy to the side and just gobbled up her pussy. I wanted to keep watching, but I had a snatch of my own awaiting attention.

I pulled the crotch of Lainie's teddy to the side, exposing her dangling pink cunt lips. I got a few licks of her sweet-tasting snatch when she threw back her head and begged me to fuck her. I wasn't about to hold back, but I needed more room for what I had planned. I led my blonde honey into the bedroom, and the others followed.

Lainie lay down on the big bed and spread her legs. I plunged my whole dong into her lovely sluice. She felt really hot and tight and we started a rhythm that got the whole bed shaking. I looked over and saw Jules's dick easing between my wife's well-spread legs. When he had his pecker all the way in her, he drove it in and out in long strokes.

I followed suit and saw that the women liked action. We pumped them for a solid fifteen minutes. At one point they looked at each other and held hands as they moaned in ecstasy. Jules and I were on the brink of coming, and by the sound of the women, so were they.

My balls tightened and I let out a moan as I unloaded in Lainie's quim. This started a chain reaction. Next came Morgan, then Jules, blasting what seemed an even bigger load than mine. Some come oozed out of Morgan's muff. Lainie's whole body shook with excitement as we all watched her come.

What happened next is what really made the evening great. Jules and I pulled our cocks out of our partners and rolled off the bed for a moment. Lainie felt Morgan's soaked slit with her hand, then lowered her head so she could lap up her husband's come. I knew Morgan had always wanted to try making it with a woman, and now was her chance.

Morgan pulled Lainie's hips up over her face and began sucking out my come from Lainie's box. They both moaned with delight, which made Jules and me rock-hard again. Morgan and Lainie were completely lost in each other. Morgan bucked her hips up against Lainie's mouth and came again. Lainie ground her mound furiously into Morgan, moaning loudly.

Jules was jerking off when he heard his wife come. The women, having finished with each other, gave their attention to us. I moved toward the bed and Lainie took my cock in her mouth. Morgan took my balls in her mouth as she massaged Jules's member. Then the women moved their sucking mouths to Jules's throbbing meat.

Lainie urged me to bring my dick closer to the action. She put it next to Jules's and the women applied their hot tongues to our privates. It was a turn-on for me to feel Morgan's mouth on Jules's sausage as Lainie fondled my ball sac with her tongue. As Jules and I were ready to shoot, Morgan and Lainie removed their mouths from us and began kissing. They embraced and rubbed their pussies together.

Jules immediately entered Morgan from behind. I took his lead and stuck my dick in Lainie's twat. I grabbed onto my wife's hips, which pulled Lainie's bottom snugly over my meat, and Jules took Lainie's ass cheeks in his hands. The women were grinding their soaked muffs together. The wet sound they made was a total turn-on.

I rammed my cock into Lainie's pussy and pushed my ring finger deep into Morgan's asshole. Soon the women were moaning and grinding their pert clits wildly against our hard cocks. The girls lost it at the same time, then us guys released our cream in their love holes.

We rested about half an hour, then spent the rest of the night enjoying one another in every imaginable way.

Since then we've become quite close to Lainie and Jules. They have a couple of other friends who are also into swinging, so it looks like we'll get to experience our orgy fantasy after all.—*R.F., Denver, Colorado*

THESE REDHEADED BEAUTIES, OFTEN MISTAKEN FOR SISTERS, SHARE A TASTE FOR CROWDS

My wife Lydia and I had been friends with Annette for about three years. We really get along well. Both Annette and Lydia are redheads with long, silky legs, and each fills a bra well. They are stunning when they are together because both have cute faces and great asses. Annette is just twenty-two, Lydia twenty-five. People always mistake them for sisters.

Lydia and I have tried to get Annette to swing with us but weren't sure how to approach her. She has always had boyfriends, but they seemed conservative sexwise. One day Annette told Lydia she wondered what it would be like to have two guys at once. When I heard the news, I told Lydia to invite her over for a night of movies—videotapes featuring me and Lydia at some of our swingers' parties.

Annette came over, and true to her fun-loving nature got all hot looking at the tapes. I put in the last tape, showing what ended up as a black-on-white swingers' party. A few minutes into it Annette's mouth dropped open, and she said she'd really love to see some naked black men up close. Lydia told her about a hot experience she'd had with a black guy and how well his dick made her come. All the while Annette had her eyes glued to the screen, where two black men were making love to my wife.

We invited Annette to go out on the town with us that Friday evening. Lydia suggested we go to a dance club where several of our black friends hang out. Both Lydia and Annette were dressed up like they were on the make. They were strikingly beautiful, and plenty of guys were giving them a good looking-over. Lydia recognized several of them. At least six had fucked her.

Gregory is a well-built guy in his late thirties with a very large cock, and Lydia will testify he knows how to use it. He has given her multiple orgasms on more than one occasion. He gave her a big hug and a long kiss. When she asked him if he wanted to fuck, all he could reply was, "Is ice cold?"

Then she introduced Annette. Gregory gave her a long look up and down and let out a low whistle. Lydia boldly said that Annette was craving black dick and wondered if he could fix her up. Gregory said he could do the job all by himself.

After that, things really went well. Everyone got in a mellow mood. Lydia took up with Mason, a professional boxer. We invited five other friends to our apartment for a small orgy, explaining that Annette had never been fucked by a black man.

Everyone was excited about seeing the orgy-virgin get it on. Gregory and Mason rode with us. The others followed. By the time we reached the house Lydia and Annette were topless.

Once we were inside, Gregory glued his muscular body to Annette. They were locked in a kiss and Gregory was feeling her all over.

Everyone watched the hot couple. Gregory continued to grope her and pulled up her skirt, giving everyone a nice view of her ass. Then he complained her panties were too snug for him to get a good feel of her pussy. She removed her skirt and he pulled off her panties.

We all watched in anticipation when Gregory moved his head down to Annette's crotch. He examined her red-haired cunt and stretched out his tongue to give it a few licks. At the same time Mason had exposed Lydia's red-haired cunt as well. The girls had both guys' cocks out and were playing with them.

Annette could hardly encircle Gregory's monster with her small hand. He sat on the couch and leaned back, helping her straddle his lap. She removed her top. He unfastened her bra and took her boobs in his big hands. She squatted over his pelvis with her back to us as she guided the fat head of his cock through the red cunt hair. Once the head penetrated her opening, she lowered herself down, crying out in intense pleasure.

When Gregory's cock was completely inside, Annette fucked him furiously, moaning out in joy. Soon they both let out a loud groan and he shot his load up inside her cunt. She threw her arms around his neck and kissed him deeply, telling him she would like to leave his cock in her pussy all night long. He laughed and said, "Baby, it's going to be there a lot from now on."

The party got into full swing. Lydia and Annette lay back on the big bed. Their red-haired cunts looked identical, except Annette was wetter from her adventures. Gregory mounted her while Mason took on Lydia. The other guys stood close by, big dicks in hand while eagerly waiting their turn to fuck those inviting snatches.

I grabbed the camcorder and recorded Annette's first gang bang as one black man after another fucked her with his massive tool. The dark wide cocks stretched her pink pussy to the limit. I watched as her face contorted in pleasure from being filled again and again.

At one point Annette cried, "Keep those cocks coming!" and spread her legs even wider.

Each guy fucked Annette good and hard until he came with his meaty balls resting against her little twat. She proved to be a sexual dynamo. She just could not get enough cock. By the end of the night she even took Mason up her pale little ass while Richie pushed his long black schlong into her quivering beaver.

Gregory told Annette she had the best pussy that he had ever fucked. Annette replied by taking his meat into her hand and sticking it back in her hot snatch. The party lasted all weekend, and Annette never had so much fun. I know for a fact that Annette still meets Gregory quite often for some good deep fucking.

I'm glad we set her up that night. What else are good friends for?—D.R., Baltimore, Maryland

FROM FIRST TEE TO EIGHTEENTH GREEN, THEY HOLE OUT IN A HURRY

As part of our effort to stay involved in each other's life, my wife Penelope recently took up the game of golf. When we had our first chance, we went away on a golf package to a resort area. There were only the two of us and we enjoyed some great golf and great sex on the first day of our stay at the resort.

My wife has a great chest and one of those personalities that guys just know make for fun in bedmates. To top it off, when she golfs she wears those sheer nipple-revealing bras with tight-fitting sleeveless shirts that button down the front. More than once I have had to mention to her that buttons have come undone by the force of her golf swing and the thrilling momentum of her beautiful 36D, button-busting breasts.

On the second day we were paired with two divorced men, Evander and Quentin, who happened to be staying at our hotel. It was apparent that they found my sexy, vivacious wife very hot, and it seemed that she really liked these two guys.

My fantasy has always been to watch my wife make love to other men. Or to be honest, to watch her fuck at least two guys like a come-sucking, cock-loving slut in heat. To feed my desires, Penelope and I have an ongoing game we call "Do 'im?" which we play when I see a guy that I think might be desirable to her. Her response is usually "No," occasionally "Maybe," but rarely an emphatic "Yes!" During our round of golf with Evander and Quentin, I jokingly looked at Penny and asked, "Do 'im?" To my great surprise she looked me in the eye with a playful smile and enthusiastically said, "You bet your balls, do both of 'em!" The tantalizing half-comic, half-suggestive banter continued as we played through our round.

On one hole Penelope launched a great drive down the fairway, looked at us, kissed the head of her driver and commented on how satisfying a big head and long shaft could be. Our two fellow golfers were speechless—their mouths dropped to their knees. Knowing her playful style, I just laughed. But even I was surprised a few holes later when Evander got a ten on a hole and seemed dejected when reporting his score to Penelope for recording. She looked up at him and said she always wanted to play with a man who needed a whole lot of strokes to accomplish his objective. Then she smiled, and ran the tip of her tongue over her upper lip.

It was cool to watch Evander's Bermuda shorts tent at the crotch as Penelope's words gave him a swift woody. On the seventeenth hole, Quentin hit his second shot only two feet from the pin. As we watched, Penelope marked his ball for him and bathed it with her saliva. That, I thought hopefully, was a precursor of things to come, come, come! After tonguing it and wiping it off, she kissed it and gave it back. She told him to stick it in the hole for a birdie and she would reward him.

By the eighteenth hole you could see spots of pre-come the size of half dollars staining the front of three pairs of pants. By the bulge each of these leaky dispensers was making, Penelope had an indication about the size of each man's driver. Call them their number one woods or number one irons, it was plain these guys were both playing with oversized clubs.

After our round they invited us to lunch and were generous with the wine and the courses of food. Given such an opportunity, my darling Penelope proceeded to drink a bit much. Soon the conversation passed from golf to sex, and in a joking mood one of the guys asked Penelope if I was better with my putter or my driver.

To my astonishment and delight she looked him right in the face, reached behind herself, slapped and grabbed her own asscheek and said it depended on whether I was playing the front or the back nine.

Then the conversation got around to past wives, or former golf widows, and the divorced fellows both said that their wives had never met their emotional and psychological needs. Before we knew it, they were almost in tears recounting the unwillingness of each wife to share and participate in their deepest desires and fantasies. I shared how Penelope had come around to the belief that whatever I wanted was at least all right to act out and role-play. As their mouths dropped again, my beautiful wife explained how she had role-played a farm girl, a maid, a waitress, a nurse, and—my favorite fantasy—a come-swallowing slut, who takes on two fellows simultaneously while her husband watches.

They revealed that this was the stuff they had always desired their wives to do: to pluck some primitive strings and make them feel like men. Then it was my turn to be surprised. Penelope looked at me and our two new friends and suggested that if I was ever going to watch my threesome fantasy she couldn't think of a better time, a better place or better company.

Within minutes we were all in our room and I, just like a caddy, instructed them in each and every contour, hazard and fairway of Penelope's body.

Ready to proceed with our own national open, Penelope went to her knees and unzipped first Quentin's, then Evander's, pants. After gently attending to their flag sticks by giving each player some sensitive head, she started to look for each golfer's sweet spot.

Penelope, like the legendary golf wife of the radio interview, was wishing Quentin and Evander good luck by kissing their balls. Not just that—she licked them, with the effectiveness of a ball washer on the first tee. She tongued the ridge below each of their dicks, as well as the heads of their cocks. Penelope later told me she could determine what would send each of them into orgasm—a hole in one, so to speak—by their reaction to her oral investigation. She turned up the tempo of her oral and manual strokes and, with their excitement shooting straight down the fairway, our buddies teed off within a few seconds of each other.

Penelope had accomplished her first double eagle. And to look at her smiling face you could tell she'd won her Masters tournament and all that was lacking was a green jacket.

"Damn!" said Quentin. "That took so much out of me I may need a cart to get to the next tee! My legs are awful weak!"

"Well, don't lose your balls in the bunker, boys," Penelope said. "Join me on the bunk instead."

She straddled the bed doggie style and asked me to make this a foursome. I was enjoying watching her in action so much I declined, saying I'd let Quentin and Evander play through. I instructed Evander to get behind her and hook one into her slice as Quentin scored a birdie in her mouth. Within a minute, they had a three-way playoff.

Evander had an easy lie. I could tell from the groans that she was about to tee off in her first threesome. She had always loved my two hands massaging her while we made love but now she had four. Instantly she gave out a loud cry, as if she had sunk a fifty-foot putt. Unlike many women, Penelope craves multiple orgasms. Now she asked that Evander take out his longest iron and link it to her. As her cunt swallowed his club from behind and squeezed it, she became perhaps the first human head cover in the history of golf. Quentin had lain down on the bed beside her and asked if his cock could have a Mulligan. She smiled and told him that Evander would be completing his round almost any second. As if to respond to her show of confidence in him, Evander let out a loud cry of "Fore!" Immediately withdrawing from her cunt, he splashed his load on her butt. As I watched him shoot his load I noticed that his dick, similar to his golf shots, had a natural fade to the right and consequently his come ended up entirely on her right cheek.

Now Quentin had the honors and began by asking Penelope to straddle his member and ride it like a golf cart on a bumpy path. Even after the golf, the drinking and their prior sex, she bounced on his club with the energy and enthusiasm of a rookie on the tour. A craving came over her as her orgasm drew close. She looked me in the eye and asked me please to fuck her in the ass. Wanting the guys to appreciate just how far she would go while she role-played a cock-hungry tramp, I asked her to ask them to satiate her every orifice. Penelope entreated Evander, who was just watching from the gallery, to put his trusty wood into her mouth. I asked her to reach back and spread her asscheeks so I could work on my backswing.

I heard nothing more from her, since her mouth was too busy for talking. But then she began to make a sound I had never heard before. As Evander stuffed her mouth, Quentin filled her pussy and I reamed her butt, she began to chortle and babble rapidly and uncontrollably. It was something to hear, as she came again and again, driven by three weekend duffers suddenly on their best game. Soon we were in a heap on the bed, our rounds completed, our nineteenth hole celebration proceeding joyfully.

After a rest and showers I decided to call room service and order a bottle of their finest champagne and four glasses. I poured each of us a glass to toast our day and our hostess. As we raised our glasses, Penelope complimented us on the fine wine we three had produced for her appreciation.

"It felt good, it tasted good," she said. "Excellent nose, smooth going down, splendid finish. I think we should declare a vintage!"

Evander and Quentin had to catch a late flight, they said, and after a flurry of effusive praise from each to everyone else, they left.

Penelope and I straightened the bed, lay down in it and slept the sleep of the contented. The next morning, we had a playoff round that broke par by a very wide margin.

Later that morning, on answering a knock on the door, we found an entire set of top quality women's clubs had been sent to us with a thank-you note from our recent partners.

"Thanks for achieving a Grand Slam," it read. "You set a course record that may never be broken!"—*C.J., Windsor, Ontario*

SHE'S TOO BUSY FUCKING & SUCKING TO FIGURE IT OUT, SO THERE'S NO NEED FOR YOU TO

Recently my boyfriend introduced me to your magazine. Needless to say, we thoroughly enjoy reading the stories together. I have a story that you just might find worthy of your pages.

Every summer I go to the beach for a week or two, and every summer I meet someone, without fail. I've had flings with lifeguards and fellow vacationers, but this summer was by far the best. I met Clay and he invited me to a party. At first I figured it would be a typical run-of-the-mill get-together, but to my delight it was anything but typical.

After a couple of hours of music, dancing and just talk, several of us were discussing Split Rock Beach, a little-used nude beach a short distance up the road. Before I knew what had happened, our discussion had turned into a dare and we were on our way.

There was Clay and three other guys, and two other girls besides myself, so the women were outnumbered.

When we got there the guys immediately got naked and ran into the water. I remember staring at this one guy and his awesome body. His penis was somewhat long and his washboard belly was thrilling to see. I still liked Clay, but I was getting wet just dreaming about this other guy atop me, his cock inside me.

The two other girls and I decided to make the guys work to get our clothes off. One girl's name was Eugenie, the other's Phyllis. Mine's Leora. When two of the guys came out of the water they started to attempt to strip us. We cajoled them not to by promising our clothes would come off in due time. We all sat around talking about sex and our experiences, until Eugenie dared Clay to touch Hal's dick; Hal being the one with the great midsection who was turning me on. He sat waiting to see if Clay would take the challenge and touch him. Clay did, and there was just no stopping what followed.

It became a game of dares, each one a little more erotic. I was dared to fake an orgasm, which I did so well the guys wondered if I hadn't been finger-fucking myself to get in the mood. Then it was to touch Eugenie's breasts. She was a petite girl with brown hair and moderate-sized breasts, with what proved to be perky nipples. She had long lean legs and a flat belly. I thought if I were a guy I would definitely be attracted to her.

The other girl, Phyllis, was a little more developed, with large breasts and a big ass. The guys kept commenting on getting a bit of her.

It was Eugenie's turn and she was dared to suck my tits. I'm a petite girl, five feet four, weighing about a hundred and two. Eugenie commented on how she liked my firm breasts and my large erect nipples—which, of course, I was showing by that time. As she began sucking, I got so wet I could barely contain myself. I started hand-jobbing my mound, but the guys soon stopped me and said I was cheating. Then we both beat off a couple of guys, Ernie and Vinnie, till they came. Clay was jerking off Hal while fingering Phyllis. Oh yes—we were all bare-ass by that time!

Then Eugenie started licking Phyllis's pussy while I was getting eaten out by Hal, the guy whose dick I had longed for. Still, I was wondering what Eugenie's tongue would feel like. I wanted her to lick my wet pussy, since she'd licked my nipples so nicely. Then, as if he had been reading my mind, Hal looked up and dared Eugenie to eat me while letting Phyllis eat her.

It was fun, and then Hal started to give me the fucking I'd dreamed about, while Clay was fucking Eugenie. Phyllis was eating Ernie while Vinnie fucked her in the ass. After a little while, a lot of switching started going on. All I can remember is four guys reaching orgasm at the same time, by any means necessary, and shooting their goo over our three female bodies.

Then as I sucked off one of the other guys, I think it was Vinnie, who was busy playing with the other girl, Phyllis, I think, we got him to come and I had him shoot it into my hand. I had Hal lick it up. He loved every last drop, yes he did!

We were all so turned on and horny that we could be called fucking machines—never getting enough, always ready for more. Eugenie started sucking Clay's cock, but I decided I wanted to also. So as we both licked our tongues up and down his dick our tongues met.

Clay seemed to dig this, because pretty soon he pulled his dick away and Eugenie and I were left french kissing. We were exploring each other as we had never done with any other guy. It left a tingling sensation in me. She knew just how to kiss me to make me yearn for more.

When I tell my new boyfriend, Wallace, this story, he gets off instantly, and begs me to tell him more. He fantasizes about me getting fucked by Hal's or Clay's limber cock and getting my pussy eaten out by Eugenie or Phyllis.

No experience I've had has been quite like this. I hope soon to be able to do this again, with Wallace and another energetic troupe of men and women.—*L.K., Olympia, Washington*

NINE WAS FINE BUT THEN CAME TEN,
TO GLADDEN GLADYS ONCE AGAIN

We live in a new apartment complex. The walls are very thin. Our bedroom is next to the next-door couple's bedroom. During our first night in our new apartment we were preparing for bed when we became aware of the squeaking of bedsprings. Moaning and passionate sighs were coming from beyond the wall. It was almost as though we were in the room with them.

The woman was sure a howler when she came. We heard her say, "Oh baby, your big dick sure makes my pussy feel soooo gooood! You m-m-make me c-c-come soooo gooood!"

Listening to them fuck was a turn-on for us. So my wife Gladys and I agreed that turnabout was fair play.

"You want me to suck your tits, honey?" I asked loudly.

Gladys replied loudly, "Oh yes, play with my tits, pull my nipples, make them stiff. Lick my tits now!"

I sucked with gusto, making slurping sounds. Gladys cried, "Oh, you make it feel so good! My pussy is getting wet! Oh yes, feel my pussy!"

"Oh baby, baby, baby, what a hairy, hairy pussy you've got!" I groaned. "God, I want to stick my face in it half the night, then stick my dick in it till dawn!"

"*Fuck* my pussy, baby," Gladys grunted. "Oh yes, *fuck* my pussy *good!* Oh, put your *big cock* in my *hot* cunt! Oh yes, that's it, you have the head in. Don't tease me, give it all to me! Fuck me hard, *hard*, you crazy bastard!"

We did our best to outdo our neighbors. Gladys groaned and bellowed with each stroke of my cock. The bedsprings squeaked in a steady rhythm. The headboard made a rapping noise as it bumped against the wall. We both wailed that we were coming, crying in turn like a couple of opera singers, tenor and alto.

I swear, she never gets enough. I reminded her of that night when we went to a swingers' party and she played a big part in an interracial gang bang.

"I'll bet you remember," I said, "that big, nine-inch black cock that you fucked five times that night."

She replied, "Now how could I ever forget that? I must have come so much I risked a hernia."

We didn't know it at the time but we had lately been setting the stage for a future gang bang. The discovery began one morning when the doorbell rang.

Gladys, being naked at the time, put on a short, belted terry cloth robe and went to the door. There was a young, nice-looking black lady standing before her when she opened it. She was wearing a baby doll pajama set and was the picture of friendliness. She invited us over for toast and coffee. Gladys said that would be nice, but we weren't dressed yet and our clothes were still packed.

"Come as you are," she said, laughing. "After hearing the way you two went at it, we feel as though we know you already."

I put on a pair of cutoffs and we joined our new friend next door.

Introductions were made. They were Ted and Cora. Ted was tall and well built, with a very dark complexion and a big, friendly smile. As Cora was pouring coffee and preparing toast, Ted leaned back in his chair, facing Gladys. It was then I noticed her robe had gaped open and her pussy was completely exposed to Ted's gaze.

Gladys glanced down and pulled her robe shut. But when Cora sat down Gladys reopened her legs and her robe gaped open again, much to Ted's delight. We made good conversation, thanked them for their kind hospitality and invited them to have coffee at our apartment the next morning. When we returned there, Gladys laughed.

"Did you see how Ted stared when I showed him my pussy?" she asked. "I'll bet he got a hard-on. I'll bet it'd be fun to fuck him!"

"Maybe you should go for it," I suggested.

"Maybe I will," she said.

Gladys got her chance a few weeks later. Ted and Cora invited us to go out drinking and dancing at a club nearby. The drinks really loosened us up. The conversation turned to sex. Ted asked Gladys to dance with him. I danced with Cora, who could really swing her hips. And I admired her shapely ass.

Ted and Gladys were dancing very close. Ted had one hand on Gladys's breast as she laid her head against his shoulder. He unbuttoned the two top buttons on her blouse so he could see her tits. A moment later, his hand was in the waistband of her skirt. Before I knew it, he was feeling her pussy, right on the dance floor. By the time the dance ended, they were locked in a tongue-tangling kiss. Back at the table, they went easy on the drinks, but kept ordering for Cora and me. They wanted us to get drunk so they could fuck.

Ted went to the restroom and presently I followed him. I found him getting condoms from a machine. Then he stood at the urinal next to me, unzipped his pants and hauled out his cock. It was very long and thick, though only half erect. I felt a frightening thrill knowing that before the night was over, he'd have it lodged in Gladys's pussy.

When we left the club, Cora was completely passed out. I pretended to be too drunk to notice. They dumped Cora in the back seat of the car. Ted drove, Gladys seated next to him. I sat beside Gladys but leaned back against the door frame. We sat momentarily in the parking lot.

Ted loosened Gladys's blouse and bra so he could admire her tits. Gladys unzipped his pants and took out his cock. She looked shocked at first at how large it was. I felt her shiver.

Gladys unzipped her skirt and worked it down over her hips. Ted admired her sexy panties. Then she pulled them down so he could play with her pussy.

My cock was hard and pre-come oozed from the head. It hurt, too; I was getting a case of blue balls, just from watching.

A car pulled up beside Ted's. It held five of Ted's friends. Ted and the driver exchanged greetings. The driver asked Ted what's up.

"My dick!" Ted said, laughing powerfully.

"I got me a white gal here," he continued, "with a fine set of tits and a hot puss wanting some big black dick. Cora is passed out and this girl's old man is so stoned he just ain't happening. Hey, honey, here's an idea. How about you take on not only me but a few of my friends?"

Gladys said okay. Ted said they would have to go to his apartment so he could put Cora to bed. When we all got there, Gladys and Ted undressed Cora completely. Her cunt, opened slightly, showed pink. Her nipples were much the darkest part of her breasts.

We then went to my apartment, where we were joined by the rest of Ted's friends. Ted completely undressed Gladys and got on the bed. He started feeding her his long, thick black cock. She took it down her throat enthusiastically.

When it was slick with her spit, he pulled free and knelt between her legs. He drove that ten inches hard into her cunt with one swift thrust. I was amazed.

"Oh yes, I love black dick!" Gladys cried.

"My dick loves your red-haired pussy," Ted crooned in reply. "Oh yes, you are so tight, but you'll be loose when I get done with you!"

Then, one after the other, Gladys had black cocks down her throat, up her cunt, and twice in her ass and cunt at the same time. When all the gang were tapped out, they departed.

The next morning Cora told me she'd heard from Ted about Gladys's getting gang-fucked. She asked me if I liked sharing her with several men. I only smiled, and refrained from asking her if she knew that Ted was the leader of the pack.

Anyway, next time will be different. It'll be Cora's turn, and I'll lead the pack!—L.C., *Liberal, Kansas*

BAND ROMPS IN THE HEATHER ON HER BIRTHDAY, WHILE SHE BLOWS A FEW HORNS

I started playing the guitar for the same reason most teenage guys start playing: to get laid.

And it works. I've had more sex with more girls than anyone's had a right to have, I swear. I've been playing since I was fifteen, drifting from one band to the next until getting with the guys I'm with now. We've been together for eight years. We're all in our thirties and know we're not going to make it big, but we still love to play. And yes, we still love to get laid.

My brother Aaron called me one Friday and said a friend of his was having a party and wanted to see if she could use our services. He asked if they could come to our rehearsal the next day to listen. Of course, I said.

Since I'm the only unmarried man in the band, we practice at my house. (I guess I needn't explain that at any length.) The next day we were warming up, playing a few songs, when my brother's car pulled into the driveway. Leander, our black drummer, leaned over and looked out the window. "Lord God Almighty! Look at this chick!" he alerted us.

Walking toward the house was one of the sexiest girls I had ever seen. Even wearing heels she was at least nine inches shorter than Aaron, who is six feet tall. Her waist-length hair framed a gorgeous face and she wore tight jeans that perfectly accentuated her curves. She wore an oversized leather jacket, so we were not able to measure her chest with our eyes.

Damian, our singer, said what we were all thinking. "I want to see her tits. Baby, loosen, better yet lose, thy bomber jacket and let us see what it's our sacred birthright to see!"

I went to the door to let them in and led them to the rehearsal room. Aaron came in, unaware of the effect his guest was having on us.

"This is Heather," the fool said simply.

She stepped forward, petite and smiling. "Hi," she said softly, making me hard.

I asked, "So, what kind of party are you having?"

"It's my nineteenth birthday party, in two weeks," she answered.

Damian said, "Well, permit me to introduce the band. I'm Damian, the singer. Kenny and Brian, guitars. Thor plays bass and his brother, Leander, drums. Why don't you sit down and let us play some for you?"

Then Leander did his part by suggesting, "Why don't you take off your jacket?"

The whole band watched anxiously and she seemed to enjoy the attention. She slowly unzipped the jacket, teasing us expertly. She thrust her chest forward as she slid the jacket from her shoulders. She wore a tight T-shirt with a cartoon character on the front. Leander couldn't help himself from uttering, "Holy shit!"

Heather smiled shyly and said, "Thank you."

Grabbing Aaron, I said, "We're gonna go get ourselves some brews." Once out of the room I said, "Brother, where'd you find that piece of ass?"

He said he had been doing some electrical work on her mom's house and overheard about the party, so he suggested my band as musicians.

Shaking his hand, I said, "Thanks, man!" Shit, I'd almost be willing to work the gig for free, if only Heather would—oh man, I told myself, now you *are* crazy!

When we got back to the room, Heather was in the middle of the band and they were crowded close to her.

She was obviously enjoying all the attention. When we got back, we got situated and started playing. After a few beers, we passed a joint around. Heather started dancing and we went into an original song, a slow one.

It had the desired effect. Her hands began roaming over her body. She kept moving closer to us and when the song ended, she dropped to her knees in front of Damian. She went straight for his zipper and pulled out his cock!

The rest of us took the cue and gathered around her, pulling out our dicks. We almost got into a fight, pulling her off each other's dick so each could fuck her mouth. She sucked us like that for about an hour. She smiled sweetly, having digested all our jism, and said, "I'll call you in a couple of days. After I clean up, Aaron honey, would you please take me home?"

A few days passed before she called and we settled all the details. I had to go to her house to pick up the check from her mom. I learned that her parents were leaving her alone for the weekend of the party.

The day of the party, we arrived and set up our equipment while Heather was rushing around, getting ready. When the guests started showing up, she emerged from her room wearing a plaid mid-thigh skirt with white lace thigh-highs and black high heels. She had on a tight white shirt with short sleeves. She came over in front of us and spread her arms. "Well boys, how do I look?"

Leander stood up and said, "I can't speak for everyone, but I'm as hard as a cleanup hitter's bat!"

There were about fifty people there and Heather must have danced with every guy among them. Everyone that I saw got a good handful of her too. After watching about a dozen guys grope her and lift her skirt, we realized she was wearing a thong. At one point she went into another room with three guys and didn't come back for twenty minutes. Somehow, the party went on without her.

After playing for hours on end, we were glad when the party started to break up. Guys were being dragged out by their girlfriends, and single girls were leaving with lucky guys. But nine or ten guys were still hanging around Heather. A couple of them still had their hands on her. We packed up our equipment and started leaving, feeling disappointed.

"You guys aren't leaving, are you?"

It was Heather, who quickly added, "I'll get rid of these losers. Wait a few minutes while I do, will you?"

Despite the chilly night, we went into the backyard, and in another twenty minutes Heather came out. Because of the cold weather, it was obvious that she wasn't wearing a bra.

Aaron asked, "So what do you want to do?"

Heather looked confused before she said, "Don't you guys want to fuck me?"

We roared "Yes!" in unison. Then Damian added, "I wanna see those tits!"

Heather obligingly took off her shirt and then dropped to her knees. We surrounded her once more and it turned into another circle suck. She stood up and all six of us towered over her. She removed her thong and said, "Fuck me, guys!"

She bent over and took my cock into her mouth as Leander took her doggie-style and sank his thick black cock into her pussy. Soon I shot my load down her throat and Leander, having held his climax back, turned her around and thrust his cock into her mouth, which was soon filled with jism. She dutifully swallowed every drop. Thor, now behind her, plunged his cock into her pussy.

We kept fucking the little vixen like that for longer than I care to calculate, until she said, "Let's go inside, guys."

We followed her into the kitchen and she bent over the table and said, "I want each of you to fuck me square in the asshole."

We complied. Bobby stepped up first and, using olive oil to lube her up, slid his cock full length into her rectum. He started ramming away, making her moan and occasionally issue a joyous yell.

Her wails brought cheers from the rest of us. Each of us took a turn in her tight ass, fucking her to the cheers of our friends until she was a bit looser.

It was starting to get light out when I flopped off to sleep. Before I lost consciousness, I saw Leander pull Heather atop himself as Thor again mounted her from behind. When I woke up a few hours later, Heather was lying with her head on Thor's belly as he slept. She was idly sucking his big sausage, at the moment limp as a rag doll. When she noticed me watching her, she asked, "Why just watch? Don't you want to put your dick in my ass again?"

This I gladly did as she got up on her hands and knees and continued sucking Thor's dick. When I was mounted, Aaron crawled over and said, "Let me get into her pussy."

We all adjusted and soon she was between me and Aaron, with me on top. After each of us came again, we all collapsed in a heap. Heather rolled over on her back and looked at the ceiling, declaring, "Jesus! That was the best birthday party I ever had! I'm going to be sore for days, but remembering the fucking that made me sore just might make me come again!"

Then Leander looked up and said, "But how about one more blowjob?"

Heather smiled and said, "All right, just one more for each of you."

Unfortunately, Aaron, Thor and I couldn't get hard again, so we watched.

Ladies and gentlemen, all names in this story have been changed to protect my friends' marriages!—*J.P.*, *Levittown, Pennsylvania*

A BEAUTIFUL DAY IN THE MOUNTAINS BECOMES A DAY TO REMEMBER FOREVER

It all began when my husband of three years was working away from home for a month. After listening to my neighbors fuck all night long, I was horny and needed a man to hold onto real bad. Not wanting to spend the whole day listening to the neighbors screw, I got my camera and headed to the mountains for the day to shoot some pictures.

I drove with the windows of my truck down, so the wind blew my long hair freely. It was sunrise, and the mountains were beautiful. I stopped by a little stream and took a nice picture of the mountains and the stream. I was feeling just great until I got back into my truck and found that it would not start. Here I was, way off the main road, with no food or water, and miles from anywhere.

I had been sitting in the truck for four hours when I heard some motorcycles coming down the road. They stopped and did the same things I had done. They lifted the hood and looked at the motor. After a few minutes of this they said they didn't know what was wrong, but they were on their way to meet some friends and I could ride along with them to the campgrounds.

I said no at first, but I was hot and dry, and who knows who would ever come this way for a while? Frank, who seemed like the head of the group, said that he would take care of me and get me back to town okay. I never could have dreamed how he would take care of me. Jumping on his bike felt great, putting my arms around his waist as we motored down the road.

I was glad to get to the campgrounds, because every time we hit a bump, my hands would bump Frank's dick. The vibration of the bike was making me horny. Or maybe it was because I had not had my arms around any man for a while. They pulled off the road and went off into the trees near the stream, but we were not at the campgrounds where I thought we were going.

I became concerned until I saw two other women there by a van with three other guys. That made three girls and eight guys altogether. We rode up, and everyone seemed to know each other. One of the girls asked me if I was Frank's old lady. I told her I had broken down early this morning and they had given me a lift.

One of the girls, who said her name was Ginny, came over and handed me a cold beer. She looked me up and down, then giggled and walked away. The guys that I came with were laughing and sucking down one beer after another.

Frank walked over to me and handed me another beer and asked if I would like a hit on a joint, but I said no. I said maybe I should walk down to the campground and find someone to help me, or call a ranger or something. I said my grandfather lives just over the mountain and he could help me. Frank said he knew him real well, and when he was done here he would take me there.

Frank made me feel at ease. He was a good-looking guy and he turned me on, so I stayed close to him. Where he went, I went. He told me everyone's name, but I didn't remember any of their names but Hog and Ginny. I asked Frank why they called him Hog, and all he would say was that if I was lucky I would find out, and let it go at that.

They completed their business and then they started to play. Soon some people were skinny-dipping in the stream, but I remained cautious and stuck to Frank like glue. A guy Ginny was making out with picked her up and carried her over to a table. He set her down on her back, put his head between her legs and then ate her out like there was no tomorrow. Everyone circled around the table and watched her get a great cunt lapping.

Frank had slipped around behind me and was rubbing his hard dick into my ass-cheeks ever so softly. My nipples were rock hard.

Next, another guy came up to the table and stuck his dick into Ginny's mouth and was fucking her mouth. A guy was jerking off nearby. The next thing that happened was that the guy they called Hog took the place of the guy between Ginny's legs and dropped his pants. Out popped the biggest dick I had ever seen. I couldn't believe it was real. I fantasized about what it would be like for a woman to take it inside her.

It was as big as Ginny's arm. It must have been fourteen inches long and at least three inches thick, and the head was the biggest of all. I just could not believe my eyes. I was in a daze. I could not move, I stood and watched that big dick move in and out of her. I had never watched anyone fuck before, but I could not stop looking.

I realized that Frank was rubbing my tits slowly through my shirt. I had not worn a bra, and now my nipples were like rocks. I was in a trance. I was so hot, my pussy was flowing.

Frank was fast peeling me out of my clothes. Someone had placed a blanket by the table, and in seconds I was naked and on the blanket, spread wide open for everyone to see. I was not only willing but eager for Frank to take me, so eager that when the head of his dick parted my cunt lips, I exploded in orgasm time and time again.

Another girl was sucking my tits, and one of the other guys was sticking his dick in my mouth. I was so hot, I wanted them all. I sucked and fucked for everything I had. I never knew it could feel so great. Frank blew his load in me and pulled out. I was telling him not to stop. He said, "You are going to get the fucking of your life."

By then another guy had taken Frank's place, and away I went again. I came time after time, with super orgasms like I never had before. Then Ginny came over and sat on my face and ran her pussy over it. Her juices with the traces of Hog's come were wonderful. I was in a state of tranquillity and loving every bit of it.

The second guy pulled out, and then Hog slid into position, placing the big head of his dick against my pussy lips and rubbing it up and down. He said to me, "Lady, are you ready for a real man?" Then he eased that giant dick of his all the way in, and I was overtaken by one giant wave of orgasm after another. He fucked me for what seemed like hours before he rolled over on his back, taking me with him.

Now I was on top and going crazy. Never in my life had I ever dreamed that sex would be like this. I kept screaming for him and them to fuck me, and I didn't care who heard. Then Hog pulled me to his chest and again with hardly any effort stuck that mighty shaft up my asshole. Another orgasm blew my mind. For the next hour or so I'm not sure how many guys or girls fucked me, but when one finished there was always another to take his or her place.

I must have passed out when it was over, because when I came back to earth, I was alone on the damp grass and everyone was gone. I jumped up, and in a split second all I thought was, how could I do such a thing? I was just a quiet housewife waiting on my man. Sweat had caked all over me. I ran to the river and tried to wash the day away.

Then it hit me. My camera and purse! Did they take them? And where were my clothes? How could I be such a fool? I was old enough to know better. I looked around and found my shorts and my torn shirt. I slipped them on, but my panties were gone. I would not be surprised if one of the men had them. I also found my camera and my purse, with all my money there. I was beginning to feel a little better. I had had the best fuck of my life, and beyond the muscle soreness you expect from any good workout, I was no worse for the wear.

I walked back to my truck and found a note saying: "We fixed your truck. If you want to have another go with us come by the biker bar on Highway 78 and they'll come up with some guys and give you a great fuck."

I got in my truck, and it started right up. I headed for home. After a hot bath and a good drink, I said to myself that I was lucky that I didn't lose my camera. I went and picked it up, and the indicator said that the film was on frame thirty-six. I went to my darkroom and developed the film, and I could not believe what I saw. Someone had taken pictures of me while I was being gang-banged.

I still have the pictures, and every time I look at them, my pussy gets wetter than wet. I wish I could share them with my husband, but I know that he would not understand. Since others have shared their joys with me and other readers, I thought you might want to hear about my experience.—G.E., *Laramie, Wyoming*

THREE ON A BOAT TURNS OUT TO BE A GOOD START TOWARD BETTER SEX

When you've been married as long as Elizabeth and I have, serious familiarity starts to take some of the joy out of the old sex life. In fact, it gets downright boring. So we talked about things we hadn't tried that might spice ours up.

We tried just about everything two people can do together, without a lot of luck. We hadn't tried anything with other partners, though, and we talked some about that. I thought it might be worth a try, but Elizabeth wasn't sure. After talking it out, she agreed it might add excitement under the right circumstances.

We booked a cruise for our anniversary. For meals I requested a table for four by the window. We were three instead of four. Our tablemate was Patrick, a recent widower. He told us he was trying to get back among the living, and thought a cruise might help.

We advised him to hang out with the singles instead of eating with an old married couple. He said, "No. I'm not comfortable with that yet, particularly women. I'd rather be with you two."

We both felt bad for him, because he seemed so lonely, and we spent a lot of time with Patrick in the coming days. The second night out we went to a variety show that was being performed on board, and afterward we stayed for the dancing. After we'd been there awhile, Patrick asked me, "Why don't you dance with your lovely bride, Leo?"

I explained, "With my bum leg, I'm not much for dancing anymore, especially when the ship is rocking the way it is now."

"Do you mind if I dance with her?" Patrick asked.

"Absolutely not—that is, if Elizabeth doesn't mind." Obviously she didn't, because she took his hand and led him to the dance floor. They danced a dozen or more numbers before we called it a night and went back to our cabins.

We spent a good deal of the next day on deck reading. I read, anyway, while Patrick and Elizabeth carried on a long, serious discussion. That night it was the show again, and more dancing. I watched as they danced, and gradually got closer and closer together.

Clearly Patrick was very much attracted to Elizabeth. Later that night I asked her about it. She said, "Yes, he had a hard-on just about the whole time we danced."

"Did you like it?"

"Yes, it felt good."

"Could this be the one?"

"I don't know. Maybe. I'll let you know."

The next day was the same thing. The three of us spent the day in port. Then they danced the night away. Very sensuous dancing, I might add. Again I asked her about it later. She responded, "He started talking about sex. He misses his wife, of course, but it's been months since he's had any sex, ever since she died, and frankly he's very horny. I told him I'd guessed as much, since I'd felt him pressing that hard thing against my belly the last couple of evenings. He was embarrassed, but he said he couldn't help it, he was so attracted to me. He told me I was beautiful and desirable and he'd give anything to go to bed with me. He said he knows he can't, under the circumstances. I told him there were no absolutes. He asked, 'What about Leo?' and I told him it wasn't up to Leo, it was up to me."

I asked, "How do you feel about it?"

"Good. I'm attracted to him, I think I'd like to try it."

"The three of us?"

"No, not at first. Why don't I go with him first, then we'll see if we can work out the threesome thing?"

"Fine, if that's the way you want it. Tomorrow night I'll say I'm tired and want to turn in early. Then you can go dancing with him and you'll be free to see what develops from there."

The next night I left them right after the show and went to our cabin. I went to bed, but I couldn't sleep. I lay there and started fantasizing about Patrick and Elizabeth and what they were doing. I saw them in his cabin in a tight embrace, kissing with mouths open, jaws working. I imagined his hands caressing her ass. Then she reached down between them and rubbed his hard cock through his pants. They were stripped naked, and he placed his hands on her breasts, then his mouth. I saw them rub each other between the legs. Then he got on top of her.

About that time I realized that my cock was hard, so I began stroking myself as I fantasized. In my mind, Patrick was fucking Elizabeth vigorously, and they were moaning and groaning. I felt my own climax coming. I heaved my hips a couple of times and went off, squirting a good load over my belly. After that I stopped fantasizing and finally dozed off.

Some time later I heard the key in the lock, and Elizabeth came into the cabin. I turned on the light. One look at her and I knew that she had very recently been laid. She sat on the edge of the bed. I asked, "Did you go to bed with him?" She smiled and nodded yes. "Was it good?" She nodded again. "Did you come?" She nodded yes and held up two fingers. "Did he come inside you?"

"Yes," she answered. "He hasn't been with anyone but his wife for years. I felt sure he was safe. And it felt so good, I wanted him to."

Then I had an urge to do something I had thought about for years. I got out of bed and pushed her gently onto her back. I pulled her skirt up to her waist. She had no panties on, and I wondered where they had ended up. I got down on my knees and put my mouth on her pussy. It was full of Patrick's sperm and I sucked it out. She started to thrash her hips.

I got up and pulled down my shorts. My cock was stiff and ready. I got on top of her and rubbed it against her wetness. She was wide open and I slipped in easily. God it felt good, with her sheath all slippery from Patrick's ejaculation. I slid back and forth smoothly, and she answered with a strong pumping of her hips.

Because of the high level of our excitement we didn't last long. I moaned, "Now, now, now," and shot my load deep into her, spurt, spurt, spurt. She responded with the great throes of a deep, satisfying orgasm.

When our breathing got close to normal I helped her off with her clothes, then turned off the light, and we went to sleep naked in each other's arms.

We slept like logs. When we woke I asked her to tell me the details of what had happened the night before.

"When you left, we got up to dance. As usual, Patrick was soon pressing his erection against me. I asked him if he was serious about taking me to bed, and he assured me with all his heart that he was. We danced for a few minutes more without saying anything. I knew Patrick was very excited, but I hadn't realized that I was too. Suddenly I realized that my panties felt wet.

"I told Patrick I was ready if he was, and we went to his cabin. As soon as he locked the door we clinched, hugging and grinding against each other and kissing open-mouthed.

"Patrick turned out to be a gentle and considerate lover. He helped me undress, stopping to kiss each bit of skin he uncovered, then nibbling and licking. When I was down to my panties I lay on his bed, then raised my hips and took them off. I tossed them to him. He held them to his face and inhaled my scent. Then he put them in a drawer.

"I lay there and watched him undress. Patrick has a good body, and when he took off his shorts I saw that he has a good penis as well, strong-looking and pointing straight up. He got on the bed with me and spent a lot of time on foreplay. He kissed me and caressed me and praised me with a constant stream of words. He nibbled my ears, licked my neck and spent a lot of time on my breasts, kissing and sucking.

"At the same time, he put his hand down between my legs and started to rub my wet openness, slowly jerking me off. Then he gently pushed his finger in and began a neat rhythm, pumping his finger in and out while rubbing the palm of his hand over my very sensitive clit. My hips joined in, and before long I came in a wonderful way. As I lay there recovering, he kept kissing my face and neck and ears, crooning words of love.

"When I was ready for more, I reached down and took his erection in my hand. It felt good, hard and hot, and I fondled it. After a moment I moved down and took it in my mouth. He gasped, then began moaning and rocking his hips. I didn't want him to come that way, so I rolled over and pulled him with me. He knelt where he could rub the head of his pecker up and down on me, from clit to opening. He was slow and thorough. He inserted his prick into me, making a series of little jabs until he was in up to his balls.

"We rested a bit and smiled at each other. Then he started to pump. I pulled my knees up to my chest and moved with him. He kept up a steady chatter of love-words as the pace picked up. Soon we were going at it very fast. I grabbed him by the cheeks of his rear and pulled him into me as tight as possible.

"We went over the top together, he with a grunt, me with a moan. He shot a hefty load, and my vagina spasmed several times. It was a great come. As we rested he kept his softening penis inside me, until it finally plopped out and his sperm poured out of me onto the bed."

As she was telling the story she was playing with my cock. It got hard again, and when she came to their mutual orgasm I went off too, pouring my semen out over her hand. Before we got up I asked her, "What do you think his reaction would be to a threesome? Think he'd go for it?"

She answered, "I don't know. Maybe I should have another session alone with him. Then I could feel him out on the idea."

I said, "Good, because I really want to do that."

Later that day, after we finished lunch, I said I was going up on the deck to read. Patrick and Elizabeth announced that they were going down to the handicraft class. After about three hours I went down to the cabin. In a while Elizabeth opened the door and came in. To use a crude expression, she looked well-fucked. I said, "Tell me about your afternoon."

"Well, we didn't go to the handicraft class, we went to Patrick's cabin. We got naked pretty quick and lay on the bed fooling around. His pecker was big and hard, and I went down on him. I gave him a good blowjob. He thrashed around, and kept telling me how good it was.

"Finally he went rigid and shot off into my mouth. I let him finish squirting, then swallowed the load. He was ecstatic over what I had done, particularly that I swallowed it. I asked him if his wife hadn't done that for him. He told me they never got into oral sex, or anal either. I asked him what did they do. He said they'd tried every position known to mankind, but that was about it. Then I asked him if they ever tried it with other partners. They had talked about it, apparently, but he was more into it than she had been. After we'd talked about all this we dozed off.

"When I woke up he was already awake. When he saw that I was awake he began hugging and kissing me and caressing my body. I took his soft pecker in my hand and asked him if he was up to another one. After all, I didn't want him to get frustrated. He told me he'd get hard again if I'd suck him for a bit. I did, and he did.

"We lay there for a while, with me stroking his erection and him fingering me between the legs. When I was good and wet, he got on top and gently put his penis into me. When he was all the way in, he announced that he'd have great control this time. 'Then make me come,' I told him. He smiled and started to hump me. I humped him back and we gathered speed. In no time I went off like a rocket, but he didn't. He stayed hard inside me while we rested.

"Soon we began again, and agreed on trying different positions. We had fun. At one point I was on my hands and knees and he was plugging away from the rear. He reached under me and played with my clit. Wow, I came again, smooth and easy. Finally, I was on top, and he challenged me to try and make him come. I started bouncing up and down, squeezing him with my pussy muscles. I was getting close myself, so I knew I had to get him there soon. I told him I wanted to feel his hot, white cream blasting deep inside me.

"That did it. He pumped very fast, then stiffened and moaned and his gushes of sperm filled my pussy. As I felt him throb, I exploded with a series of strong contractions.

"It was a beautiful orgasm for both of us. We cuddled for a while, and he told me he was crazy about me but was worried about you finding out. He didn't want to lose me. I assured him I'd figure something out and left it at that."

I asked her, "Is his load still in you?"

"Oh yes. I can feel it oozing out. I haven't even gone to the bathroom."

"I want to suck it out of you again."

She took off her clothes and lay on the bed with her legs over the edge. I got on my knees and spread her legs. The lips of her pussy were creamy with his sperm. I leaned forward and lapped it up. I put my mouth on her opening and sucked. As I ate her out I opened my pants and brought my very stiff prick out in the open and stroked it. She built to a powerful climax. While she pounded her way through it, I came as well, blowing my wad out onto the carpet by the bed.

As we rested in afterglow I commented that Patrick had certainly added spice to our sex life. Elizabeth agreed, explaining that she felt she had set him up well for the next step. She planned to talk to him about it as soon as she had a chance.

The next day after breakfast the three of us went up on deck to read. After a while, Patrick and Elizabeth said they were going to take a walk around the deck.

Later on, down in our cabin before lunch, she told me they had stood at the stern of the ship and she'd told him everything: that I knew about them, that I was in favor of it and that I wanted a threesome. Patrick went from shocked to hurt to intrigued to being fully in favor of a threesome. At lunch we talked about the idea in some detail. I became quite aroused, and felt sure they did too.

When we finished lunch we all hurried back to our cabin. This being our first threesome, it turned out to be a bit awkward. Not so much the situation, because we were pretty excited from discussing it at lunch. It was the logistics that were awkward, who does what to whom and what does the odd man out do.

For example: We sat on the couch first, fully dressed, with Elizabeth in the middle. She and Patrick went into a clinch, and there wasn't much for me to do except maybe stroke her ass. So I watched. I watched their open mouths moving against each other. I watched his hand under her T-shirt caressing her breasts. I watched her rub the bulge in his pants. When we got naked and lay on the bed it was the same thing. If I wanted to kiss her, he was already there. If I put my hand between her legs, I felt the back of his hand. At least we each had a breast to play with.

Finally we brought some order to the process. We shifted around so that Patrick worked the top and I worked the bottom. He stimulated her breasts and I got between her legs and went down on her. With this dual stimulation, Elizabeth became highly aroused and had a powerful orgasm.

After we rested a bit I offered Patrick the first shot. He nodded, got in position and gently inserted his hard cock into her pussy. The sight of it was so stimulating I almost came. When he was in to the hilt he started to pump in a leisurely way. I watched them screw for a while. Then they changed positions. She lay on her side and he got behind her, spoon fashion. She put her upper leg up over his hip, and he had easy access to her pussy.

I had a clear view of his cock pumping in and out, and there was a kind of swooshing sound as it did. Elizabeth apologized for my being left out, and asked me to move up so she could suck on me. I declined, explaining that I would come in an instant.

I could see that their humping was getting more intense. Elizabeth suggested that she get on top. When they were in position, I got down close so I could see his prick as it pumped in and out of her. The pace had really gotten faster, and I knew it wouldn't be long.

The climax was spectacular from that angle. His balls spasmed as he shot his sperm into her. Her entire groin area throbbed as she went off. I hadn't realized so much visual stuff happened down there during orgasm.

They rested awhile, with Patrick soaking contentedly in her. But I was impatient and finally asked if I could go. They both apologized, and Elizabeth rolled off him onto her back. She wanted to clean her vagina, but I shook my head no, saying I wanted it just like it was.

I moved up and slid my hard prick into her. She was wide open from the recent activity, hot and slippery from Patrick's emission, and it felt terrific. After all that stimulation, my control was not the best, but I managed to hang on long enough for her to build to another peak. I shot off, adding another load of semen to what was already squishing around in there. As I squirted, it felt like her spasms were sucking the come out of me.

We all settled down to take a nap. Movement woke me. I realized that they were kissing passionately, and she was playing with his pecker, which was again completely erect. I watched as he got between her legs, then plugged himself in. Their hips began moving together, and she locked her legs around his waist.

I realized I had a semi, and I took it in my hand. It soon stiffened, and I jerked myself off in time to their rhythm. At the end they appeared to go off at the same time, thrashing and moaning, and I felt my ejaculate pour out of the tip of my cock onto my hand.

The next day, when we went down to our cabin after lunch, Elizabeth announced that her vagina was tired out from so much use, and offered to take care of us in some other way. Patrick and I had no problem with that.

We all got naked, except Elizabeth kept her panties on. We fooled around for a while on the bed. At one point she was jerking us both off in unison. But then she got down and started to suck Patrick's cock. He clearly loved it, and I did too. I got extremely excited watching her blow him. She'd bob her head up and down a bit, then take it out of her mouth and stroke the shaft as she licked the head, only to plunge it back into her mouth again. She was able to take nearly all of it in, her lips brushing his pubic hair at times. As she sucked on him she fondled his testicles. It became obvious he was going to come. Then he did, with a stiffening and a breathless gasp. I could see the throbbing as his sperm shot into her mouth. She sucked him until he was finished.

Then she rose up, pushed me down on my back and leaned over to spit her mouthful of white semen on my hard prick. It was the most exciting thing I had ever experienced. When she grasped my sperm-covered hardness and squeezed, I came instantly in great bursts, high in the air.

In terms of adding spice to our sex life, yes indeed, the threesome has worked in a big way.—*L.M., Harrisburg, Pennsylvania*

BEAUTIFUL WIFE DISCOVERS STRIPPING AND SWINGING ALL IN ONE NIGHT

I guess it all started when Randall and Sue moved next door. They are a very friendly black couple. My wife Sandy and I introduced ourselves, and we soon became friends, sharing drinks and playing games, having a lot of fun.

Randall, it turned out, was the assistant manager of a nightclub. We were invited out to an evening as his guests. The place had a good dance floor, and also had topless waitresses. Randall greeted us and ushered us to a table marked "reserved." From time to time Randall came and talked to us. He asked Sandy if she would care to dance, and she said sure.

He had in mind some serious dirty dancing. Sandy rode his leg as it massaged her crotch, her tits pressed hard against his chest. Randall liked her style, and told Sandy they were always looking for new talent at the club. Sandy laughed and said she was afraid her tits weren't big enough. The thought of having my wife show-ing her tits really turned me on.

As the evening progressed, the drinks got us in a mellow mood. Randall told us that after closing there was going to be a private strip show for selected patrons. He informed Sandy that if she entered the contest she'd be paid a nice sum of money. Sandy said she'd never done anything like that before.

Randall said, "Don't worry. As attractive as you are? Your pretty auburn hair is nicely styled, and from what I can see your tits are lovely. I'm sure you have a nice ass and pussy as well. You can just come on stage dressed as you are. Prance around a little and slowly take off your clothes. There will only be men in the audience. Show them your tits and pussy, and don't be in a rush to get offstage. They'll love you."

Sandy agreed to give it a try. The doors were locked and a closed sign put up. All the lights were turned off except some huge floodlights aimed at the stage. Several girls stripped and strutted their stuff. Then Randall took the mike and announced, "Tonight we have a beautiful married lady who will, for the first time ever, strip and show her beautiful tits and pussy for your viewing pleasure. See how beautifully her auburn hair is styled. Is the hair on her pussy red as well? Let's welcome Sandy to the stage."

As Sandy climbed to the stage my cock was hard and throb-bing. The crowd welcomed her. Sandy slowly did a teasing strip, copying what she could remember from the earlier strippers. When she dropped her bra she lifted her tits and held them out as an offering.

My, but she was hot and beautiful when she was down to her panties. She really teased the guys, pulling those panties up tight into the crack of her ass. Then, turning to face the audience, she pulled them down almost to the hairline of her pussy, then back up, turning her back to the audience.

She pulled her panties down to below her crotch, bending over and wiggling her ass. The crowd cheered, but before she faced the audience again she pulled her underwear back up, to the great disappointment of the men. I knew there wasn't a limp dick in the audience. Finally she pulled her panties off and tossed them to the audience. Her auburn-haired pussy was completely exposed.

Randall said, over the mike, "Okay guys, how about it, doesn't she have a lovely little pussy? Anybody want a better look?"

He asked Sandy if she would lie back on the stage and spread her legs wide. Sandy lay back, her legs spread wide. Her clit was red and swollen. It stuck out like a miniature cock. It was all wet and shiny. She remained in that position for a few minutes, while the audience applauded wildly.

Sandy received a fair amount of money for her performance, and we celebrated with a few more drinks. Sandy was dressed again, except for her panties, which some man had made off with.

The manager asked me if we wanted to have sex. He asked Sandy if she'd ever fucked a black man. Sandy replied that she had, but only once. The thought of watching Sandy fuck these two black men caused me to actually come in my shorts.

It turns out that in the office of the club there was a very spacious bed. We all undressed and Sandy got in the middle of the bed. Her nipples were hard and standing out. Her cunt was really wet. Both of the black guys had full erections.

Randall went first. The monstrous head of his cock penetrated her pink cunt. Sandy moaned as he drove it all in with one hard thrust. His cock plunged in and out of my wife's cunt. He gave it to her long and hard. I had never heard Sandy moan so loud. Sandy and Randall finally came together, then lay there panting and spent.

The three of us took turns fucking my beautiful wife. Once, Sandy had a cock in her cunt and one in her ass, while Randall knelt in front of her so she could suck his cock. Never in our marriage had I seen my wife so hot and wanton.

The next day, Sandy quit her job as a waitress. Now she makes more money in one night stripping than she made in a week being a waitress. Randall's wife Sue has no idea that Randall frequently fucks my wife. Maybe sometime I will get a chance at Sue's black pussy. I sure hope so.—*B.N.*, *Orlando, Florida*

SAILING TO PARADISE WITH TWO BEST FRIENDS AND THE ANCHOR DOWN

I have been a subscriber to *Penthouse Letters*, off and on, for many years, and I think it is time to share some of my many experiences. I have found that fantasies can become real, but you have to take advantage of every opportunity. It sure helps if your partner shares in the enthusiasm. In my case, my wife and I both believe that if it feels good you should go ahead and do it. We've also found that developing friendships is very important, sex only being good when it's an extension of that friendship.

We have been married since October of 1978. Shortly after we married, we decided to open our relationship. Our intention was, and still is, to keep our marriage exciting. Some people may not agree with our ideas, but it has worked for us. From time to time we will send you a letter telling you of our experiences.

Our best friends, Kit and Nancy, have lived on Lake Erie most of their lives. After purchasing a new boat, they invited us out for a sail.

Wendy and I packed a picnic basket with fresh fruit, sandwiches and plenty of champagne. We also took a few "roll your own"s just to take the edge off.

I had never sailed before, but was anxious to learn. As soon as we were out far enough, Kit began his lesson. I was certainly no expert, but was able to handle the tasks he assigned me. While Kit gave me my lesson, the girls stripped to their bikinis and poured each of us a tall glass of champagne. At ten in the morning, it didn't take long to have an effect. When we added a little good grass, we were all feeling great. Wendy and Nancy decided to lie in the sun naked.

Nancy is a little more petite than Wendy, but both look absolutely great. The four of us have traded partners many times, and I figured that day would be no different. The girls are both bisexual. They'd never put on a show, but they had always enjoyed each other's touch.

It looked like this day was going to be different. The girls were kissing, licking and touching each other more than usual. As we sailed, Kit and I had a hard time both controlling the boat and watching. Wendy has always been the more aggressive of the two. As she positioned herself to lick Nancy's pussy, Kit handed the rudder over to me and joined the two girls. Kit sucked Nancy's nipples as Wendy licked her to orgasm.

Kit pulled Wendy on top of him, and Nancy stuffed his big cock into Wendy's pussy. She loves getting on top, because that way she has more control. Kit's cock is a good eight inches, and when she's on top she can control how far it goes into her. She loves to tease Kit. That day there wasn't any teasing, though. She was pumping away in no time, and Kit and Wendy both went over the edge.

As they lay there, bodies glistening from the sex and sweat, all I could do was watch and control the sail. It wasn't long before they all came back to greet me. The girls both kissed me as Kit took the helm. They sat me on a bench. Nancy straddled my lap and rode me as Wendy had Kit. What sent me over the edge was having Wendy lick my balls and Nancy's asshole, alternating back and forth. Both girls licked the come off the fingers they had been using to touch themselves.

What a day for sailing, and it wasn't even noon yet. We pulled down the sail, dropped anchor and all went below for a nap. About an hour later we all woke up to drink more bubbly wine and start where we had left off earlier.

The sex with our friends is always good, but on this particular day it was absolutely great.

We never really tried to duplicate the details of that day. It wouldn't have worked. The sex, the sun, the sailing, everything was perfect. Especially our friendship with two good—best—friends.

We did a night sail not long after that. Someday we'll share this adventure too with our friends at *Penthouse Letters.—S.I., Buffalo, New York*

UNTIL SHE'S READY TO SWING, HE HAS A VIBRATOR AND A DREAM

Although I am a longtime subscriber, I've often wondered about the validity of the letters. I thought the best way to determine was to submit one of my own.

My wife and I are both forty-one. While neither of us is any great beauty, we have a strong love for each other. She is just over five feet tall, weighs about a hundred and twenty-five pounds, has short brown hair and a nice pair of 36Cs, with nipples that point out when she is excited. We've been married for twelve years. Our sex life is good, but I often fantasize about her being seduced by someone who is extremely well endowed. In reading your magazine, this seems to be a pretty familiar fantasy for men.

After many years of marriage, I finally introduced her to the joys of adult toys. Her favorite is now an eight-inch clear vibrator with a knob that rests against her clit. Often, after I have her wet from my average-size cock, she will ask for our toy. I recently started to ask her to picture herself getting fucked by a large cock as she works the vibrator around inside. I nuzzle her neck and ears as she writhes in pleasure. I rub my cock over her breasts and lick my pre-come off her nipples as she begins to moan.

I've asked her if she enjoys getting fucked by a large cock. At the same time, I get behind her and rub my cock against both her ass and her well-oiled pussy. I inquire if she would love to have two cocks working her pussy over, and she moans her affirmation. She normally comes after about fifteen minutes of this verbiage, and then she loves to make me come.

I often wonder what she is thinking when she has her eyes closed, her pussy full of cock, her ass moving as she squeezes that cock. I fantasize that she is getting laid by someone with a huge cock while I caress her lips, neck, ears and nipples and help her rotate that huge cock in and out of her.

Since she was a virgin when we met, and had a very conservative upbringing, I am doubtful she would ever let this fantasy happen. I love watching her pussy get stuffed full of cock and seeing her facial expressions as it goes deeper. She has gotten to the point now that she can tell me she loves having a huge cock in her pussy. I have recently started to tell her to talk to her imaginary lover, to tell him to pump her, to come in her pussy or that she wants his cock deeper and harder.

When she comes, she is often very loud, and uses a pillow to cover her cries of passion. I often shoot my come on her tits at the same time, which is a great turn-on for me when she rubs it into her tits and then licks her fingers clean. Although she doesn't read your magazine, at least not yet anyway, I plan on showing her this letter to see if she will start reading the letters with me. They always get me hard and ready to make love to my beautiful wife.

We're planning a cruise in the near future, and maybe a massage can turn a fantasy into a reality. I hope so.—A.M., *Platte, North Dakota*

IT TAKES TWO FOR TANSY, AND THIS COUPLE IS HAPPY TO OBLIGE

I worked late one night. When I got home and let myself in, I was met by Tansy, completely naked. Tansy is a twenty-five-year-old, dark-haired beauty who works with my wife Ruth.

Tansy is married, and has visited us often. I had always admired her firm tits and tight ass, but I was taken aback by her appearing so unexpectedly—and totally naked too.

Tansy said I should get undressed and come into the bedroom to join her and Ruth. I quickly stripped in the living room and followed her into the bedroom.

To my surprise, Ruth was already in bed with a guy I had never met. Tansy explained that they had been out drinking and had brought this guy home with them. They couldn't go to her place because her husband was there. I've always been open-minded with Ruth, and not put many restrictions on her.

Tansy told me they had brought Tom home with them. They had all taken a shower together, and ended up in bed. Tom was now concentrating on sucking Ruth's big tits, and barely looked up as we entered.

Tansy got into bed beside Tom, and I got in beside her. As my cock came in contact with her smooth ass it immediately shot up erect.

Tom was sucking intently on Ruth's tits. She had her arms up over her head, and was obviously enjoying every minute of it. She barely acknowledged my arrival, other than to say that Tansy would take care of me.

Tansy's hand went down and grasped my cock, stroking it, while she massaged her pussy with her other hand. I reached over and put my hand with hers on her snatch. Her crack was already quite wet as my fingers penetrated her box.

I slowly removed my hand from her pussy and moved it up to

cup one of Tansy's tits. She didn't have tits as big as Ruth's, but they were firm and tipped by saucy, perky nipples.

By now my cock was totally rigid, and I desperately needed to plunge it into a pussy. I rolled Tansy over on her side, grabbed her hips and sank my weapon into her box from behind. My hand moved back up to grasp her tit. Her cunt felt heavenly as my cock sank farther and farther into her secret depths.

While I was making the journey into Tansy's womanhood, Ruth had straddled Tom, and was lowering her pussy onto his huge cock.

The look on her face was one of sheer pleasure as Tom's hard pole filled her. This caused me to ram Tansy's cunt even harder as she thrust her ass back toward me. Ruth's tits bounced violently in front of Tom as she jumped up and down on his cock.

As my load pumped into Tansy's cunt, Ruth continued to work hard to achieve her orgasm and flood Tom's cock with her own juices.

Just as Tansy and I were finishing our climaxes, Ruth let out several loud moans and then collapsed onto Tom's chest. She just lay there, her hips slowly gyrating, with his cock still inside her. The insides of Tansy's thighs were drenched with the come my cock had released as it was coming out of her box.

After a few minutes of resting, Ruth asked me if I would like Tansy to suck my cock. I said that would be wonderful, and without any further discussion Tansy obligingly took my prick into her mouth.

As Tansy began sucking and licking my tool, Ruth left Tom and came to straddle my head with her legs. She lowered her dripping pussy down onto my face. I was obliged to open my mouth and extend my tongue to receive her hot cunt.

As my tongue passed her lips I licked her erect clit, which was obviously very sensitive. Then I slipped my tongue into her opening, which was ripe with the accumulation of juices, the product of her fucking with Tom. Her hole tasted exquisite, though perhaps it is an acquired taste, and I found myself eagerly licking as much of the nectar from her cunt as possible.

In the meantime, Tom had positioned himself behind Tansy, who was doing a fantastic job of blowing my cock, and he was ramming her from behind. I don't know if his cock was in her pussy or her ass, but she was obviously enjoying it. While he was doing this, his hands were all over Ruth's tits, squeezing them gently and playing with her large, pink nipples.

Between my efforts and Tom's, Ruth quickly reached another orgasm, and her juices and Tom's washed down into my waiting mouth. This caused me to release my second load into Tansy, this time into her warm mouth. Tansy did not retreat, but continued to suck, drinking my come. At about the same time, Tom was depositing his load into another part of her.

After Tom removed his cock from Tansy, it went directly into Ruth's waiting mouth. Tansy moved up to position her cunt on my face. While Tom was busy fucking Ruth's face, I was tasting his come again, this time from Tansy's wet pussy. Tansy's cunt wasn't as big as Ruth's, and her dark pussy hair felt strange against my lips, as I was used to Ruth's softer down. Tansy's cunt tasted different from Ruth's, too, but I could detect the familiar taste of Tom's come. He had left a large quantity of it inside Tansy, on her thighs and around her snatch.

Tom and Ruth got up and left the bedroom, going to the living room, leaving Tansy and me alone in the bed. I rolled Tansy onto her back and spread her legs apart to the maximum. I drove my hard cock straight into her until it was entirely buried inside her. She lay with her legs open, accepting my dick with pleasure.

By this time I could hear Ruth moaning from the living room, where she was obviously getting her pussy fed full of man-meat.

This caused me to feed my cock harder to Tansy, as I thought how good Ruth's cunt must feel to Tom's cock. I drove Tansy hard until she reached her climax.

There was so much moaning coming from the other room that

I decided to leave Tansy, who had fallen asleep, and go take a look at what was happening in the living room.

I stood in the doorway, where they wouldn't notice me. Ruth was on the floor on her hands and knees and Tom was ramming his big cock up her tight ass. She had never let me up her ass, but apparently was prepared to give Tom anything he wanted.

As he rammed her, she begged him to give it to her harder. He was saying "Fuck me, bitch," which seemed to make her hump even harder. I noticed my cock was getting harder. I started stroking it while watching my wife's ass get fucked. They were at it for quite a long time. When I was ready to come I went back to the bed and released my load while staring at Tansy's face and tits. Then I got into the bed beside Tansy and, putting my hand on her wet pussy, went to sleep with her.

When I woke up, Ruth and I were in bed together. Tansy and Tom were nowhere in sight. They must have left together while I was sleeping. I thought that maybe I had been dreaming, until I checked Ruth's pussy. It was totally soaking wet with come, and her pussy hair and thighs were still wet with come. I knew by the quantity that I had not been responsible for putting all of it there.

The next morning when I woke up, Ruth was already up and had showered. She made no mention of the previous night's activities as she made toast and coffee.

I casually asked her if she would be seeing Tansy again. She said that as a matter of fact they had been planning to go out again that very weekend, but only if I was a good boy. As you can imagine, I'm being as good as I can.—*J.R.*, *Auburn, Alabama*

A WALL AWAY, HE'S ALL EARS FOR HIS SEX-LOVING WIFE AND HER TEAM OF LOVERS

My wife Jane and I must be two of your most devoted fans. I buy each issue of *Penthouse Letters* on the newsstand as soon as it comes out, and then both of us read it cover to cover.

We enjoy letters about husbands sharing their wives with other men. It is so refreshing to see these letters from couples who have opened up their marriages this way.

Before I tell our story, I will tell a bit about us. I am twenty-eight and Jane is twenty-five. We have been married a little over five years and have three wonderful children. When we were married, I was twenty-three and a year out of college, with limited sexual experience. Jane was twenty then, and still a virgin.

Starting on our wedding night, however, she took to sex like a duck to water. She did not climax the first time, but she did enjoy the experience. Within two weeks, she was saying it was too bad that she hadn't known sex was so much fun, or she would have started much sooner.

About the third time she said this, she laughed and added it was probably a good thing she hadn't given in to one of the many young guys who had done their best to get into her pants.

"As much as I like sex, I would have turned into the biggest slut around," she said. "I would probably have been the single mother of four kids and living on welfare by the time you met me."

With Jane's sexual awakening and emerging sexual curiosity, it was only natural that the idea of trying it with someone else would eventually pop up. When I first brought home a copy of *Penthouse Letters*, which was already a favorite of mine, she instantly became interested in the letters from men who shared their wives with other men, which were always my favorites.

We were soon talking about bringing that scenario into our

marriage. Within a month we agreed that she would take a lover or lovers, and either tell me about it or even let me watch.

That was five years ago, and I have still not seen my wife making it with another man. She feels she would just be too self-conscious making love with someone watching.

I trust Jane and know she would never deceive me or hide anything from me. I think couples like us, with half-open marriages, actually have closer, more honest relationships than most supposedly monogamous marriages where people feel it necessary to keep secrets from one another out of fear that the relationship will be damaged or destroyed.

Now I may never have *seen* my wife with another man, but I have *heard* her making passionate love, more times than I can count over the years.

I am able to do so for two reasons. First, because most of her liaisons take place in our home while I am there. Second, because of the layout of our house. Through careful saving, we were able to come up with a down payment for our lovely four-bedroom ranch-style house only two months after our wedding.

All of the bedrooms open off a long hallway that stretches out from the living room. As you leave the living room you come first to two bedrooms and a bathroom that are occupied by the children. As you continue down the hall, you come next to my wife's and my bedroom. This leaves the farthest bedroom for use ostensibly as a guest bedroom. In actuality it is used mostly by my wife to entertain other men.

Jane's first extramarital encounter, in what she refers to these days as her "adult playroom," occurred only a couple of weeks after we had decided she would try sex with someone new. When we discussed it, she did not have a ready candidate, so we agreed that she would go out to a local night spot, seek one out and then bring him back to the house. She would have sex with him in the spare bedroom at the end of the hall.

Anticipating her first time with another man, she felt uncomfortable at the prospect of having an audience. She did allow, however, that if I were to hide in our bedroom, it was possible that I could hear what went on through the wall.

When she made that suggestion, I jumped right into action. I made a small structural modification, cutting a square hole in the wall that separates our bedroom and the guest bedroom. The hole is about sixteen by twenty-four inches, about a foot from the floor.

I then put air-vent grates over the hole, so that from both sides it looks like just an ordinary air-return vent. You can't see much of either room, and you can't see the beds at all. But you can hear anything that goes on in either room from the other. The vent in our bedroom has been my frequent listening post, week in and week out, over the past five years.

That first night that Jane went out, wearing a short, tight wraparound skirt and a white see-through blouse, I had no doubt she would be able to pick up any man she chose. She is five-five, with shoulder-length blonde hair, a beautiful face and big brown eyes. In her sexy attire, her 37-24-35 body looked incredible. Today, at twenty-five, after having three kids, she has a 37-25-36 figure and can still attract any man she wants.

That first night Jane went out at eight, and when she returned shortly after ten, I was waiting in our darkened bedroom with the door closed. Not long after, I heard footsteps coming down the hall—two sets, hers and a man's.

I heard the door to the spare bedroom open and close, and I waited breathlessly, sitting there on the floor beside the vent. It didn't take long for me to learn that the guy's name was Eric. I heard the rustling of clothes and my wife's soft moans and sighs as she became aroused.

I then heard her crying out, "Yes, oh God, oh my, oh my," and I knew that he was eating her out.

He said, "Oh God, you taste incredible. Oh wow! Do you use a flavored douche, or what?"

"No," my wife said, chuckling. She added, "Thank you for saying that, though. I do try my best to keep myself very clean."

Next she was crying out, "Now, Eric, now! Oh God, Eric! You've got me so hot! Now, Eric, fuck me! I want to feel you inside me! Do it! Put it in me! Fuck me! Fuck me right now!"

Eric then surprised me and, I must say, even earned some grudging points from me. Instead of just shoving his cock right in her, he took the time to ask Jane if she wanted him to use a rubber.

"Not unless you want to," she replied. "You don't have anything, do you? I know I'm clean."

"And I know that I'm fine," Eric said.

"Okay," Jane said, "then why don't you go ahead and put it in me? One thing, though. You'll have to pull out before you finish. I don't want to take any chance of getting pregnant."

The next thing I heard, she was letting out a deep moan. I knew that Eric was inside her. As he proceeded with his fucking, she became extremely vocal. She cried out repeatedly in pleasure. She told him how big he was, and how great it felt to have his big, beautiful cock inside her.

"Am I bigger than your husband?" Eric groaned.

"Oh God, yes!" Jane said. "You're much, *much* bigger!"

Then he asked, "You like this better with me than with your husband, don't you?" And she cried out, "Oh yes, yes, I do, yes! Yes!"

She then kept telling him how she loved having his huge cock inside her. I was beating off like mad as I listened to my wife tell her lover how she loved him fucking her. The bedsprings squeaked as Eric pounded in and out of her.

Next Jane cried out, "Oh God, I'm coming! Come with me, Eric! Come on, baby! Do it now! Come on, honey! Fill me up, baby!"

Eric groaned and cried out, "Shit, coming, coming, I'm coming!" They moaned together as he emptied his balls in my wife's pussy. At that same instant, I spurted gobs of come all over my hand and thighs. For a few moments there was silence. My heard was pounding so hard, I was afraid they could hear it.

Then I heard the spent lovers talking.

Eric sounded quiet but confident as he asked: "So you liked my big, bad fuck tool? Liked it better than your husband's?"

"Uh-huh," Jane cooed. "Until tonight, I had only done this with him. It felt so much better with you."

Eric said, "Maybe you just graduated up to better and bigger things?"

Jane giggled and said, "Maybe so. Though I doubt I could have got your big thing in back when I was a virgin. I guess my husband's prick was the perfect size for a beginner. But I don't think his prick will ever be enough for me now."

Eric sounded triumphant. "So you *have* graduated to bigger and better."

Jane laughed and said, "I guess I have."

It was no pleasure to hear my bride tell her stud he was a much better lover than me, and not a whole lot of fun to hear her describe me as being much less of a man in the penile department than he was. But it still excited me sexually to be eavesdropping on their postcoital conversation. I was riveted.

A few minutes later, I heard Jane moaning again and the bedsprings squeaking again. I beat off again as Eric fucked my wife a second time. He fucked her four times before I finally heard him leave, a little after two in the morning.

When Eric left, our bedroom door opened and my still-naked wife crawled in bed beside me. Jane snuggled against me, rubbing her wet pubic hair and slit against my thigh. In less than five minutes she was snoring. I put my arm over her and fell sound asleep, holding my gorgeous, very sexually satisfied wife.

Eric became a regular visitor to our house. Then, a week after she met and bedded him, Jane brought home Sam, a guy she met at a local shopping mall. Two weeks later she brought Anthony home. She now had three stud lovers she would bring home and screw in the spare bedroom while I listened through the vent and jacked off in our darkened bedroom.

Jane has now slept with an even dozen men during our marriage. She still sees Eric about twice a month or so. Sam and Anthony each screw her on average once a week, and she has a couple of other steady gentleman friends she gets it on with in her "adult playroom."

I have listened to her couple with all these guys regularly over the past five years. I still get off, not only on listening to the erotic sounds of the passionate lovemaking, but on the pillow talk after they make love.

I have never directly met any of my wife's boyfriends, and, as I said at the beginning, I've never actually seen any of them make love to her. But I've listened to her couple with each of her boyfriends many times, and I've overheard their conversation as they lie there in the satisfied afterglow. I've shared the intimacy of their talk after they're all done fucking.

When Jane's lovers leave, she comes into our bedroom and snuggles up to me, rubbing her wet snatch and groin against my thigh. Some of the men do sleep over on occasion. In that case, most of the time she still manages to slip into our bedroom at some point. She takes my hand and puts it on her slot so I can feel her snatch. If her boyfriend is not spending the night, she will then cuddle with me, falling asleep in my arms, drifting into a deep, contented, sexually satisfied sleep.

Jane and I continue to be two of *Penthouse Letters'* biggest fans, and we will keep on buying and reading it, just as she will continue her extramarital liaisons and I will continue listening when she does. I am a big fan of your magazine, so keep printing all those wonderful, intimate letters.

I am not a wife-watcher, as many men who write to you are, but who knows? Maybe someday I will be. I am something else, though. I am a *listener*. I may not get to watch my wife's lovemaking, but I love listening to her make it with other men.

So to all those horny wife-watching men out there, I have this message: Keep watching, and please keep those letters coming to *Penthouse Letters* so my wife and I can read all about your adventures and enjoy them along with you.

I'll be eagerly watching for more of your letters. While I do, I may not be watching my own wife, but I can promise you this: I'll be *listening* to the action.—*C.T.*, *Durham*, *North Carolina*

A "PRIM, REPRESSED GIRL" RECALLS A COLLEGE AFFAIR THAT WAS ANYTHING BUT

My husband thinks of himself as daring and uninhibited in everything, including sex—though I suspect he prefers talking about adventures to living them.

After ten years of marriage he thinks he knows all about me. Since I'm not comfortable talking about sex, I know he's sure I'm a prim, repressed Catholic girl who would never indulge in forbidden fruit. However, there's a side of me he doesn't know.

Early in our married life, when I was still in graduate school, I had an affair. Chris was tall, athletic, very handsome—and also married. We met in a class and spent a lot of time together when we were assigned to collaborate on a project.

One evening, after an afternoon of research, he asked me to his house for dinner. He revealed on the way that his wife was away for the weekend, but the news made no impression. We were just friends!

After dinner we sat by the fire in his living room and talked for some time. Somehow—I still can't say what happened—we found ourselves kissing passionately. He reached under my skirt and I instinctively opened my legs, wanting his hand against my crotch, his fingers inside my panties.

I unzipped his pants—something I had never done before—wanting to hold his penis. We didn't go to the bedroom or even undress. I lay back on the couch, lifted my hips so he could remove my panties and spread my legs. He mounted me, his pants still on.

I'd had a few lovers, but the sensation of his cock in my vagina was like nothing I'd ever felt before. It was as if we had been made to be together. We fucked quickly and both climaxed. Soon I felt his soft penis harden again. We both stripped, and fucked nude for a full hour until he exploded again.

That was just the beginning. We were so desperate to touch and had so few opportunities to be alone that we never had the time to be inhibited or self-conscious. In our frenzy, we did things we had never done before.

I had never sucked a cock until one night when we met at the library after a week apart. We went back into the stacks. I was so horny, I reached in his shorts for his cock, and before I knew what was happening, they were around his ankles and I was kneeling on the floor sucking his cock and playing with his balls.

He had the most fabulously sensitive balls of any man I've been with, and he just went through the ceiling when I squeezed and licked and caressed them. I remember him leaning against a shelf moaning as I sucked the juices from his luscious cock. He shouted with pleasure as he shot his load into my warm, wanton mouth. I held his cock in my mouth for at least two minutes, not wanting to let it go.

Even today I can't help smiling when I think of myself kneeling in the library with his cock in my mouth. Perhaps my husband will read this letter and realize I'm not the innocent Catholic girl he thinks I am.—*E.L.*, *Santa Monica, California*

THEIR HUSBANDS LEARN THAT THE SWINGING GAME IS PLAYED BOTH WAYS

My name is Debbie. I work in a Midwestern gym as a receptionist. I am twenty-four, medium height, with long, strong hair, and I am very fit. Working in a gym helps keep me in great shape, and a generous husband helps keep me draped in the height of fashion.

My husband Warren and three childhood friends of his have a long-standing routine of getting together once a month for fun and drinks. They have always brought their wives along. Warren, Buck, Rex and Martin have many things in common—financial success and foxy wives half their age, to name two.

One particular Friday night, we stayed out a bit late and drank a bit too much. The men had us going with suggestive conversation, and before long persuaded us to make the following Friday night a night of swinging.

I got together with Mia, Honey, and Cheryl the next day. None of us had any great interest in making it with the other husbands. Wife-swapping was *their* fantasy. As we kicked it around, we wondered why only they should indulge their fantasies. A plan formed.

What if we each invited a good-looking young man for Friday night? Our husbands might freak at the sight of them and abandon their plan, which was fine. Or they'd have to play along, allowing *us* to play with studs our own age. The more we talked, the more it sounded like a plan by which we could only win.

We were all looking forward to Friday night. I think it was Honey who suggested a prize, to be decided later, should go to the one of *us* who showed up with the hottest date.

I called the girls from the gym Friday afternoon to see that everything was in order. I was amazed to find them chickening out! I gave each an earful. How could they let the husbands get away with this sexist behavior?

"Well, not me," I told them.

I rallied all of them, but it was too late for them to find men, I said I would bring a couple of well-muscled hunks from the gym. On Friday the guys are usually pumping themselves up for weekend action. So I watched as all those fit young men walked in and out of the gym. There were lots of studs, but I was looking for strangers who would make me melt with desire.

I got nervous as my shift neared its close and I had found no candidates. I decided to hit the weight room on the way out and extend invitations to the best men I could find. But the gym was almost empty. I began to regret some of the guys I had passed over.

Then I heard noise from the basketball court. Four guys, maybe eighteen or nineteen, were finishing a pickup game. They were in high spirits and sweating so heavily I could just about smell them from across the court.

They were all about six feet and packed with beautifully sculpted muscles and not an ounce of fat. In their rugged way, especially with those athletic juices flowing, they were gorgeous. I could not have gotten my eyes off of them if I had wanted to.

Their speech, with lots of "dese"s and "dem"s, said they were all working-class guys. I figured that that, in combination with their youth and hot looks, would drive the husbands crazy.

They were slapping and teasing each other, the winners of the game obviously taunting the losers. As they caught their breath they finally noticed me. As I mustered my courage, I realized they were looking at me with deference. I was an "older woman" to them, and they had all flirted with me unsuccessfully in the past.

I spoke with confidence. "Nice game, guys."

They mumbled in confusion and embarrassment, thinking back, wondering what exactly I had seen.

Their wet shirts and shorts clung to their powerful bodies. I turned the sexual heat way up. "Have you used up all your energy?" I asked.

They looked confused.

"Because I need some real men tonight," I continued. "Men who can take care of some real women. You guys know any men you think might be up to the assignment?" From the attention they paid to their groins, it looked like they might indeed be "up" to it.

A brave one found his tongue. "We've never had any complaints," he said, clutching his crotch.

Perfect, I thought! He had a dimple that was making *my* crotch wet. I chided myself for not noticing him before, or his cute friends.

"Well, it looks like I might have to settle for you guys," I said. I had written out copies of the address earlier. I handed them to the guy who had spoken and gave him the most suggestive smile I could manage.

"There's the address," I said. "Be there at nine. Don't disappoint me. I hate to be disappointed *by men*."

I stared all of them up and down. There was lots to look at. "Okay?" I said finally.

The talker had passed the address slips around, and they took pains to keep them from being soaked in the sweat that still poured from their overheated bodies.

"We'll be there," said the talker. "We're curious to see if you know any real women."

"See you at nine then," I said. My heart pounded and my head swam as I turned and slunk away. I barely made it to my car.

That night I wore a one-piece backless dress, with six-inch strapped heels. I painted my face and did my hair like a princess. Arriving at the hotel room, I noticed the other girls' seeming relief that I had no men in tow. I informed them that their dates were on their way, and our husbands wouldn't like it—or them.

After a few drinks our husbands began to talk openly about how they were into the wife-swapping. Warren had his sights set on Honey, who jumped to answer when there was loud knocking at the door.

"Debbie," Honey called from the foyer. "There are four men here to see you."

I crossed halfway to the door and said, "It's okay, Honey, I invited them, please let them in."

My hoops buddies, all dressed in T-shirts and shorts, sauntered in. I greeted them with hugs.

"What the fuck is this?" Rex shouted.

"We thought you wanted to swing," I said innocently. "Now we can!"

The husbands talked among themselves nervously, occasionally warning us not to go near these hoodlums. Warren approached me and tried to speak, but I ignored him. I fixed my new friends drinks and turned on the stereo.

I called the other girls over, and when they arrived whispered, "Let's dance with these guys, and see what happens. Don't even look at your husbands. Just have fun while they watch."

I danced with Vinnie, who had been the group spokesman. We danced innocently at first, but it became sexy. I couldn't take my eyes—or hands—off his beautifully muscled body. I was really turning on. I could hardly stand, so I asked him to sit with me for a bit. He sat on a bench with his back to the husbands. I sat on his lap.

"For God's sake, not on his lap!" Warren whined.

"Baby, it's a swing party, remember?" I said. "Don't worry, we're just going to be kissing for now."

Vinnie got brave and pulled the pin from my hair, allowing it to cascade down his chest. We stared in each other's eyes. He took my head in his hands, pushed it back gently and kissed my neck and chest so wetly, so sensuously, I began to coo. I licked his lips, then felt a fat cock pressing up between us. I gyrated against him, my heels on the floor, my weight leaning into him.

I rode high in his lap till his rising cock was under my dress. I slid high up on his chest, pushing off with my heeled toes. Taking the cue, Vinnie unzipped his shorts and, reaching under my dress, pushed my underwear aside. With both hands I worked his hot cock into my cunt. As it broke the threshold of my vagina, I lurched and grunted. I was already coming as I began the most glorious down stroke I've ever felt.

There was no misunderstanding about what was happening, but the hubbies were quiet—speechless, I imagine. All pretense gone now, I rode Vinnie in almost continuous orgasm.

"Oh yeah!" he groaned. This hot young athlete, in his sexual prime, was in me so deep, it gave me a new kind of orgasm. Had he hit the famous G-spot?

I lifted my feet off the floor and locked my heels tightly to Vinnie's waist. My full ass pressed down on his cock. My orgasms became even more powerful. He held my hips and pumped me full and hard. My long hair flew wildly, and I encouraged him, repeating, "Oh fuck me, fuck me!"

When Vinnie exploded, I could actually feel his powerful gushing inside me. After a minute or so of ejaculating, he dropped to the floor. I took his beautiful cock in my mouth and cherished it.

When my senses cleared, I saw all my friends coupled around the hotel room with my hoops studs. Honey was spread-eagled on a couch with one of them devouring her pussy and gliding his fingers in and out of her asshole. In time Cheryl and Mia were on the other couch engaging the other two young athletes.

Our husbands remained spectators for the rest of the evening. Perhaps they had no desire to be compared with the young studs who were having their way with us. Eventually the party broke up, and we fondled and kissed our virile guests good-bye. When Warren and I got home, I tried to make it up to him. He's my husband, after all, and I intended to hold on to him for a while!

He and the other husbands did seem to get the message, that swinging is a two-way street, and in time we found some rather imaginative ways to explore those possibilities. But that would be another letter!—*Name and address withheld*

"PART OF ME WAS HURT, PART OF ME JEALOUS, PART OF ME CURIOUS"

My wife and I have been together almost fourteen years. We married our senior year in college. I knew she was a free-spirited woman. I felt, as most men do, that I could always keep Connie happy. How wrong I was.

Two years ago, I returned a couple of days early from a week-long business trip. It was very late, and when I drove into my driveway I noticed the reflection from the windshield of another car parked next to my wife's in our two-car garage. Connie had not said anything about company staying over.

In the depths of my mind I sensed what might be happening, and I can't explain the rush that went through my body. Part of me was furious, part of me hurt, part of me jealous. Yet another part was feeling a strange pang of curiosity.

I had had a few flings in the past few years myself, which I did not think it necessary to share with Connie. We were not practicing an open marriage relationship.

At this point I had to confirm things, but I knew I needed my composure before facing Connie. We weren't having the greatest sex as of late, but after twelve years of marriage, not many couples experience the same passions they had when they first met.

I checked into a nearby motel for the night. Early the next morning I parked several houses up from mine and called Connie to say I had just arrived at the airport and would be home in a half hour. Sure enough, fifteen minutes later a man in his late twenties (my wife was then thirty-one) drove a blue BMW out of my driveway.

When I walked into the house, Connie acted as if nothing had happened. Instead of confronting her with my discovery, I found myself with a raging erection and a desire to fuck my wife silly.

She was as receptive as always to my sexual advances, and in no time we were stretched out on the sofa. As we kissed, my left hand found its way between her legs and touched a soaking wet pair of panties.

I was dying to confront her, but my investigative nature required me to go further. I rubbed her clit through her panties, then snaked a finger under the elastic and into her wet hole. She was squirming almost uncontrollably and whispered for me to fuck her now.

That was unusual, since Connie always loved for me to spend time sucking and licking her pussy before fucking her. She pulled at my belt and zipper to free my cock and urged me to mount her. I lifted her legs, pulled her panties off and opened her legs wide as if to prepare my entry. I continued to rub her clit, noticing the unusual redness of her pussy lips.

The air was filled with the smell of sex. With my fingers I opened the lips to her cunt. I noticed a milky secretion. Holding her cunt lips open with my thumbs, I dropped my head to her lap and ran my tongue into her hole.

Connie kept saying, "No, fuck me, Wayne," trying to push my head away. But I knew what it was, and kept licking and sucking her. My cock wanted to explode. I actually felt my heartbeat through my cockhead.

I stepped out of my trousers and plunged my cock in her slick cunt. I lasted about fifteen strokes, then added my semen. Interestingly, my cock stayed as hard as a brick. Connie repositioned herself on top of me and began to move slowly up and down on my cock again. Within only a few minutes we shook in what became one of many orgasms. We fucked like teenagers the whole day.

The following morning I took off from work, and Connie and I talked. I told her what I had discovered, saying that I had been more stimulated than anything. I found out that the "visitor," as she put it, was one of her boyfriends from college whom she used to ball before me.

She confronted me with a few of my flings and said she was not happy with our fucking only once a week, and if I could fuck around, so could she. She said she'd started having affairs over five years ago and was having sex almost every day, sometimes twice a day, with several men.

While she was explaining, the telephone rang. It was one of

her lovers. She made small talk, then told him she would call back later.

Since that day, Connie and I have opened our marriage up. We have experienced orgies, swap parties and two-on-ones with a few of her lovers. Last year she was the center of attention at two bachelor parties.

At the last one, the month before Christmas, she fucked and sucked off fifteen guys, including the groom and his younger brother. I fell asleep around one in the morning. When I awoke, around seven, I found the groom's brother on top of my wife, groggily humping away.

He said he had fucked her three times already, and he had never fucked a more beautiful woman. Then he made a couple of more plunges, pushed as far into her as he could and emptied his fourth load.

As I cleaned Connie up for the ride home, she said she'd lost count of how many times she'd been fucked. She fucked or sucked everyone, including myself, once. Then several guys came back for seconds. The groom fucked her twice, then asked her to suck him off once more before he left the party, at three.

This year promises to be much of the same. One of the attendees at the last bachelor party has already booked Connie for his wedding in May.—W.C., *Springfield, Massachusetts*

IT TAKES A BIG MAN TO SATISFY
HER FANTASY OF SUPERSIZE SERVICE

Before my wife and I started reading *Penthouse Letters*, we thought that there had to be something wrong with a man who had the desire to see another man fuck his wife. We were fascinated by the acts described by your readers' letters, which we devoured eagerly.

They led us to start watching amateur fuck videos. Georgette commented that she has a shapelier body and is certainly more attractive than the women in those videos. But what fascinated her most was the size of some of the really big cocks she saw in the amateur videos. The biggest of them was several inches longer and a great deal thicker than mine.

I asked her if she would like to have one of those men with a super-size cock fuck her pussy. She hesitated, then replied, "Oh, I could never do that! He might not find me attractive, and besides, if I did, you might stop loving me."

I told her that she didn't have to worry about me, that what I wanted was for her to be satisfied sexually. I reassured her that I would always love her, no matter who she might fuck.

Once the subject was opened, we continued to discuss the possibilities of her having an opportunity to fuck a superstud. But after several such discussions, I decided that if it was ever going to happen, I was going to have to help it get started. I sought the help of a friend who in turn introduced me to a promoter who had connections in the underground sex world.

I explained to this fellow that my wife would like to fuck a man with a huge cock but felt embarrassed, and we didn't know how to proceed from there. I had a picture of Georgette with me. The promoter took a look and said he didn't think there would be any problem. He would just make a couple of calls to people who owed him favors.

He assured me he would not only find a superstud to fuck my wife but would provide her with a night she would remember the rest of her life. He gave me the card of a club that catered to people who wanted to "get together" with other people. He said for us to be there the following Friday no later than ten.

He told me to have her dressed sexy to the hilt—heels, hose, garter belt, revealing panties, nice lacy bra and, most of all, a nice expensive dress. Have her hair styled. He said that our party would contact us at the club Friday night.

As we got ready to go out, Georgette was very nervous, afraid the panties were too revealing. She admired herself in a full-length mirror. The garter belt made a perfect frame for her pussy hair, and the panties were so sheer that she appeared to be naked. The pink folds of her cunt were plainly visible.

Her dress clung to every curve of her figure, and the high heels of her pumps really set her off. Her firm tits stood out, showing the outlines of her large nipples.

There were a lot of unescorted women drinking and dancing with men they had met in the club. Everyone was dressed very neatly and in expensive clothes. I ordered champagne, and the bubbly got Georgette in a festive mood. She and I danced several times.

Eventually a tall, powerfully built man dressed in an expensive suit and wearing large diamond rings approached. He addressed us by our names and introduced himself as Pedro. He asked if he might dance with the lovely lady.

Georgette blushed but stood up. Pedro took her hand and led her to the dance floor. While they danced, I was surprised to see the promoter who had arranged this for us. He hadn't said anything about being at the club that night. He approached me and asked if I approved of the man he had chosen to fuck my wife and give her the thrill of her life.

"He's a sexual athlete with ten inches of dick," he said.

I replied that he seemed fine, but I didn't know if Georgette would go along. The man laughed and said, "Don't worry. Leave that to Pedro." He had absolute faith in Pedro's powers of persuasion. He added, confidentially, that I would get to see everything, which I found unaccountably exciting. What he didn't explain was that everyone in the club "would get to see everything."

Georgette and her "date" came back to the table. The promoter ordered drinks for all of us, including a special one for

Georgette to pay tribute to her beauty. We all drank up, and very soon Georgette began to get very passionate, deep-kissing Pedro. The promoter smiled and said, "She is ready."

Pedro suggested they go to a back room so they could have some privacy. Georgette looked at me, and I said okay. They stood up. The promoter suggested that Georgette hike up her dress and show her pussy, and to my surprise, she did so.

When her dress had reached waist-high level, she pulled the crotch of her panties to one side.

"Nice," Pedro said. "*Very* nice indeed."

Georgette moaned, "Will someone please fuck me?"

"Oh, I am so hot, you bet I will, baby," said Pedro. "Let me give you some of my big fat dick."

As Pedro led Georgette to their back room, the promoter got up and whispered a few words to her. (I later learned he told her what was going to happen.) Then he had the lights dimmed in the club, and he flipped a switch. A giant TV screen lit up. On it everyone in the club saw Georgette and Pedro enter a room containing a giant bed.

He helped her take off her dress. Then she faced the TV screen as he removed her lacy bra. Her tits were firm. Her nipples were long and hard and looked like cherries. Pedro commented on how nice her tits were.

He suggested she remove her panties and commented on how nice her large mound of pussy hair looked. Next he had her spread the folds of her clit so he could see how large it was.

"That pussy is going to be tight," he said, "but I'll be able to get my dick in there."

He stripped and lay back on the bed, his cock sticking straight out. He invited Georgette to suck his dick and make it good and hard. She could barely get the head inside her mouth. She licked up and down the full length of his shaft. She even sucked his balls—something she had never done for me.

Everyone could see my wife sucking that big dick. How could I not feel a pang of jealousy when Georgette straddled him and guided the head of his cock to the opening of her cunt? She lowered herself slowly until she had his whole cock up her cunt. She bounced up and down furiously.

Soon flecks of come could be seen clinging to Pedro's cock. Georgette moaned loudly, then lay back as his slick cock slipped out of her cunt. He then mounted her from on top. He buried his big cock completely up her cunt and fucked her furiously.

With a groan, he pumped a large load of come deep inside her cunt. She lay with her legs spread wide, her cunt gaping, and drops of come leaking out of her.

Then there were two more giant cocks in front of her. We all watched her hungrily suck those three magnificent members, taking on one after another. Then, one after another, she was fucked by all three of the men who were attached to the jumbo cocks. Finally she took one of those supercocks in her ass and another in her pussy at the same time.

Georgette had a wonderful time. She was delighted when she saw a copy of the videotape, and said that her excitement had doubled when the promoter told her about the cameras.

Georgette is no longer embarrassed to be naked with a super-endowed man. In fact, she welcomes it. So, thanks to *Penthouse Letters*, we had the courage to try something different and exciting.—*F.D., New Orleans, Louisiana*

HIS FANTASY COMES TRUE WHEN HE ENCOUNTERS A COUPLE OF SWINGERS

My biggest fantasy has always been to have a threesome, either with a couple or with two women. Though I did once go to bed with two women, that session did not go beyond heavy petting, and it was a hell of a disappointment. So for the past few years I have been trying to find ways to meet other people who might desire a three-way. After all, you only live so long, and I was intent on enjoying the pleasure of multiple partners before my dick and I were consigned to our eternal rest.

Last month my dream finally came true. I answered an ad in a swingers' magazine, placed by a couple who were looking for another man. They contacted me by phone and invited me to come to their house for a drink and to see how we all got along.

My initial reaction on meeting Ralph and Jan was one of disappointment, because although they were not unattractive, they were not the ultra-glamorous types I had been picturing. But after a few drinks I began to get excited at the thought of having Jan suck my cock in front of her husband. We seemed to hit it off well, and finally Ralph said what the hell, let's just get undressed and go from there.

Well, that was all I needed to get my cock hard, and in a minute we had all taken off our clothing. It was a little awkward at first, but then Jan grabbed my cock and started sucking me like there was no tomorrow. Ralph sat on the couch beating his six-inch cock, until I suggested that he come over and go down on Jan as I watched.

The shyness and awkwardness had left me already, and I positioned myself so I could enjoy the blowjob Jan was giving me and at the same time spread her pussy lips while Ralph sucked her clit.

Soon we were all moaning. When we took a break, Ralph suggested we move into the bedroom, and once there he asked me if I wanted to fuck his wife. I suggested that he go first, while I watched. As Ralph sank his cock into Jan's dripping pussy, I reached around and grabbed his balls. That drove Ralph over the edge, and he blew his come forcefully up into her twat, then pulled out to shoot more of it onto the bed.

He rolled off her then and lay back, but was soon beating off as he watched me fingering Jan's hot sticky pussy. Jan was moaning and begging me to fuck her hard. I turned her over and mounted her, slipping my dick into her from behind, and began to pound away at her, doggy-style. The feeling of her wet box and

Ralph's hot come drove me wild. As she came I unloaded my jism all over her pussy and asshole, and I knew that at last I was getting what I had so long desired.

As we lay there exhausted, Ralph reached over and started fondling my cock, which was all it took to get me hard again. Jan suggested that he get down and lick me clean. This was another fantasy I had long secretly dreamed about. As Ralph sucked my cock, Jan positioned her pussy over my face. Though I was a little hesitant at first, I dove in and was soon slurping all of our come out of that squirming pussy. In a few moments I was blowing my load into Ralph's mouth, and Jan let out a loud scream as she climaxed again.

All three of us fell onto the bed and lay there in happy amazement over what had just happened. We were slowly coming to realize that our lives had just changed radically. As we cleaned up we decided to continue this new and exciting friendship. They are planning to invite one of Jan's girlfriends the next time we get together. That, I am sure, will be another letter.—R.G., *Trenton, New Jersey*

SHE IS A REDHEAD WITH A RED-HOT NEED TO SUCK COCK. ANY COCK

My name is Fran. I am forty-two years old and a real redhead. I weigh a hundred twenty-five pounds, have long legs, and my tits are just big enough to fill a man's mouth. I always wear bright-colored sheer underwear, and I love to tease men by sitting with my legs open just far enough to let them see up my skirt to my panties.

By doing this I can get just about any man I want. When I see a man looking at me in a bar, for example, and I know he is interested, I will open my legs wide, so he can get a view of my silk-covered red-haired pussy. I also make sure he can see my tongue licking my lips, and it usually isn't long before he comes over and asks to sit down with me. A few minutes later his hand is between my legs, going up under my skirt to my panties. By this time the bulge in his pants will be in clear view. I will give it a good feel and tell him how nice and big and hard it is, and that I would like more of it. I then suggest we go to his car. I can tell you that I don't often get turned down using this approach.

Once we are in the car, I know that his nuts are hot and he is ready for fucking. But I am not ready yet. I want foreplay. I want him sucking my tongue and feeling my tits and hard nipples. I open my legs wide, squirming around so that my skirt goes up to my hips, again showing him my hot pussy through the sheer panties.

Now I take his hand and put it down between my legs, pulling the crotch of my panties aside; but as his finger starts to enter my love hole I stop him and tell him to take my panties all the way off, raising my hips for easy removal.

When my panties are off I allow him to massage my hot pussy. As his finger enters my swollen cunt lips I pump up and down until he has finger-fucked me to orgasm. His hand is now soaking wet with my come, and I bring it to my mouth and suck all the hot sweet juices from his fingers.

Meanwhile I have been playing with his hard swollen cock through his pants, and by now it is ready to explode. As I open his fly to let his prick out, I tell him I don't want it up my cunt, since he has already satisfied me with his finger. At this his pussy poker usually starts to go soft; but I quickly stiffen it up again by telling him that his cock is so nice and hard, with its throbbing veins and the little hole in the purple head, that I can't wait to get the whole thing in my mouth and suck him off.

I lean over on the seat with my legs wide apart, so he can play with my slit and asshole while I go down on his red-hot swollen love stick. I take that prick slowly into my mouth and work my tongue over every inch of it, from the top down to the balls, and then I suck it like a vacuum.

His finger is in my cunt, making me want to come again. I feel the prick in my mouth starting to twitch, and I suck harder and faster, lashing it with my tongue, until I feel his pearly-white jism shoot out into my eager mouth. I swallow every bit of his nectar, and then I tell him I want more. I know if he wants to qualify as a real man he'll find a way to manufacture another load and deliver it to me. And usually he does.

I have sucked small pricks, big pricks, young pricks and old pricks. Right now I am keeping a seventy-year-old man happy by sucking every drop of juice from his balls at least four times a month. So now you can believe me when I tell you, I love sucking cock!—*F.W., Topeka, Kansas*

HE SERVICES HER LAWNMOWER, SHE SERVICES HIS LOVE TOOL

I'm a nineteen-year-old girl, a year or so out of high school. My father is very strict and religious, and even though I am of age he is still very protective of me. He's never fitted me with a chastity belt, but maybe that's because they're hard to find these days.

Until about two years ago, I was short, shy and awkward, with a flat chest and bad skin. Recently, however, my skin cleared, I sprouted to five feet six, and grew a pair of perky 34B tits with pointy, upturned nipples that always seem to catch the eyes of the guys at work. I have long brown hair that I wear in a ponytail, and green eyes.

My dad never lets me wear sexy clothes and won't let me go out with guys. He gives me lectures about morals and sex all the time, and makes me come straight home every day after work. On the weekends he usually makes me stay home and work around the house. It's so embarrassing. I've been asked out a couple of times, but I always have to say no because of Dad. Most of my friends have steady boyfriends, and I've heard a lot of stories about their sex lives, but I've never even been on a date. I wish I had a boyfriend and could fool around, but Dad says I can only go out with my friends if an adult is with us at all times. So my life has been pretty dreary—until recently.

This summer Dad has decided that it would be my job to take care of the yard. Every Saturday he goes off to his church meetings, and I stay home and mow the lawn and trim the bushes. If the work's not done when he gets back, I'm grounded for the week. At first it was total drudgery, but a few weeks ago it all changed.

It started while I was outside pushing the mower under the hot sun. I was wearing faded cut-off shorts, a white T-shirt and work boots. I was almost finished with the lawn when the mower suddenly died, and I couldn't get it started again. I tried pulling on the cord and playing with the controls, but nothing worked. I was hot, sweaty and frustrated, and worried that Dad would yell at me when he got home. Just then one of the neighborhood boys drove by and saw me kicking the mower.

Randy had kind of a bad reputation; he was the kind of guy Dad would hate. He's tall and thin, with slicked-back hair, and likes to wear an open shirt with chains around his neck. I knew Dad would go crazy if he found out Randy had been around, but I was sick of being trapped in the house, so I was hoping he would stop and help. He pulled into the driveway and got out of the car. As he walked over to me, I looked down at my white T-shirt and realized that I had sweated right through my bra. My shirt was clinging to my breasts, making my pointy nipples stand out.

Randy looked me over and smiled. "Need a hand?" he said. I did, and I could tell he wanted to give me one.

I have to say I loved the feeling of Randy checking out my tits. I smiled back at him, and purposely bent over to show him something on the mower, giving him a good view of my ass beneath the brief cutoffs. Straightening up, I said that my dad would give me hell if the lawn wasn't done when he got home. I put my hand on his shoulder and gave him a sad, wide-eyed look. "I would be so grateful if you could help," I said.

Randy smiled. "I'll see what I can do," he said. He bent down to fiddle with the mower and I knelt down next to him, with my nipples just a few inches from his arm. I could feel a sexual tension between us, and it made me scared mostly because I was worried about Dad.

But I couldn't help feeling excited at the same time. I could see a bulge growing in Randy's black jeans, and at one point he glanced back and caught me eyeing his crotch. When he stood up his arm brushed my breasts, and he looked into my eyes. Then he pulled the cord on the mower and it started right up.

I let out a cheer, put my arms around Randy and gave him a quick peck on the cheek. His right arm circled my waist and held me to him, and I felt my sweaty nipples poking his chest through his open shirt. "Is that all I get?" he asked.

"What do you mean?" I answered innocently, but I didn't pull away. He looked around, grabbed my hand and led me to the garage. I pretended to protest, but I went along. Once we were in the garage Randy wrapped me in his arms and kissed me.

I had never been French-kissed before, but I guess some things just come naturally. My mouth opened right up and our tongues intertwined. The feeling was indescribable. I had never even been alone with a guy before, and now here I was in a wet, clingy T-shirt, sucking on Randy's tongue in my dad's garage! Randy held me to him, and I felt his stiff prick poking into my side. I wanted to see it and touch it, but I was shy. We kept kissing with wet, open mouths, and Randy's hands went to my breasts. He pulled my sweaty T-shirt over my head, removed my bra and rubbed my soft mounds. He tongued his way down my neck and sucked on my tits for a long time, kissing and licking them and lightly biting my nipples.

I was soaring up to heaven, leaning back against Dad's workbench, and I felt my pussy begin to tingle. Randy was rubbing my ass and lapping my tits as I held his head in my hands. Suddenly he stepped back and looked me over. I was standing there in my boots and shorts, with my glistening tits fully exposed, and with a look of raw inexperienced lust in my eyes.

"Well," he said, "are you ready to reward me for my services?"

"What do you mean?" I asked, pretending not to understand what he had in mind. Randy stepped forward, put his hand on my shoulder and gently pushed me to my knees. He looked down at me and slowly undid his belt and unzipped his pants. I knew what was coming and what he wanted me to do, and I couldn't wait. My heart was pounding. I helped him pull his pants down to his knees, and then I discovered that he wasn't wearing underwear.

The garage door was still open and we could easily be seen from the street, and I was on my knees with my face only inches away from the first hard, throbbing cock I had ever seen. I wasn't sure what to do, so Randy held my head with one hand and rubbed his cock all over my face. I loved the smooth feel of his penis against my cheeks, lips and eyebrows.

"I serviced your equipment," he said. "Now you're going to do mine. You're going to give me a nice long blowjob. Have you ever done this before?"

I shook my head no, closing my eyes in rapture as he continued to rub his cock on my face. "Are you ready?" he asked. I nodded, feeling like I was in a trance. I couldn't wait to taste him. He put the tip of his cock against my lips and I opened wide, allowing him to ease the length of it into my mouth. "That's good," he said. "Now start sucking." I wrapped my lips around his rigid tool and bobbed my head back and forth, sucking on his dick and rolling my tongue around the head. "Yeah," he groaned. "Now play with my balls." I kept sucking as I reached to massage his balls with my hands. I looked up at him, smiling around his cock and moaning softly to myself. It was wonderful. I never knew I could be so turned on. I took that stiff cock out of my mouth and licked all the way from the tip to the base, and then down to his balls. I put each of his balls in my mouth, swirling them with my tongue as I pumped his saliva-covered shaft with my hand. "You are one fine cocksucker," Randy said.

I was crazed with lust. "I love your cock," I replied in a sultry voice, looking into his eyes.

Randy asked if I would be his cocksucking slut from then on, and I moaned in agreement. "Man, everyone thought you were such a good girl," Randy said then. "We never knew you'd go crazy with a big cock in your mouth. You keep this up and I'll have a nice surprise for you."

I looked up at him again and smiled as I licked his cock up and down like a lollipop and massaged his balls. Randy reached down to play with my tits, and then he took my head in both hands and began pumping his cock in and out of my mouth. I held on to his thighs and tried to breathe through my nostrils and relax my throat as he pumped.

"That's it, girl," he said. "Take my cock all the way in. Suck on it." I kept taking him until he had pushed his cock all the way into my throat, and he groaned in ecstasy. My nose was buried in his pubic hair and his balls were slapping against my chin. I loved the sensation of having his cock all the way in me. He continued to pump back and forth, fucking my mouth until he cried out. His knees buckled and he held my head tightly as his dick spewed a load of white-hot semen into my throat.

That only got me more excited, and I kept sucking and licking the cream from his rod until it was all shiny and clean. Finally he pulled me up, gave me a kiss and pulled up his pants.

Randy finished mowing the lawn that day, and now every Saturday, after Dad leaves, he mows the lawn and I suck him off. Dad is so happy with the yard he says he might have me paint the house this summer, to keep me out of trouble while he's at work. Randy says he can do the job for me, but he'll have to bring a few friends along to help out. I can't wait!—M.J., *Pensacola, Florida*

HE RETIRED TO GET SOME PEACE,
BUT THE WOMEN HAD OTHER IDEAS

My wife passed away last summer after thirty years of marriage, so I sold my business and moved to a nice retirement community in California. Given the fact that I am fairly well off, and still pretty attractive, I guess word soon got around that I was available.

The first woman to hit on me was Sally, a lonely lady who had lost her husband a few years back. I told her from the start that I wasn't ready for any permanent arrangement, and that was fine with her. By our third date we were into some heavy petting. At the end of the evening we went back to her place, and were soon down to our undies. She said she didn't fuck because she was afraid of disease, but that she would like to give me a blowjob. I said that was fine as long as I could reciprocate by eating her pussy.

She gave me a great blowjob. When I told her I was coming she put her hand on my ass, taking just about all of my cock down her throat. The other hand pumped my balls till they were empty. I lay down on the floor and told her to sit on my mouth. She was a little hesitant, saying that her late husband had never been into eating pussy. I told her to relax and let me take care of everything.

I worked my tongue up and down her slit, pausing with each stroke to suck on her clit. After a few minutes she started moaning and saying how good it felt. Soon she was sliding her cunt back and forth over my lips and tongue, screaming, "Oh, yes!" as her hot cream oozed out her cunt and into my mouth. After her orgasm subsided she started to get up, but I held her there and managed to bring her to two more orgasms before I was through. We both had quite an enjoyable evening.

A few days later I was sitting by the pool around noontime when Donna, a married lady of about forty, came over to me. "Boy, it sure is hot," she said. "Would you like to come up to my place and have a beer?" I said sure.

We were drinking our beer and making small talk when she came out with, "I hear you're quite the man when it comes to pleasing a woman." When I didn't make any reply to that, she stood up and unhooked her bikini top, then pulled off the bottom.

My seven-incher got as hard as a rock, but I said, "Donna, don't do this. I play golf with your husband."

"Are you going to tell him?" she said. "Because I'm not. Come on, Peter. I hear you really know how to please a woman with your tongue."

Donna still had a fantastic body. She was five feet six inches, and about one hundred and twenty-five pounds. Her boobs were about 34B, and her nipples stuck out invitingly. I thought, what the hell, and took off my swim trunks. Donna lay down on the couch with her legs spread. She reached for my cock as I went over to her. "Let me take care of that first," she said, and slid my tool into her mouth. I put one hand on her tit and the other on her cunt. Donna had evidently had lots of practice, because she really knew how to give head. She had me blowing my load in about five minutes, and she swallowed every last drop.

I knelt on the floor, putting one of her legs over the back of the couch and the other on the floor. Her cunt was spread wide, the outer lips all puffed up. I put two fingers in her cunt and thumbed her love button. I leaned over and started sucking energetically on one of her big hard nipples.

She started moaning, pulling my head tight to her tit. Her cunt muscles tightened around my fingers and her ass came off the couch, her cream coating my fingers. Her orgasm seemed to last for a full minute. When she was finished I pulled my fingers from her cunt and licked them clean.

Then I got between her thighs and started feasting on her pussy. She came three more times before she stopped me, saying she was drained. We had another beer, and then I left.

I was having the time of my life. I hadn't realized that there were so many women out there who had never had their pussy eaten by their husband. I went to most of the community functions with Sally, who was the only single woman I was making it with. She knew I was making it with some of the married women, and she was also fucking a few of the husbands.

One day Sally told me that her daughter Lorna was coming to spend a week with her during her college vacation. I figured we would have to be discreet, but Sally didn't seem too worried. "Hell," she said, "at eighteen, I'm sure she knows what fucking is all about."

The night after Lorna arrived, Sally and I went out to a dance, then back to her place. Lorna had gone to bed early, so we retired to Sally's bedroom.

"I hope that tongue of yours is ready for some action," Sally said, "because my pussy is hot and ready!" She had her clothes off and was lying on the bed with her legs hanging over the edge before I even had my pants off. I knelt on the floor. Her cunt was shiny with her pussy juice. I started lapping up her liquids, and it wasn't long before she started moaning and humping her cunt at my mouth while I licked up the sweet honey as it flowed out of her cunt.

"Fuck me, honey," Sally moaned. I had never actually fucked her before, so this would be a first. I got between her legs and slowly slid my seven inches into her slick, tight hole. I was soon in up to my balls and it felt like a velvet glove around my cock. Her cunt muscles squeezed my prick, and her legs wrapped themselves around my ass, pulling me in tighter against her. She started moaning, "Fuck me, honey, fuck me, it's been so long!" I fucked her hard and deep, and she soon screamed, "I'm there!" and dug her nails into my back. I put my hand over her mouth to stifle her scream. Her cunt milked my cock and I let go with a good load.

The following morning I got up about ten o'clock, put on my robe and went down to get a cup of coffee. Sally had left a note saying that she had gone shopping with a few of her friends and would see me later. When I walked into the living room Lorna was there, reading a book. I did a double take. She had on the smallest thong bikini I had ever seen. Lorna was about five feet tall and maybe one hundred pounds. Her tits were small, but her body was firm and curvy as hell.

She looked up from her book and said, "Good morning. Is Mom a good fuck?"

I was taken back by her bluntness, and told her she shouldn't talk about her mother that way. "Christ, Peter," she said, "the way she was moaning last night, I knew you guys were at it." Then, before I could move, she stood up and pulled off her bikini! God, she had a hairy little cunt. "Do you think you could make *me* moan like that?" she said.

"Damn," I said, "your mom would kill me if she ever found out I touched you."

She just smiled. "Mom and I had a long talk before she left. She told me how good you are." I was now looking at her tits, which were about the size of small oranges. The areolae had to be at least two inches across, and the nipples stood out a good half inch.

All I had on was my robe. My cock was as hard as a lead pipe. I leaned over and took one of her nipples in my mouth. She reached through my robe and grabbed my cock. "Oh God, you feel big," she moaned. "Do me like you did Mom last night."

I sat her on a chair and draped her legs over the arms. Her pussy was all puffed up and wide open. Her little clit was peeking out from under its hood. Creamy juice was oozing out her hole. I started licking her thighs, not touching her pussy, until finally she pleaded for me to lick her cunt.

I looked up at her face. Her eyes were closed and her tongue was licking her lips. Her hands were on her tits, pulling on her nipples. I moved my tongue to her clit, and her ass came off the chair as though she had gotten an electric shock. I put my tongue at the bottom of her slit and licked up the nectar that flowed out. It wasn't long before she was twisting and moaning, "Oh God, it's happening! I'm there!" I put my hands under her ass and stuck my tongue in her hole.

Her stomach muscles tightened and a gush of pussy cream flooded my mouth. Her fingers plucked at her nipples as though she was trying to pull them off. Her shrieks echoed around the apartment.

I never stopped eating her pussy, and was soon rewarded with a second burst of cunt cream. "Oh God, Peter, fuck me!" she begged. "Fuck me, I need to feel your cock in me!" I straightened up and positioned my throbbing tool between her thighs. Her cunt juice was still flowing, so I had no trouble easing it deeply into her tight hole.

When my seven-incher hit bottom she moaned, "Oh God, you're so big! Fuck me good. I'm almost there!" Her cunt muscles started squeezing my cock. I took one of her nipples into my mouth and sucked it hard.

Her little ass came off the chair and her legs wrapped around my waist, pulling my cock in up to the hilt. I felt that tingling sensation in my balls, and in a minute I was spurting hot come into her cunt. She was yelling and squirming, and tears of joy were running down her face.

When we were both finished I pulled out, my cock limp as a wet noodle. Lorna got up and went to take a shower. A minute later, Sally came in. As soon as she saw me she started taking off her clothes. "I hope you still have some juice in that cock for me," she said. "Because I'm ready!"

I knew right then that this was going to be one week I would never forget.—*P.T., Sacramento, California*

HE GAVE HIS WIFE A FUR COAT
AND IT KEPT THEM BOTH HOT

My name is Kris and my wife's name is Peggy Anne. About five years ago, when I was forty-four and my wife was thirty-seven, I bought her a knee-length fur coat for Christmas. It was a light-colored mink with white fox fur on the sleeves.

Why am I telling you about my wife's fur coat? Because it turned out to be one of the best buys of my life, considering that it led to one of the greatest sexual experiences I have ever had.

I would like to describe my wife. Peggy Anne is just barely five feet tall. She has dark blonde hair that she highlights to great effect and wears in a short stylish cut. She has firm, well-shaped tits that sag very little for her age. While her breasts are not large, they are more than proportionate to her petite size-six body. She fills out her blouse very well, and when she goes without a bra she draws many looks from those around her. Her tits are capped with large nipples that respond quickly to any stimulation.

Peggy Anne loves it when attention is paid to her breasts. Sometimes while she is watching some of those stupid TV shows I hate, I will lie across her lap and suckle at her breasts. She is very content to sit there and let me mouth her tits for an hour or more. While she has never had an orgasm from breast stimulation alone, she has come within seconds when I rub her pussy after one of these sessions.

Peggy Anne has a narrow waist that flares out gently to great hips. She has a magnificent ass, consisting of two of the softest, firmest, roundest cheeks anyone has ever grabbed. They fill out the seat of her jeans very well.

Then there are her legs. They are well shaped from years of athletic activity. Her thighs are satin-smooth and firm. Her calves look fantastic when she has on a pair of high heels. I love to have those legs wrapped around my back, or even better, around my head as I play with her pussy. In short, Peggy Anne looks at least as good in the nude as she does with clothes on.

We were living near Chicago at the time of this experience. During the winters there, a fur coat is very useful. Also, I loved the way it looked on her when she tried it on in the store, not knowing I was going to come back later and buy it. She sure was surprised when she opened the package. Being the sort of woman who responds well to favors, she returned the surprise a couple of weeks later. Here is how it happened:

We had planned to go out for dinner and then take in a show, so it was a perfect occasion for her to wear her new coat. I got home from work about five o'clock, planning to take a shower and get dressed for an elegant evening out. When I walked to the door, Peggy Anne appeared ready to go. She had on the fur coat, hose and high heels. Surprised, I asked if it was time to leave already.

She replied that we had plenty of time. I commented that she seemed very eager to wear the coat, and asked if she wouldn't get hot wearing it while I got ready. She just chuckled and handed me a cold beer. Then she stepped back and opened the coat. She didn't have anything on underneath. My mouth dropped wide open. I asked her if she planned on going out like that. She smiled and said that what she was planning right then was to relieve the tensions of my day.

I took a very long drink of my beer. My wife was standing there in nothing but her fur coat, a pair of thigh-high hose and her heels. She could have been a model who had stepped from the pages of *Penthouse Letters* right into our house. I could tell that she was already aroused. She had a seductive look in her eye and her turgid nipples stuck stiffly out from her tits. She advanced toward me, took the beer from my trembling hand and kissed me passionately. She began slowly unbuttoning my shirt, kissing every inch of flesh that she uncovered. When she was finished with the buttons, she slipped the shirt off my body.

Peggy Anne then led me to the den, where she had the fold-out bed set up. There were candles burning everywhere, and music was playing softly on the stereo. She had planned this well. She sat me down on the edge of the bed and slowly removed my shoes and socks. I sat there watching my beautiful wife's naked body wrapped in fur as she did this. She had me stand up so she could remove my pants. She then slipped down my jockey shorts, and my hardening dick popped free. Peggy Anne quickly engulfed the mushroom head of my cock with her hot mouth. She started sucking on it, her head bobbing slowly up and down.

While she was doing that she began to stroke my lower ab-

domen, thighs and groin with the soft fur of her coat. My dick got
so hard I thought it was going to lift her right off the floor. It was so
hard it almost hurt. She was flicking her tongue against the underside of my sensitive tool while she kept fucking me with her mouth.
My legs were trembling so hard I thought I would fall down. She
kept this up until I was on the verge of exploding. Then she stopped
this mouth magic and slipped her ruby-red lips off my pole. My
cockhead was more swollen than I ever saw it, and I almost expected it to burst open from all the blood that had pumped into it.

Peggy Anne then stood and pressed her naked body against
me, kissing me passionately while the fur coat brushed against my
skin. She then pushed me back on the bed and slowly dragged her
hot twat up along my body until it was positioned above my face,
then smashed her wet swollen cunt lips down on my mouth. My
nose was buried in her pussy fur while the softer fur of the coat
brushed against my face.

I reached up and started playing with my wife's tits, which
bounced up and down as she humped my mouth. I held them so
the nipples thrust out between my fingers, and Peggy Anne raised
her arm and rubbed the fur at her sleeve over those vibrating nipples. Between my thrusting tongue on her clit and the sensation
of the fur on her tits, she soon erupted in a violent, noisy orgasm,
rubbing her twat fiercely against my lips and screaming as the
waves of pleasure flowed through her body.

As she eased the pressure on my mouth, I continued to suck
the love juices flowing from her pussy. Her body twitched each
time my tongue flicked over her rigid clit. After a minute she
pulled away and slid back down my body, dragging her wet cunt
across my skin and leaving a slick trail of dew.

Peggy Anne now reached for my steely shaft and positioned
the head at the entrance to her dripping love tunnel. Then, with
a quick downward move, she engulfed my throbbing meat to the
hilt. I felt my dick crash into her cervix as those velvety walls
tightened around my shaft. Peggy Anne gave a soft moan and
ground her cunt into my pelvis.

She was keeping my dick buried as deep as it would go while stimulating her clitoris on my pubic hair. She kept stroking my chest with her fur coat. My skin was tingling. The fur on the bottom of the coat was tickling my thighs and groin. I groaned with delight. The sensation was unbelievable.

Peggy Anne now began to move her hips, first slowly, then faster and faster, till she was riding me for all she was worth. She was moaning loudly and rocking wildly on my dick. I knew her orgasm was close.

The sight of my wife's beautiful breasts swinging with her movements, the touch of the soft fur brushing against my skin, and the sensation of her hot pussy sliding up and down my cock were all too much for me. I felt my nuts start to tighten. Then, just as Peggy Anne screamed out that she was coming, I erupted. Surge after surge of hot come pumped out of my dick and into my wife's cunt.

Her spasming twat sucked every drop of jism from my body. Slowly her hips stopped rocking and she leaned down to kiss me as I told her how much I loved her.

"Okay," Peggy Anne said. "I guess we can go now." Then she ran upstairs to shower. I lay there for a moment, wondering what had hit me. Then I slowly got up on my weak legs and joined my wife in the shower.

We had to rush a little to get to the show on time, but the delay was certainly worth it. Every time Peggy Anne brushed me with that fur coat during the evening, my dick got hard again. Peggy Anne knew that and did it often; smiling slyly as she did. What a night!—K.O., *Cicero, Illinois*